PENGUIN BOOKS

The Spanish Doctor

Matt Cohen was born in Kingston, Ontario in 1942 and educated at the University of Toronto. He taught religious studies at McMaster University before becoming a full-time writer.

His first novel was published in 1969. Since then, he has received critical acclaim for many books, notably "The Salem Novels" – *The Disinherited, The Colours of War, The Sweet Second Summer of Kitty Malone,* and *Flowers of Darkness. Café le Dog,* his most recent collection of stories was published in the Penguin Short Fiction series. In addition, he has contributed articles and stories to a wide variety of magazines including *The Malahat Review, The Sewanee Review* and *Saturday Night.*

Matt Cohen now lives in Toronto, Ontario.

THE SPANISH DOCTOR

MATT COHEN

ESQUIMALT
USED BOOKs

Penguin Books

Penguin Books Canada Ltd., 2801 John Street, Markham,
Ontario, Canada L3R 1B4
Penguin Books Ltd., Harmondsworth, Middlesex, England
Penguin Books, 40 West 23rd Street, New York, New York
10010 U.S.A.
Penguin Books Australia Ltd., Ringwood, Victoria, Australia
Penguin Books (N.Z.) Ltd., Private Bag, Takapuna, Auckland 9,
New Zealand

First published by McClelland and Stewart Limited
Published in Penguin Books, 1985

Canadian Cataloguing in Publication Data

Cohen, Matt, 1942-
    The Spanish doctor

ISBN 0-14-007710-3

I. Title.

PS8555.038S52 1985   C813'.54   C85-098464-5
PR9199.3.C63S52 1985

For P.A.

THE SPANISH DOCTOR

Baltic Sea
Novgorod
Vilna
Minsk
Lublin
Prague
Mainz
Cologne
Paris
Lyon
Avignon
Montpellier
Barcelona
Bordeaux
Madrid
Toledo
Cordoba
Granada
Lisbon
Fez
Algiers
Tunis
Bologna
Venezia
Roma
Naples
Kiev
Black Sea
Constantinople
Mediterranean Sea
Atlantic Ocean
N
W
E
S

Jean Affleck

BOOK I

TOLEDO
1391

PROLOGUE

In the fall of 1347, an unwelcome visitor arrived in Europe. Its bearers were sailors: some dead, others suffering from black swellings in the armpits and groin, fevers, breath so foul that even the sympathetic were repelled. From the ports the Black Death swept inland. Within two years over twenty million were struck down.

Among the victims was, in the year 1350, King Alfonso XI of Castilla.

When Alfonso died, his eldest son, Pedro, inherited the throne. To ensure a peaceable kingdom and an uncontested succession, the newly crowned King Pedro sent assassins to poison, stab, and drown his numerous brothers and cousins. But despite Pedro's careful plans, one man who might have been their victim escaped: his half-brother – Henry the Bastard. While his more royal siblings were being sent to eternity, Henry the Bastard beat a tactful retreat to France. There he became the friend and accomplice of Bertrand Du Guesclin, a French general instrumental in France's successes over England in the Hundred Years' War and the leader of the mercenary armies – Les Grandes Compagnies – that became Europe's second plague.

Meanwhile, in Toledo, Pedro the Cruel reigned and life went on.

Even in the Jewish barrio no one doubted that Toledo – the New Jerusalem for hundreds of years already – would continue to be a secure home for the followers of the Hebrew God. Pedro the Cruel, like his father before him, soon came to depend on the Jewish financiers of Toledo to collect his taxes and keep his army loyal. So tolerant was Pedro of his Jewish helpers that Toledo became a refuge for Jews from all over Europe. By the time Ester Espinosa was married in 1355, the Jewish barrio of Toledo contained as many inhabitants layered family onto family as its gardens contained flowers. Including the new luxurious temple just built by King Pedro's chief financial adviser – Prince Samuel Halevi – the city had a total of twelve synagogues. Some were in the original Jewish quarter, where Ester lived with her new husband, a distant cousin to the Prince Samuel. Others were in the new quarter, where fifteen thousand Jews lived under the shadow of the great wall that had surrounded the city since Roman times.

Three months after the wedding of Ester Espinosa and Isaac Aben Halevi, Henry the Bastard led an army of mercenaries back to Castilla and laid siege to Toledo. Soon the bellies of the soldiers began to rumble with boredom and hunger. Finally, one of Henry's aides found a guardsman willing to be bribed: the gates to the new Judería were opened and while the inhabitants of the old quarter collected their weapons, almost every Jew in the new quarter was butchered.

But when the forces of Henry the Bastard tried to capture the rest of Toledo, they met a determined resistance. After suffering heavy losses, Henry retreated.

In 1369 — fourteen years later — Henry's chance for revenge finally came. Since his last visit, the kingdom of Pedro had shrunk until Toledo was almost all that remained. Small and weak, it tried to prevent the destruction of Toledo by meeting Henry's forces on a plain well removed from the city.

After only a brief battle, Pedro's army was routed. Utterly humiliated, Pedro had to wait — surrounded by his half-brother's forces — while Henry himself came to demand the terms of surrender.

One of the officers of Pedro the Cruel was Isaac Aben Halevi. A soldier who had never killed anyone, the husband of Ester Espinosa was reputed for his devastating powers of debate concerning arcane theological points. Hovering nervously at the side of his king, he watched as Henry the Bastard dismounted from his horse and, wearing his full armour still, approached his half-brother.

"Halt," Pedro cried out.

"You should have killed me with the others."

"In the name of Christendom I demand — "

"Fool," Henry said. As he advanced, barely able to walk in his encumbering armour, he was followed by the man who had become his shadow, the famed Du Guesclin: dark and flat-nosed, self-possessed in the French way, bandy-legged from riding horses, and so short that his huge sword made him look like a child.

"This is my last warning," Pedro said weakly.

But without replying Henry the Bastard leapt forward and threw Pedro to the ground, beating his head against the sandy earth.

Pedro, coming to life for the first time since the battle had begun, suddenly let out a loud roar and began to tear at his brother's armour.

11

For a few moments the two middle-aged men wrestled in the dirt, scratching and clawing at each other, their voices transformed to semi-human moans and howls as their lifelong hatred finally spurted to its climax.

Then Bertrand Du Guesclin stepped forward and, as the two kings rolled like alleycats in heat, lifted his bright and shining sword. When the opportunity presented itself, he brought the blade down with all his force, sending the head of Pedro the Cruel rolling in the dust.

Isaac Aben Halevi tore his eyes from the jagged neck of his former king. He felt his stomach lurch. Then he slipped back through the crowd and began to run.

It took Isaac Aben Halevi two days to reach Toledo again. The advance of Henry Trastamara's army was a slower one. Daily marches were followed by nights of celebration. From his lookout on top of Toledo's great wall, Isaac Aben Halevi kept track of the slow progress of the troops.

On the evening when only a day's march separated the army from the city – which had already formally surrendered – Isaac was at his post. Around the city itself meandered the Targa River, and as Isaac tried to calm himself, the setting sun threw its violent colours onto the surface of the water. When the sun dipped entirely below the far horizon, the great sky's bowl itself was filled with blood – a gigantic heart waiting to be released – then slowly it began to drain into the blackness.

The sky grew darker, the cooking fires of the army began to blaze, soon the air was filled with long and shining ribbons of smoke.

Isaac Aben Halevi uncrossed his legs and stood up on the wall. Tonight the soldiers would eat and drink until they passed out. Tomorrow would be soon enough to worry about the battles to come.

That night, reassured by her husband, Ester Espinosa de Halevi plunged into a deep and dreamless sleep that ended only when she was woken by the noise of heavy battering at the gates of the barrio. While she was dressing herself and the children, her brother Meir burst in, barely able to speak: his house, bigger, fortified with stones and logs, would protect them all.

Meir hurried back to his family, leaving the Halevis to make their final preparations. Moments later they stepped outside. The street was absolutely silent.

When the mob swept around the corner, Ester, her three daughters, and Isaac Aben Halevi were standing in a sedate little circle. "Look," Ester said, pointing to the men who were rushing towards them like red-faced demon-clowns from a great and gaudy Purim play. Then the bubble of innocence burst: as she shrieked in fear, her husband was cut down.

The street that had been an empty tableau was suddenly filled with nightmares. Cries of pain and dying echoed in the narrow spaces between the houses, which themselves were being put to the torch. What first happened to Ester was over so quickly that as she struggled to her feet she was hardly aware of her violation, drowned as it was in what she was seeing: the mutilated bodies of her family on the road beside her, her husband's dead eyes trained open in her direction, a forgiving witness, clutching his daughters to his chest so that they need not know.

Down the street she ran, searching for death, but the soldiers refused her the sword, only raping her

13

again and again until finally the imprint of her husband's staring eyes was erased.

The next thing she knew it was dawn. She had crawled back to join her daughters in her husband's arms, and was lying across their bodies. Steeped in the cold smell of their death, she believed she had died with them until she felt a blanket being thrown over her back.

Twisting slowly, not realizing the truth, she saw a stranger's face crumple in horror. He screamed, but she kept silent: like a card being overturned, the memory of the night came back to her. "It's all right," she said. She wrapped herself in the blanket so as not to offend his eyes. "You don't have to worry about me."

The next few weeks Ester occupied herself – like most of the other Jews of Toledo – in mourning. Although she felt no shame for what had been done to her, she could not understand why she had been doomed to live, while the rest of her family had been permitted to die. But when she discovered she was pregnant, all doubts about herself ended. The child, wanted or not, was the future. "We are condemned to life," she told her friends who were also created mothers on the night of terror. Among them were her best friend, Naomi de Hasdai, and her sister-in-law, Vera, who had been dragged from the house of Meir Espinosa while he, unknowing, cowered in a closet.

The rabbis of Toledo were not pleased to hear that the sentence "We are condemned to life" had become a watchword to the women who were about to bear – according to Jewish law, which had long ago learned to cope with such eventualities – Jewish sons and daughters.

"Life is not something you are condemned to," said the Rabbi David de Estibbah, "life must be lived with hope."

"Hope!" Ester exclaimed, hardly able to believe she had heard this ridiculous word. "What do you mean by hope?"

"Human life is hope," replied David de Estibbah.

"What about God?"

There was an awkward silence while the rabbi, a famous jurist, searched for his answer. Ester felt a heavy and gloomy shadow descend, as if God Himself were sourly waiting to discover how these tiny mortals, these specks whose doubting hearts were like faltering birds in His sky, saw Him.

"God is God," the rabbi said.

When her son was born, Ester felt her heart break open. Even she, who had dared to stand in public and praise the coming of these strange children before they were born, was shocked by the strength of her love for the infant. It was like a river that flowed from her heart to his own, a river that not only was renewed every time she held him to her breast, but was present from the moment he struggled free from her body, one that stayed with her, changing, but undiminished ever since.

Avram Espinosa Halevi, she called him: he was not the son of her husband, but he would grow up to avenge him.

Nor did Ester Espinosa de Halevi forget the words of the rabbi. "We are condemned to life," she now said, "but we must allow the children to know hope. If they are mistakes, let them be known as God's Mistakes."

And that was what they were called as their mothers — banded together for solace — watched the children playing in the rubble of the New Jerusalem

15

of Toledo. Three of these children – Avram Halevi, Gabriela Hasdai, Antonio Espinosa – were born on the same day.

Seven years later, on the anniversary of the night of terror, the barrio was attacked once more. This time the mob was made up not of soldiers, but of peasants who blamed the Jews for the high rents that were ruining them.

Once again, Ester Espinosa de Halevi was dragged from her house. This time her arms were around Avram and in her hand she held a dagger, ready to plunge into her own and her child's hearts. But before she could act, Avram was jerked free and sent to the ground with a blow so violent that Ester could see the blood spurting from his nose as he fell.

"Crawl," the peasant bellowed. "Crawl to the Virgin."

As Ester watched, Avram shook his head in refusal until finally she started to go forward in the desperate hope that he would follow.

While one of their attackers held out a cross and a statuette of the Virgin Mary, the other raised a sword above the skull of Ester Espinosa de Halevi, threatening to split it in two if she interrupted Avram as he swore fealty to the Father, the Son, the Holy Ghost. . . .

ONE

LIKE AN ARMY OF TEN THOUSAND GHOSTLY SPEARS, SMOKE FROM THE COOKING FIRES OF TOLEDO ROSE IN THE DARK EVENING AIR; AND FROM HIS PERCH ON THE STONE WALL AVRAM Halevi could feel his belly respond to this chorus of roasting food. Beyond the wall steep grassy banks sloped down to the Targa River. In the dimming light the grass was dark as pitch, and a few children could still be seen urging their straggling goats and chickens towards the safety of the walls.

The night-time whimpers of the animals mixed with random voices from the city into a long soothing murmur. Across the river, the giant encampment of the summer fair sent out its own signals that the summer day was ending. Just home after two years at the medical school in Montpellier, Avram felt his body settling into the familiar rhythms, fitting itself into them like a knife in its master's hand.

Two years in Montpellier: now the time was gone like a cough. But the view had changed. Before leaving Toledo he had looked out from the city's surrounding wall and seen a surrounding knot of river, then plains stretching to the horizon of the world. Then he had been a baby protected by the darkness of his mother's womb. A baby blindly praying that beyond the darkness of fear and superstition lay a new and brighter world.

"Don Avram, please, I have an urgent message for you."

The voice startled Avram Halevi and he swivelled towards it, his hand reaching automatically to the dagger he always carried.

"Don Avram, please." On the steps below him was a boy, his face half hidden.

"What is it?"

"A certain person has asked me to bring you to his house. You will need your doctor's instruments."

Avram stood up. In his cloak were hidden his surgeon's knives; tied to his waist was a pouch with bags of the powders that Ben Ishaq made from recipes that had been handed down to him, he assured Avram, through dozens of generations stretching back until the beginning of time.

"I am instructed to tell you," the boy said, "that it will be dangerous because you must go outside the barrio."

As they descended the steps and began to walk, Avram saw the boy more clearly. Only ten years younger than himself, with a moustache just beginning to make its shadow along his upper lip, the boy was vaguely familiar. No doubt, Avram thought, he would have recognized him easily enough in the old days. But it was less than a week since he had arrived back from Montpellier, and children whose names had once been on the tip of his tongue were grown into a gang of teenagers who had their own secret games to play through the crowded streets of the Jewish quarter.

Soon, walking quickly, they had almost reached the gate that separated the Jewish quarter from the rest of the city. The boy's words, Avram knew, were not as mysterious as they seemed. From them, he was supposed to understand that a wealthy Christian was requesting his services. Because he was officially a Marrano, a converted Jew, travel outside the ghetto was not expressly forbidden. And yet, should something go wrong, the consequences could be anything from a fine to death by the torture used to extract confessions.

They moved past the gate, which was already locked and guarded, and into the tangle of barrio streets that followed the course of the wall.

"Who has asked for me?"

"The merchant Señor Juan Velásquez. Do you know the name?"

Velásquez. There was no one in Toledo who did not know that name. Juan Velásquez was a merchant with palaces in every city of Spain. His brother, Rodrigo, was a cardinal to the Avignon pope, and it was said that if the papal schism could ever be healed, and the two popes became one, Rodrigo Velásquez – the famous "barefoot cardinal" – would give his lifeblood, or better still that of a thousand rivals, to become pope of all Christendom and restore the power of the battered and divided Church.

"If you like," the boy offered, "I will take you to the home of Velásquez."

"No," Avram said. "I will go alone." He had already reached into his money pouch to find a coin.

"I am not afraid," the boy boasted. "One night I stayed in the Christian quarter until dawn."

"What is your name?"

"Isroyel Itzhak," the boy replied. He said his name loudly, and when he grinned with his pride, his teeth showed a gap along one side. If nothing was done for the boy's mouth, it would one day begin to cave in towards the missing teeth, like a mountain whose

19

sides have been mined for gold. In Montpellier, Avram had learned to do a new operation, one in which the teeth of dogs and cats were implanted into human gums. There were surgeons who had claimed their implants could last even longer than the life of the animal from whom they had been taken.

"Go home tonight," Avram said gently. "It takes more courage to comfort and obey your parents than to sneak around the houses of the Christians."

The boy looked at Avram, appealing, then turned and fled.

Avram stepped deeper into the shadows. As a boy he, too, had spent nights in the Christian quarter – sometimes on a dare, sometimes in order to steal food for himself and his mother. Velásquez had his palace, he knew, not too far from the wall that was supposed to separate Jews from Christians. Like the palace of Avram's deceased and distant relative – Samuel Halevi – it was famous for its terraced gardens, but unlike the walled palace of the Jew, its gardens had a view of the Targa River.

That Velásquez had sent for him secretly was no surprise. For his brother Rodrigo and Ferrand Martínez – the queen's confessor, a ferociously anti-Jewish archbishop – had already proclaimed their support of the pope's ban against Jewish physicians. Asked what he himself would do if threatened with a mortal illness, Cardinal Rodrigo had replied: "It is better to die than to owe your life to a Jew."

Soon Avram came to the place where he liked to scale the wall. It was behind one of the warehouses that used to belong to Samuel Halevi: but the warehouse guard was an old friend, and in a few seconds Avram was inside the locked door and crossing a courtyard thick with the smell of foreign cloth and spices. As he was climbing the wall, his feet found the familiar niches that he himself had helped to chip out.

The wall was so wide that he could lie on the bed of stone that divided the city. For a moment he paused, old fears circling through him, and from his cloak he withdrew his dagger. Slowly he closed his palm around the handle. The knife was a gift from his cousin Antonio, to be carried, Antonio had said, whenever he was in the quarter of the Christians. *Now*, Avram said to himself. Then he leapt the twenty feet down into the street. It was the first time he had crossed the wall since his return; a sharp tingle of pleasure ran through him as he landed on his hands and feet together – like a cat – in the way every boy in the ghetto had practised since childhood. Minutes later Avram Halevi was gently rapping the handle of his knife against the iron bars of the gate to the palace of Juan Velásquez.

The gate swung open a crack and Avram slipped inside. Instantly he was slammed into the stone wall, cold steel pressed against his throat. A lantern was held to his face, and in its light Avram saw two men: a hunchback whose floppy hat failed to conceal a round and beardless face, and the guard whose sword held Avram in place. This guard was a giant, with the neck and shoulders of a bull. He bent his head down and blew into Avram's face. His breath was rank with garlic and burnt meat, his body gave off the odour of an animal too long caged.

The hunchbacked man began to search him. His hands soon stopped at the bundle of knives in Avram's cloak.

"Leave those," Avram said.

The hunchback, without answering, inserted his hand into the cloak to feel for the pouch.

Avram brought his knee up quickly, and the hunchback collapsed onto the ground in front of him. At the same time the giant, surprised by such impudence, stepped back. Avram moved away from the wall and into the open area of the courtyard. He still held his dagger, and now he extended his hand from the sleeve of his cloak so that the metal would catch the light of the lantern. Without a word the giant stepped towards him, waving his huge sword effortlessly. The blade swished through the air like a fan. In the wake of the giant crawled the hunchback, cursing as he struggled for breath.

"What are you doing?"

Immediately the two servants turned towards their master. "Don Juan –"

"Don Halevi?"

"Yes."

"I am Juan Velásquez. Welcome back to Toledo." The merchant came into the circle of light and Avram saw a middle-aged man who was tall and corpulent, with a face that – in contrast to his fleshy body – was carved and rigid. His cheeks and chin were shaven, but he wore a moustache that emphasized his wide and thin-lipped mouth. His eyes, like his hair, were jet-black. For a moment he stood still, a man who was used to making an impression. Then he put an arm around Avram's shoulder and began to draw him towards the house. Juan Velásquez had a certain reputation for swagger, and as they moved into the lit corridors Avram could see that he was wearing a gold-brocaded white tunic with a red cape slung over his shoulders, as if this medical emergency had interrupted his attendance at an important dinner.

"You will forgive my rudeness in reaching you so late," Juan Velásquez said, "but I have had a boy looking for you since noon today."

Avram doubted this. Rich merchants did not like to have doctors from the barrio seen entering the house: a rich merchant who was the brother of a cardinal would be no exception.

"And you will forgive my rudeness in interrupting your evening. I know that you have just returned to Toledo, and you must have friends to visit."

Avram restrained a smile. If Juan Velásquez was anything like his brother, who had preached that the very air breathed by Jews became contaminated by their refusal to believe, his only wish for Avram's friends would be to see them brutally dispatched to their own special Hell.

"Ben Ishaq gave me your name."

How curious that Velásquez would explain how he came to know the name of Halevi. As if there might be any other surgeon crazy enough to cross at night into the Christian quarter.

"My wife has been in labour for three days now. I have had the best midwives in the city, but they are useless. I have no children. You understand?"

"I understand," Avram replied, understanding that if there was a choice to be made, the infant must be saved before the wife. A good Christian sentiment, Avram thought, but one he had never been able to accept fully.

"Ben Ishaq was here this afternoon. He told me that there were three possibilities."

"What were they?"

"He said that first of all we could do nothing and that perhaps the baby would be born before my wife died in labour."

Perhaps born dead, Avram thought, but said nothing.

"Second, he said a surgeon could reach into my wife's womb and –," here Velásquez's voice broke,

23

"— and cut the child up, so that it could be removed. In this case my wife might survive."

Avram nodded. To reach into the womb and kill a living child was a task for which, despite his medical training, he had no taste. But now that he understood that it was surgery that was going to be required, he knew why Ben Ishaq had passed the case to him: surgery was the one area in which this Muslim doctor refused to practise. He claimed that his old man's hands were too awkward, but Avram knew the truth: Ben Ishaq had smoked so much hashish that he could no longer bear to watch blood flow from wounds he himself had made.

"And the third?" Avram asked, already knowing.

"The third is that you cut open the womb of my wife and lift from it the living child."

Avram was silent.

"Ben Ishaq tells me," Juan said, "that Julius Caesar was born in this manner."

"His mother had died during labour."

"But," Velásquez insisted, "wouldn't there be a better chance for the boy to be alive if the mother was still living?"

"How do you know it's a boy?"

"The midwives told me."

"And how do they know?"

"How does anyone know these things?" Velásquez snapped back, irritated. "If I were a surgeon, I assure you that you would be at home with your mother, I would be having dinner with the queen's foreign minister, and my new child would be happily suckling at the breast of my wife."

When Velásquez had married his young bride, shortly after his first wife had died following twenty years of infertile misery, it was said that the flour used to make the cakes for the wedding could have fed bread to the whole of Toledo for a week.

24

While talking they had arrived at a door, which Velásquez now opened. At the end of a bedroom large enough to be a dining hall was a four-postered bed, overhung with canopies whose gold brocade pulsed in the light of the candles. Guided by Velásquez, Avram walked slowly forward; suddenly two women that Avram recognized emerged from the shadows, their faces cringing and eager to please.

"Don Halevi," Velásquez said, his voice heavy with sarcasm, "may I introduce you to the fair midwives of Toledo."

The crones giggled nervously. It was a tradition that the rich rewarded midwives well when their labours – and their patient's – were successful. When they were not, their patient's poor luck could spread like a disease.

"Perhaps the Señoras will tell the doctor about the problem that has prevented the birth of my son."

"Excuse me," Avram said, and stepped away from Velásquez with the two women. They had been up with Isabel for nights; their eyes were red and the lines on their faces had deepened with fatigue.

The older Señora de Cisco, who was always the one to do the talking, leaned mournfully on Avram's arm. "She is too thin. A big man like the Señor, and the lady is as thin as a bean grown in the desert."

"Many thin women have children."

"But the baby is sideways," protested the midwife. "You cannot move a sideways cart through a narrow door."

"You tried to turn the baby?"

"For three days."

"And the opening?"

The midwife held up two fingers, pressed tightly together. "That is not even a window, Doctor, let alone a door."

"What did Ben Ishaq do today?"

25

"He asked questions like you, Doctor. He consulted his astrological charts. And he gave the Señora a potion of sunflower seeds."

"What happened?"

"Her stomach went as hard as wood. Then she had an hour of violent labour. During that time Ben Ishaq tried to change the baby, but with no result. After this he consulted his charts again and advised Señor Velásquez that he must send for you, because you could do a miraculous operation that would save both the mother and the child."

"Ben Ishaq is a man of great faith," Avram said drily. The charts were, Avram knew, no more than a special piece of theatre that Ben Ishaq reserved for rich patients.

"Yes, Doctor."

Avram turned back to the centre of the room, where Velásquez was waiting impatiently.

"They have done everything they can," Avram said.

Velásquez glanced at the sisters as if they were a pair of courtyard dogs he was about to kick, and they slunk back into the shadows. Looking satisfied at their fear, Velásquez took Avram's arm and led him towards the bed. Above was a niche containing a gold statuette of the crucified Christ. The wound in His side was studded with tiny rubies, which formed a bright drizzle of blood descending to His gold loincloth. Sitting beneath the statuette, holding the hand of Velásquez's young wife, was an old woman dressed entirely in black and shrouded by a veil.

Despite the dozens of candles, the huge room's stone walls easily absorbed the light. Avram was virtually upon the bed before he could distinguish the face of the patient herself, Isabel Gana de Velásquez. As he bent over her, the mother and Velásquez melted away. Isabel's black eyes were dull and without hope, her ivory skin had turned a sallow colour and was covered with layers of sweat from the violence of her labours, the hollows of her cheeks were dark caves of impending death.

Avram drew the curtains around the bed, enclosing himself with his patient. He smiled at her, trying to reassure, but though her lips parted in return, it was hard to know if what she was returning to him was a smile or simply the grimace of total surrender.

"May I?" Avram murmured. "Please excuse me," and he drew down the sheet that covered the belly of the Señora de Velásquez.

The first thing he saw was that on top of her protruding navel, at the very height of her stomach, an eye had been placed.

This would be the work of the superstitious midwives: for some reason they believed that the eye of a hare, taken in March and dried in pepper, had the power of drawing out a baby whose birth was difficult. Every spring hundreds of rabbits fell victim to this hope, dying in the snares set by the old women who religiously climbed around the rocks at the riverbank, trying to trap a new supply of guarantees for the coming year. These same women were convinced that if couples should fail to conceive babies – thus leaving the poor midwives with a glut of dried eyes in their pepper-pots – the nether parts of the unsuccessful couples should be twined with the pubic hair of wolves.

Avram gently lifted the eye away from the white and tender skin. Its months in the pepper-pot had given it a dried and shrivelled look – surely it would frighten any infant unfortunate enough to see it through the walls of the womb. As he watched, the muscles of Isabel's womb contracted, pushing the

27

baby up and forward like a huge ball that refused to be thrown.

Avram put his hand on her inflated belly, the womb distended with the unborn child. As the midwives had said, the baby was lying crossways. But it was still alive; Avram could feel it struggling under his palm.

The curtain parted and Velásquez entered the enclosure. He had a cloth moistened with wine, which he held to his wife's mouth.

"Will you do the operation?"

"It is dangerous. I cannot guarantee the result."

"Only God can grant miracles," said Velásquez. This in a practised voice, as if he meant to imply that his brother had made the necessary applications.

"The patient must consent," Avram insisted.

"She consents."

Avram looked at the face of Isabel de Velásquez. She was nodding to confirm this, but as she tried to speak another contraction gripped her, and the muscles of her mouth distorted in pain.

"With God's help," said Avram, "I will try." They stepped outside the curtain and Avram requested boiling water, a brazier of coals and a cauterizing iron, a new bottle of wine, a supply of linen to be used for soaking up the blood.

"Should I call the priest?" Velásquez asked, his voice suddenly changed from that of a confident merchant to that of a scared boy.

"Not yet. The child is not yet ready to be baptized."

While Velásquez was ordering what was necessary from the midwives, Avram brought a table to the side of the bed, and on it he laid out his surgeon's knives, all of them bought at Montpellier, and his pouch of powders from Ben Ishaq.

Where it was that Ben Ishaq got his potions, Avram did not know. But the old man, with his cynical jokes and his superstitious routines, made the best sleeping powders and herbal remedies of any doctor in Toledo; and he was at least willing to supply them to the younger man in return for Avram's taking on the surgical jobs for which he himself did not have the taste.

Into a glass of wine Avram emptied a quarter of a small vial of powder. He wanted to force Isabel into a sleep – deep enough that she would feel no pain, not so deep that the baby would die. "Of course," Ben Ishaq had said, "I have tested all of these myself." He looked at Avram and smiled. "But I prefer hashish, because it allows you to stay conscious and enjoy your dreams." There was another potion he offered Avram, one that made the patient forget all the pain, though during the actual operation he might shriek with agony. Ben Ishaq, who had learned his surgery tending wounded soldiers in the south, once described doing an amputation while the soldier screamed and begged, above the sound of the saw going through bone, that his leg not be taken off.

Without question Isabel de Velásquez accepted the wine and drank it. She must have been beautiful when Velásquez first saw her, but the long labour had made her face into that of an old woman, and her neck was corded with the effort of days spent struggling with her pain. Why, Avram had sometimes wondered, do some babies choose to spite the bravery of their mothers by trying to be born feet first, upside-down, curled into shapes that should never have been invented? Did they not realize what agony and danger attended their birth? Or perhaps this was the true original sin of children, to come smiling into the arms of the mother who endured such torture in order to receive them.

"You will fall asleep," Avram said. "But during the operation you may wake up. I will give you more to drink and then, in a few minutes, the operation will be over and the child will be born."

Looking first to see whether Velásquez had returned, Isabel motioned Avram to bend over.

"Will it hurt?" she whispered.

"No," Avram said. "I promise you that it won't hurt."

But seconds later Velásquez set the glowing bowl of coals on the floor by the bed. Isabel flinched and turned her head away.

"We begin," Avram said. He had three more glasses, each filled with wine and sleeping potion, on the table beside the bed. As soon as Velásquez had closed the door behind him, Avram gave Isabel the second glass of wine. She was barely able to swallow; as she did, Avram stroked her throat to make the liquid go down. Against the tips of his fingers, her skin was silky and warm.

The younger Señora de Cisco carried forward the basket filled with baby blankets while out of sight of Isabel, the elder de Cisco sister held the cauterizing iron in the coals.

"Count to ten," Ben Ishaq had told him, "and then, ten seconds after the second glass, you have whatever chance you're going to get. Go as quickly as you can, don't touch unnecessarily because you know how little you would like your own insides to be touched, and pray that because of your speed, the God of the Jews will forgive you for tampering with what He Himself has been unwilling to effect."

Avram moved his hand from the smooth throat of Isabel de Velásquez to her mouth, carefully parted her lips. Above them, he held the largest of his silver knives. A slight mist settled on the metal. He changed the knife for a steel scalpel, small and sharp. For a moment he hesitated, wondering what would happen to him if the operation failed. Then he pressed the sharp tip of his scalpel to the belly of Isabel de Velásquez and all else left his mind. In Montpellier he had done this operation several times – but always to women who had already died.

The skin parted, revealing a red sheet of underflesh. Wiping away the blood, Avram drew the knife through the thin marbled fat, wiped again, pressed into the muscle of the belly until the womb itself was exposed. As he took a linen cloth to wipe the blood, Isabel de Velásquez opened her eyes.

"Sleep," Avram murmured. Then he turned to Señora de Gana, who was holding the next glass, awaiting Avram's instruction.

"Not yet." Because since the second glass, the baby had not moved. He put the cloth down and cut again, deeper. This time there was a contraction, accompanied by a shriek, and blood spurted up from the cut flesh, spattering Avram's face and clothes. He sponged the wound, wondering if he should have bled her from the ankles before beginning. A new contraction tore the womb further. Isabel moaned and her jaw began to clatter. Death rattle, Avram thought, and fear burst through him. Suddenly, through the torn flesh, he caught a glimpse of something new, scarlet and twisted. He pushed the wound apart to examine it: an infant's ear.

"Give her more wine."

Even as the Señora de Gana was forcing the wine into her daughter, Avram was reaching for the baby – it was alive, he knew it; as his hands closed around it, Isabel screamed, but this time the midwives were holding her still and crying with her. Avram felt first the baby's shoulders, slippery with its mother's blood, and then suddenly he had it free, lifting it up from the open belly of the mother and into the light of the candles.

"Alive," Isabel's mother choked, "Isabel —"

But Isabel groaned so loudly that her mother's voice was cut off.

The baby was blue. Avram slapped it and it coughed out its first breath. He hit its back again and this time it cried, a loud high note.

Avram set the baby in the waiting basket. With one hand he kept mopping up the blood, with the other he held the cord, which was still pulsing wildly.

"Now," Avram whispered, "give her the fourth glass now." He felt a fierce elation: in his hand the cord was turning from blue to white, and as his fingers flew, first tying it twice and then cutting between the knots, he knew he had done the operation more quickly this time than ever before.

The younger Señora de Cisco took the baby and wrapped it with cloths. While its loud cries like crashing music filled the room, Avram turned back to Isabel de Velásquez and pressed her wound closed. He realized that he should have waited for the afterbirth, but just as he was cursing his stupidity the womb contracted gently and the afterbirth released.

As he bent back over Isabel, the older de Cisco sister brought the iron towards her wound. "Not yet," Avram whispered, but not soon enough to stop Isabel de Velásquez from opening her eyes to see a red-hot iron travelling towards her. Once more she screamed, so loudly that Velásquez came rushing into the room.

But Avram, oblivious, was sewing the wound with the thread Ben Ishaq had given him. He was faster than a seamstress, his teacher had joked, and every few stitches he stopped and gave a few rubs to Isabel's belly, noting each time that miraculously the womb was shrinking as it should.

Soon the inner layers were closed. And then, when the outer ones were closed too, Avram was finally ready for the iron.

With Isabel's final shriek, the room was filled with the smell of burning flesh.

"It's all right," Avram murmured, but now that everything was over, his arms had begun to tremble. "It's going to be all right." Using the last of the linen cloths, he shakily wiped clean the wound. Then he put his hand back on her womb. It was growing harder and shrinking just as it should. Soon it would be no larger than a fist.

The next time Isabel opened her eyes, the baby was ready to be offered to her. She weakly extended her arms and, with her mother's help, lowered it to her breast. At this moment there appeared on Isabel's face, as there did on the face of every mother he had ever attended, a sweet but passive smile. "Why," Avram had once asked Ben Ishaq, "is the smile always so restrained? Are the mothers afraid to show their true face to a heathen?"

"No," Ben Ishaq had replied. "The women of Toledo have a universal face that is formed by excessive contemplation of the Virgin." And then he had made his own sly smile, while looking suspiciously behind himself to make sure that no one had heard a helpless old Muslim making an anti-Christian remark.

As the new infant lay against his mother's breast, Halevi wiped the blood from his knives. Steel and flesh: every time he cut the skin he was afraid that he was going to kill. He closed and tied the leather pouch of his knives, inserted it in the inside pocket of his cloak. The safest thing, Avram knew, would be to wait in Velásquez's house until daylight. But his own mother would remain awake until he came home; and if she spent the whole night awake, it would be days before she had caught up enough on sleep for her pain to be bearable again.

The infant was a boy. His name, Juan Velásquez had proudly declared, would be Diego Carlos Rodrigo Velásquez – the name of his grandfather. Meanwhile the lips of the new Diego Velásquez had slipped away from Isabel's nipple, and he had fallen asleep. For a few months of such drooling contentment, Avram thought, a child and its mother are tied for life; and yet even the thick walls and the heavy oak shutters of a merchant's house could not guarantee the safety of such a relationship.

Halevi took the brandy that Velásquez offered, and gulped it back.

Velásquez, surprised, offered him a refill from the crystal decanter. Halevi accepted. Careful, he warned himself, Jews and Marranos don't drink. Christian merchants drink. Peasants drink. Armies drink when the blood is boiling with the sound of houses burning.

The brandy had formed a fiery pool in his stomach and was sending flashes of heat to his blood. On the surface of his skin Avram felt a slight burning, a reminder of the scorching summer sun under which these grapes had matured.

"You are skilful," Velásquez said. "And you are quick. That is how they told me you would be. You will come back tomorrow, to make sure she is well?"

"Yes."

"She will live?" This question asked in a voice that tried to seem careless, man-to-man, as if to say that the rich merchant Velásquez, who could buy his way in and out of many a silk-sheeted bed, at least valued his wife in the moment of childbirth, even if he did not love her. Perhaps Velásquez did not realize how lucky *he* was to have lived to see his own child – to have lived himself to make sure that the child he saw was his own.

"God willing," Avram said, "she will live to be a grandmother."

"Your God or mine?"

Avram smiled. The brandy must be heating Velásquez, too. "I am a Marrano," Avram said. "I was baptized by the sword when I was a child."

"To be baptized by the sword," Velásquez said, "is not a pleasant experience."

"Many experiences are not pleasant."

"And you live with your mother, in the Jewish quarter."

"My mother had no wish to change."

"And yourself?"

"I was a child," Avram said. "I had nothing to change from." There was still brandy in the glass he held, but he did not move it towards his lips. Some Marranos had used their conversions to shed the restrictions hindering Jews and to rise to high positions in the king's service. Others dared to enter the Church, using their Hebrew education to become favoured priests, even bishops, whose specialty lay in convincing the wayward Jews of their error in failing to recognize Christ as the true Messiah. But most – like himself – had been forcibly converted and were left, as a result, in a no-man's-land.

Velásquez was testing him, he knew. Like most tests he had experienced, there was little to be gained from passing; but to fail could be very dangerous. So far, he had not failed.

35

"It is hard," Velásquez said, "being a Marrano. The Marrano does not have the comfort of being a Jew, yet he shares the inconvenience."

"In such difficult times, there are many inconveniences to share. I am thankful to have so few."

"You should have been a diplomat," Velásquez said sharply, "not a doctor." What he meant, Avram knew, was that Avram was being not at all diplomatic, but rude. The great and wealthy merchant Velásquez had invited him into his home, permitted him to save his wife and his future heir, and then had done the Marrano Halevi the great service of inviting him to unburden himself. Instead, the ingrate was fencing. Well, Avram thought, he would keep fencing. Let the merchant buy his knowledge elsewhere.

Avram put his glass on the mantel and turned to the bed. Isabel's eyes were closed, and the blanket over her was moving with the slow rhythm of sleep. Avram slid his hand beneath the sheet and felt her belly. Then, while the midwives watched, he lifted the covers and inspected for bleeding. If the wound healed and there was no post-natal fever, Isabel would be healthy. But she would not be able to have another child, because after the incision he had made in the womb, it would never be strong enough to bear an ordinary birth without splitting open like an overcooked squash. Ben Ishaq, who had taught him the operation, had told him of such incidents.

Avram reached for his cloak, which had been hanging by the door, and drew it over his shoulders. It was black, as was the broad-brimmed hat he now held in his hands: the physician's uniform he had won in Montpellier.

Velásquez opened the shutter. The last dark veils of night hung over the city, waiting to be stripped away.

"Tomorrow night," Avram said, "I will come after dark to see your wife."

"I will be here." Velásquez extended his hand to Avram to seal the bargain: in Velásquez's palm was a silk handkerchief that surrounded a dozen gold coins. Avram allowed the weight to sink into his fingers. Money was safety, freedom and danger, all in one shiny place. He put the coins in a special inside pocket of his cloak, padded so that their jingle could not be heard.

"Until tomorrow," Avram said.

"Shalom," Velásquez replied. "Go in peace." He clapped his hands to Avram's shoulders and he squeezed – the grip of a powerful man. "Thank you," he said. "You are everything Ben Ishaq promised: courageous, skilful, polite. I am in debt to the wonderful science you have brought back with you from France."

A few minutes later Avram was scaling the wall that separated the quarters. When he reached the top he lay on the wide stones for a moment, sucking the night air deep into his lungs.

What a triumph!

To have penetrated the house of Juan Velásquez, to have opened the belly of the most treasured woman in all Toledo, to have plucked from her womb a living child –

The sweet feel of the child's head, the warmth of its tiny shoulders, came flooding back into Avram's hands. For six years he had prepared for this moment – four years as an apprentice to Ben Ishaq, then two years at the medical school of Montpellier – every night telling himself that he would be a doctor, a surgeon, that with his surgeon's skills he would pare away superstition, the clouds surrounding his own life, the earth laid upon the grave of the medical knowledge of the ancients –

37

Feeling foolish, a young boy overwhelmed by his hilarious and ridiculous pride, he wanted to stand up on the barrio wall and trumpet his triumph out over the sleeping city.

Instead, like a man swearing allegiance, he held his hand to his chest. Beneath his palm he could feel his heart pounding: alive, alive despite all the warnings that, with the shadow of the plague still hanging over Europe, no Jew could survive the trip from Toledo to Montpellier and back.

For six years the dream had been forming inside him: the dream of becoming a new man for a new age, the dream of being a Jew with the intelligence, the knowledge, the will, to escape the tiny, fearful enclave in which his life was destined to be lived.

Now, a few cuts with the knife and the bonds were gone forever, his great journey begun.

TWO

THE EVENING AFTER HIS TRIUMPHANT DELIVERY OF THE VELÁSQUEZ HEIR, AVRAM HALEVI WALKED HAPPILY THROUGH THE BARRIO. HE HAD SPENT THE DAY SEEING PATIENTS AND each was eager to praise him for the miracle he had performed on the wife of the rich merchant. Now he was waiting for nightfall so he could pay his return visit to the house of Juan Velásquez. In order to ensure that visit, a letter had already arrived at his house, containing more gold coins and sealed with the Velásquez stamp.

Though the hot afternoon had scarcely begun to expel its breath, in the narrow and crooked streets the angled light played tricks on the stone and wooden walls of the jammed-together houses: some had been transformed into a smooth and living gold, as if the city had finally been raised to Heaven; others were already plunged into the shadow of night. He stopped and looked towards the sky: a faint sickle moon was visible.

Above him, Avram could hear the sounds of shutters slamming closed. As dark approached, it always seemed that the houses grew wider as they rose from the streets. Often the third and fourth storeys were so close that the windows opened virtually onto the

39

rooms of the house opposite and two neighbours, talking, could lean out and pass cups of tea back and forth – or, if they were on bad terms, throw their slops into each other's kitchens.

From the open windows came the sounds and smells of dinner: like a huge and ancient beast Toledo was beginning to settle its stiff bones and creak and twist its way into sleep.

A beast, that was how Avram liked to think of Toledo, a huge scarred beast with a wrinkled hide in which lived its multitudes of parasites, colonies that had staked out their territories in corners from which the beast's mind had retreated centuries ago. And though the beast had once, millennia before, stretched its body like a young and supple maiden dancer, now it was a dowager so crusted with the centuries that its jewels had turned to worthless rock. Even its memory had turned to stone. Its great hairy ears were filled with coarse sawgrass and heard sounds that its dim great-grandmother's brain never registered – and that brain itself was a hollow cave so filled with broken dreams, unforgotten hours, strange and glorious oases, too, that it no longer realized that its purpose was to direct the beast. But now the beast needed no direction. It was slumped in the doze that would eventually carry it to eternity.

But despite everything, Avram knew, the city of Toledo was at peace. And why not? he asked himself. Was there anywhere in Spain where the Jews were so prosperous? Women and men alike wore clothes imported from countries whose names twisted the tongue. Even the street he was walking on was adorned by the newest and fanciest synagogue in Spain – the Synagogue of the Tránsito: a gift to the Jews of Toledo from the wealthy Samuel Halevi, a gift made with the express permission of the same king who had banned the construction of new synagogues elsewhere in his kingdom.

Through the temple's high diamond-shaped windows, each one a mosaic of expensive Italian glass, Avram could hear a ragged chanting. He stopped in the square for a moment to listen. Inside, he knew, old men with prayer shawls around their necks were swaying from side to side, singing prayers whose words had long ago been memorized and whose meaning they had spent their lives disputing.

Hundreds of times, Avram had heard these prayers as he passed. Tonight, obeying a new and sudden impulse, Avram walked quickly up the steps and swung open the heavy door.

In the corners of the tall building, a few candles burned, sending yellow shafts of light to the carved wooden ceiling. At the far end of the synagogue stood an old hazzan, a singer hired to lead the prayers, bent over his book. His back was to the congregation, which was itself only two dozen men scattered through a space that could have comfortably held two hundred.

Avram closed the door behind him.

The sudden gust of wind made the candles jump, sent new sheets of yellow light across the walls and ceiling. But not one of the men turned. As he walked to one of the benches, Avram was aware of a slightly musty odour, as if the skins of the old men were emitting, even in this new temple, the smells of their ancestors. He picked up the prayer book. Because he had been converted, he had never gone to the Hebrew school, but living in the barrio and studying medicine had forced him to be fluent in Hebrew, and he had heard the prayers being chanted so often around him that their words were as familiar as the popular minstrels' songs. Without at first joining in, he let

41

the prayers surround him, settling like a new weight on the cloak he still wore.

The voice of the hazzan was high and whining, on the narrow ledge between beauty and self-pity. Avram was just about to join in the chorus when he looked up to see Gabriela Hasdai sitting in the balcony reserved for women, a dozen feet above the benches where the men prayed.

Before he had left for Montpellier, there had been a tearful scene during which he had explained why he must risk his life and follow his dream wherever it led him. But in his whole time away he had written her only once, and since he had come back to Toledo he had neither sent her a message nor gone to visit her. Now he could feel his heart diving in on itself. Fear? Love re-awakened? Yes, there was a way in which he loved Gabriela Hasdai, but whether with the love for a sister or for a wife, he could not answer.

For a moment Avram looked directly into Gabriela's eyes. Then, flushing as if his thoughts had written themselves upon his face, he turned back to the prayer book. His voice, sibilant when he spoke Spanish, took on a guttural sound with the Hebrew words. The events of his childhood might seem far away, but the Hebrew of God and the prophets was buried in the earth itself. Four thousand years: sometimes Avram tried to imagine how life must have been in Israel. He pictured a southern desert, like the desert near Cordoba: fanatical old men with their skin baked to splitting, stumbling out of caves and into the blinding white sand, begging God for a sign.

But when the sign was given, Avram had always wondered, were their cut lips healed? Did their cracked skin become whole again, their faces youthful, their hair shining and flowing, their gowns and garments white and dazzling? Or were they still the same as they had been: a bit dazed by having had the lightning of God's voice rip through their veins, and eager to spend another twenty years waiting for the next encounter?

The words rushed through him like the stone rivers that flowed down the mountains. Now all the voices blended together, pulsing like a great heart inside the synagogue, like God's heart as it hung above His worshippers, ready to open up and give the divine kiss to His own chosen people.

"Listen!" a voice suddenly shouted.

The singing continued.

"LISTEN!"

Later Avram remembered that when he had turned to the door, there was a blackness to the air that no August night should be able to hold.

"LISTEN!"

This time the singing stopped and all the men, even Joshua, the mosquito-voiced hazzan, turned to the open door.

A short man, hooded, stood with his arms spread wide, panting with the effort of his journey. Behind him in the courtyard of the synagogue, a dozen children were gathered, perhaps waiting to see what this insane profaner of the synagogue would do.

He was dressed in the costume of the south: a bright hooded tunic over a white blouse, torn red cape half hanging from his shoulders, baggy leggings tucked into leather boots that were wrinkled and scuffed. All the cloth he wore was soaked in sweat. From under his arms spread large black patches, and his chest, too, had a dark island.

"It is forbidden to interrupt the service without permission," Joshua said in the silence.

The hood that had covered the stranger's face was now thrown back. Antonio Espinosa: even in the dim light Avram recognized his cousin at once.

"In Sevilla," Antonio Espinosa began, "in Sevilla this happened. They broke into the Judería at the door of San Nicolas. It was Ferrand Martínez in the lead, followed by Rodrigo Velásquez, and they had two thousand men." This was recited in a monotone, the way that memorized commentaries are recited by students, and as he spoke he looked not at any of his listeners, but at the ark at the front of the synagogue.

"We heard them coming and we closed the gates, but they had brought logs to break them down. For two hours the gates held, and we hoped for the royal guard to come to our rescue. When the gates collapsed, the archbishop was the first to enter, carrying a cross. His followers poured in behind him, enraged by the hours they had been detained.

"Some of us were killed in our homes, others as we cowered on the street. To each was offered freedom in exchange for conversion. But none agreed although the archbishop held his cross in front of every man before he was killed. This process took a long time; soon the mob decided to herd the rest of us into the Jardines de Murillo.

"While we were being held there, listening to the sermons of Martínez and Velásquez, we could hear the dying of those who were being caught as the invaders went from house to house, searching for gold and for jewels. When they were finished, they came to the gardens and began to kill us. We numbered at least a thousand persons, including children.

"By this time it was dark. I and a few others managed to fight our way to the edge of the gardens and escape over the wall."

His eyes stayed fixed on the ark, but his voice had stopped. Then Joshua began chanting the mourner's kaddish, his dry and wavering voice fluttered towards the ornate vaulted ceilings.

"This happened two weeks ago," Antònio said. "There were four of us who escaped from the whole Judería, and each of us has carried the news in a different direction."

"And the others?" asked Samuel Abrabanel, the self-proclaimed chief rabbi of Toledo. "What about the others who survived? Is there anyone to take care of them?"

"None survived."

"No converts?" Abrabanel insisted.

"None."

"Some might have converted after you escaped."

"If heads carried on spears can convert, then perhaps they bowed down. If children split in half can be reunited by the Christians' God, then perhaps they became whole again. If hearts carved out of their owners' chests can learn to love a different God, then perhaps they learned to love the God of the archbishop. If bodies, dead and mortally wounded, heaped together and burned so that the smell of their flesh spreads over the whole countryside, can learn to see Christ in the flames, then perhaps they were resurrected in a new faith. But aside from these miracles, and others for which my tongue has no name, there were no conversions."

For a moment he was silent. Then Antonio Espinosa slowly drew off his tunic and opened his blouse. Carved into his chest, the wound an angry red, was the sign of the cross.

"They said," continued Antonio in his flat voice, "that as a special favour they would give me this before they killed me, because this was the sign of the true explorer and seeker after God; and that with this on my body, perhaps St. Peter would have mercy

45

on me when he saw the soul of a Jew." He closed his shirt and drew on his tunic once more. "Forgive me for uncovering myself before God. Forgive me for interrupting the prayers. And beware what has happened in Sevilla, because there is not a city in Aragón or Castilla that will be different." And then, as suddenly as he had come, Antonio Espinosa turned and walked out the door. As soon as he was outside, he ran at full speed across the square and in moments was lost in the narrow maze of ghetto streets.

A few minutes later, everyone was standing in the square. Rumours had already begun to fan through the quarter. Every Jewry in the south, it was said, was now in flames. Armed mobs, hundreds of thousands strong, were marching like a new and expanded crusade through the land.

Avram stood briefly on the edge of the crowd. Then, suddenly realizing that the sky had become completely dark, he began walking quickly towards the Christian quarter and the house of Juan Velásquez.

THREE

TO THE WORLD, THE HOUSE OF MEIR ESPINOSA PRESENTED A FACE OF QUARRIED STONE. IT BELLIED UP FROM THE NARROW MUD ALLEY-WAY, SURROUNDED A HEAVY WOODEN DOOR that was reinforced with iron, and rose several storeys to a sharply pitched roof covered in tiles of orange clay.

In the night-time, no windows were visible, and a passer-by could not see even the tiniest crack of light through the heavy wooden shutters. "These shutters must be closed," said Alfredo Meir Espinosa, "in order to keep out the spirits of the dead."

"Don't be superstitious," Avram had protested. "The spirits of the dead must have higher ambitions than haunting poor Toledo."

"Other spirits, too," Meir Espinosa insisted. "The spirits of golems that have never been born are so jealous that they can poison the heart and lungs. My own mother died after a night when she slept with her windows opened."

"She was ninety-six years old," Avram said. "And in any case, if it is so unsafe, how do you dare to walk outside at night?"

"I wear an amulet."

"The claw of a wolf," Avram had laughed. "I thought that you believed in science."

"I believe in science," Meir agreed. "I believe in everything."

The night Toledo learned of the massacre at Sevilla, Ester Espinosa de Halevi sat in the house of her brother and contemplated her own bitter thoughts.

Through the wall she could hear the unstoppable weeping of Vera, her brother's wife. In Sevilla, Antonio had been visiting his grandparents. He had escaped but they had perished.

For a few hours the whole family mourned together. Then Ester had gone to her own rooms to await Avram.

Though her son was now twenty-one years old, Ester could still say that she had heard the song going from herself to him for her whole life – even if the tune sometimes changed from love to pain, it never deserted her; even if he died, it would not desert her, only turn from love and pain to grief and despair.

And yet, while her sister-in-law cried and her own heart twisted, Ester could not help feeling the sweetness of the summer night. One of her husband's ancestors had been the grandfather of Samuel Halevi, but another had been a poet, famous for his verses in praise of nights such as this. Ester had always thought that Judah Halevi must have been a fool to spend his time arranging silly words about the weather. Now she was no longer sure.

It was past midnight, but the warmth of the sun was still in the air. She remembered how Toledo had smelled twenty-two years ago, and knew that now Sevilla would be smelling the same, the smoke of wood and human flesh mixed into a nauseating and acrid wind that swept through the windows of the sacked houses, rustling in the corners of the empty

48

rooms in a dry echo of the voices that had once lived there.

Her own house was anything but empty. Through the wall that adjoined her brother's bedroom, she could hear that the cries of her sister-in-law were now punctuated by the rough-edged tones of her brother's voice. Soon their heavy bodies would collapse on the bed. When they performed the rites of marriage, their weight made the ropes that held their mattress squeak like a family of terrified mice.

But the houses in Sevilla would not be empty for long. Within a week, the peasant who had burned and looted them would find that their city cousins had moved in, expanding out of their own cramped quarters to what was left of the city of the Jews. That, too, had happened in Toledo after the night of terror.

She was aware of the soft kissing sound of the downstairs door opening. The weight of Avram's step on the stairs was the feeling of her own body coming home to itself.

"You're still up."

"Not a night for sleeping."

"I would have come home earlier, but I had to go to a patient."

"Such a dedicated doctor," Ester de Halevi said sharply. Avram was swinging the cape off his shoulders as she spoke, but she could see his neck stiffen with her words.

He turned around to face her. The happiness she had felt about him was already replaced by irritation — at herself for her foolish tongue, at Avram for reacting so quickly.

"I'm sorry," Ester said. "But tonight, of all nights. Were you in the city?"

Avram nodded. She could see the guilt passing like a shadow across his face – another night spent in the service of his new Christian patrons. As if there was something to be bought with the money he so proudly brought home.

"You might as well have stayed. It's dangerous to come home."

"I wanted to see you."

"Antonio was here," Ester said. "He saw you at the synagogue. He waited up for you, and then he went out to meet with some of the other men."

"How did he travel?"

Ester shrugged her shoulders. For two years Antonio Espinosa had been warning of impending attacks. Now that they had begun, he was full of rage and violence.

"And you," Avram finally asked, "how do you travel tonight?" His voice was soft, and she could feel herself feeding from it as if it were honey.

"Not so well," Ester said.

She let her eyes settle on Avram's face. There were times when Avram deserved his nickname: *el Gato* – the Cat.

"I'm going to wait up for Antonio," Avram said. "You should go to sleep."

"I'm not tired."

"It's best to sleep," Avram said, his voice solicitous. "Let me give you a glass of wine."

"I can sleep without wine," Ester said.

"Of course you can."

"All right then, a small glass."

As Avram turned his back, Ester felt a tension that had existed in her the whole night, dormant, spring into life. It was always like this before the wine; there was a sudden gripping in her stomach that admitted she had been waiting the whole evening

50

for this glass. Not simply the wine, of course, but the powders that Avram mixed in with it.

The powders were from Ben Ishaq; like any of his gifts, it had many sides, and at the thought of the old man, Ester had a sudden picture of his face: his beard, which had been black only twenty years ago, was now a pure and woolly white; the lines that had been starting on the surface of his cheeks had become deep carved trenches; his lips were thinner and stayed frozen when once they would have jumped to laugh; his brown eyes, which used to search outwards, curious about everything that lived, had become dark and luminous as they turned inwards. Like the rabbi whom she had asked about hope, Ben Ishaq no more believed in God than an ancient heathen. But instead of being empty and frightened inside, he was full of the desert he had been torn away from as a boy; his dreams of the life he had never quite lived had become the prison that possessed him day and night.

But he had always helped Avram, and when Avram went to Montpellier, he had returned to her for a while.

She opened her eyes. She was holding the glass, empty in her hand. It was often like this: a sudden black-out from the first sip of the wine to an hour later, when she woke up. It was the powders, Avram had told her, they let her sleep, but she knew the black-outs were something else – little souvenirs of the morning she had awakened to find herself in the stiff arms of her dead husband.

Now the room was dark but for one candle. Through the wall she could hear Meir snoring. If he knew what a donkey he sounded in his sleep. . . .

Across from her sat Avram, still waiting for Antonio. The half-light set his face in gold; with his

51

fringed black beard, his cheeks still hollow from travelling, his wide, bowed lips, he looked like one of those tall and elegant statues of the Christ that the Christians bought so eagerly at the markets. Looking at his man's face, in fact, Ester was suddenly unable to remember him as a baby. That was, she knew, another trick of the powders: some nights they obliterated the past; others they re-created it in a smooth and sentimental glow.

"The fortune-teller came today," Ester said.

She watched as Avram's face turned towards her. The candlelight floundered in his dark eyes, sparking back towards her as if to tell her that this remarkable son was so fiercely protected that even his eyes were like the walls of a garrison city.

"Do you want to know what she said?" Avram nodded. "She told me that this week you would meet the woman who is worthy of you."

"And who would that be?"

"She didn't mean," Ester found herself saying, "that you should be so hard to match. She meant that it would take a remarkable woman to drag you up from the gutter." This pronounced, she felt her lips vibrating with surprise at the words that had passed through them, just as she had felt her ears vibrate with the shock of the words they had heard when Meir told her that Avram was performing operations in the Christian quarter and then releasing his tensions in the brothel-tents at the fair.

"And Gabriela Hasdai has sent a message," his mother continued. "She says that she would like to see you tomorrow evening." There was a new, almost victorious, note in her voice.

"Gabriela is a very eligible young woman," Ester added.

"She is," Avram agreed, "though you didn't always think so."

"Even a mother can change her mind. I see in Gabriela Hasdai a young woman who should be married."

"It is time she had a husband," Avram agreed. "She is twenty-one years old."

"And so are you. You have been a man for eight years."

"I was away studying medicine. And I should still complete my studies."

"One day," Ester de Halevi said, "there will be time. But meanwhile, perhaps you should start a family. You could do worse than to marry Gabriela Hasdai."

"This is quite a recommendation," Avram said drily.

"She is very beautiful and very honest."

Avram was silent.

"Do you hear what I am saying?"

Ester reached to the table and filled her glass one more time. It was a sin to drink too much, she knew, but she knew also that there would be nights when there was no wine at all, no wine and no powders, and on such nights she would be able to congratulate herself for not sinning. Meanwhile the powders were like Ben Ishaq, the man who made them for her: they turned inwards, too, and they made her blood burn. Where there had been the terror of emptiness now was a flame. In such a state she had once said to Meir: "Is it not written in the Zohar that 'God conceals Himself from our minds, but reveals Himself to our hearts'?"

"The Zohar," Meir had sputtered, "was written by cabbalist heretic idiots. They should be scourged."

"Now Meir —" His wife, Vera, like the most timid of birds, grey hair with downy bird-like tufts under her chin, had given birth to Antonio with such cries of happiness that the whole barrio had heard him coming.

"Where did you get it?"

"Avram gave me a copy."

"Avram," Meir said, and then added, sarcastically as always, "Avram, the man of science, the new man of the new age: the Jew who is afraid to go into a synagogue."

Ester sipped at the wine again. Only a few seconds before, she remembered, she had been thinking of the power of God to touch the heart, and now she was going over arguments that had happened at the supper table that evening. Only Antonio's entrance had prevented Meir, after a soliloquy on the value of meekness and suffering, from once more asking Ester why she did not send her converted son, her Marrano, out to find his own home — so that if he could not give her peace, he could at least grant her privacy.

Ester rose from her chair. She saw Avram's head turn towards her, but she knew he wouldn't speak. Then she walked, slowly and numbly, to the alcove where her bed was. For one last moment she looked out at the room, at her son nursing his hurt, the smoke from the candle vibrating in the summer night. When she was a girl, there had been nights like this when she and her friends had stolen down to the river, boys and girls alike, to swim naked in the silvery Targa. Their bodies had shone like white spirits in the moon. Ester reached and drew the heavy curtains across the alcove.

54

FOUR

AVRAM SETTLED DEEPER INTO THE CUSHIONS. WHEN HIS MOTHER REPRIMANDED HIM, HE FELT HIMSELF CONSTRICTING INSIDE, AS IF HIS STOMACH WERE CLOSING AROUND ONE of his own sharp steel knives. She was afflicted, Ben Ishaq had diagnosed, by a form of nervous disease that caused both her inability to sleep and her periodic attacks of lethargy. These attacks, long sieges when she was wrapped in a fog of misery, left her so weak that she could do nothing but sit panting in her room, grey as death, barely able to navigate the abyss from one shallow breath to the next.

According to Ben Ishaq, every few months the poisons in the powders built up to the point where Ester Espinosa de Halevi seemed about to die from them. Then the powders were taken away, and for a sleepless week Ester struggled through a strange coma until her body was clean again, ready to be drugged once more.

"In one of those comas," Ben Ishaq had warned, "your mother will die." He had looked at Avram, who was silent, and then added: "She will miss her son, but otherwise she will be grateful."

Through the heavy curtain Avram could hear the rasping breath of his mother's sleep. In Montpellier he had often feared that she would die in his absence, wondering on her deathbed why her son – to whom she had devoted her life – was not there to wish her well in the next world. But he had come home to find her unchanged: some days with the energy of a young girl, others groaning about like a crone of a century or more.

What, he wondered, would she have thought if she had known what had passed through his mind when he saw Gabriela at the synagogue this evening? Because, almost as if the fortune-teller had been reading his heart, Avram had been comparing Gabriela to the Portuguese woman he had discovered at the fair. But although he had been thinking that Gabriela was more beautiful, would surely make a more suitable wife, his heart froze at the idea of fulfilling his promise of marrying her and starting a family.

The thought of Gabriela, the memory of the night he had told her he was going to Montpellier, the tears she had cried, and the promise he had made in order to stop the tears made his stomach clench tighter.

Uncomfortable and cramped on the cushions, Avram stood up and stretched. The candlelight threw the shadows of his long arms against the wall. As his shoulders and spine cracked into place, he could hear his mother complaining in her sleep. And then, as her breathing settled again, he heard the sound of running on the stairs.

By the time he had turned to the door, Antonio was in the room, embracing him.

Avram, gasping for breath, had to push him away. "Still as sickly as ever."

Avram laughed. "We sick ones live forever."

"You are well?" asked Antonio. "Tell me you are truly well."

"I am. And you? But I don't need to ask. I saw you at the synagogue tonight. Your wounds would have killed another man."

Antonio laughed again. "I will die when I am ready, not before. Now find us some wine and we will go down to the river to talk, the way we used to."

When they went out onto the street, darkness had sealed the ghetto into a coffin. But by the time they reached the river, Avram's eyes had adjusted. The moon that had been a pale crescent in the twilight was now bright silver, and the sky around it glowed like the richest of velvet.

Crouched at the edge of the river, Avram could see up the rocky precipice to the wall, and the hundred feet of the wall itself. That such a barrier had been breached was difficult to believe. Yet the walls of Toledo, celebrated by the Romans themselves, were like a woman too easily courted: they had fallen to everything from well-organized armies to angry mobs of peasants. On the night of terror, the furniture of the Jews had been thrown from the windows of their houses into the streets to start fires, and in the heat of these flames the screams of killers and victims had mixed together in the long primal howl of the beast.

How many had died? Legend said ten thousand. Some of those bodies had been buried, others dragged down to the river and burned. As children, Avram and his friends would sometimes sneak out of the barrio to play among the charred skeletons that littered the bushes by the riverbanks. Little mounds of bones – hips, thighbones, whole hands with their fine structures – were preserved in this unintentional museum.

Avram's first operations were with these bones: squeezing bulbous joints into sockets that didn't quite fit, searching among the twisted and the crippled and the smashed to find an arm or a leg – or, rarest of all, an unbroken rib cage – to put together a whole new entity. The rib cages and the skulls were the worst: some had huge craters where iron fists or boulders had smashed; others were twisted and fractured to mark the entry of a sword or a spear.

Broken necks from the gibbets, bodies torn apart entirely as though they had been quartered, oddities beyond even the most bizarre explanation – these left even more to the children's imagination.

Like the discussions about the night itself, the skeletons' playground was a secret among the children. But eventually it was discovered, and then one night all the bones mysteriously disappeared. How they were disposed of, no one ever said.

The answer came to Avram in a dream. He announced it gravely to the other children: the beast, one night while they were asleep, had woken up hungry and discovered these uneaten skeletons on the riverbank. In one lazy gulp it had swallowed them all, barely pausing to chew the men and women in its gigantic rotted teeth, swallowing the dead children without even noticing – their bones were as tiny and delicate as the bones of cats – swallowing all evidence of the night of terror in darkness, swallowing a whole universe full of remains that had once laughed and eaten and sung and prayed, swallowing them in such complete and thorough happiness that the children – who had never cried through the most lengthy and the most gruesome of the reconstructions – burst into bitter tears at discovering that their playground and true heritage, their museum of bones, had been stolen away from them.

"The wine is sweet," Antonio said. "I did not think I would live to taste the wines of Toledo, or to sit again with my cousin on the banks of the Targa."

They were at a place where the river fell over a series of small rock cliffs, so that flowing around their conversation, supporting the sounds of the night birds that swooped over the river's surface and hunted among the trees that lined its banks, was the serene and endless music of the bubbling water.

From the moving surface of the water was reflected the light of the moon. Across the river could be felt the giant heart of the fair, thousands camped in tents in the great market that visited Toledo every August, but as Avram sat with Antonio and let himself be drawn into the night, he was gradually aware of his own steady heartbeat, of his own peaceful breathing as his body settled into the soft grassy bank of the Targa.

Avram turned to Antonio and watched as he pulled out the pouch Avram had seen often enough before leaving for Montpellier. From the pouch Antonio took his clay pipe and his flints to light it. With a quick and practised turn of his wrist he struck the flint and ignited the hashish in the bowl of his pipe, the way Ben Ishaq had taught him. Then he sucked in the smoke with sharp gasps before passing the pipe to Avram. For the first time in two years Avram felt the acrid blast of power that hashish sent into his lungs, a power he had seen his teacher succumb to. Then his throat began to burn and he coughed the smoke into the night air.

"I love this city," Antonio whispered. "While you have been away, studying, I've travelled all over the peninsula – from Barcelona to Valencia, to Sevilla and Granada – warning of the massacres to come.

And yet, when I come back to Toledo, I feel that I am walking back into my own heart."

Antonio's mention of the word "heart" made Avram again aware of his own: like those he had dissected, it would be a gigantic muscle, invaded by canals that were filled with blood. There had been a lecturer at Montpellier who claimed that in some mysterious way the heart controlled and regulated the blood, sending it in cycles around the body. What a strange idea – that the blood from the feet would be, at another minute, in the hands or even the brain. His own heart's blood, Avram felt, was special and permanent. When he had seen Gabriela in the synagogue he had felt it come to a sudden boil, like a pot into which had been plunged a red-hot stone.

Now, too, his heart felt warm and excited. In the light of the moon he could see Antonio's face: the familiar face he had seen every night of his boyhood now hardened and changed into the face of a man.

"Tell me," Avram said. And then he paused to gather his courage. "Tell me about Sevilla again."

"It was a nightmare, that is all. A nightmare worse than other nightmares. Something a man prays to forget."

Avram leaned forward. The night was warm but he could feel his bones clacking and shivering, as if they were suddenly in a great hurry to leap into the river and join the bones it had swallowed twenty-two years before.

"Even to you," Antonio said, "I can't tell more." He sucked on the pipe, then violently exhaled before passing it to Avram. "Who knows God's designs? If not for the night of terror, we would not have been born. The Jews of Sevilla are dead now – we should mourn them, but use their lessons to protect ourselves."

"That is a hard thing to say. Do you really believe that the living must climb on the backs of the dead?"

Antonio laughed, this new laugh, Avram noticed, that kept erupting despite himself, a laugh that was not happiness but an outburst of bitterness and anger. "Yes," Antonio said, "I believe that some of us must die so that others may live. And I know, too, that I am one of the ones who will die. But you, Avram, you must have faith in life, even your life, or you would not have spent six years training to be a doctor."

Avram looked out at the river. Blue and silver in the daylight, nightly turned scarlet by the setting sun, it was now a barely visible black snake shimmering before them.

"I hope," he said, "but I don't believe." The triumph — only twenty-four hours ago — of his operation on Isabel de Velásquez now seemed a whole lifetime away. "I hope there will be a better world — one free of plagues, of superstition, of man's insane desire to murder other men. In such a world I would be happy to be a doctor, to heal those whom I could."

"The man with the silver knife," Antonio said.

"What?"

"The man with the silver knife. That is what you are called now, in the barrio. Even in my few hours back, I have heard of your daring in the houses of Christians, your miraculous operation. Congratulations, my brilliant cousin. You wagered your life going to Montpellier and you have come back an instant saint."

"Thank you, my sincere cousin."

"The knife you used to wield was a sword, remember? In our games, no one could ever knock the sword from your hands."

"I remember."

"I still have a sword," Antonio said. "With it I have killed real men. Three at Sevilla. And others before. Have you ever killed a man?"

"Never."

"Thou shalt not kill," Antonio pronounced. Thickened by smoke, his voice had taken on a terrible echo. The echo, Avram knew of the cries of the dying in Sevilla. "I have killed, Avram. I killed to protect my people, even myself, and soon I will have to kill again. You will also. Because soon enough there will be an uprising against the Jews of Toledo. The archbishop Martínez will pay one of his charming visits, and those who are not converted will be killed. The same thing has already happened in a dozen other cities. Now Rodrigo Velásquez, who is the brain and right arm of Ferrand Martínez, wishes to jewel the crown with Toledo. He is confident that the Jews of this city are so attached to their wealth and their power in the court that they will convert by the thousands rather than die. But this time, instead of there being a community of Jews for the Marranos to fade back into, he wishes to make sure that every Jew is killed, every synagogue turned into a church."

Antonio's voice had taken on an edge that Avram knew well: it was the edge that gave the challenge to whoever was listening – the challenge to dare whatever Antonio was proposing.

"Don't worry," Antonio added gently. "I know that you and I are destined for different paths. I am a soldier by nature – perhaps I have too much of my father's blood. But you are different, you have the gifts to be a leader, not simply a fighter."

"I don't want to lead anyone."

"But you will, whether by design or by chance. Because you are the one who has broken the mould:

protected by neither Christian or Jew, you will spend your whole life in exile. But the man who is given no shelter grows his own walls. You are no warrior, but your surgeon's knife will be your sword." Antonio clapped his hand onto Avram's shoulder and Avram felt his cousin's strength flowing into him.

Once more Antonio sparked the flint. The hour was now so late that the cooking fires across the river had all gone out, and even their smoke had been absorbed into the night. All that was left was the glowing embers, the last feeble traces of man against the burning white light of the moon and stars. His eyes pinned to the stars by long needles of light, Avram felt himself explode in answer to the sky, old nightmares shooting from his skin until the air was thick with demons and his ears buzzed with their crying.

Protected by darkness, he crouched with his back pressed against a tree. This was how he sometimes found himself: sitting with his knees pulled close to his chest, arms wrapped protectively around. Like the child's embryo he had once watched Ben Ishaq remove from the womb of a pregnant woman who had died in her fourth month; like himself when he had been a child in his mother's womb, a mistake planted on the night when Mars and Venus fused into a single star; like himself when he had been a child, cowering under the sword.

The noise of his memories faded and then, as it always did, the attack of fear passed by, and Avram found himself breathing grateful swallows of the cool night air.

He opened his eyes. Antonio was leaning forward, looking intently at him.

"So, my cousin, are we going to be able to save the Jews of Toledo?"

"Do they need to be saved?"

"Even tonight, at the fair, the friends of Rodrigo Velásquez have been planning their attack while we have been lulled to sleep by the rushing of the river."

"You are sure of that?"

Antonio nodded. "There is a traveller who is an old friend of mine. A Christian, but a man to be trusted. Tonight, while you were at the house of Velásquez, I was at a secret meeting, disguised as a monk."

Avram could not help smiling. Antonio, always travelling from town to town, an unofficial general rallying his troops, was famous for his disguises. Once he had come home dressed as a priest and Meir Espinosa, startled at such an apparition, had nearly fainted on his own doorstep.

"Toledo cannot escape," Antonio said. "You have come home to a battle."

"I came home to take care of my mother," Avram replied. "To take care of my mother, and to pay my debts to my teacher Ben Ishaq."

"And," Antonio added, "you must admit that you do not mind the idea of being a success in the city where you were born."

Avram leaned closer to Antonio, grasped his sleeve. "Listen, my cousin. There is more to life than battles of the sword. In Europe a new movement is abroad, a desire to throw off the blinkers of darkness and return to the teachings and the clarity of the old empire. For a thousand years now the Church has had its hands wrapped tightly around the throat of the masses. Even now, we in Toledo have reason to fear its power. But the Church is dying. With its two popes the Church has become a two-headed dog, running in both directions at once while being attacked by heresies and enemies of every description. In a few years the Church as we know it will be dead: in its place will be an age of reason, of science, an age when the central force of the universe is not terror but man and his understanding of himself."

Avram stopped, surprised himself at what he was saying. But the words rang true: after all, when he had dissected corpses in Montpellier, had the heavens crashed down to destroy him? And when he used the knowledge he had gained from his secret explorations of the body, had not the results been the spectacular saving of lives? Was it written in stone that every disease, every illness, must end in horrible suffering? The Church had used its power to bend the human mind into a twisted mass of superstition. Now the Church itself was falling to pieces.

"In Montpellier," Avram said, "I cut apart bodies in order to see what they were made of, how they worked."

"So," his cousin murmured, "you do not kill, but you, too, have use for the dead."

"Antonio, *listen*. Despite everything, I was myself so superstitious that the first time I opened a body, I believed that I would find not simply a heart but some miraculous trace of the soul."

"And did you?"

"No."

"And do you now believe that man has no soul?"

"I believe that man has a soul," Avram said. "But whether the soul of man is something he makes for himself, or whether it is divinely given, I do not know."

Hearing himself pronounce with such certainty, Avram felt suddenly embarrassed. If only the river could carry away his words, if only he had not so quickly exposed his inner thoughts to Antonio's cynical judgement. But, unwilling to contradict himself,

65

Avram stayed silent and watched as Antonio reached for the wine bottle and drank deeply from it.

"I have also heard the idea," Antonio began, "that the Church is dying and that a new era begins. And I, too, have heard the saying that while there is a papal schism, no man or woman can go to Heaven. But I do not think this means the end of the Church. The Church is weak now, it is true: with one pope in Avignon, another in Rome, it is divided and con-fused. But confusion is part of growth: the Church is like a child half-way to manhood – with strength so great it has not yet been tested, waiting for some-one to lead it. But I believe it will find that leader – the leader will be, in fact, none other than Rodrigo Velásquez; brother of your patron, cardinal to the pope of Avignon, and ruthless hater of Jews. Nor will he stop his campaign against the Jews – for that is the one issue that can unite the Church. Jews are the worst heretics, and the Inquisition that has started in other countries will soon come here, ready not only to burn disbelievers but to demonstrate and strengthen the power of the Church. Yes, my cousin, I admit that there are some forces of reason. But they are like nothing in the face of what opposes them. And like a heresy, reason will be crushed.

"Now, you ask me, where does this leave the Jews? It leaves us not in a new age of reason, but in an era of persecution. With each year, each decade, the Church will regain its old strength. And thus we will be chased, persecuted, driven underground. If we fail to resist and to cling to our faith, we will be exter-minated like the races who have only the history books for their homes. Our only hope of surival is armed resistance."

"I thought," Avram said, "that you believed Jews are the chosen people, protected by God."

Antonio barked out his new laugh. "Chosen, yes, we are chosen to be an example of suffering and death. If we are to survive, it is by our own wits, not by God's protection. God will protect those who protect themselves."

"And how, by their own wits, are the Jews of Toledo to save themselves?"

"By defeating their enemies," Antonio replied.

"But the Jews of Toledo have no weapons. You know it yourself: since the night of terror, it has even been forbidden for a Jew to own a sword."

"Then, my cousin, we will have to use our minds." Antonio leaned closer and Avram, in the grip of the hashish and the wine, felt the years slipping away. As in the old days, they were down by the river, plotting their strategies. But the children's games they used to play, fought against rival gangs, had become adults' wars; and instead of the joy of victory, the stakes were life and death.

"My friend," Antonio said, "the traveller has told me he could get enough crossbows to arm at least two hundred of us."

Avram remembered the day he had seen crossbows being used in Montpellier. The bolts had shot forth with such power that even targets of thick oak had been split apart by their force.

"Would two hundred crossbows have helped the Jews of Sevilla?"

"With weapons," Antonio answered, "they could have defended themselves."

"And driven away the invaders?"

"No."

"Here, if you are correct, there are ten thousand peasants preparing to tear apart the barrio. Even if two hundred — four hundred — are killed, the rest will smash down the doors."

"And so what do you propose, my man of science? A sweet surrender, begging the good cardinal to show mercy to his gentle Jews?"

"I have an idea," Avram said. An image of the cardinal was fixed in his mind, he had seen a portrait at the Velásquez house: Rodrigo Velásquez's official portrait in his new cardinal's robes. "We have not enough men to fight the army, but if there is no leader, perhaps there will be no army to fight?"

"Tell me," Antonio said.

"Rodrigo Velásquez," Avram said. "Suppose we captured him and held him hostage for the Jews of Toledo."

"Capture Velásquez?"

"He is going to be staying at his brother's house. I go there often, to see my patient. One night, when he is walking from the church to the house, we could capture him and bring him to the Jewish quarter."

Antonio wrenched the bottle from Avram's hand, then threw it across the stones and into the swirling centre of the river. Then he brought his hands to Avram's shoulders and squeezed them until Avram gasped.

"You're crazy," Antonio whispered. But his voice was filled with love, and Avram felt, finally, home again. "Kidnap the cardinal? Only Avram Halevi could think of such an insane idea. But wait — I have an easier way. My Christian friend is also a driver of carriages. If one night he were to substitute himself for the driver of Rodrigo Velásquez —"

Even after walking home, Avram was still not tired. Sitting in his mother's room, listening to her breathing, he closed his eyes and let his conversation with Antonio spin through his mind.

FIVE

THE PANIC BEGAN WHEN GABRIELA HASDAI SAW AVRAM IN THE SYNAGOGUE, HIS ARMS SO NEAR THAT SHE COULD HAVE LEAPT INTO THEM. WITH ANTONIO ESPINOSA'S NEWS OF Sevilla, fear and nervousness melted together into a chant. *Run, run, run.* The refrain hammered through her, ever louder, a crazy drummer that didn't know how to stop.

It beat at her through the long night, distracted her all morning while she tried to carry on business at the fair. When the sun was almost directly above her awning, she made her decision. Then, from her stall near the fair's centre, where she bought and sold silks to pamper the skin and conceal the bodies of the most respectable Jewesses of Toledo, Gabriela Hasdai walked through the heat and the dust in search of the one means of escape she could think of. The press of the crowds was so heavy that it seemed each member of the throng was a finger belonging to the same gigantic hand, and that this tens-of-thousands-fingered hand was itself being crushed in the grip of the sun so that sweat ran between the bodies of strangers, like a secret shared between husband and wife. Despite the heat Gabriela Hasdai was wearing cloak and headdress, not only for the sake of modesty

69

and to hide her features from the curious, but also to indicate – if such demonstrations could be of use at the disreputable edges of the fair – that here was a wealthy woman, one whom it would be foolish to harm.

Finally she found the ragged tent she had been told about. In front of it stood a man so short that Gabriela found herself looking down towards bloodshot eyes and a domed forehead corrugated by a lifetime of worry and fear.

"I am looking for Carlos."

The peasant lifted a broad hand and scratched his chest through his filthy tunic. Then he dug his bare feet deeper into the ground, as if he were a mule preparing to be stubborn, as if he had sensed the drummer inside Gabriela and was determined to tease him out.

"I am Carlos," he said. His voice was surprisingly smooth, an unexpected jewel in a badly made setting. "I am Carlos," he announced again. "Carlos himself I am." He made a deep bow. "Call me simply Carlos, Carlos the Mouth, Carlos the Famous, call me even Carlos the King – I was named after one – call me and I am pleased to be at your service. Whoever you are or are not, whoever you are pretending to be, Carlos is eager to be your servant, at your service, pleasant and honest without fail, Carlos will sell you a horse." After this long and dazzling chant the peasant smiled widely, a hyphenated welcome featuring a very few teeth – but each one brilliantly polished, and gums and tongue of such a startling crimson colour that Gabriela Hasdai could not help seeing why at least one of his names, Carlos the Mouth, had been given. "Carlos will sell you a horse, a horse that Carlos guarantees is a horse that rides faster than the wind, a horse —" From nowhere the man called Carlos withdrew a swollen wineskin, which he offered to Gabriela.

She shook her head, and even as she wondered if it had been safe to refuse his offer, Carlos uncorked the bag and, cocking back his chin as if to crow, squirted such a stream of wine into his mouth that it might have been a drunken midnight rather than a broiling afternoon.

Having drunk, swallowed, and spat, Carlos wiped his mouth and wriggled his toes deeper into the earth. Meanwhile, Gabriela let his words wrap themselves in the silence, a silence she had learned made up for whatever disadvantages a woman might have in striking a bargain with a man.

Waiting for her reply, Carlos opened his eyes wide, staring at her as though hoping his crimson tongue had woven a spell around her still one. Then, after taking another drink from his skin, he rubbed it fondly and cradled it in his arms like a baby.

Gabriela withdrew her hand from her cloak, letting her rings flash briefly in the sun. The rings were crowned with chipped and worthless stones, but they were shiny enough to impress a desperate trader from the north.

"The horse is for my husband," she said. "It is to be a gift for his birthday."

"The wife who buys a horse for her husband is a wise woman. What kind of horse does the wise woman wish?"

"A wise woman," said Gabriela, "is a woman with the wisdom to hear the advice of a wiser man."

But Carlos did not reply. Instead he, too, lapsed into silence, as if to show that even Carlos the Mouth, Carlos the Famous, could use the trick that this brash woman horse-buyer was trying to fool him with.

Beyond Carlos, Gabriela could see the horses themselves. Their coats looked healthy enough, but they were not glossy like the coats of the purebred mares and stallions displayed under gigantic multi-coloured canopies at the centre of the fair.

As opposed to their superior brethren, sheltered by awnings of bright silk, these horses were enclosed by nothing more than rope-joined stakes that had been pounded into the hard earth. And for shade they had only a giant plane tree that made up one of the corners of the paddock and also had the duty of guarding the ragged tent near which Gabriela now stood.

It was Carlos who spoke first, but not before lifting the wineskin one more time to wet his famous mouth. As he squeezed it between his palms, the sun shone through the dark purple stream.

"A certain woman comes to Carlos," Carlos said, "and she comes to him walking alone, unprotected by a man. At first Carlos is surprised to see a woman alone. Then he thinks she must be a whore, come to sell herself to the famous Carlos. But Carlos rubs the sleep from his stupid eyes and sees that the woman is rich and respectable. Having opened his eyes Carlos then opens his mouth and asks the woman her business. Can you blame Carlos for asking such a question? He is only a simpleton, anxious to please. The woman says to him that she is buying a horse to give her husband for his birthday. Carlos is so happy. What a generous wife, Carlos thinks, what a fortunate husband. Carlos himself has had two wives, so he knows that one woman can be even more generous than another, God forbid it should be necessary. And then, having opened his eyes and his mouth, Carlos opens his ears. Why does Carlos open his ears? Is it so the birds can fly in and deposit their little shits and secrets? Is it to give wax to the bees? All of these are worthy pursuits that Carlos has at other times pursued. But today, Carlos opens his ears to hear what horse the woman wants to buy. Can she tell one beast from another? And when does she intend to buy this horse, because there are many people who are always begging Carlos to do business with them, but Carlos loves his horses and sells them only to those who will love them well. But excuse Carlos, Carlos the Mouth, Carlos the Famous. Here is Carlos, drunk on hope already, and there is the woman he wishes to serve, yet she will not speak. Has Carlos offended? Has Carlos failed to offer her mouth the wine he puts in his own?"

"The fame of Carlos is so great," Gabriela said, "I could not bear to make this gift for my husband without making also a gift to myself, the gift of hearing Carlos speak."

"When Carlos sees the buyer is ready to buy," said Carlos, "then Carlos must ask for the price that the buyer is ready to pay."

By the time she left the trader's tent, Gabriela's stomach was so tense that she could hardly stand. After two hours of conversation and haggling with Carlos, she had arranged to buy a horse. Not once had he mentioned the word Jew, yet the price of the horse had been insanely high. Then, walking back to her own sales-stall, she had twice overheard remarks about the overfed Jews of Toledo, and the fate that the Jews of Sevilla had met.

The Catholic Church, she knew, had taken upon itself to divide Christians and Jews forever. Not only were Jews in the northern cities taxed into poverty and forced to wear the yellow badge so that Christians need never be fooled into commerce with them; they were also the first victims of anyone's rage —

be it the rage of peasants from whom the Jews collected taxes or the rage of the kings and princes on whose behalf the tithes were taken.

"A Christian may not enter the house of a Jew. A Christian may not employ a Jew as a physician or a surgeon. A Christian may not speak to a Jew on the Sabbath or Holy Days. A Christian may not invite a Jew into his own house save as a servant. . . ."

Every month the papacy in Avignon announced new restrictions. According to the Hebrew elders, the Christians had succumbed to a mysterious religious plague, a spiritual sequel to the Black Death that had afflicted them with a state of total religious confusion. That confusion, they said, was what had caused the Christians to divide their church in two parts, just as the Roman empire had divided into two before its collapse.

But though the wise men of Toledo diagnosed the malady of the Christians as confusion – and what could be more confused than a race of people who took their Messiah to be a man planted by God into the womb of a virgin? – Gabriela and some of her friends had their own explanations.

For a millennium the Jews had been the servants of Muslim rule. Merchants, traders, bankers, travellers: while the Muslims had provided the army to conquer the lands around the Mediterranean, the Jews had been beside them, holding and controlling the purse-strings. So close was the association that it could even be seen: inside almost every synagogue in Spain, the mosque-like minarets of Muslim temples were to be found gracing and expanding the vaulted ceilings, as if both races reached towards a common heaven.

But the Age of Islam was over. Some said it had ended with the arrival of the Black Death, a signal that the world was about to be reborn. Others argued deeper and more complicated causes, showing through charts of the stars that the fate of Islam had reached its zenith with a certain conjunction too mysterious to be explained, and that now the very cluster of stars and planets that had held the empire together was dissolving. Meanwhile, new planets were moving towards each other. These were the planets of the kings of Castilla and Aragón. Together with their brethren in the Church, they had formed a new coalition to drive the Muslims south. Their leader and emblem of supremacy was the pope of Avignon. Today a Frenchman was pope; but eventually, Gabriela knew, the French pope would die and a Spanish pope would succeed. A pope with ambitions of his own, old scores to settle against those who had ruled and those who had been the rulers' willing servants.

"Gabriela."

The voice of her sister was harsh, insistent. Gabriela looked up to see Leah inspecting her, as usual, for any fault that might need to be corrected, any slip in propriety that might bring down an accusation of disrepute.

"Gabriela, did you know that Avram Halevi was back in Toledo?"

"Yes."

"Have you seen him?"

"I saw him in synagogue last night."

"In synagogue," Leah repeated. "Did you speak?"

Leah had a round face that had once been described as a moon of melted cheese. If the description had been cruel to Leah-the-child, it was worse to Leah-the-wealthy-matron: for the features that had once been small and defined now wavered under the unsure and shifting flesh of cheeks and chin. Only her eyes, a hard emerald green, resembled those of her beautiful but unmarried sister, Gabriela.

As Gabriela was still deciding whether to reply to her sister, Avram Halevi suddenly appeared. He smiled, and then he took off his doctor's hat and bowed. But before he could speak, there appeared beside him Rabbi Samuel Abrabanel of Toledo's Jews.

For a moment Gabriela suddenly saw herself as part of one of those cruel puppet shows about Jews: the matron, the businesswoman, the doctor, and the rabbi — four preposterous Jews overdressed in their multiple fineries, dancing and curtseying like madmen in the broiling sun. Finally Rabbi Abrabanel, who had already told both sisters that Gabriela's unmarried state was a shame that the Jewish community of Toledo could hardly bear, broke the silence: "And so the famous doctor has returned to his home village to perform his duty?"

"Just so," murmured Avram.

"And you have made a good beginning. Last night I was pleased to see you in synagogue."

"And what did you think," asked Avram, "of the news that you heard there? Are you not worried that Toledo will be next on the list?"

Rabbi Abrabanel laughed. "An old man knows. Why would the Christians attack the city that is their most important capital, the city that contains the home cathedral of the great Cardinal Rodrigo Velásquez? Even he will not cut off his nose to spite his face. The man who wishes to be pope does not open the gates of the city to those who would destroy it."

"You reassure me," Avram said. He turned to Gabriela, once more lifted his hat from his head. "Goodbye." And then he was gone, his wide-brimmed black hat visible as he walked through the crowded throng that streamed amongst the merchants selling silk and wool. Nonetheless, before leaving, his eyes had met hers: in them she had seen the promise that he would come to her that evening.

Rabbi Abrabanel turned to Gabriela. "Marry a believer. Have children. Trust in God."

Gabriela was sitting on a stool, peering at her store's accounts by the smoky light of an oil lamp. When she heard Avram's knock at the door she could not help feeling a foolish burst of happiness, as if all that had gone wrong might be miraculously undone.

Before she could get up, Avram had slipped inside and was locking the latch behind him. At least his hands, Gabriela thought wryly, had remembered what his heart found so easy to forget. He moved to the edge of her lamp's circle of light. There he stood, as though waiting for her admiring remarks on his new outfit: the young Marrano doctor who had survived his years at Montpellier and was now back to practise his craft on the rich Christians of Toledo.

"Your shop is full. Business must be going well."

"Well enough. And every day there are new songs about the miraculous man with the silver knife."

"Very humorous." Avram took off his hat and set it on the counter. When she had fallen in love with him, Avram's face had still been soft and unformed, the hopeful face of a boy who dreamed of becoming a hero. Now the baby fat had melted away and his bones had started to show more clearly: high Castilian cheeks, black eyes, a strong proud nose – if he lived to be an old man, Avram's face would travel farther down the same road: with each decade his skin would draw more tightly around his bones, and his features grow more pronounced, his black eyes larger.

77

"It's good to see you. I was afraid that I might not be welcome."

He had grown taller in Montpellier. But his voice had not changed. Soft and persuasive, it reached out for her heart, offering to surround it in warmth and safety.

"Am I welcome?"

Despite herself, Gabriela felt a brief burst of bitterness. "Of course you are." She felt awkward and formal, a wooden statuette. The last meeting in this shop – the time Avram told her he was going to Montpellier to study medicine – had been full of tears, unforgivable accusations whose details she had already forgotten.

"Am I?"

"Will you leave if I frighten you?" Then she laughed, the tension broken, and put her hand on his arm. "Zelaida is asleep. But if she woke to find out I'd sent you away, she'd kill me. Come into the back and I'll give you some tea." Gabriela picked up the lamp and led the way through a thick set of curtains to the room that was her kitchen, her living room, and her sleeping room. With her sudden movement, the wick was partially drowned, and for a moment the light was entirely gone, but she knew Avram would follow well enough. They had called him the Cat because, of all the children, he was the fastest at getting over the wall. But she had been as agile and years before, when they had been just children, they had easily enough slipped out of their parents' houses and over the wall so they could thread their way past tents of soldiers and peasants down to the river at night.

In a few moments she had tea heating in a copper pot above the alcohol lamp in the middle of the floor. As they used to, she and Avram sat on the floor on either side of the lamp. Now there were new layers of soft carpets, and the barely visible hangings that covered the stone walls were richer and more exotic. But with only these few minutes of familiarity, Gabriela found Avram's face softening again; looking across at him in the light, she could almost convince herself that they were close once more, their souls twined the way their children's souls had been.

With the memory of the closeness came the memory of the nights she had spent alone here, nights she had not amused herself thinking about the charming way they had eluded the soldiers on the way down to the river to celebrate their precocious love: those nights she had first learned to cry, and then learned to feel so bitter that there was no place left for tears.

"I should have come to visit you before."

"You've been busy."

"This week since I have been home has passed like a single day. Ben Ishaq has made me see every surgical case in Toledo."

"Did you like Montpellier?"

"I missed Toledo. But it was good to go away. I would have stayed two more years, but it became impossible."

"I heard." In the barrio, there were no secrets; even before Avram himself had the news, Gabriela had known that his uncle was unable to keep sending him money. Out of an only slightly malicious sense of charity, she had been tempted to offer to take on the burden herself. But before she could decide whether to actually beard old Meir Espinosa and do the outrageous – a woman offering money to a man – Avram had returned.

Now he was back where his journey had begun, in the room of the love he had denied in order to go.

A breeze through the cracks of the shutters made the flame of the lamp waver. With it, Gabriela saw, Avram's face wavered too: between that of the adolescent boy he had once been, tormented equally by nightmares and hopes, and that of the man he was becoming.

"It's good to visit."

"You've grown oil on your tongue," Gabriela said. "Did they teach you that, too, at the famous University of Montpellier?" Then, seeing Avram's stricken look, she reached for his arm. For a moment her hand stayed hovering above his sleeve, stretched out across the teapot like the tiny and vulnerable advance of a foreign army. Then Avram covered her hand with his own.

"Your tongue is sharp enough."

"I'm sorry, Avram."

"I deserve it. I should have come to see you right away, but – "

"But you were afraid, because you had rejected me."

Now she had said it and, despite herself, her hand jerked in fear.

There was a silence, but Avram did not move away. Gabriela could remember dozens of nights when she had wished for a moment like this: herself and Avram sitting close in the dark.

"I should go soon," Avram said abruptly. "My mother will be expecting me back." But he did not move, and Gabriela now felt the beginning of a sensation she had entirely forgotten: the feeling of an actual door in her heart opening, a door opening and the wind of her love blowing through her soul. In those earlier days, without even asking, she had assumed that when her heart opened, the love that she felt flowing between them was felt by him as well, the sensation of their souls' joining, two people becoming one in God's eye.

"I'm glad you came," Gabriela said. "I wanted to tell you that this time I'm the one who is leaving. I've arranged to sell my business and I'm leaving Toledo."

"Leaving Toledo?"

"For Barcelona, before this quarter is burned to the ground. Which it will be, I am sure, before the summer is out."

"And you really believe you're safer there than here?"

"I do. And you would be, too."

Avram laughed: his mouth had a downward turn now that it had lacked two years ago. "And what are you going to do, when you're in Barcelona?"

"I'm going to work for the merchant Velásquez, who bought my store here."

"Velásquez!"

"He is an honest man," Gabriela said. "At least I believe he is. Do you?"

Avram pushed his fingers through his black hair, the way he used to when he was about to propose some amusing prank. But now he simply shrugged and said, "I don't know."

"You don't know? Avram Halevi has no opinion on the honesty of his own client? Surely they didn't change you *that* much at Montpellier."

"I suppose he's honest enough in matters of money."

"And in other matters?"

"I don't know," Avram said.

"Are you afraid," asked Gabriela, "that he is not to be trusted in matters of the heart? Are you afraid that he is going to seduce the vulnerable young Gabriela Hasdai with his gold coins and his Castilian eyes?" She knew she should hold her tongue, but what had been unsaid for years was now boiling up in her, demanding to be released: "Do you think, great doctor, that everyone is so easily seduced by the promise of money and a place in the houses of the Christians?"

Avram sat without moving or replying.

"I'm sorry."

"Don't apologize."

"I won't be seduced by Velásquez. I want you to come with me."

"Me?"

"Yes." Now that the opportunity had arrived, Gabriela launched into the speech she had been composing and reciting to herself since the moment Avram had greeted her at the fair.

"Avram, I want you to come with me to Barcelona. Your mother would be welcome to come too. You say that you are not sorry you left Toledo to study. I am willing to admit that you did the right thing, and I am willing to admit that I have not yet recovered from my love for you. We trusted each other once, and it is the law of the community that we cannot stay single. So why not marry? We could live together in decent harmony as man and wife, you would be free to pursue your studies, and your mother would have a secure place with us." She stopped, breathless, and realized that her eyes were shut. All the elegant and compelling phrases she had memorized had fled, and the words she had said echoed foolishly. She opened her eyes. Avram was still sitting cross-legged, waiting.

"That's all," Gabriela said. "You can take it or leave it."

"Gabriela."

"You don't have to answer me tonight."

"Gabriela, I can't leave Toledo. My patients already depend on me."

"By the end of the summer they'll all be dead. You, too, if you stay."

Gabriela was not going to admit that an astrologer who had read her palm had advised her to travel after asking an old love to accompany her. She herself would not have taken seriously such a prediction if, for three nights in a row, she had not dreamed of the sack of Toledo and the slaughter of its Jews. The morning after the last dream, Velásquez had sent for her.

"Gabriela," Avram said, "you are a wonderful woman. My dearest childhood friend."

"And you," Gabriela said, "are also *my* dearest childhood friend, my first and only lover. But you are also a fool. If you loved me, you'd find a reason to come with me."

Avram sighed. These days, it seemed, everyone was full of advice for him: Velásquez, Gabriela, his mother – all had plans for the future, which was supposed to be such a mystery.

He took Gabriela's hands, held them in his own. She leaned towards him, and in the light he could see the swell of her breasts, smell the beginnings of her desire. While he was away she had turned from a nervous girl into an assured and confident woman. He felt a sudden jolt: the force of her love against his unprotected heart. As she came towards him, her lips parted for his kiss, he kept his eyes open, fixed on hers.

Then they were lying on the carpets together, he was still looking into her eyes, but he had pulled her against him and could feel her belly pressing to his own, her legs stretching to twine about him. Love was her master: love and the need to be loved in

83

return. Yet, despite everything, she had saved herself for him. He felt his heart respond to hers, his chest aching as if love were a prisoner too long underground.

"Tell me what you want." Her voice, a whisper claiming him.

"You leave for Barcelona first," he said. "Send Zelaida and your belongings ahead, right away. I'll follow, bringing my mother and my uncle's family. When we arrive, you and I will marry."

"Marry me now. Then we can travel together and keep each other safe."

"No." For a moment Avram considered telling her of the plan he and Antonio had discussed. But in the light of morning the plan to kidnap Rodrigo Velásquez had seemed too daring to succeed, and yet he had not been able to find Antonio to talk about it again.

"You go ahead," Avram said. "Go now, while it is still safe."

"Come, too, Avram, please?"

For a moment he hesitated. "I can't desert Antonio. If he would come with us —"

"Antonio will never leave Toledo alive. He is eager to fight, eager to die."

"Gabriela. Please do as I say. Go now, and let me follow you as soon as I can." But her hands were under his tunic, caressing, bringing him back into the net of desire. It was impossible to think of Antonio, of Rodrigo Velásquez, of anything but his sudden burst of passion for Gabriela.

But when they were under the blankets and he was lowering himself down to her, he had to close his eyes. Gabriela gave such a cry of vulnerability that Avram found himself crying out with her. A flash of anger and despair tore through him, and as

84

her body yielded to his, he wanted to writhe and stab her deeper until by desire and wanting alone they could shoot free of the shadow of the beast.

SIX

AVRAM WOKE IN THE MORNING TO THE SOUND OF ZELAIDA'S SINGING IN THE NEXT ROOM. AGAINST HIS BELLY WAS THE WARM BACK OF GABRIELA, IN HIS SLEEP HE HAD cupped a hand around her breasts. When he raised himself to his elbow, he saw that Gabriela was still sleeping: over one smooth shoulder her black hair fell like a veil. Then, as if aware he had been watching her, she opened her eyes to his.

"I thought you'd never come back to me."

"Don't say that."

"The wound is healed now."

"I didn't mean to hurt you. I had to –"

"I know, Avram. I know." She extended her hand to his cheek, caressed it gently, and despite himself Avram felt something flare up inside himself: a warning, a desire not to be possessed.

"You will follow me to Barcelona as fast as you can."

"Yes, Gabriela."

Once, twice, she lifted her head to his and kissed his lips. "In Barcelona we will get married," Gabriela whispered. "Every night we will lie together and make children, every morning we will wake up happy. Do you promise me that?"

"I promise you."

That afternoon Avram went to the house of Velásquez. It was now the third day after the operation
on Isabel de Velásquez – and two days since Antonio
had brought the news of the massacre of Sevilla.

Every hour since then, the hysteria and fear in the
Jewish ghetto had mounted. On his way home from
Gabriela's, and again on his way to the house of
Velásquez, Avram had heard the cries of mourning
seeping like blood from the high, barred windows of
Toledo's synagogues. After a tragedy, Antonio had
once remarked, the synagogues were more like dungeons emitting the cries of the tortured than temples
dedicated to the worship of God.

As for Antonio himself, since the night of their
conversation by the river, Avram had not seen him.
Each time he returned from a patient, Avram asked
his mother if his cousin was home yet. And Avram
had just spent part of the morning at the fair, looking
not only for his cousin but for the Christian traveller
of whom he had spoken.

By the time Avram made his way to the gate of
Velásquez's palace, the sun was high in the sky,
burning with such violence that the air itself was
bleached with the heat.

When he knocked on the grill, Avram was greeted,
as always, by the hunchbacked dwarf. This greeting
came not in words, for since Avram's attack on him
he had refused to speak, but in the form of a wicked
smile and a bow accompanied by his hands crossing
over his groin. To this charming gesture, Avram raised
his hat in recognition, not without thinking that he
must never turn his back on this malevolent spirit,
and then crossed the courtyard to the house.

Today Velásquez was sitting on the small patio outside the bedroom of his wife. In the cool shadows of the hanging plants, and holding a glass of the sherry with which he liked to move from afternoon to evening, he was dictating a letter as Avram arrived.

"Sit down. I was just finishing."

Velásquez concluded his message with his eternal prayers and compliments and then the scribe, plying the quill awkwardly and slowly over the parchment, scratched out the remaining words. This scribe, the same giant who had almost slit Avram's throat on his first visit, then got to his feet and made his own mute bow to Avram, before begging the permission of Velásquez to be dismissed.

"Go," Velásquez said. "But the finished copy must be brought to me before evening." Then he turned to Avram: "May I offer you a drink?"

"No, thank you."

"The doctor never drinks on duty."

Avram was silent.

"Once you drank on duty. The night you operated on my wife."

"I was very tired," Avram said.

"Perhaps you were nervous, too?"

"Perhaps."

"Well," Velásquez said abruptly, "I have just heard of another cause for nervousness. There has been a new massacre of the Jews, this time in Barcelona. It is said that thousands have died, and that tens of thousands have converted. The letter I was dictating gives instructions to my business partners in Barcelona to take over the wool trade that has now been vacated by the Jews. We will now be shipping woollen goods to Italy and points east."

From his chair on the patio, Avram could see past the columns of the house to the red tile roofs of the

88

city below. It was a pretty view. Others lauded the lusher beauties of the more southern cities, but Avram liked the dusty colours of Toledo, the dirt streets, the brown-grey stone, the semi-desert stretching out from the city.

"You must know," Velásquez said, "that Ferrand Martínez has the support of the people."

"He is the queen mother's confessor, but he is also a fanatic."

"Why is he a fanatic?"

"Ferrand Martínez," Avram said carefully, "is a fanatic because he wishes to eliminate an entire race of people. He wants to kill or convert every Jew in Spain."

"And what is wrong with that? Why should a Jew stay a Jew? Why should he not be happy as a Christian? Why should he not join with everyone else and make this the most splendid of all kingdoms?"

The two men had been sitting at the table, talking but hardly looking at each other as they made their predictable arguments. But now Avram felt suddenly engaged by Velásquez. To unite, to become one: the great community of man linked heart-to-heart, soul-to-soul, God-to-God, that was a vision even Antonio has espoused. He looked at Velásquez. The older man was smiling at him, a warm invitation to come out of his own strange fearful world and into the safety of the Christian city.

"I ask you as one man to another," Velásquez now said. "You, your friend Gabriela Hasdai, why should you spend a life divided against yourselves? After all, what was there before Jews? So many wanderers in the desert who had no idea of God. And then came Abraham, and with him the knowledge of God. Those who had faith became Jews. For a time the Jews ruled their own destiny. *Then* was the era to be a Jew. But the Jews grew corrupt, they lost their power. Finally God sent the Messiah to save the Jews. And now it is the Christians who are in the eye of God. Join us."

Velásquez poured himself more sherry, extended to Avram the glass he had already refused.

"I am a merchant. I know how to judge the value of things and of people. When Ben Ishaq told me of the miracle you could perform, I was desperate. I bought your services because I needed them. But now I have had a chance to judge you at leisure, and although I owe you the lives of my wife and my son, I still cannot say what value you have. Now I want to know more about you, so please, feel free to answer me as one man to another. After all, though I am a Christian and you are a Jew, and we each have our separate places, each of us is trying to change our destiny. But to change is to sacrifice. So tell me, please, as one man to another, why do you not join us? We are all children of Abraham."

"To be a man is a strange fate," Avram said. Even as he pronounced the words a chord of fear and danger sounded within him. "Because I am not only a man, a blank man who might be any other man, I am also a certain and specific man, Avram Halevi. This man, Avram Halevi, knows that you are honest and sincere. And he knows, too, that the Christian heart is as real in God's eye as the heart of the Jew. But Avram Halevi also knows that the man who should have been his father was killed by a Jew-hating mob, that even tonight such a mob could attack the Jewish barrio of Toledo. And so you ask me to speak to you, Don Juan, man to man, one son of Abraham to another, but we must also talk Jew to Christian, because that is what we are."

Velásquez swirled the sherry in his glass. Avram watched the sun's light shoot through the liquid.

"Now," Avram said, "it is I who have spoken and you who remain silent, Don Juan."

"That is because you have spoken with great eloquence, yet have still not answered my question: why should a Jew stay a Jew? Why should he not be happy as a Christian? And don't tell me that I should ask some rabbi that question. It is *your* answer that I want, because you are a man I respect. Or can you yourself not answer me? Do you think your people should give up their religion? As have, so you say, you yourself?"

"You ask me," Avram said, "why a Jew should not be happy as a Christian? But if all Christians were happy, why would they rush about killing their neighbours? Perhaps the Jews are happier, because they do not feel such a need."

"And yet," Velásquez said, "according to the historians, the Jews, when they ruled the land of Israel, were willing enough to use the sword."

"That is true," Avram admitted. "But every country must defend itself."

"Then so must Spain," Velásquez said, "defend herself from its enemies inside."

"But the Jews are not Spain's enemies; they are her servants."

"They are the enemies of the people," Velásquez said, "because they are the ones who break the backs of the poor by collecting taxés."

"But the taxes are not paid to the Jews. They are paid to the landowners and the king. The Jews are merely the collectors."

"They are the visible face of tyranny," Velásquez insisted.

"When the plague came," Avram said, "in some countries, they accused the Jews of poisoning the wells. In Germany, they made the Jews build wooden houses, and then they herded them into the houses and set fire to them. Then the Jews were gone. But the plague remained."

"But the people felt better," Velásquez said, "because they had cast out the demon."

"Those who set the fires felt better," Avram said. "Those inside the houses were also people, and they did not feel better."

Velásquez set his glass carefully on the marble table. It made a very slight click, and for some reason that dry noise reminded Avram of the sounds that fractured bones sometimes made when they were being set.

"You have the mind of a Greek," Velásquez said.

"My mother used to claim," Avram replied, "that I had the mind of a rabbi."

Velásquez smiled. "Well, if you were a rabbi, I would be giving you a message to take to your people. That message is: leave Toledo. So far Martínez has not dared to come here. But he will, and very soon. And when he does, my Marrano rabbi, it will be very, very bad."

The anger that had been building up inside Avram during this whole conversation now forced him to his feet. He paced from the table to the outer wall of the patio. Outside Toledo there was no refuge for her Jews – this city, the New Jerusalem of modern times – surely it was the place where the Jews must stay to face their destiny.

Velásquez broke the silence. "In my new business, I will need someone who speaks Arabic as well as French and Italian to manage the affairs of trade. He will live in Barcelona, there will be risks to be taken, fortunes to be made. It is a chance for a new life."

"I already have a new life."

Velásquez laughed. "You have a temper. Only the very young and the very stupid can afford to have a temper like yours. Anyway, I would rather you got killed trying to further my interests than at the sword of some peasant. Think about my offer and we will talk about it again." He stood up. Velásquez had, Avram realized, something no Jew could ever possess: confidence in the future.

"I have a surprise for you," Velásquez said. "After all this serious discussion I hope it will be a very pleasant surprise." Velásquez opened the door to his wife's chambers and called her name, so that she might be warned of their coming.

Isabel was sitting up in bed, wearing a white dress that pushed up her swollen breasts, white gloves that covered her slender arms to the elbows, a tiara of precious jewels on her brow.

"Don Juan, Don Avram, don't stare so, you are making a sick woman embarrassed."

"We are staring in happy surprise," said Velásquez. "Even the doctor must be surprised to see you so well."

"Not surprised, only happy."

Avram stepped closer, took the hand of Isabel and kissed it as if they were being presented at a formal dinner. Twice he had already opened and drained the wound, but today he could see that despite the ordeal she had undergone, Isabel de Velásquez was beginning to recover. Still, her face was amazingly frail — fine bones that stretched wide and proud at the cheeks, transparent white skin through which could be seen pulsing the blue veins at her temples, glossy black hair with coppery-tinted tips that curled into tendrils where they rested on the clear white skin of her shoulders.

"Don Avram, my husband and I are hoping that just because your surgery has been so successful, you will not cease to be our friend and come often to the house."

"Of course not."

"We would be honoured if you would join us three nights from now, for dinner. My husband's brother, the cardinal, will be visiting us and he is curious to meet 'the miraculous Marrano,' as my husband calls you, the Marrano who wields the silver knife."

Avram flushed, despite himself, as inside his chest his heart squeezed in violent reaction to this unexpected twist of fortune. Now, urgently, he needed to find Antonio: the plan that had seemed so unlikely had suddenly become possible.

"Come at sunset," Don Juan instructed. "We will sit on the patio and watch — as your countryman poet, the one who lived in Barcelona, liked to say — watch the sky bleed into the river. And afterwards, when my brother has returned to his duties at the cathedral, you will tell me if you have decided to become my partner in Barcelona."

SEVEN

TWO NIGHTS LATER, SITTING AT THE OAK DINING TABLE THAT HAD BEEN IN THE VELÁSQUEZ FAMILY SINCE THE SIXTH CENTURY – SINCE BEFORE THE VERY FIRST MUSLIMS HAD even thought of invading the Iberian Peninsula – Juan Velásquez looked across the burnished wood and into the eyes of his brother Rodrigo, and tried to decipher the meaning of his words.

In the time since their boyhood, his brother had grown more powerful than even his high ambitions could have led him to forecast. Like all the Velásquez men, he was powerfully built: a barrel-like torso with wide shoulders set on long spindly legs. His hair, too, was black and combed straight back, but Rodrigo's high forehead gave him, Juan thought, a cruel and stony look: an aspect, no doubt, that he liked to cultivate.

"It is rumoured," Rodrigo said, "that the Jews of Toledo are preparing an armed uprising."

Dinner was long over. The dishes had been cleared away and Isabel had gone to her bedchamber. Only the Velásquez brothers were left at the table, and between them was a bottle of the musty claret that Rodrigo's vineyards excelled in producing.

"The Jews of Toledo," said Juan Velásquez, "are like frightened chickens. They have spent the last few days dreading the hour when they must receive what has already happened to the Jews of other cities."

"Ferrand Martínez is a harsh man," said his brother. "But the Jews are not being killed by him, they are being killed by their own money. Why should the Jews be rich and dress in fancy clothes while the nobles and the Church are starving?"

"You are not starving, my brother."

Rodrigo Velásquez pushed back his chair. His voice, as always when he grew impatient with his younger brother, grew louder. "Why are you arguing with me, Juan Velásquez? Why do you doubt what I say? Are you such a lover and defender of the Jews? If you love them so much, why are you so happy to take over their trade in Barcelona?"

"I don't love them so much, my good brother. I love you, my brother, and I love the Lord."

"And that physician of your wife's, Avram Halevi. I suppose you love him, too?"

"Halevi is a Marrano. In fact, I have invited him to dinner tomorrow so that you can meet him."

"Pig," said Rodrigo, leaning across the table. "He is not a Christian, he is a pig."

"And what else do your informants tell you about Avram Halevi?"

"Nothing about him, my good and trusting brother. But his cousin, Antonio Espinosa, that is a different man. A man," Rodrigo said, "who did not give up his religion under the sword."

"And?"

"And he was kind enough to visit my office," Rodrigo said, "where we had a little conversation."

Velásquez could not help cringing inside. He, too, had visited his brother's Toledo office, but not as one of the prisoners who paid their respects naked and after a week of starvation.

"There was no violence," Rodrigo said, "nor did he confess, even when asked more than one time. But there will be further conversations, and when they are complete, I am confident that we will have the information we need."

"He is in your prison now?"

"My dear brother. The Spanish Church has no prisons. We do not even have, like our sister Churches in other countries, an Inquisition."

Juan Velásquez reached for the claret and refilled his brother's glass and his own. This was the third bottle that had been opened in the past few hours, and there were several more at the end of the table, waiting for their attention. The more, it seemed, his brother drank, the thirstier he got. And the thirstier Rodrigo Velásquez became, the louder grew his voice and the more strident his pronouncements.

For Juan Velásquez, however, the claret had a different purpose. He drank it to dissolve the hatred he felt for his brother, for his role in the Church, for his pompous words and his unconcealed delight in the privileges of his office. "Why should that make you hate him?" Isabel had once asked, when Juan had confessed these feelings to her. "After all, he talks too much, but no more than many others; and if his position has given him wealth, it is still not as much wealth as that of a successful merchant, like yourself." About the torture chambers she had said nothing; Juan Velásquez himself had used the chambers to extract information from a rival's messenger. Moreover, both of his most trusted servants – the hunchback and the giant – had been tested by the chambers before he had admitted them to the intimacy of the household.

Now Juan let his eyes drop to the table. His brother had emptied his glass and was reaching for a new bottle. The brothers came from a family that had once been almost large. Both their parents and their two other brothers and two sisters had been killed by the plague, all in the space of one week as the Death raged through their home in Barcelona.

That had been decades ago, when he and Rodrigo were still boys. Their uncle had first taken them in, then passed them over to the Church to be educated. Juan had left as soon as he was old enough to take his place in the family business; Rodrigo elected to stay with the Church. But twice a year he and Rodrigo would meet, the survivors. As children they had been six years apart and buffered by the others but now, alone like the two remaining fingers of a maimed hand, they were forced to accommodate and depend on each other. "We must tell each other everything, all our secrets, all our dreams," Rodrigo had insisted. "Otherwise what use is it having a brother?"

In the polished surface of the table, Juan watched the reflection of Rodrigo's strong arms as he twisted the cork from his claret. He had cultivated his cruel look, his brutal reputation: ten years ago, when a new group of the wandering flagellants had shown up in Valencia, Rodrigo had been the priest to put it down.

He had waited until the flagellants gathered enough courage to perform their ritual in the centre square of Valencia. While his disciples lay on their stomachs, men and women alike half naked, chanting their prayers, the master confessor and flagellator had in full scarlet-robed costume raised his whip to scourge their scarred backs.

Only then, while the whole town watched, had Rodrigo acted.

Without a word, he broke through the circle of spectators. And then, with one blow of his open palm, he sent the charlatan master reeling to the ground. When the master raised his whip to Rodrigo, Rodrigo tore it from his hand and scourged the master himself until his scarlet cloak surrounded him in a wreath of blood-soaked ribbons. That evening, when the body of the master was burned, Rodrigo himself had preached to the watching crowd. The smoke of a heretic's corpse may rise to the sky, he had said, but his *soul* would be consigned to an eternal Hell a thousand times more terrible than the fate he had tried to inflict on the poor innocents whom he had led astray.

And when the corpse and the wood that burned around it were reduced to ash and bone bits, Rodrigo released the flagellants, gave them white robes, and allowed them to partake in the communion of the Church. Their only punishment was that each of them lost his or her left ear, so that they might in future be deaf to the temptations of the Devil.

Juan raised his eyes to his brother again, and watched him as he poured the claret into their glasses. It was said that Rodrigo had allowed his personal barber the privilege of cutting off the ears of the misled innocents.

"So," Rodrigo said, "you hear that the Jews of Toledo fear what might befall them."

"Yes."

"Does your Marrano doctor, whose cousin is a Jew, speak to you of such things?"

"He speaks of those things of which a doctor speaks."

"It is a great honour to be the personal physician of Señor Juan Velásquez."

"It is an even greater honour," said Juan, "to be the physician of the wife of Señor Juan Velásquez."

"But now she has recovered?"

"She is on her way to health."

"And Diego is well?"

"My son grows in strength every day."

"And so it is not necessary that the physician who has gained such a great honour continue to live in the city of his most illustrious patron."

"But he does live here," Juan said, "and when you and he look at each other across my dinner table, I hope you will forget your harsh words so that he may enjoy the honour of meeting the illustrious cardinal of Castilla."

"I am the one to be honoured." Rodrigo was at the stage in the night, Juan recognized, when his drinking accelerated and his words grew more flowery. Soon he would reach the next and final stage, the point to which each of their very occasional and very formal evenings were dedicated; and that was the time when he would reveal whatever little surprise he had prepared.

"It will be an education for the doctor, too," Juan persisted, "for perhaps he can learn, from you, the advantages of staying faithful to the Christianity he has adopted."

Rodrigo laughed. "You want me to extend to this pig the protection of the Church?"

"That's right," Juan said, "now that you put it so bluntly."

"And why should I do such an irregular thing? Because my brother asks me?"

"Because, my good brother, I do not fancy having my wife die before she has had the opportunity to watch her child – your nephew – become a man. And – "

"Enough," Rodrigo interrupted. "A priest has the grace to stay out of the marriage bed of his brother. Neither your wife nor your doctor will be inconvenienced. And I will be delighted to meet him, at *your* table."

"Thank you."

"But I would suggest, dear brother, that, if you wish to keep him alive, you persuade him to take a trip very soon."

"I have already done so."

"And where is he going?"

"Valencia," Juan said. The lie surprised him even as he spoke it. And yet he knew that he liked Halevi. Perhaps it was his youth and the stupidity of his ambition. Or perhaps it was simply his own long-frustrated desire for a son. "I would like him to go to Valencia and be my emissary to certain Arab traders there. Perhaps he could even learn to do something useful for me." Now the lie was wrapped in a truth; it would be harder to detect.

"They are gathering now in Madrid," Rodrigo said. "The archbishop and his friends wish Toledo to be next. It bothers them that such a delicious and mature fruit has not yet been harvested."

"The Jews of Toledo have been here for a long time," Juan said. "Surely the king should protect his loyal subjects."

Rodrigo laughed again, and refilled his glass. "The king is twelve years old," he said. "Even royal blood flows weakly at such an age."

There was a knock at the door; then it swung open and the hunchback entered.

"A messenger for Cardinal Velásquez."

"Send him in."

A small man scurried like a mouse across the room. Standing, he was barely tall enough to whisper into the ear of his master. "Go," Rodrigo said, "we will be with you soon." And then he turned to Juan with a wide smile on his face. "We have eaten and drunk enough to make younger men proud. Perhaps we should leave the table for a moment. Would you care to walk with me in the night air?"

EIGHT

IT WAS WELL PAST MIDNIGHT, AND THE SQUARE OP-
POSITE THE GREAT CATHEDRAL WAS EMPTY. BUT
IN THE LIGHT OF THE HALF-MOON, THE WIDE STONE
STEPS AND THE CARVED PORTICO WERE A SILVERY
eternal white; and looking up at the majestic series
of spires that had just been completed after a full
century of work, Juan Velásquez could not help putting his hand across his brother's broad back: surely
this cathedral, its stonework, the dazzling sculptures
of Christ and the Virgin so perfectly wrought that
they hung in the air the way angels must hover in
Heaven — surely these acts of worship were great
deeds. If Rodrigo was cruel, he also had the courage
to touch the marrow of a man's life.

Yes, courage and daring: the same Rodrigo Velásquez who had erased the flagellants of Valencia had
also, in defiance of the pope, fasted for *three months*
on his pilgrimage to Santiago de Compostela: stopping every night where St. James himself had stopped,
he had refreshed his body with a single glass of water
and then spent the whole night praying in preparation for the journey of the next day.

"A holy fool," it was said that the pope whispered
to his advisers.

But the "holy fool" made sure that all of Christian Spain heard of his feat. And afterwards, when he threw his support to Ferrand Martínez, there was no one to doubt his sincerity — or his political astuteness.

"Look at it," Rodrigo now said. "One of the most beautiful churches in Spain."

"Like a great ship."

"Exactly, my good brother. It is like a great ship with indestructible stone masts, and it is going to carry us to a new world."

"A new world?"

"A new Christian world where the Church is not a tiny minority battling against the tides of millennia of ignorance and fanatical opponents, but where the Church and the state are twins, united. Where they provide the ground on which the people can walk, where innocents are led not into heresy, but into faith."

Juan had heard Rodrigo speak like this before: now, as in the past, it always sounded faintly rehearsed, like an extract from a speech he had given to the college of cardinals, like the dogma that he himself, as a shrewd and rough boy, would have labelled as pompous hot air.

"Such a wonderful land must be very far away," Juan said.

"Spain will be such a land," replied Rodrigo, "as soon as the Muslims have been driven out of the peninsula."

The summer air was sweet and warm. Before their parents had died, such nights had been spent sitting in the gardens of their father's house, listening to the grown-ups talk and playing games with the cousins. But the Black Death had taken almost everyone, and the bodies of his family were buried together in a single grave that Don Juan had never once had the heart to visit.

"This way," Rodrigo now said. And he waved Don Juan towards a side door of the cathedral. With a large skeleton key, the messenger opened it – it seemed to take all his frail strength merely to turn the lock – and then, once inside, he lit a taper and led them down a narrow set of stone stairs to the rooms where treasures were kept.

As they descended the steps, Juan Velásquez smelled that familiar mixture of dampness, money, and fear that always seemed to drift upward from the dungeons of the great cathedral.

"There is nothing wrong with force," Rodrigo once said. "Force is the right arm of God. And has there ever been a civilized country in this world that has existed without it?"

"Perhaps," Juan had countered, "a country that depends on force is not truly civilized."

But Rodrigo had only laughed. "In that case, my dear brother, there has never been a civilized country at all. Because those who have not been able to defend themselves – as well as those who have not been able to use armies to expand their territories – have disappeared like so many swallows into the night of history."

Now the cardinal led the way down a hall that had as many twists as the back streets of Toledo, until suddenly they found themselves outside a large vaulted room. Juan paused in the doorway, while his brother went inside.

Seated at a large table, writing with utmost calmness, each letter a flourish, was one of the monks who worked with Rodrigo. He was wearing a judge's robe and cornered hat, and in his hand he held a large quill pen that, periodically, he lifted from the page and refreshed with his tongue before dipping it into the ink.

At the back of the large room, lining the wall above wooden benches, were several iron rings, hooks, and chains. From these, however, no one was hanging. In fact, the only persons on the bench were perfectly comfortable: they were two of the other monks in Rodrigo's service, and they sat casually at ease, waiting to see what would now develop.

But even more quiet than these resting monks was the figure in the middle of the room. This person was lying belly-up on a table; the skyward-pointing toes helped to identify the direction of the body's repose. The body was covered with a blanket, and beneath it, Juan could see a familiar bulge: it was the shape of the hands clasped together on the chest – the position they were put into by the monks after a victim of the interrogations had been lucky enough to die. Looking closely at the feet, Juan could see now that two of the toes were swollen into grotesquely purpled carrots.

As Juan stepped closer, Rodrigo drew back the blanket and exposed the face.

It was a large, square-jawed face with a black curly beard. The man's eyes stared resolutely at the ceiling.

"Why is Antonio Espinosa in the position of the dead?" Rodrigo demanded.

"To bring him closer to God, Your Eminence."

Juan watched as Rodrigo threw the blanket back across Espinosa's head.

The pen continued to scratch on paper, like a chicken happily eating while his fellows are decapitated for the stew-pot. Now, looking at the wall, Juan could see where Espinosa had been. Blood had congealed on the bench over which he had been hanging, and placed on a tray were instruments of torture in the use of which Rodrigo, after acquiring them in Italy, had instructed his followers.

"Well," Rodrigo asked, "what has he told you?"

"Nothing, Your Eminence."

"He will," Rodrigo said. Juan saw his brother step forward again, but this time to the desk, where he began to read what the clerk had written down.

"Look at this," Rodrigo exclaimed to Juan, handing him the first papers. "Do you remember what I told you tonight? About the Jews wanting to defend themselves? They were planning to kidnap me and demand as ransom free passage for all the Jews of Toledo to Valencia, and from there a boat to Italy. Have you ever heard anything so moronic?"

"It's not such a bad idea," Juan said drily. "You are a valuable member of the Church."

"Pigs," said Rodrigo. "Pigs like this should be roasted on a spit, not sent to Italy. Do they think I am so afraid to die?" He turned to the monks on the bench. "Chain him to the wall again. We will see what the brave Antonio Espinosa has to say."

For the first time the priest at the desk stopped writing. "He cannot be questioned further, Your Eminence, without serious risk of death."

"All of life is a risk," Rodrigo said. "Since Señor Espinosa was prepared to risk my life, surely I have the right to risk his."

Juan looked carefully at the papers. According to them, an itinerant merchant had been overheard bragging that the Jews of Toledo had a plan to outwit Ferrand Martínez. When questioned, he admitted nothing, until a child was brought in and threatened in front of him. Then he had confessed that there had been a meeting in the square of the synagogue and that the participants in the meeting had stabbed a communion wafer until it bled. When all present had drunk of this blood, they had decided on the plot to kidnap the archbishop's favourite cardinal. He had not given any other names of conspirators, saying that he knew no one in the town, but had admitted finally that he had once met Antonio Espinosa while in Barcelona.

Naked, Espinosa now was lifted from the table and his wrists raised to the iron rings. When he was strapped into position, he crossed his feet so that he hung above the bench in a parody of the crucifixion.

"Look at him," Rodrigo spat out. "You would think he hoped for God to bless him, too."

Juan did not reply. If Espinosa was not guilty of this plot, he was undoubtedly guilty of others. He deserved to die, of that Juan Velásquez was certain; and even, he told himself, if Antonio did not actually *deserve* to die, his death was probably inevitable. The only unfortunate thing was that this would be unpleasant – at least he might have been lucky enough for a quick and easy end. He turned away from Espinosa. Rodrigo had picked up a scourge – since his great victory in Valencia, it had been his personal trademark.

"You don't have to stay, dear brother."

"I will stay."

"But even if the sight of Señor Espinosa's descent into Hell would not make you squeamish, you might not enjoy what will happen if his cousin is equally stubborn."

"Avram?"

"Avram Halevi, yes, the former physician to the wife of the illustrious Señor Juan Velásquez."

Juan felt his chest thump, as if a huge fist had punched him in the breast. "Where is he?"

"In the next room."

Then the air was cut with the whisper of leather. A long sibilant whisper that ended with a loud slap and the sound of flesh tearing. A second later, the next whisper began. At its end, a small sigh escaped Espinosa. "Go and see your doctor now," Rodrigo said. "Perhaps you will be able to console him."

Juan stood, undecided for a moment. One of the monks came close to him. "If you would permit, Don Juan, I will show you to –," and then the monk, very lightly, put his hand on Velásquez's arm.

"Fool," shouted Juan Velásquez. The paralysis that always descended upon him in the presence of his older brother suddenly broke open, and with it, his rage at having been tricked. Grabbing the monk by the collar, he threw him with all his strength across the room. But by the time Juan was in the corridor, the monk was already at his elbow again, apologizing obsequiously and leading him to the cell where Avram was being kept.

That room was another level down in the church basements. It had been pitch-black until the monk, holding his taper to a candle at the doorway, sent a weak yellow light through the barred doors and onto the bench where Avram was sitting.

"Open the door," Velásquez commanded.

"It is not permitted – "

"Open the door, or you will envy Antonio Espinosa."

"Yes, Don Juan."

The iron door creaked open and Avram rose to his feet.

"Don Juan Velásquez, an unexpected pleasure."

Juan turned to the monk in the doorway. "You can leave us now."

"It is not permitted – "

109

"Tell my brother that I commanded it. And light the lamps in the hallway."

Velásquez waited until the footsteps of the monk receded, then drew Avram towards the stronger light of the hall. One of his eyes was bruised and swollen, and he walked with a limp, as if his leg had been injured.

"My brother tells me that the Jews of the barrio were planning to kidnap him. That is why they are questioning you and your cousin."

Avram nodded.

"My wife would not have survived without you. Nor would my child. We owe you a great debt."

Avram only nodded again. Velásquez put his hand on the doctor's shoulder. Not only had the child been born, but in Halevi he had met the man whom he wanted to be his manager until the boy was old enough to begin working in the business.

Ben Ishaq had told him that Halevi wanted to be a great surgeon. But very soon there would be no Jews for a surgeon to practise on. And after the Jews, Rodrigo had already told him, the Marranos would be eliminated.

"I am not going to ask you whether this ridiculous accusation is true. We are men here, and we know that men must have honour between them."

Now Avram smiled and pushed back the hair from his forehead. There was revealed a long and ugly gash, travelling almost from the middle of his forehead to his temple. Juan's hand, of its own accord, darted towards it.

"It is nothing to be concerned about, Don Juan. The blood of a doctor flows just the same as the blood of another man."

"You are hurt."

"Only my pride."

"Avram, I want you to go to Barcelona, as I asked you to. Have you thought about it?"

"I have, Juan Velásquez."

"And what have you decided?"

"I have responsibilities here, in Toledo. For the moment, I cannot leave. But perhaps later, when the current danger has passed, we could – "

Here Avram's voice stopped. But Velásquez, about to question him further, now heard a rush of footsteps in the hall. He looked up to see Rodrigo's monk running towards them, candle sputtering in his hand.

"Don Juan, yourself and the doctor, your brother requests you come right away."

"Excuse me," Avram said, and went back into his cell for his cloak and hat. In a moment, garbed as if for a formal visit, he was walking down the hall beside Velásquez.

When they reached the interrogation room, Velásquez could see that his brother's whispers had not helped the health of Antonio Espinosa. He was still hanging from the wall now, but his head lolled to one side and his whole body had slumped lower, as if the sockets of his shoulders no longer had the strength to hold him. From the neck down, he was wrapped in a blanket, but through it, like narrow islands pushing their way up through the surface of the sea, were mapped little trails and lakes of blood.

Rodrigo, who was standing and looking at Espinosa, turned to the doorway to greet them. "My dear brother. And Don Avram Halevi, the great doctor and surgeon of Toledo. What a pleasure it is to meet you."

Juan watched as Avram bowed in response to Rodrigo's greeting. Then as the cardinal stepped forward to shake the doctor's hand, Juan saw that Antonio's eyes had opened very slightly.

"I am delighted to be presented with you so soon," Rodrigo said. "My brother has already told me that we would have the pleasure of your company."

"The pleasure would have been mine."

"But now," Rodrigo continued, "we have a more urgent problem. Your cousin is in a most unfortunate situation. He refuses to talk and he refuses to die. You are the great doctor, perhaps you will give him medicine so that he may revive himself."

"It would be my privilege," said Avram. Juan saw him reach inside his cloak for the pouch of medicine that had been a familiar sight in the Velásquez home. Then he stepped forward to Antonio, whose eyes had closed once again. "May I take off the patient's blanket?"

"In this hospital," said the cardinal, "the doctor must be supreme."

The blanket was stripped away. Despite himself, Juan felt his chest constrict once more. Espinosa had been flayed like a reluctant beast. The skin of his chest and stomach had been reduced to ribbons, that of his thighs, too. His genitals were a clotted lake of blood. Now Avram turned around to confront Rodrigo. His face was, Velásquez noticed, perfectly calm and serene, the way it had been when he had begun the operation on Isabel.

"Take the patient from the wall," said Avram, "and place him on the table, please."

"My pleasure, Doctor," said Rodrigo, and nodded to the monks.

When Espinosa was lying on the table, covered again by the blanket, Avram turned once more to Rodrigo.

"The patient cannot talk because he is in shock. May I have permission to administer a small stimulant?"

112

"Will this stimulant stimulate him to tell the truth?"

"The patient wishes very much to tell the truth. I am sure he will comply as soon as he is able."

"Very well."

From his pouch, Velásquez saw Avram withdraw a small envelope. He pried open Antonio's mouth and then, after requesting some wine, placed the powders on his cousin's tongue. Cradling his head in his hands, he lifted him slightly from the table, so that he could swallow. As he did, Velásquez heard Avram whisper something to his cousin.

"What did you say?" Rodrigo demanded.

"I said, 'Shalom, Antonio.'" He was still cradling his cousin's head in his arm.

"Tell me what that means."

"Sometimes it means 'Good day, Antonio.'" Now Velásquez saw Espinosa's face contort. His skin was suddenly covered with sweat and his body jerked and convulsed.

"The patient is responding to the stimulant," Avram said.

Now Antonio's arm flew back, like a bird desperately trying to fly. The blanket slipped off and to the floor. Velásquez's eyes went automatically to the bloodied lake between his thighs. "Cover him," Juan said, and himself bent for the blanket. But even as he raised it, Espinosa's body quivered and shook, like a man in the last moments of the plague.

"The patient is still responding to the stimulant," Avram said.

Suddenly Antonio's convulsions stopped, and his head lolled back in Avram's arms. Avram took the blanket from Velásquez and covered his dead cousin.

"The patient has now responded to the stimulant," he said.

"When will he talk?" Rodrigo demanded.

Juan turned towards the wall. Avram had fooled Rodrigo. But what Rodrigo had done to Antonio's manhood: the image was like rat claws scratching at his eyes.

"Unfortunately," he heard Avram say, "the patient's response to the stimulant was so successful that it overcame every other desire."

Velásquez turned back to watch his brother's face tightening with rage. "Very well, we'll see how you do in your cousin's place." Rodrigo waved forward the monks. "Strip him."

But as the monks stood up, Juan Velásquez moved also.

"Touch him and you die." From his sheath he drew a long knife, and there now stepped into the doorway his two bodyguards, the giant and the hunchback.

The monks looked to Rodrigo in confusion.

"You are protecting a Jew from the Church?" Rodrigo asked. But Velásquez saw that his brother's face had begun to regain its normal colour.

"I am protecting my own property," said Juan Velásquez, "the personal physician of myself, my wife, and my child. Do you have an objection?"

There was a moment of silence. Juan could sense the giant moving closer.

"I am pleased," Rodrigo finally said, "to see that the house of Velásquez has the grace to shelter its own servants."

NINE

BY THOSE WHO LOVED HIM, THE FACE OF BEN ISHAQ WAS SAID TO BE THE SAD FACE OF WISDOM. HIS FEATURES WERE NARROW AND LONG, A WHITE FRINGE OF BEARD SURROUNDED THE dark and leathery skin, his mouth was turned down slightly at the corners. But on an evening in early August, exactly one week after his favourite pupil had performed a miraculous operation on the wife of Juan Velásquez, the mouth of Ben Ishaq had relaxed from the frown it had worn all day while seeing patients, and might even have been said to be entertaining the idea of a smile. He was sitting on the rock that was his private preserve, a niche in the wall that separated the Arab quarter of Toledo from the sun-scorched orchards sloping to the Targa below. With the aid of two pipefuls of hashish, he looked out to the desert, and what he saw gave him the feeling of a golden and dusty serenity.

Below him, the Targa River doubled back on itself so deeply that the silver ribbon looked as though it had been tied into a bow. And just beyond the river, reaching its peak after a month of growth, was the huge encampment of the fair.

It was while travelling with such a fair that Ben Ishaq had served his apprenticeship with the herbalist who had adopted him as an infant in Tunisia.

Those years in the desert were the exotic flowers in the garden of Ben Ishaq's mind: each was cultivated and re-visited, watered with nostalgia, inspected for signs of deterioration. It was during those years that he had become a man, had first learned the dream-trance in which he discovered new curative herbs, had married and had children.

By the time circumstances forced him to Toledo, the children had been long buried, and his dreams had started to lose their potency. Aside from the treasures in his memory, only the yearly visit of the fair could remind Ben Ishaq of the magical happiness of his youth.

From his position on the wall, Ben Ishaq's eyes could encompass the entire span of the fair. At this twilight hour the complex jumble of thousands of tents and pavilions, dotted with columns of smoke from roasting pits, was a feast to his sentimental eye. At this very moment, Ben Ishaq knew, the improvised streets of the fair would be filled, and the smoky smell of North African sauces would be mixed with raw wine and gossip as the thousands of merchants and traders and hangers-on prepared to celebrate their last night near Toledo.

Later, when the dusk had deepened to exactly the proper point, Ben Ishaq planned to leave the city and cross the river to the tents where he would spend the night talking to old friends. But for now it was enough to look out across the river and the desert, and to remember the same view from other years, other final evenings of the fair when he had slipped out of the city to join in the celebration.

After his wife had died, but when he was still, at least in retrospect, a young man – that is, a man who was mature but had the appetites of youth – he had wanted in one or two nights of violent carousing to

116

make up for a whole year of the abstinence he practised in Toledo. In those years he had been a wild man: fortified by his own carefully selected aphrodisiacs, he would drink brandy with his friends and then rush over to the gypsy caravans where two certain sisters would be waiting for him.

But one year the sisters were missing. They had died in the Pyrenees when their cart, catching on an unseen patch of ice during a storm, had plunged into a canyon. All this was explained graphically to Ben Ishaq by the mother, an old prune of a woman who told the story vividly enough that he was forced to see the cart overturned, its wheels spinning slowly in the dark rainy air, burro thrashing in the traces. It had fallen so far, the crone explained, and the storm was so bitter, that they had not been able to descend into the bottom of the canyon for two days. After crawling down the slippery rocks they had made a fire from the brush in the valley and boiled water to soften the ground for digging.

"I know what you want them for," the crone had said, when her story was concluded. Ben Ishaq now noticed that her stooped body was wrapped in gauzy purple layers, and that the odour of death that he had smelled during the entire tale was not the unfortunate fate of her daughters but the perfume that the ancient mother had bathed in. "You can have me if you like," she added.

"You are too kind," Ben Ishaq said.

"Half-price, because there's only one of me."

"In fact," Ben Ishaq said, "I stopped only to say hello and to tell them that I have been ill, a disease, you understand, of the –"

The next year, ashamed, he had gone to the gypsy tents again with a gift for the old crone. But she too had disappeared.

The hashish circled in his blood the same lazy way that smoke from the fairground cooking fires was beginning to rise into the sky. In the afternoon there had already been started the roasting of whole cattle and pigs, and even now the smell of cooking meat hung, sweet and succulent, over the city of Toledo.

In the early afternoon, he had seen his oldest friend from the fair. Yussel Al Khan, twenty years older than himself, was becoming so frail that the skin rode over his bones like a blanket lying uneasily on a fevered sleeper. One year soon, those bones would find themselves in a grave beside one of the trails that connected the great cities of Spain. "My last burro," Yussel had said, introducing Ben Ishaq to his new donkey.

"You are even more stubborn," Ben Ishaq had said. "In the end it will be *you* who is carrying the beast on *your* back."

Ben Ishaq heard the scrape of sandals on the steps. He looked down: a young woman was climbing towards him. She was hatless, with long black hair that was parted in the centre of her head and fell about the shoulders of her white cotton dress.

Ben Ishaq turned away, his eyes suddenly running with tears. These last years he had become too sentimental, the least reminder of his wife enough to make his eyes gush. He breathed deeply, turned back to the desert until his tears had stopped and the dry air had wiped away their traces. By the time the sandals had drawn closer, he was composed again, the doctor ready to hear the trouble of others.

But this woman was silent; when Ben Ishaq finally turned to her in the dusk, he could see that she, too, had been crying. It was Gabriela Hasdai. In the twilight, her face was like living gold, her eyes deeper than the Targa.

118

"I am sorry to bother you, but Ester de Halevi said that I would find you here."

Ben Ishaq nodded. The hashish had emptied his mind of the present. Now he remembered that Avram and his cousin, Antonio, had been missing for several days, and were presumed to be in Rodrigo's prison.

"Avram is back," Gabriela said. "Ester said you would want to know that."

"Yes," Ben Ishaq said. Something inside of him unclenched – the tension he had been feeling ever since Avram was arrested – and the dusk seemed to breathe more easily. Avram: at the moment he heard of his disappearance, he had given him up for dead.

"Antonio is not back," Gabriela said.

"He is still in prison?"

"No."

Ben Ishaq uncrossed his legs. He had met Antonio many times with Avram. A young man with Avram's temper, but without his calculation. Avram, Ben Ishaq had always thought, had been born with enough cunning so that he might, if he was very lucky, survive long enough to regret living to be so old. For Antonio, such regrets were not in the stars; he would need not luck, but a galaxy of guiding angels.

"And Avram?" Ben Ishaq asked. "Is he well or is he hurt?"

"He is well enough," Gabriela said.

"But he would accept a visit from an old man who is his friend?"

"Yes."

The sky was turning dark enough that the red glow of the fires was beginning to spot the night.

"You were there today?" Gabriela asked, pointing to the fair.

"This afternoon."

"Are they going to attack the Judería? Everyone says that there are hundreds of followers of Rodrigo Velásquez and Ferrand Martínez."

Ben Ishaq had wondered about that same question during the afternoon. Though the fair was even more crowded than usual, everyone there seemed to have a purpose. Yussel had sworn that he had heard nothing unusual. But even he had admitted that should the cardinal himself come down to offer to lead an attack against the Judería, should the soldiers follow him, there was the chance events might flow out of control. A tiny chance. Ben Ishaq had been ready to dismiss the possibility until, as he was leaving the encampment, he overheard two men discussing the sack of the Jewry in Valencia. They were talking not simply about the news but about how they had paid sympathizers to hide inside the walls during the day so that when night fell, they could force open the gates.

Without answering her question, Ben Ishaq got to his feet and followed Gabriela down the stairs. Shortly after his wife died, he had stopped fearing his own death; and when he had stopped fearing his own death, he had somehow reduced his worries about the deaths of others – bad news was like a rain falling far away from the edge of his own desert. "You're an old man," Ben Ishaq would whisper contemptuously to himself at such times, "a withered cynical old stick. *Die*."

A few minutes later, Ben Ishaq was sitting cross-legged on the floor of the apartment of Ester Espinosa de Halevi. Opposite him were Avram and Ester herself, who had been frozen all evening in a deep and silent depression.

"We must leave tonight," Gabriela was insisting. "The longer we wait, the more stupid we are. Now is the time to go — while we are alive to make the journey. Everything is ready: my servant has already gone and I have bought a horse and a carriage that has room for us all."

The bruise on Avram's forehead had turned a dim yellow and purple colour, and Ben Ishaq had already wound tape around his ribs. "I killed him," Avram whispered, when they were alone. "I couldn't stand to — " Then he had stopped and Ben Ishaq had looked into the eyes of this boy whom he had spent years teaching, this unlikely Jewish student whose ambition shone so brightly that it was like soft gold, begging to be corrupted. And when Avram had told him how he had killed Antonio, Ben Ishaq, who knew that in his place he would have done the same thing had he dared, could not reach out to the boy and reassure him, because the doctor's task was to love life, not to take it away even in the cause of mercy. Had he not ended his own wife's suffering? And yet, by ending her suffering, which he himself could not bear, he had only plunged himself into that desert of aloneness that Avram was now entering. "A doctor cannot play God," he had told Avram dozens of times. "A doctor's duty is to use his dreams and his craft to save the lives of others." Now Avram was suffering from his disapproval.

"I don't want to go," Ester said, breaking the silence. "But you and Avram should leave without me. Marry, make a new life together. To know that you are safe, together, having children — that is what I want."

"You know I can't go without you," said Avram. "If you want me to go to Barcelona, you must come, too."

121

"I will die here," Ester said, her voice flat, barely audible. "Let me die in my own house, not in a peasant's cart on a road to nowhere."

"Then I will stay here with you. Gabriela will go ahead. She has arranged transportation at the fair and if we have not joined her by midnight, she will leave without us."

Ben Ishaq watched as Gabriela struggled for control. She was right to insist on leaving, and Avram was a fool not to go with her. But no one who knew Avram Halevi could imagine that he would leave his mother to die alone. And no one who knew Ester de Halevi could imagine, no matter what her words, that she would cut the cord that bound her son.

"Ben Ishaq, can't you – " But then, in mid-sentence, Gabriela suddenly stopped. "Goodbye," she said abruptly. Stiff with anger, she bowed first to Ester Espinosa de Halevi, then to Avram, and finally to Ben Ishaq. Then she turned and started down the stairs.

Once more Ben Ishaq found the eyes of Avram searching his, wanting reassurance.

"Go after her," Ben Ishaq said. The hashish was still in him and he could hear her step hesitating at the door. "At least you could see her home."

Avram stood motionless.

"Go," Ester said, "do as your teacher says."

For a moment, Avram looked like the uncertain young adolescent he had been when Ben Ishaq first met him. Then he took his black cloak from his couch and strapped on the dagger he always wore at night. "I was about to leave in any case. There is a patient I must see."

Ben Ishaq stood at the head of the stairs and waited until he heard the two voices mingle. Then he turned back into the room. Ester had fallen asleep, one of those sudden dives into unconsciousness that she seemed to be making these days. He went and knelt in front of her. Her head was slightly to one side, her fine-featured face set in a mask of peacefulness. A wisp of hair had fallen loose and was touching one eye. Ben Ishaq reached up and tucked it behind her ear. Her face was not unfamiliar to his fingers. After the night of terror, when every Jewish doctor in Toledo had been killed, he himself had gone into the Jewish quarter to tend the wounded.

"You think they should get married?" Ester's eyes had suddenly opened. Ben Ishaq was still kneeling in front of her, his hand on her face. He started to take it away, but her own hand reached up, held his. "We should have married, you and I." Her voice was dreamy and slurred.

"Jew and Muslim," Ben Ishaq said. But he knew Ester was talking out of her dreams and would not hear him.

"I want to go to sleep."

"Sleep," Ben Ishaq said. He stood up and, struggling, lifted her from her chair to the couch, where he put a pillow under her head and a light cover over her. Then he sat beside her, stroking her forehead as she settled back into a deep and regular breathing. His hand was like old leather now, her brow felt as satiny and smooth as the skin of a girl, but looked as transparent and old as the skin of his old friend Yussel. To imagine that he and Yussel had once made the gypsy girls dance. But now Yussel was enamoured with his last donkey, and he, the insatiable widower, was more than content to stroke the sleeping brow of a woman whose greatest love was for her son.

Ester's arm reached up and surrounded his knee. Ben Ishaq felt sweet and peaceful. He began to doze, his mind filled with the sounds of their breathing and the long silvery ribbon of the Targa at sunset.

TEN

"YOU MUST HAVE SOME MORE LAMB. THE COOK WILL BE INSULTED." THE VOICE OF ISABEL DE VELÁSQUEZ WAS TAUT AND WORRIED.

JUAN VELÁSQUEZ HAD EXCUSED HIMSELF from the table to fetch another bottle of claret, and now Isabel leaned over and whispered to Avram, "I was afraid you wouldn't come tonight."

"It is an honour, as always."

"*As always.* Must you always sound so formal?"

"I'm sorry."

"*I* am sorry. It is terrible that they killed your cousin."

Avram did not answer. Juan Velásquez had insisted that he come this evening, his first free from prison. "I am your benefactor," Velásquez had said, "and you are the benefactor of my wife. She is dying of fear for you. You must come, if only to reassure her."

"And what about your brother?" Avram had asked. "Will he also be reassured to see me?"

"My brother is busy tonight."

Now Avram looked at Isabel again. It was only a week since the operation, yet she was well enough to be sitting in a comfortable armchair beside the dining-room table. Instead of the wine with powders she had drunk for the operation, she was now sipping the famous Velásquez claret. The woman so near death when he had met her must have, Avram thought, a truly magnificent life-force to have survived such an operation and then exploded into bloom in only a few days. Life-force: that was what Ben Ishaq always said was the true secret of health. Life attracts life, just as the willow tree by the water contained the essence that cured rheumatism caused by damp, just as flowers that bloomed in the sun gave sweet pollen and honey. Doctors and surgeons could encourage or frustrate this force of life, but they no more than astrologers or necromancers or alchemists could make it exist where there was none.

"You're like one of the family," Isabel said. Among the doctors of Toledo it was a common joke that female patients were attracted to the hands that healed them. Avram felt his cheeks reddening at the spectacle of himself flirting with the beautiful and desirable woman whose brother-in-law was Rodrigo Velásquez. And as she smiled at him he saw that her cheeks, too, were flushed.

From their chairs on the patio they could see the fair across the river. A great campfire had been built and from it dozens of torches had been lit and were waving in the air like so many fireflies.

Juan Velásquez returned, a smile on his face, carrying two bottles. Avram stood up to welcome him, sweat springing to his skin. In this courtyard he felt a prisoner, suddenly more afraid than when he had been in the cardinal's prison. The gates to the courtyard were locked, he now noticed, and the hunchback and the giant were sitting like ill-matched twins, guarding the portals.

"To the health of Señora Isabel de Velásquez and the new heir to the Velásquez fortune," Avram said, raising the glass that Velásquez had offered him. He had remained standing. Truly Velásquez was, as he had claimed, his benefactor. He had saved him from Rodrigo, who surely would have had him killed, and now, to further polish his honour, he had insisted that Avram come to his home for dinner. He had also given him, by the simple act of offering his wife's belly to his knife, a reputation that a dozen years of work among the poor in the Jewish and Muslim quarters could never have brought. A reputation that after the Jewry was attacked would be as worthless as a debased coin.

After leaving his mother's apartment Gabriela had walked quickly, making Avram lengthen his strides to keep up with her. When they had reached her door, Avram followed Gabriela inside. But then, once in her sitting room, Avram had announced that he could only stay a few minutes, because he was expected for dinner at the house of Juan Velásquez.

"Velásquez?" Avram saw Gabriela's lips tighten so quickly that white lines appeared in the skin around them.

"I owe him that."

"Avram, his brother *killed* Antonio."

"*I* killed Antonio."

"You know what I mean."

"No, I'm afraid I don't." Avram felt his own anger mounting. "Perhaps you would like to explain."

"Actually," Gabriela said, "I don't think I want to explain fine moral points to the brilliant young surgeon of Toledo. Or perhaps I should call you a rabbi, too, since you seem to have such wisdom that you know your debts to the brother of the man who would like all the Jews of Toledo murdered."

"A few days ago, you yourself announced that you were going to Barcelona to work for Juan Velásquez."

"A few days ago," Gabriela said bitterly, "you were planning our wedding. You said it would take place in Barcelona, and that is where I am going, my future husband. Furthermore, I think you and your mother are fools for not coming with me."

Avram, feeling sudden shame, backed away. In Rodrigo's dungeon he had thought of his night with Gabriela as a miraculous oasis, and had promised himself that if he ever escaped, he would marry her immediately.

"You know," said Gabriela, "paying a debt to the Devil is nothing to be proud of. Better to throw away his gifts."

"And what do you mean by that?"

"What I mean, Avram Halevi, is that sometimes you are a bit too eager to sell your soul. Perhaps it is not me you want to marry, but the riches of Juan Velásquez."

Avram stood without moving. As he watched Gabriela he could see her anger gradually fading, and her defiant posture slowly changing into an appeal. A response had come into his mind: if he was the one who was so eager to sell his soul, why was he the one who was staying in Toledo, ready to face almost certain death, while she had agreed to save herself by running to Barcelona? But he could not speak. Not because he was too kind, but because he knew well enough that Gabriela's real accusation was that he refused to love her as she loved him.

"Well, Avram, thank you for seeing me to my house."

"Travel safely, Gabriela. I will see you soon. I promise you."

"I will travel safely," Gabriela replied. "And I will tell you, also, how much I trust our friend Velásquez. He offered me his carriage but I decided to go my own way, to be sure I was not betrayed. I advise you, my future husband, to take similar precautions."

She turned away and Avram felt a sudden pain in his heart, as if he had just witnessed her death. He stepped towards her, ready to say that he *did* love her, that he wanted to travel with and protect her. Then into his mind came the image of Antonio, hanging by his wrists from the iron rings of Rodrigo's chambers. He rubbed his eyes: *Antonio*, he had begged Avram to help him die. *Antonio*: he had been flayed by a madman. *Take my life*, he had begged, *avenge me how you will*.

"Avram. *Avram*."

He was swaying on his feet. Gabriela had caught him as he was about to pitch forward.

"Are you all right?"

"Tired," Avram said.

"Do you want some tea?"

"I should go."

And then he had kissed her goodbye, quickly and casually, as if this was a parting barely worthy of the name. And yet, the whole way to the palace of Juan Velásquez, Avram kept pausing, wishing that somehow God would strike him down with love for Gabriela and force him to keep the promise he had made in Rodrigo's jail.

The claret had found a home in the eyes of Isabel de Velásquez. In the light of the candles they glittered as brightly as the enormous ruby that hung from a gold chain around her neck and rested on the flushed skin of her breast. At Juan's insistence Avram had been telling of his two years at Montpellier, and during his description of the dark nights when students and professors alike crept to the lecture halls to perform illegal dissections, Isabel had laughed so hard that the previously sombre courtyard had taken on a brilliant and shimmering air. Avram, drinking one glass of claret after another, felt himself floating in his own eloquence, in the paternal approval of Juan Velásquez, in the pealing laugh and the sympathetic eyes of his wife.

"You must be so brave," she said, "to go to school under such conditions."

"But Isabel," Velásquez protested, "our good doctor is a specialist in the art of the narrow escape."

From across the river, the fires of the encampment now burned a phosphorescent red. By now, Avram hoped, Gabriela would have reached the place where the horse was waiting for her. For the first time it occurred to him that he had not even asked how a woman could make such a difficult arrangement.

"Tell us more," Isabel demanded.

But Avram felt suddenly depressed. Isabel was glowing, incandescent; she shone in exactly those ways in which Gabriela was dull. "Everyone knows," Ben Ishaq had said once, "that there are women who lose their lives in the hopeless love of men. But there are men, too, who lose themselves to love. Desire is what you should feel towards women. Take advantage of them when you can. Love is better saved for children."

The torches Avram had noticed an hour ago now stretched in a long avenue from the encampment to the city. From the table it was impossible to see, but he suddenly wondered if the bearers were massing outside the walls of Toledo.

"Have you noticed," he asked, "that there seems to be a procession marching from the fairgrounds to the city?"

Velásquez nodded, then stood up. "Let us go to the wall and see."

He began walking across the patio to the stairs that led to the highest point on the wall surrounding his residence. Avram followed him. When he got to the ledge he looked over and saw that hundreds of torches were milling in circles on the plain between the city and the river. Almost the whole of it was lit now; it would have been virtually impossible for Gabriela to cross unseen if she had not set out immediately after he had left her.

"My brother was sorry not to join us tonight," Velásquez said. "He said that he, like my wife, admired your courage."

Sometimes it is dangerous to have such admirers, Avram thought. But instead he simply bowed to his host. The claret, which had made the night so dazzling a few minutes ago, seemed to have evaporated from his blood. Instead of drunkenness, his senses were drowned in the alarms of danger, and his heart had begun to pound: tonight was going to be the night of the attack. That was why Rodrigo was absent. His eyes automatically circled the courtyard, taking note of the fact that the hunchback and the giant were still sitting in their places by the locked gate, weapons beside them on their benches.

"But your brother is busy tonight."

"He promised that he would go to the fair."

"And now the fair has decided to come to us."

"That's true," Velásquez said. "Now the fair has decided to come to us, to pay a visit to Toledo."

"What sort of visit?" Avram asked, wondering what polite words Velásquez would use for the slaughter.

"A visit that is unfortunate," said Velásquez, "but necessary." Isabel had now reached them. "My wife and I would be honoured if you remained our guest tonight. We have already prepared a chamber for you."

Avram looked from Velásquez back to Isabel. "I *am* sorry," she said. Exactly the same words she had used to console him about Antonio. "This must be difficult for you."

This, Avram repeated to himself. What did she mean? That it was difficult for him to be imprisoned again? Or that while he was safely locked in the guest room – would it be the same room that Rodrigo used? – he would have to listen to the distant sounds of the slaughter in the barrio?

"Another glass of wine?"

"Thank you," Avram said. "But despite your kind invitation, I'm afraid I must go home. You see, my mother can't sleep without the drugs I give her, and at her age one sleepless night can ruin a whole week."

"Your mother," Velásquez said. "That's a problem I had not thought of."

From where he was standing, Avram could see that the torches had congregated at the lowest point of the wall that separated the Jewish quarter from the Christian. Soon scaling ladders would be propped against the wall. He turned to look again at Velásquez's gate. The two guards were standing now, too.

"Good night," Avram said. "Please ask your servants to open the gate."

"Your mother could be brought here," Velásquez offered.

Avram turned away. The ladders, with astonishing speed, had already gone up the wall. A huge cross was being erected on the ledge. *Antonio*: if he were alive, he would have known what to do. Avram glanced down from Velásquez's wall to the street,

131

almost thirty feet below. The two servants were coming towards him now; the hunchback was grinning, walking with mincing steps, his hands over his groin.

"Well?" Velásquez asked.

Avram clasped his hands, trying to still their trembling. His heart was beating so strongly that he could feel the waves of blood battering against the insides of his ears.

"A generous offer," he replied. "But I will go to fetch her. Please get me my cloak."

As Velásquez turned and started walking towards the house, Avram saw the cross burst into flames. In his cloak were his knife and his medicines. The giant and the hunchback were closer now.

Isabel, too, was staring at the burning cross. "You will be careful," she said, "but my husband's servants will protect you."

Avram bowed. "You are very kind." His heart was like the Targa rushing over the rapids, so loud he could hardly hear Isabel. He wanted to look down from the ledge again, but did not dare. The hunchback was standing beside him, and Avram could smell the sour sweat of his clothes. The giant was a few steps back, watching Juan Velásquez as he approached with Avram's cloak.

"You still insist on going? My servants could go without you."

Avram took the cloak from Velásquez and wrapped it around his shoulders. As he returned to the ledge he could feel the weight of the knife against his stomach. The hunchback stepped up beside him, and was reaching to take custody of Avram's arm.

"Goodbye," Avram said. Then he turned and looked down from Velásquez to the street. The hunchback's hand reached his arm. Avram's knee swung up once more, the hand flew away as the hunchback doubled over, Avram saw the giant's huge arm sweeping towards him, but it was too late: he had stepped off the ledge and was falling towards the street, arms spread so the cloak would catch the wind. *El Gato*, they had called him, and he had jumped like this every day for years. When he hit the street he rolled once; there was a loud shriek as the hunchback simultaneously hit the ground, bones breaking on the cobblestones; and then Avram was racing down the street without looking back. As he disappeared into the maze he thought he heard Isabel's voice calling his name above the cries of the hunchback.

Even while Avram was running towards the burning cross, the streets had been virtually silent; but by the time Avram got to Samuel Halevi's old warehouse, the barrio was lit in a new scarlet daylight of torches and burning houses, and the shouts of fighting mixed with the crackling of flames and the groans of soldiers splintering battering logs against the stubborn doors of the houses in the Jewish quarter.

In the yard of the warehouse he stopped to take off his cloak — only a Jew would be so formally dressed tonight — and then rubbed blood from his cut hands onto his white linen shirt and his pants. Then he ran to hammer on the door of Gabriela's shop, shouting her name. But there was no answer, and so he continued on towards his own house. At one corner three peasants bumped into him. They were drunk, staggering through the quarter, and Avram joked with them about carving Jewish meat until he had a chance to continue running. But from the next street he could see down to the synagogue. From that square, flames were leaping into the air — and for a moment Avram stood transfixed: perhaps the attack was not going to be as bad as he had feared; despite the noise and the flames there still seemed to be whole streets that were empty and calm. Perhaps Rodrigo would content himself with burning out the inside of a few synagogues and making a few fine speeches over the remains of the prayer-books.

Then from behind he heard shouts. A crowd was charging up the street towards him, waving torches. Avram shrank into a doorway, and then, when the street was full, mixed in with the surging mob and let himself be carried towards the square. When he was in front of the synagogue he saw that it had been surrounded by soldiers, and that in its centre benches and prayer-books had been heaped together in a huge fire. Forced to gather round the pyre were the elders of the congregation. They were kneeling in the dirt while standing above them, reading loudly from a Bible, was Rodrigo Velásquez.

Moving back to avoid being recognized by the cardinal, Avram struggled to the edge of the square and started running again, down through the maze of alleyways that would lead to his own home. In some of those alleyways groups were clustered; peasants from the fair who had managed to break down a house door were looting the house and forcing the Jews to the street. These places Avram avoided, and despite the rapidly filling streets he managed, running with his knife in his hand, to gain his own street and the entrance to his uncle's house.

The door had been shattered and as Avram ran up the stairs he could hear Ben Ishaq shouting, incomprehensible Arabic curses flying forth like a volley of arrows from a crossbow.

And then he was standing at the entrance to his mother's room.

Ester was sitting up in bed, her head slumped against the wall. Standing between her and Velásquez's giant was Ben Ishaq, waving a small knife as the giant slowly advanced upon him, his huge sword still tucked into its belt, his hands held open, ready to throw the old man aside.

For a moment Avram paused. Then he leapt forward, onto the giant's back, one arm around his back and the other carrying his razor-sharp knife towards his throat.

But the giant must have heard him coming, for as Avram leapt, he turned, and Avram was thrown off balance; even as he was falling back, the giant's fist came smashing into his face and Avram could feel his nose being squashed into itself, splintered bone and cartilage grinding together.

Trying to shake his head clear, he rolled away from the feet of the giant. In his hand Avram still held his knife, a long, curved dagger that he had never actually used. As he struggled to his feet he could feel his nostrils filling up with blood, could remember, from the night he had been baptized, the incredible urge to sneeze out the blood and bone before he choked.

The giant had drawn his sword and was looking back and forth between him and Ben Ishaq, who was still screaming curses.

With a casual glance of contempt at Avram, the giant clasped both his hands around the handle of his sword, flexed it briefly, fluttering it back and forth so delicately that it might have been a bird shaking dry a rain-drenched wing, then with a sudden backhand motion swung the cutting edge of the sword full into the belly of Ben Ishaq.

The screams ended. Ben Ishaq doubled over like a stalk of wheat bending to the scythe. As he fell,

Avram felt his eyes bulging out of his sockets to follow the apron of blood that gushed towards the floor.

In the air without thinking, catapulting towards the giant who now was lifting free his sword, Avram reached out with one arm to delay the moment of his own death. With his free arm he carried the curved knife forward, letting its point dive just as it entered the giant's leather tunic. Expecting at each second to be sent to join Ben Ishaq, convinced that the pressure against him was the giant's sword slicing open his own flesh, he let the knife make its way through the tunic first, then the shirt, and then, talking to himself in this second that would not stop, reminding himself of the dissections he had done, of the exact place where he must pass through the ribs and then jerk the point upwards so that the heart would be torn open, he discovered that he, too, was screaming; that his mouth was open and he was shouting out the long savage howl of the beast.

And then he was lying on top of the giant, the dagger buried to the hilt, his broken nose choking with blood. When he looked at the giant's face he saw that the mouth was open, dribbling blood and saliva.

Avram struggled to his feet, pulling the dagger free with a slight popping sound. The two of them had collapsed across Ben Ishaq, whose blood and intestines were forming a dark and corrugated lake. Avram stepped to the bed. His mother was lying in the same position she had been in when he came into the room. He reached his hand out to her forehead. It was cold, the skin frozen into place. She must have died in her sleep, hours ago, even while he was drinking claret at the house of Juan Velásquez.

He kissed her lips — they were cold and stiff — and then, unable to look at her face any longer, covered her with her best blanket.

There was a pitcher of water on a table. He washed off his face and nose as best he could, then tore strips of linen from one of his shirts and packed the nostrils. The break was not bad; this time, it would have to get better without Ben Ishaq to set it.

From the giant he stripped the bloodied leather tunic; this he threw over his shoulders to hide the doctor's tools and the knife he had strapped to his waist. On the way downstairs, he went into the rooms of his aunt and uncle. They were sitting on the floor, side by side, their smashed skulls lolling towards each other in disbelief.

At the doorway of his house Avram paused. The mobs were still growing, running from one street to the next. At the fairground there would be clothes and horses, waiting to be stolen. Avram began walking quickly; with each step fingers of pain gripped his skull, and every time he stopped to rest, the image of Ben Ishaq, his insides diving to the floor, filled his mind. He circled around the synagogue, the wailing filled the air like loud rain, and then he made his way to the gates of the Jewish quarter. These had been battered open and were now untended. A free man, he walked out of Toledo and, after a few moments, began running towards the river.

Kneeling on the bank, he felt his nose carefully. The tip of his nose had been flattened and the bridge now bent towards his upper lip. With his eyes closed he gritted his teeth and tried to push the bones back into place. When his nose started bleeding again from his efforts he washed it out once more and changed the dressing.

Then he turned around for one last look at Toledo.

The fires that had been set were starting to join together: after five hundred years the New Jerusalem was becoming its own funeral pyre. Avram tried to pull the giant's tunic closer for warmth. As he did, he felt the rip that his knife had made. At least, he thought, the giant might be pleased to know that his own blood had been well mixed with his killer's. From inside the walls, only a few hundred yards away, Avram could hear the sounds of burning, the shouts of victims and mob mixed together. The beast was roaring now: its voice was the chorus of life and death, its throat the hollow streets and alleyways, its tongue the licks of flame that shot up to caress the sky.

ELEVEN

LIKE THE SITE OF A PARTY THAT HAD MOVED ON TO A NEW AND EXCITING HOUSE, THE FAIRGROUNDS HAD BEEN ABANDONED. WHILE THE NEW HOUSE, THE JEWISH BARRIO OF TOLEDO, burned its welcome to the celebrants, Gabriela circled the old. For hours she had hidden in one of the wall's secret niches, waiting for her chance to escape. Now, dressed like a man, her hair chopped short, she made her way through the ruins of the fair.

Fires still smouldered in the pits where animals had been roasted. In one pit, she saw, a giant ox was being stripped of its meat by a group of children so tiny they looked like half-human wolves. As she threaded her way towards Carlos's paddock she was reminded suddenly of the followers of Moses, camped at the base of the mountain.

By a miracle Carlos was easily found, sitting in front of his tent and looking into his fire as he drank. Behind him, in the paddock, were his horses. Gabriela crouched in the shadows at the side of the paddock, trying to decide which one she could take. The horses were moving about restlessly, as if they were aware of the slaughter taking place on the other side of the wall. After a few moments her eyes finally found what they had been looking for, a well-muscled roan mare – not too big to control, strong enough to carry her far into the night.

The mare came close to her. It had, Gabriela noticed, no harness or halter. Bareback and holding onto the mane, she would be unable to jump over the paddock rails, let alone ride to safety. On her first visit she had seen several sets of harness hanging inside the tent. Now, moving stealthily, she crept forward. Suddenly a dog leapt to its feet, barking as it threatened to throw itself at her.

"Carlos."

"Who calls?"

"Carlos."

And then he was beside her, pulling back the dog and dragging her towards the fire.

"I came to get the horse," Gabriela said. "I brought the money."

"What money? Carlos remembers no –" He seized her more tightly and inspected her face in the light. "*You.*" An explosion of laughter, gapped white teeth. "Now Carlos remembers: the lady whose husband is to receive a horse for his birthday."

"His birthday has arrived."

Carlos laughed again. "What a fortunate husband to have such a wife."

"I am a fortunate wife," said Gabriela, "to have such a husband." She shook her arm free, stepped back a pace. The drumming of her heart had started again, but this time it was no slow fear, but a total panic. She breathed deeply, tried to push out of her mind that if not for the dog, she might already have escaped.

"Carlos has a wife," Carlos said suddenly. "A wife with a tongue more dangerous than a dagger."

They were standing near the fire; Gabriela could feel its heat blasting against the side of her face. If she had stayed where she belonged, with her sister in Toledo, she would already be dead. But she would have died in her own home. Now she would be killed by Carlos, her body would lie undiscovered and lonely until the birds found it and picked it clean.

"Carlos wants to know, how does a husband live with a wife who has such a tongue?"

"A husband has his own charms," Gabriela said.

Carlos laughed. "Carlos has no charms, except the charms that cannot be seen." He looked at Gabriela. "Give me your money," he said.

"First, the horse."

"You want the horse now?"

"Yes."

"I see." He held out his hand. Gabriela shook her head. There was a sudden lightening in the sky and they could see that new and higher flames were shooting from the Toledo Judería.

"Give me the money," Carlos said. "Then I will give you the horse."

"A man named after a king should not try to cheat an innocent woman. Give me the horse you promised, then go join your friends." But she reached into her cloak and passed Carlos a small handkerchief filled with coins. Without counting them he stuffed them greedily into his money belt.

"Thank you," Carlos said. "Now, Carlos wants to know why you aren't with *your* friends. Aren't you afraid to be out alone on a night like this?"

"Give me the horse." Gabriela could hear the desperation in her own voice. "You're missing the party."

Carlos laughed. "Carlos has no taste for killing Jews. Does that surprise you?"

"Why should that surprise me?"

Carlos held out the bladder, still half full of wine. "You may have a drink," he said, "a drink that is a gift from a thief who will not kill Jews to a woman who is not so helpless."

"Since you put it that way," Gabriela said. She took the skin and held it away from her face, squirting the raw red wine into the back of her throat: once for thirst, twice for courage, her father used to say.

"A drink, I said, not the whole thing. What kind of woman are you?"

"A woman like all others," Gabriela replied.

Carlos took back the wineskin. "Even a married man can be tempted."

"And if Carlos the Famous was tempted, what would the famous Carlos be tempted to do?"

"Who can say?"

"I cannot say," said Gabriela. "Perhaps another sip of your wine would bring it into my mind."

"Carlos's skin is almost empty, look." He held out the deflated sac. "If you wish to have more of Carlos's wine, and more of Carlos's hospitality, you will have to come into his tent."

"A woman hesitates to enter the house of a stranger." From Toledo could be heard a constant roar, punctuated by the occasional explosions of oil casks and high-pitched noises that Gabriela thought might be either screams of the murdered or simply the fear careering inside her own skull.

"The house of a king," Carlos said, "is safe for all his subjects." He extended his hand and Gabriela, who had been crouching by the fire, accepted it and allowed Carlos to pull her to her feet. Still holding her hand he walked her forward, into the tent.

"A woman fears the dark," Gabriela murmured. She had thought she would have to seduce him.

"No need." And then with a sudden motion he was pressed against her, his lips against hers, arms wrapped tightly around her.

"No," Gabriela protested. But effortlessly he held onto her, dragged her one step further into the tent, and then sent her sprawling onto her back.

He landed on top of her. "Do not struggle with Carlos," he whispered. "Carlos is too strong for you."

"Please."

"Be my wife. I will help you escape."

"Help me now."

"I am helping you. I am helping you to make Carlos happy."

Carlos had his knee between her legs, was pushing up her tunic. Gabriela forced herself to lie still, unresisting, moving in no way at all except to slowly slide one hand down to the belt where she had concealed her knife.

"You will be Carlos's wife now, a beautiful wife for Carlos. He will make you happy, keep you safe. Carlos wants you, Carlos has you, now you know what a man Carlos is, Carlos the Man, Carlos the King, Carlos, Carlos, Carlos – "

Gabriela wrapped both her arms tightly around him, pulled him deeper, grasped the handle of her knife firmly with both her hands, and then plunged it with all her strength deep into the centre of his back.

"Carlos – ," he mumbled one last time. His arms shot straight out with such force that she could hear his joints cracking. She was still plunging the knife through his back, towards her own chest, when his hands wrapped around her throat. But even as they lay across her skin, she could feel the strength draining out of his fingers.

When she finally rolled over and extricated herself, her hands and wrists were soaked with Carlos's blood, her thighs with the leavings that not even death had interrupted. Revolted, she bent down to the ground and began furiously rubbing dirt on herself – face, hands, thighs, and groin.

In the tent she found the harness she needed, an extra set of man's clothing. But it was only after she had been riding for an hour that she remembered that she had neglected to cover the nakedness of Carlos.

TWELVE

IT WAS NOVEMBER WHEN AVRAM REACHED BAR-
CELONA. HE HAD TRAVELLED MOST OF THE DIS-
TANCE ON FOOT, GOING INTO THE FORESTS TO SLEEP
BY DAY AND THEN WALKING AT NIGHT. IN THE
mountains he stopped for a month to work at a vine-
yard. He explained that he was a medical student on
his way to the great university in Montpellier. "Do
medical students always suffer so many wounds?"
the workers teased him when they saw him bathe.
But at night they were kind to him, waking him
when he screamed in his sleep, and by the time the
month was over, the nightmare of Toledo had begun
to recede.

In Barcelona he found Gabriela without having to
try. When he walked into the Jewish market of Barcelona, she was behind a counter of brightly coloured
rolls of cloth. Despite the disaster that Velásquez
had related, the quarter seemed to have sprung back
to life: the square was teeming and Gabriela was
right in the midst of it all, surrounded by admirers
whom she was transforming into customers.

"Avram."

Before he'd had a chance to finish inspecting her,
she was in his arms and he felt his heart twist.

145

"Avram, I've been waiting for you for months. Don Juan told me that you left Toledo the same night I did. I thought you must have – "

"You're looking well." In the months that he had been making his slow crawl from Toledo to Barcelona, tortured every night by nightmares of his dying mother and teacher, Gabriela had bloomed into a veritable queen: under her shawl he could see that she was wearing a fancy silk dress that cinched in her waist and pushed her half-revealed breasts forward; her long white neck was decorated by a necklace studded with enough jewels to advertise even Velásquez's considerable fortune; her hair, dark and coiffed, was sprinkled with emeralds to match her eyes and to help wink her beauty and happiness to the dazzled beholder.

"You're the one who's looking well. I was so afraid you were dead." And as Avram glanced down self-consciously at his ragged outfit, Gabriela squeezed his arm and laughed. "Forgive the way I'm dressed today. I was supposed to impress two of Señor Juan's business associates from Montpellier –"

And now as Avram looked around, he could see that Gabriela was no longer in charge of a single stall as she had been in Toledo, but that an entire square of counters selling silk were united under one large awning.

As he looked back to Gabriela, two men approached. The first was middle-aged, but thin and spindle-limbed, with the kind weak face and silvery hair of a diplomat who has carried too many unpleasant messages.

"Avram, I would like you to meet Robert de Mercier and François Peyre. Gentlemen, this is Señor Avram Halevi, of whom I have already spoken."

146

"My pleasure," said Robert de Mercier as he bowed. He spoke in French and as Avram bowed in return, he remembered well enough that the de Merciers were one of the wealthiest families in Montpellier, a family that had even given considerable endowments to the medical school.

"I, too, am honoured." The second of Gabriela's partners was much younger: a large and soldierly-looking man who broke into a wide smile and took Avram by the arm: "Mademoiselle Hasdai has told us that you were a medical student in our city. But she must have been too modest to inform you that we are not only her associates in the cloth trade, but her most enthusiastic admirers."

Avram looked from one smiling face to the other. While he had been travelling through his nightmares, Gabriela had sprung into a world of luxury, wealth, and good feelings.

The silence extended itself and grew uncomfortable. Avram saw Gabriela watching him. Her face had become thinner, almost nervous.

"It is my pleasure to meet you," Avram finally said. "And I must congratulate you on finding someone so worthy to admire."

The apartments of Gabriela were as sumptuous as her clothes. But Zelaida was there, the faithful old servant who had been with Gabriela ever since her birth, and while Gabriela went back to her market square, Avram soaked himself in a huge steaming bath prepared for him by Zelaida.

To have a private bath was even in Toledo a luxury almost unknown. Lying in the water, looking out the window to the bright autumn sky, Avram could see, as if on a gigantic fresco, the journey he had made from Toledo.

Still wearing the giant's leather tunic, slippery with blood, he had galloped a stolen horse to a small settlement of Jews who worked as tenant farmers for a landlord who had agreed to allow these heathens the pleasure of tilling his soil. Unknown to the landlord, the Jews under his patronage repaid his generosity by harbouring refugees from Madrid and Toledo.

It was a settlement Avram had been to once before, with Antonio, but since that long-ago visit the tiny village had surrounded itself with a palisade. The raw spiked logs stuck up in the air like so many spears, and at his approach a dozen dogs began barking furiously from behind the wall.

A few moments later a door opened in the wall and three men cautiously emerged, carrying crossbows. They were dressed in peasants' tunics, with their legs bare and their feet protected by gigantic wooden shoes.

"Dangerous times," Avram said.

"Dangerous for strangers," said the largest of the men.

"I am Avram Halevi, cousin of Antonio Espinosa," Avram said in Spanish. Then he repeated it in Hebrew.

At each mention of Antonio's name the men relaxed, and finally, hearing Avram speak in Hebrew, they lowered their crossbows.

While they rubbed down and fed his horse, Avram inspected the splint on the broken leg of a man who had been injured by a falling tree. Then, after asking his hosts to wake him in an hour, he slept. They had seen nothing of Gabriela, and though the villagers offered to let Avram stay as long as he liked, he decided to try to stay ahead of the dispersing fairgoers. Before he left, they gave him directions to the

148

next Jewish settlement. That was how Avram travelled: from one point of safety to the next. Each day the horse grew weaker and Avram's stops became longer. Finally, after a week, the horse collapsed.

Everywhere Avram went, it was Antonio's name that gained him entry. Antonio — where had he not gone to visit his fellow Jews, to rouse them to arms, to trade tales of bravery and hope for the future? It began to seem that half of Spain's Jewry had sat up night after night, discussing the noble deeds that would be done, the gigantic legends that would be created. Yet the news of Antonio's death was always received fatalistically. A shrug of the shoulders, eyes cast down to the dirt. Avram learned to break the silence by saying Antonio had died trying to defend the barrio of Toledo, and that for each of the many wounds he had sustained, a soldier had paid with his life.

"Avenge me how you will," Antonio had whispered at the end.

As he got out of the bath and dressed himself in the silken robes that Zelaida had laid out for him, Avram wondered what Antonio would think if, from the warrior's heaven he surely deserved to be in, he could see his cousin swaddling such recent scars in cloth so soft, if he could see him standing in front of a mirror ornate enough for Cleopatra, trimming his beard and his hair with a razor sharp enough to cut an enemy's throat with one stroke.

"Have you ever killed a man?" Antonio had asked.

Three now, Avram thought. First Antonio, and then the servants of Juan Velásquez. Now he was in the home of another of his servants, his own betrothed.

During the days of his journey, while he slept, he had dreamed of the horrors of the massacre. But during the evening and night, as he walked, he had thought often of the conversation he had had with Antonio about the different roads a life could take. The road he was following was to Barcelona, where Gabriela was waiting. But the road to Barcelona was also the road to Montpellier, where the medical school awaited him – the medical school and the dream of freedom about which he had boasted so enthusiastically to Antonio.

Now, after Antonio's death, after the sack of every Jewish quarter in Spain, only a fool could believe that a Jew could be free – whether by grace of knowledge or by conversion. But, equally, only a fool could settle happily back into the old ways of life, believing that the storm of the summer had passed for good.

That evening Gabriela gave a formal dinner for her associates from Montpellier. With each toast, and between toasts, Avram found himself reaching for his wineglass. By the time the guests had left, he was dizzy from the wine that tasted like honey after the foul vinegar his mountain hosts had supplied.

Then, finally, he was alone with Gabriela, seated on the cushions of her new luxury while Zelaida discreetly disappeared to the kitchen.

In the wink of an eye, Gabriela had become beautiful and rich, a woman of the world sought as mistress or perhaps even wife by wealthy landowners: as he grumbled to himself, Avram could almost hear Ben Ishaq laughing, as if to mock him for being more interested in Gabriela now that she threatened to be unattainable.

But when Gabriela told him of her own flight from Toledo, her use of Carlos, Avram felt a sense of growing confusion.

"It was a terrible experience to kill a man."

"Terrible," Avram murmured. He tried to look at her. Yes, she was as beautiful as ever, seemingly untouched. Neither her lips nor her caresses had changed. "And yet I have also killed. In fact, I have deprived your new master of two of his best servants."

Even as he spoke, he could feel Gabriela flinch. At least, though she was without shame, she was still capable of feeling pain.

"Avram, tell me the truth. Has the man who wanted to marry me now decided I am too unclean?"

"I haven't decided anything," Avram said.

"Then let me decide," Gabriela said, her voice suddenly harsh. "All day you've been staring at me as if I were the whore of Gomorrah. Either you love and marry me, or you leave me alone."

Avram stood up.

"We could still have something," Gabriela said. Her face had softened and she was crying, the way she had cried years ago.

But the sound of her tears only turned his confusion into anger. He could feel the wine assaulting his skull, mixing in with his thoughts before they were formed.

"May I ask you," Avram suddenly found himself saying, "if François Peyre has asked you to marry him?"

"And if I said yes?"

Avram's heart stopped in his chest. There was a moment of darkness while he turned towards Gabriela – and then, like a cloak ready to be discarded, the wine fell away from his mind: once he had feared darkness, but now, he realized, he had spent three months in its centre. Walking under the black sky every night, the darkness he had once feared had become his home.

"Perhaps," Avram said, "you should marry François Peyre. Or if not him, then another who is even more convenient to your plans."

Now Gabriela was on her feet, tears suddenly finished. "When I marry, it will be for love." And then, standing so close to him that he could see the flecks of iron in her green eyes: "And what about you, my old friend Avram? What plans have you been making for yourself? And do you make them as a Jew? A Christian? Or a man without faith?"

"Do I have a choice?"

"You'd like to think so."

"I would indeed. In fact, the death of Antonio has made it clearer and clearer every day. If I am not willing to direct my own life, then it is a worthless thing that will be tramped out carelessly. If I want to survive, I must choose to live, and if I value my life, I must choose a course worth living. The last time I talked to Antonio, I told him I wanted to become a great doctor. He said that some men were warriors, and that some men must do other tasks. He was a warrior, he said. I was to be a man of science. And now what has happened? The warrior has died. And who killed him? I did, the man of science — that is what my years of medicine were good for — I was able to poison my own cousin and brother while he was being tortured to death by Rodrigo Velásquez.

"Twice, walking here, I was robbed, almost killed. Each time I found myself alive, I had to ask myself what I was living for, whether my bitterness over Antonio's death must make me change my decision — or confirm it. But perhaps, I now realize, I have struggled all these months in vain. Perhaps Gabriela Hasdai could have saved me all these problems and has found the answers to my life along with her new silk clothes."

"Hardship has made you too proud, old friend. Nothing will change the fact that you were born a Jew. And the room in which a Jew lives must always be confined."

"You were born a woman. A fate about which the same might be said."

"It is true that I was born a woman. Sometimes, when there is great danger, I disguise myself so that my weakness is invisible. But still – at all times in my heart I accept that I am a woman. That is my destiny and my fate, and it is what gives my life meaning. Also, my life is given meaning by the other aspect of my fate, which is to have been born a Jew. You – you were born a Jew, were you not?"

"My mother was a Jew. I don't know who my father was."

Gabriela flushed. "You're so proud of it," she said bitterly, "you're so in love with your misery that you want to believe that your father was a heartless barbarian with the blood of Genghis Khan rampaging through his veins. What a way you have chosen to repay your mother –"

"Bitch," Avram shouted. His arm flew up, out of his control, backhanded Gabriela in the face, and sent her stumbling across the room. "Apologize for what you said or I'll kill you." Where they had hit her teeth, his knuckles throbbed with the desire to lash out again.

Gabriela laughed. "Kill me," she said. "It would be a great favour." She got to her feet and crossed to the door. "You're a great debater, Avram Halevi. I suppose you would like to claim that you speak with your father's hand. Forget being an ordinary Jew, you should have been a rabbi specializing in the great disputations." She dropped the latch so that the door was locked.

But when she came back to him she was weeping again.

"Is it finished with us?"

"I don't know."

Gabriela's hands came up to touch his shoulder. "If only you had come with me from Toledo – " She stepped closer, pressed herself against him. "You know I don't want you to leave. You are my lover, my future husband who has finally arrived."

With her weeping Avram felt his own heart finally open. The time had come to speak, to forgive, but when he tried to start, his mouth refused to move. Instead, so stunned with exhaustion he could no longer think, he let Gabriela pull him down into the cushions, strip away his clothes, and press her own naked warmth against him. Even as he embraced her, her story continued to grow in his mind, and mixed in with memories of his journey were unwanted pictures of her humiliation that carried him into sleep.

Hours later he was dreaming that he was standing naked in the desert. At first he thought it was the barren land between Toledo and Barcelona, but as his awareness of his nakedness grew, and his flesh grew prickly and nervous, wanting to shrink in on itself, he realized that this desert was the more ancient one, the Sinai desert outside of the kingdom of Canaan; and as this certainty came over him, his bare toes dug into the ground as if they could grasp the truth out of the sand itself. From the corner of his eye he saw that the sky had turned a deep and humming scarlet, the deep new red of the inside of a baby's mouth; and he knew that if he looked straight ahead he would see God Himself: not God disguised as a man, as a burning bush, as even an animal, but

God in His pure unseeable self, a figure that would tear the eyes right out of his head. He squeezed them shut, shaking his head in refusal, putting his hands over his face even as the voice of God started its rumble, which shook the earth and frightened Avram so much he felt as though the cauterizing iron had singed his soul; and even as his own hands changed their mind, trying to force open the unwilling eyes so that the unseeable presence would be seen, he felt his brain exploding into consciousness and he bolted from his bed, the rising sun burning into his wide-open eyes.

"Forgive me," he heard himself say aloud. His nose ached, he was on his knees: "Forgive me." That was, he remembered for the first time, what he had said the night the soldiers broke his nose and made him crawl across the street to be baptized in the new religion. His eyes were open now, his words echoed in his chest, the sun searched its gold way into the shadows – lighting the whitewashed walls, the oak trunk, the ornate Persian carpets, the bed beside which Avram now knelt, and on whose silken sheets Gabriela Hasdai still slept, her own skin as golden and as shining as the golden calf itself, her long wavy hair glowing in a dark sunburst around her head.

God was in the room: the dream was over but God's presence filled the room like a giant predatory hawk, His heartbeats rebounding off the walls and crashing into Avram's ears, buffeting his chest and ringing through his skull. Then He was gone and Avram found himself standing up, alone, the colour draining out of the morning, his skin dressing itself in goose bumps, Gabriela Hasdai rolling onto her back and smiling sleepily at Avram, the sheet slipping down to reveal her breasts, the gold chain with the star of David that hung in the valley between. He knelt beside her, hungry to touch her, but then the dream began to fade and he remembered the story she had told him.

Two hours later Avram Halevi sailed from Barcelona to Montpellier.

BOOK II

MONTPELLIER
1400

ONE

SINCE THE ARRIVAL OF THE BLACK DEATH IN MONTPELLIER IN 1350, THE CITY HAD BEEN STAGGERING FROM ONE MISFORTUNE TO THE NEXT: SUCCESSIVE WAVES OF PLAGUE, FAMINE, and drought made the next half-century seem, to the poor inhabitants of Montpellier, a period better placed somewhere between Purgatory and Hell.

Each time the Black Death returned, it selected favourite victims. In the fall of 1399, it was children who were chosen to die. So desperate were the citizens of Montpellier that they burned, round the clock, a candle as long as the entire circumference of the city's walls. This candle, famous throughout France, took three and a half years to exhaust itself.

In case the candle itself would not burn brightly enough to save them, the inhabitants of Montpellier made crusade-like processions around the walls every day: beggars, maimed of all ages, priests, children, even housewives with their attendant goats and chickens joined in these parades. Carrying banners of the ducal families, the priests would lead the faithful on the well-beaten path, singing hymns and crying improvised prayers to God, stopping only to harangue the pitiful mob for its failure to be pure of heart, or to implore the king of France and the kings of Aragón, Castilla, and Italy to finally end their bickering and unite the papacy once more.

For who could doubt that God's wrath had been raised by the spectacle of a corrupt and incompetent Church, a Church that could not even agree on God's one representative on earth? After all, it was agreed, there was only one God. If one God was enough, why should there be two popes?

And yet the pope of the people, Benedict XIII, who had once been Pedro de Luna, was virtually imprisoned in Avignon by the French king. For six months his papal palace had actually been besieged by an army. And now that the siege was lifted, the pope was still a prisoner in his own house, unable to travel to nearby Montpellier to implore God to relieve the suffering of faithful Christians.

Near the end of November, in the midst of one of the largest processions, while the priests looked up to the baleful grey sky and begged God to end the drought that had famished the fields of Montpellier for two years, the heavens finally responded. There was a gigantic clap of thunder and a blast of cold whistled down from the mountains with such force that the banners were torn right out of the hands of the faithful. Then, within minutes, giant hailstones began to descend. At first these were occasional, like playful cannonballs being sent down by an amused angel. Then their intensity increased until the whole town was fleeing for the safety of the stone church as the storm of fist-sized stones smashed down on the city, breaking roofs, destroying vineyards, and pounding what remained of the crops into the ground. The next day the temperature shot up, as if God's wrath was finally exhausted, and for two weeks the town basked under summer-like skies and lazed in the warm and benevolent sun. Then, at high noon,

came an eclipse followed by an earthquake. Again
the faithful rushed to the church, where they spent
the whole night in prayer. Then next morning, when
they emerged, they saw a covering of snow upon the
ground, and their laundry hanging like white boards
from the lines. In January, 1400, when the new wave
of plague struck, half the population was already
torn apart by coughs and pneumonia.

White hair crowned the patrician face of Jean de
Tournière. With his ice-blue eyes, aquiline nose, strong
features, and forehead lined with the vertical furrows
of wisdom, de Tournière had come to resemble one
of those ancient Roman senators whose rhetorical
style he had studied so carefully.

Like a senator, too, Jean de Tournière had a voice
that was deep and sonorous. At council meetings of
the University of Montpellier it was able to domi-
nate the room, rolling forth long Latin sentences that
marched to the cadences of Virgil and Caesar.

But today he was singing of neither war nor love.
The year was 1400 and Jean de Tournière, chancellor
of the University of Montpellier and personal physician to three popes, was reassuring the distraught
Madeleine de Mercier that her precious son would
soon be well. Yet even as the words became more
elaborate, their resonance more perfectly calculated
to amplify in the large room, his thoughts plunged
out of control.

Of course he had once desired her. Who had not
admired the brilliant façade of beauty and youth pa-
raded by the renowned Jewess, Madeleine de Mercier? When she had leaned up against him at dinner
parties, brushed her lips enchantingly against his ear
as she pretended to whisper flowery secrets down
the hot stream of her sweet breath; when she wore

161

the perfume he had nervously given her, wore it so that its intimate scent wafted up from her hidden places through the cleavage of her inviting velvet gown – then she had been adorable. When she was young, ungiven, unwasted.

But by the time she had finally seduced him, still barren after how many nights and years in the narrow veiny arms of her inbred husband, the ripening fruit of her body had already turned into a thick and salty husk. The night of her triumph had been followed by several weeks of dead silence; but as the months went on, there were inevitable social meetings, and to de Tournière's horrified eye it became clear that Madeleine de Mercier was swelling in a maternal way. Nine months after the unfortunate event, Jean de Tournière received a message requiring his urgent attendance. The baby – a boy, it turned out – had been born with the caul over its head and Madeleine, afraid of the omen, had been crying hysterically for two hours.

The baby became a child, the child a boy. The boy was pretty but also, it had to be admitted, the boy was sickly. Every winter he coughed his lungs out from Christmas to Easter; every summer, the moment he was let into the sun, his skin commenced to peel and splotch. With the colds, the mysterious fevers, the strange massings of bruises that the boy perpetually collected under his pale and transparent skin, came continual calls to Jean de Tournière for help.

But neither doctor nor father could offer a cure. "The problem is his general health. He's like a tree that grows feeble branches."

"But Jean, can't you do anything about the tree?"

Madeleine spent fortunes on the crushed flowers and bee pollens of the herbalists; she consulted astrologers until the stars were worn out from being inspected; every midwife in Montpellier was brought in to render her verdict; she forced de Tournière to bleed the boy frequently — especially on the first of May and at the fall equinox.

But every time the boy was bled, he threatened to drain away altogether. As soon as the veins in the legs were opened, his blood, a bright and merry red, spurted out like a fountain, eager to make its escape.

One of the wounds in the ankle had never properly healed. Constantly it re-opened, turned ugly colours, emitted unhealthy smells. De Tournière progressively cut away the worst flesh, slathered it in unguents, wrapped it carefully in cloths imported from different ends of the earth. For two years he even bled the boy by placing leeches on his stomach and chest. But still the ankle refused to heal. Instead, it got worse. The infection spread up the leg, the boy had a fever all the time. Finally, desperate, de Tournière sent for Avram Halevi, the Jewish doctor who had repossessed surgery from the barbers, and whose daring knife had spread the fame of the Montpellier medical school all the way to Paris.

And now that he had finally arrived, this slim Marrano with his permanently broken nose and his long hands, Madeleine was making up to him with the full force of her disgusting charms: fifty years old and she could still shamelessly flirt with a boy half her age. Just to see the woman now, coyly extending her ungloved hand to Avram, bending to offer him a glimpse down the unwanted canyon, brought back the entire revolting calamity of the flesh.

How had it happened? She had gotten him alone, to be sure: but although an hour alone with Madeleine de Mercier was an impossible event for which he had once fervently hoped, it was a hope of which time and her beauty's decay had joined to cure him; for he had seen, in a reversal of nature, that from

163

this butterfly's promising youth, a distasteful larva was threatening to emerge.

But she had trapped him just the same. Telling him that her husband was away – but that was an old saw, and in any case he was always away – Madame de Mercier had invited de Tournière to one of her famous winter dinner parties.

Of the worthies of Montpellier, gussied, powdered, cinched, and slathered into their best faces, only the archbishop had been worth talking to. After the dinner, itself disappointing because normally Madeleine set the best table in Montpellier, had followed one of the usual boring contests: a joust to see who could compose the wittiest and the most flattering stanza in honour of the hostess. De Tournière had won: as a prize he was given the right – unwanted duty – to kiss Madeleine on both cheeks. At that instant he smelled – for the first time in years – the perfume he had once given her rising from places he no longer wished to contemplate.

The tone of the party had been set by this unwanted odour. Following the contest came another of Madeleine's amusements: curtains were lifted from the walls of the dining hall to reveal not the religious paintings that usually adorned them, but *tableaux vivants* – servant girls, naked except for silk scarves about their necks, were grouped in scenes depicting the adoration of the Magi, the Annunciation, Christ in the manger, et cetera.

What a pulsating market of pink buttocks, quivering thighs, breasts of every size, shape, and texture. The gaping minstrels and sycophants were so struck by this novelty that they forgot about the inadequate meal. Instead they began to pinch and tickle the servant girls, who filled the hall with giggling as they tried to hold their poses. Meanwhile, in the company of the archbishop, de Tournière walked from one trembling sculpture to the next, inspecting the ample Madonnas with Jesus dolls pressed to their pink nipples, the rolled eyes and hairy armpits of the worshipping shepherds, the open mouths and dyed pubic hair of the astounded witnesses to the Resurrection.

"Thus man's basest desires are uplifted," said de Tournière sarcastically.

"Uplifted and satisfied, too," said the archbishop, his eyes fastened on a pubescent Jesus whose wound was being carefully licked by an idiot poet. "I believe I shall pay my compliments to Madame and then retire."

At this moment de Tournière had felt a warning tremor. But the archbishop was an old man, whereas he himself was only sixty and hardly prepared to be seen as an invigorous prude, retiring early. Instead, he began to satisfy his stomach's need to be full by drinking wine. Soon de Tournière, drinking straight from the bottle, could hear the actual wind of his evil fate gusting in his ears.

On the pretext of showing him a masterpiece by a certain young Dutch painter, Madeleine de Mercier, the vampire witch, conducted him to what she called her "treasures room." In fact, de Tournière realized as he stood holding the huge silver goblet she had substituted for his most recent bottle, the so-called treasures room was only too transparently a boudoir totally lacking in art. Boudoir? But no, surely even that suggestive word was too virginal for the riot of red and purple velvet that hung from the walls, for the piles of satin cushions strewn in such heaps upon the floor that an entire nursery of naked servant girls could happily bounce about.

The name of the painter was Hubert van Eyck, and his picture was propped incongruously against the wall, like a Bible abandoned in a brothel. He had portrayed, in glowing detail, a woman fully dressed; but such care had been given to her rendering – her hair like real hair, her eyes so deep that de Tournière himself wanted to sink into them, the small mole at the side of her neck so delicate that the lips were drawn to press against this dark imperfection – that de Tournière felt himself stir in response as though she was living and breathing.

"*There*," de Tournière wanted to shout, "*there* in your very own painting, which you have entirely misunderstood, lies true beauty, true innocence –"

But suddenly the room darkened as with an eclipse: the witch had blown out every taper, leaving only the light of the fire. Then his goblet was filled again and the overpowering scent of her decaying perfume washed over him in a rancid wave. As he tipped back the goblet to console himself, the wave rose in a new crest and he, too, was tipped. Whether he had stumbled or she had actually pushed him was not clear – suddenly he was on his back, humiliated, lying in the endlessly deep and swallowing satin cushions.

"You've spilled all over yourself," she trilled.

Madeleine knelt over him, her hands cleverly unbuttoning his doublet, laying themselves like branding irons on his chest. He could feel her rubbing salaciously against his bare skin and yet he was so drunk that he did not care. Desire, he had once confessed to the archbishop, had never been a constant companion: but the more she caressed him, the more he could feel his resistance melting away – he was melting into nothing – he, Jean de Tournière, His Lordship, His Worship, physician to three popes and chancellor of the most celebrated university in the world, was being rubbed and dubbed and scrubbed into an infant again. His skin grew smooth and glowing, his stiff bones turned radiant and supple, even

166

his twisted and lumpy toes became, in the witch's mouth, soft pink gems with perfect little pearls of nails at the tips. Soon he was reduced to a soft ball of wax and the vague memory of his mother's breast began to swim through sixty years of wine-soaked cells: finally the image surfaced – himself, a little white-bearded being in velvet robes and crown, being cooed and suckled at the enormous white breast of a sweet and vaguely familiar Madonna.

Not even knowing what he was doing, de Tournière leapt gleefully on top of the witch. His hands circled the patchy wattled skin of her throat as he joyfully strangled her. Only then did he realize that the twin pains in his chest were caused not by knives but by her sharp nipples, that the legs wrapped around him were not strangling him in return but were drawing him closer, that the pumping fire deep in his belly was not simply rage but was part of another, more mysterious and voluptuous activity that his body was secretly engaged in. "Whore," he shouted at the top of his lungs.

Today the room, *the room*, with its disgustingly faded velvet curtains, its satin cushions that had supported God knew what naked buttocks, was centred by the bed of the boy: raised on a platform, draped in silk, its décor was so overdone that it had somehow slipped from being a bed to become a funeral bier.

On either side, sitting on silk hassocks, musicians were playing lutes and singing to the poor patient; of course they were out of tune. In addition, Madeleine had summoned her two favourite astrologers; they were drinking wine as they pretended to pore over the mass of lines and squiggles that they called their charts.

De Tournière moved towards the window, but Avram and Madeleine intercepted him.

"Monsieur Halevi."

"Your Excellency."

"Have you examined the patient?"

"I have, Your Excellency."

"And what did you think should be done?"

"The wound in the ankle is very serious." Halevi had a precise, Spanish-tinged French that sounded as if each syllable had been rolled and tasted in the mouth before it was spat out.

"Yes, it *is* very serious."

"It is surrounded by gangrene and the infection is spreading up the leg."

"Yes, Doctor, one can see that."

"Therefore, the leg must be removed."

"Yes," de Tournière agreed. "The leg must be removed. The only question is where. And also, there is the question of whether the boy could survive such an operation. He is eleven years old, but he has been sick half of his life." Even a year ago, de Tournière had known that the leg should be amputated. Until this week he had decided it was better to let the boy die in peace rather than to kill him with an agonizing operation. But when Madeleine had insisted, de Tournière had called in the renowned Spanish doctor. If he succeeded, de Tournière would get the credit; if, as was more likely, the boy died, then Halevi would be seen for what he was, one more doctor who thought he could play God with the knife but simply sacrificed the lives of his patients to his own ambition.

"The good doctor has been telling me," Madeleine de Mercier said, "that many patients have benefited from such surgery. He has also invented a new kind of artificial leg, one that even a boy could wear without difficulty."

"A new kind of artificial leg?"

"Yes," said Halevi. De Tournière found himself looking directly into the black eyes of the Jew.

"You are a carpenter now, too?"

"A surgeon is many things."

"Jean." Madeleine had laid her hand on his arm and he felt his flesh jolt with the revulsion he had still not learned to control. "Jean, he has brought the leg with him, so we could see it."

On a chair beside the window was a long wooden case, which Halevi now opened. Inside it, de Tournière saw a leg that was not made from a solid piece of wood, but was instead cleverly constructed of glued-together struts that made a basket to support the stump. He bent down to lift the leg from the case. Beneath it was a gleaming steel saw.

"Look, Jean, he has even brought tools to adjust the length of the leg."

De Tournière looked down to the face of Madeleine. Her eyelids quivered. The poor woman was hysterical with fear. "Have you asked the astrologers their opinion?"

"I have asked," Madeleine said, "but they have not yet spoken."

The two men moved into the light from the dark corner where they had been making their calculations. Since the day of the eclipse, the astrologers of Montpellier had enriched themselves on the fears of the citizens of Montpellier. Chief among them was Leonardo Montreuil. He had a white face with a swollen chin cratered with pocks that turned scarlet whenever his word was disputed.

"Leonardo, you tell us what you have decided."

"We have concluded," Leonardo said, his voice as grave as an Inquisitor's, "we have concluded and we have judged that the proposed operation is neither safe nor unsafe. The boy is a Sagittarius and Saturn

169

is in his house, which is a very poor conjunction. But Aries resides there as well, at this moment, and Libra is in a most favourable position. Furthermore, the surgeon is a Taurus, which makes him suitable to treat a Sagittarius; and yet it must be added that this is not the most favourable time for Taurus, although it is also true there have been much worse, even in the recent past."

Leonardo Montreuil stopped and smiled at Madeleine, who was so transfixed that she had loosened her grip on de Tournière's arm.

"And therefore?" she asked.

"And therefore," said Leonardo, "it is in the hands of God."

"Thank you," said de Tournière. Trust Leonardo Montreuil, cousin of the principal rival of Robert de Mercier, to make such a forecast. Of course he would hope that the operation would go ahead, and that the consequences would be evil.

"And Monsieur Halevi," asked Madeleine, "have you done many such operations?"

"A few."

"You see," Madeleine said to de Tournière, "I told you it could be done safely."

"It is not a safe operation," Halevi said.

The musicians were still singing, the boy was staring impassively at the ceiling as though he were too witless to understand what was being discussed.

"But you are a doctor," Madeleine persisted. "A graduate of Jean's school. Isn't he your best surgeon, Jean?"

"He is," de Tournière said.

"But," Halevi insisted, "even with His Excellency himself here to direct the operation, the result is unknown."

"You," de Tournière said, suddenly remembering the story, "you are the one who did the Caesarean on the sister-in-law of Cardinal Velásquez."

"Yes."

"Then spare us your false modesty, if you please, and be kind enough to arrange the removal of the leg of Jean-Louis de Mercier."

De Tournière wrenched his arm from the grasp of Madeleine and strode over to the bed where he looked down at the face of the boy. His son, the sole and feeble remnant of his sole and feeble attempt at reproduction.

TWO

LIKE MOST OF THE OTHER HOUSES IN MONTPELLIER, THE HOUSE OF AVRAM HALEVI WAS FRAMED IN OAK. CROWNING THE WOODEN WALLS WAS A THICK ROOF OF THATCH, AND through that roof projected the stone chimney that led from the kitchen's gigantic hearth.

The ground floor was softened by a renewable carpet of straw, and aside from two small rooms at the back – one of which was a root cellar and the other his servant Josephine's tiny sleeping cupboard – the space around the hearth served simultaneously as a kitchen and as shelter for the scrawny collection of livestock that was Josephine's great treasure.

Upstairs was Avram's private refuge: a ladder from the kitchen led to the one bright place in the house – a combination bedroom and study. Here he kept not only his instruments, his powders, his notebooks filled with anatomical drawings and designs for new surgical tools, but also the treasured books that he owned – copies made for him by needy students in exchange for free tuition.

With such students Avram was well supplied, because by the winter of 1400 the Jew from Toledo had made a certain success. First, at the university, where he had become a master of medicine with full privileges of teaching and dissection. And secondly, with the town's burghers, whose golden approvals had provided him with the luxury of having his own house, conveniently located in the university district.

The house, to be sure, was a tiny one, but it was also new. When he lay in bed at night he could smell the raw wood of the pine plank floor. If he wanted, he could also exercise his mind by trying to calculate how many years would have to elapse before all the wood's naked pores became sealed by tiny particles of chicken-shit and the weekly fish-and-bean stews that Josephine made with such religious zeal.

In his house Avram Halevi had assembled the trappings of the man: the days when he was an impoverished student wearing broken white wooden sabots and stealing bits of tallow to make himself a candle for studying were now securely in the past. But it was at the university that the dream of the scientist had taken shape.

In a small shed off the main wing of the medical faculty was his workroom. Along one wall, shelves contained dozens of bottles of blood. These represented an unsuccessful two-year attempt he and a colleague – Claude Aubin – had made to isolate the famous "animal spirits" of which Galen had written more than a millennium before. According to Galen, blood that passed through the brain combined with some mysterious substance, which was then sent through the nervous system, directing the movements of the body. These "animal spirits," Aubin had decided, must contain the essence of life itself: Avram, with his surgical skills, had dissected the brains of representatives from almost the entire animal kingdom, drawing blood from each and setting it aside to be tested and purified by Aubin. But Aubin had died before he could complete his experiments and Avram, whose interests lay elsewhere, simply left things as they had been at Aubin's death.

Beneath the single small window of the shed was the drafting table on which Avram did his most important work. Using the notes from his dissections and operations, he was putting together a series of drawings of the human body. Eventually, he hoped, the entire human anatomy would have passed under his knife, and been recorded in his drawings. But the task was going slowly: the drawings for the chest alone had taken six years.

In the middle of the workroom was the table Avram used for his carpentry. As a result of his labours and his students', a dazzling array of artificial limbs were piled beneath the table, leaned against the walls, hung from the cabinets that contained his instruments.

On the day set for the amputation of the leg of Jean-Louis de Mercier, Avram spent the morning in his workshop, going over the drawings he had made of the leg and estimating at which point it could be cut off while still retaining enough of a stump to be suitable for an artificial limb.

Before setting out for the de Mercier mansion, Avram packed all the supplies he would need in two wooden boxes, which he gave to his assistants to carry. He then folded into his pouch – the one he had carried since his days as a student – his favourite scalpels, and put that pouch into a special pocket of his cloak.

As always before a big operation, his mind seemed to retreat into itself. Walking across the city, mounting the steps of the mansion, greeting the waiting Madeleine de Mercier and Jean de Tournière, he felt as if he were in a dream, scarcely able to breathe or see. It was only as he leaned over the boy himself, and lifted the sheet off the poisoned flesh of his leg, that his mind snapped into focus: the smell of gangrene, the boy's laboured breathing, the pale girlish skin of his thigh. The boy had already been given two glasses of distilled wine and was dead unconscious. At a nod from Avram, one of the assistants cinched tight the straps that held the boy to the table. Then Avram, after staring intently at the leg, took his scalpel and drew it quickly across the skin. Almost instantly a narrow ribbon of blood sprung to the surface, marking the point at which the leg would come off.

It was two hours before Avram raised his eyes.

On the table, moaning but unconscious, lay young Jean de Mercier. His right leg had been reduced to a stump cut off at mid-thigh and wrapped in a dozen layers of soft cotton. Beside Avram, on a special bench, were the tools that had been used for the operation. Like the floor and the sheets under the boy, the tools were spattered with blood and fragments of bone.

The deathly silence of the room was broken only by the whimpering of the boy. But Avram could still hear the echo of the surgical saw cutting through bone, the hiss of the red-hot cauterizing iron as it touched the jagged blood-wet flesh. De Tournière, his face gone the sickly white of a loaf taken too soon from the oven, had long since been led away by Madeleine de Mercier. Now, aside from the boy, there were only Avram, his two student assistants, and the young woman who was advancing towards him.

"I am Jeanne-Marie Peyre, the sister of Madeleine. I was waiting outside for news of Jean, then Madeleine said I could come in and watch." Her face was heart-shaped, her brown eyes large and luminous.

175

Avram immediately wondered how she had found the spectacle of the operation. Even he had never overcome his fear of violating the body. Because although his science had learned to tear flesh and bones apart with the aid of surgeon's tools, God was still required to heal the wounds that surgery had made.

"Will Jean live?"

Her voice was soft, so pure it was almost bell-like, and Avram felt himself responding to Jeanne-Marie as if she were a woman offering herself, not a young lady enquiring after the health of her nephew.

She was standing above the boy. And then Avram saw her do something very curious: after a moment of staring at Jean and touching her fingertips lightly to his cheek, she bent down and kissed him on the lips, a full and passionate kiss. Again Avram felt himself respond, as if, this time, the bell had rung deep in the centre of his chest.

"The worst is over," said Avram.

"I admire you, Monsieur Halevi, for having the courage to do what you did."

"It is the child who is to be admired –"

"No, Monsieur Halevi, it is you, because you had a choice and Jean did not."

Avram took the boy's arm in his hand, held the wrist carefully. The boy's pulse was weak but regular. Now was the time to take an intermission, to drink a glass of wine and eat to gain enough strength for the vigil of the next few hours. But Jeanne-Marie seemed gripped by some other curiosity; because she was still looking at him over the table on which her nephew lay, her large eyes drinking in his until Avram realized that the girl was not inquiring but was announcing, was telling him that she knew what he wanted, and that the desire was returned.

Out of the room, the intimacy was thinned but not broken. Holding him innocently by the hand as if he were a kindly uncle and not an eligible bachelor, she led him down the wide and curving stone stairway to the large room where the others were waiting. Even as they approached de Tournière and Madeleine, Jeanne-Marie held tightly to him.

"Monsieur Halevi says that Jean will live." Then she let go his hand and Avram felt suddenly cast adrift.

"He will live if he is lucky," amended Avram. He had learned to be at ease in the houses of the rich; but that was because he had also learned that he was an outsider tolerated so long as he told the truth and observed the barriers separating himself from his Christian clients.

When Jeanne-Marie brought his glass of wine, she stood so close that he could see the pulse of the vein in her temple, the freckles that were scattered over the bridge of her nose.

"Do you do this every day? Saw off legs, cut into the belly, perform gory operations? I thought that surgery was reserved for barbers."

"It used to be," Avram said. "But now it is recognized that surgery is part of medicine."

"What do you do when one of your patients dies?"

"I am very sad," said Avram. "I am so sad that I go to the graveyard and I dig the grave." In fact, this winter it seemed that digging graves was the only way he could combat the terrible depression that had come over him with the arrival of this latest wave of the Black Death. Every morning at sunrise he would go from his house to the graveyard and work with the shovel until his muscles were too sore to continue. By that time there were students from the medical school to continue the work of the digging.

"If I were a man, I wouldn't be a doctor."

"What would you be?"

"I would be a miller, and grind wheat into flour so that the hungry could have bread to eat."

Avram looked at Jeanne-Marie. She was slender, deep-bosomed, her fingers fine and graceful. Her neck arched up like the stem of a fast-growing flower, her skin so pale and smooth that the details of her bones could be seen: a kitten, gathering herself to pounce on a piece of glitter that had caught her eye.

"If you were a miller," Avram said, "you could live beside a river and sing songs to the pretty wenches all day."

"If I were a miller," said Jeanne-Marie, "I would be too polite for *that*."

By the time Avram left, it was after midnight. Before de Tournière saw him to the door, Jeanne-Marie had thrown her arms around him and embraced him in a burst of tears.

Now, restless and dissatisfied, Avram walked where his footsteps always took him when he could not sleep, to an old and half-rotted wooden house on the edge of the university district. From the windows there was no sign of light. But Avram did not even try the door to see if it was locked. Instead he vaulted the low stone wall and went round the back of the house. There, also dark, was a set of shutters that he knew well enough. Reaching in between them with a knife, he pushed up the latch. Then he peered in carefully, making sure that Paulette was alone.

"Who is it?"

"The Spanish doctor."

A laugh and Paulette had sprung out of bed, was at the window pulling him in.

178

"You're crazy," she whispered. "How were you to know I wouldn't be busy tonight?"

"A man dares to hope."

"A man should be good for more than hoping. Take off your clothes."

"In a moment." She had clambered back into bed and under the blankets, but only after plunging the room into blackness by closing the shutters. What he wanted, Avram knew, was to talk. But talk to Paulette? She was famous for her good company, but not for her tongue. In the whole city, in fact, there was no one with whom he could talk. Claude Aubin, his only true friend in Montpellier, had been killed in a foolish duel six months ago. With Aubin, Avram had been able to spend whole nights talking, listening, refining with words the surprising circle of self-knowledge that seemed to be starting within himself. And when they were not using words, they had fenced with swords. Avram, who had learned the rudiments from Antonio, became an expert under the tutelage of Aubin: but when Aubin himself had accepted the challenge to a duel, saying that he would simply toy with his opponent, he had slipped on wet grass and fallen to his back.

"What's wrong with you tonight?"

"I cut off a boy's leg this afternoon."

"And now you feel sorry for yourself? What kind of a doctor are you?" Paulette pulled him down from behind, began taking off his clothes. "Come into bed and get warm. Then you will feel better."

But when Paulette had done her duty and gone back to sleep, Avram felt no different. True, his skin was buzzing and for a few moments the circle of his aloneness had been broken. But even as he lay staring at the invisible ceiling, he could feel the walls of his solitude rising once more. Who was there to speak

179

to? What were the words to be said? Paulette had once accused him of using her like a rag and then throwing her away until the next time. The accusation was true, he saw her only as she was: a servant girl who supported her crippled parents by consoling the frayed nerves of Montpellier's over-educated bachelors.

Gabriela, Paulette, a few prostitutes at the fairs: he was a man of the world with barely more experience than a virgin. And yet, who was there to marry? One of the young Jewesses of Montpellier? In order to survive at the university, he had stayed entirely separate from the tiny cluster of Montpellier's Jews. Over the years he had learned his role well enough: it was to be a highly trained and self-controlled eunuch, a machine at the service of those who could afford him, a physician to the rich who would not threaten them by saying words they did not want to hear or by publicly flaunting beliefs that would outlaw him from their homes.

And in the meantime the life he had made was carefully cupped and protected, like a flame being sheltered from the wind.

Looking back at himself as he had been that last summer at Toledo, the summer the barrio was razed and he had finally broken from Gabriela, he saw a boy who had believed himself to be a man. The boy, delighted with his marvellous new skills and the vision of a world waiting to be broken open, had boasted of science to everyone who would listen – most of all himself. The night he had operated on Isabel de Velásquez, he had truly believed that he would perform operations that no one had dreamed of for centuries. After all, even Ben Ishaq had agreed that for more than a millennium, medical science had been buried in a dark age of superstition, and that that millennium was now coming to an end.

Now, it was true, the face of medicine had changed. In Avram's nine years at Montpellier, dissection had emerged from being a secret event to become a public display attended by hundreds of students. His own courses in anatomy, his lectures on the science of the ancients, were attracting dozens of followers.

His ambitions were being fulfilled, but the world was indifferent: for every soul saved by surgery, ten thousand were lost to the plague; for every mind opened to science, ten thousand screamed with delight when a heretic was burned at the stake.

A man grew older, a man began to know himself: even Ben Ishaq had not warned him that a dream come true could become a dream gone stale. And where, he could hear Antonio asking him, where is the new age you predicted with such certainty? After almost a decade of unremitting work, what had been achieved was no new age, no renewal of man's faith in himself and God – but only a constant procession of the sick.

"Take off your clothes," Paulette had whispered in delight. She, Avram thought, had surely found a more rewarding profession; for when one of *his* patients undressed, Avram felt no happiness at the prospect of the cure his profession could offer – only dread at what new insult to the human condition would be revealed.

Jeanne-Marie was someone new, someone different. Even as he lay beside Paulette, Avram felt growing in his mind the memory of the richer and rarer flesh of Jeanne-Marie. When she had hugged him, in gratitude for saving her nephew, he had felt the promise of her innocence. The memory of her hips, unknowingly candid against his own, her child's lips that had kissed her nephew with more passion than they kissed his doctor's, made desire ring through him like the clear, high sound of her voice. The man who married Jeanne-Marie would have something to live for. Not only the wonderful castle of her desirable self, but money, protection, even the hope that an heir might survive to a life of luxury and ease.

Suddenly catching himself at his own thoughts, Avram was startled to find himself dreaming of having children. What would Antonio think to see his idealistic cousin giving up one dream to pursue another?

When Paulette had already sunk back into sleep, Avram, his line of thought unbroken, was thinking still of Antonio. From his cousin he had learned that a man must live and die by the choices he makes. But from the return of the Black Death to Montpellier this winter he had learned something equally bitter: that his ambition and his successes – no matter how great – were nothing more than the dream of a boy determined to costume his life in adventure and glory.

When the first grey light worked its way through the cracks of the shutters, Avram was lying awake, watching the room take shape with the dawn. Soon he was walking briskly towards the cemetery, his arms and shoulders already anticipating the weight of the iron shovel, the smell of the moist black earth opening its maw to receive the daily gift of the death wagons. Sometimes he felt, when his bones and muscles screamed with exhaustion, that he was carrying on a personal struggle with the Devil, a battle to see if he could bury as quickly as the Black Death could strike down.

THREE

ON AN EVENING AT THE END OF FEBRUARY, AS AVRAM WAS SITTING DOWN TO DINNER, THE DOOR OPENED AND A WOMAN BURST IN, ASKING FOR THE DOCTOR HALEVI.

"Let me have just one moment," Avram said without looking up. He hastily swallowed several spoonfuls of congealed stew and washed them down with a glass of wine.

"Monsieur Halevi, please, don't you recognize me?"

Avram realized that he had been dozing with his eyes open. He had long lost track of the amount of sleep he got – three hours a night was beginning to seem like a lot – and at dawn that day he had been in the cemetery again, taking advantage of a change in the weather, from snow to rain, to hack out a grave for a whole family that had perished of the plague. So great had been the number of deaths that the cemetery had almost run out of room, and he had been forced to use a space between two trees. Pausing in his work he had looked up to see a giant crow sitting on one of the bare branches – a crow such as he hadn't seen since Spain, and in its black eyes, like tiny night skies, he had seen a look of such satisfaction that his stomach had clapped in on itself.

"I am Jeanne-Marie Peyre, you remember –"

"Of course." He leapt to his feet. When he had gone to check on Jean the morning after the operation, he had been disappointed to find that Jeanne-Marie had already returned to her home in the country outside Montpellier. But the moment of vulnerability had stayed with him. Now it was happening again. Even standing awkwardly in front of her, his mouth still full of the bread he was chewing, he could feel his heart pounding, could see her blushing response.

"I've come to the city to take care of young Jean. My sister and her husband went to Italy and their return has been delayed by the bad weather. Now Jean has fallen sick, I didn't know whose help to ask for, the servants are sick, too –"

"I am glad you came to me."

All the way to the de Mercier mansion she clung to his arm. And yet, Avram kept trying to remind himself that nothing could be more dangerous, more useless, more stupid, than to fall in love with the unattainably rich Jeanne-Marie Peyre.

When they entered the child's room, Avram was immediately overwhelmed by the stink of the plague, the smell of inevitable death. It was a month since he had been to see him, and that day Jean had shown off his health by running about the room on his wooden leg. Since then de Tournière had taken on the task of bathing and checking the stump.

Avram put his hand to the boy's forehead. It was already so inflamed that the blood inside the brain must be steaming hot.

"He got the fever this morning. I went to your house, but they said you were at the university. This afternoon he seemed a bit better, but now –"

"It's all right," Avram said. "You did the right thing." He slid his hands under the boy's armpits. The glands were forming into swollen rocks.

"Is it the Death?"

He turned to Jeanne-Marie. Her face, too, was beaded with sweat, and her hands, clutching each other, were trembling. "I think so," Avram said gently.

He took the candle and held it to Jean's face. His skin was as smooth and translucent as a baby's, but it was shining wet. The boy opened his eyes. They were blank and confused. "Papa," he said, holding out his hand.

Avram took the hand in his own.

"Papa," the boy repeated. He closed his eyes. "Can I go to sleep, Papa?"

"Yes, go to sleep. When you wake up, all your bad dreams will be gone." That is, Avram thought silently, if he was lucky and died before the fever got worse. Otherwise he would wake up screaming, his glands like cannonballs inside him, cannonballs ready to explode.

From inside his cloak he took a small envelope of powders. A few years before, when he had run out of the medicines he had brought from Toledo, Avram had searched the district to find plants resembling those used by Ben Ishaq. Looking at a wild herb growing by the river, or its dried counterpart on an apothecary's table at the market, he would curse himself for not having paid more attention to Ben Ishaq's medicines. Finding little that satisfied him in his searches, Avram had turned to growing his own plants. Then, according to proportions he remembered vaguely from Ben Ishaq, he would try to grind the plants into mixtures that would somehow fight the mysterious demons of the Black Death.

"You're like an alchemist with your plants," de Tournière had needled him. "You should have been a witch, singing chants over your brews."

"And what do you suggest?"

"A doctor has only two things to offer: the limits of his science and impeccable behaviour."

"Impeccable behaviour?"

"If you cannot trust the man, you cannot trust his cure."

This de Tournière had said on one of their visits after the operation, and Avram knew perfectly well what he meant – for when Jeanne-Marie had embraced him at the door after the operation, de Tournière had raised his eyebrows like a priest hearing damning evidence at a trial.

"Will your medicine work?" She was standing beside him again, her hands on his sleeve. She was seventeen years old, he had discovered, old enough to marry.

"I don't know."

"You don't promise very much, do you, Doctor?"

"I don't promise what I don't have."

Jeanne-Marie laughed. It was the first time he had heard her laugh and her laughter was a sudden chorus of high bells.

"Uncle Jean said you are the one doctor in Montpellier whom he trusts."

"I will try to be worthy of it."

"Is that the medicine?" She touched the envelope of powders; her fingers grazed Avram's, then drew away.

"It should be taken with a glass of wine."

"I'll get it. And may I tell the cook that you will stay for dinner?"

"I would be honoured." He took his eyes away from Jeanne-Marie's, looked down at the boy. He was breathing heavily, but had fallen into a deep sleep. Avram drew down the silk sheet that covered him, then lifted the boy's nightgown to look at the stump. On its butt was a massive interlacing of purple scars. He ran his fingers over them, feeling the callus that had started to form. It was miraculous, truly, that the boy had survived the operation and that his health had improved enough for him to learn to walk again. And now the miracle was being taken away. He circled the stump with his hand. An absurd thought came to him: if he declined the favours that Jeanne-Marie was surely offering him, perhaps the balance of good and evil would be tipped, the boy cured.

"I'm so glad you're staying. I've been thinking about you."

"I'm sorry," Avram said. He turned away from her. "I have other patients to see."

"But —"

"Another time. Please leave me now while I give the medicine to Jean."

"And if he gets worse?"

Go for the priest, Avram wanted to say; *go for the priest and ask him why such pious people must all die like rats.*

"Come see me," Avram said. "If I'm not home, you can leave a message with Josephine."

When he woke in the morning, the sun was already so high that it had climbed above the houses opposite and shone directly into the unshuttered windows. Downstairs in the kitchen, a fire burned in the hearth and the smells of smoke, salt air from the sea, and cooking meat mixed together. Josephine, who had been his first patient when he started practice, was sitting at the table, carefully trimming flowers and putting them in a vase.

187

Avram scooped a cup of broth from the stew-pot, then took a chunk of dark bread and some cheese from the shelf. He felt starved, as though he had just woken up from a winter's hibernation.

"You like the flowers?" asked Josephine. She had come to him with a compendium of the complaints of the elderly: Avram had recommended that she reduce her consumption of wine to a litre a day and that she drink better water.

He sat down at the table and began slicing the cheese to put onto the bread. Every week he put whatever money he received into a jar, from which Josephine helped herself as necessary. But since the most recent attack of plague, most of his patients had been too poor to pay with money; if they survived they would bring instead an addition to the little collection of ragged animals that Josephine led, one by one, to the ever-boiling stew-pot.

"It's so bad now," de Tournière had complained to Avram, "that even the town council has shrunk in size. There are only enough merchants now to elect a handful of councillors. And the number of houses that pay taxes is now ten thousand. It used to be forty thousand. The only place that is growing in this city is the cemetery."

"You remember the beautiful young woman who came here last night?" Josephine asked. "She came again this morning, and she brought you these flowers and the message that the child was a bit better. She said that last night you sent her from the child's room and that when she went back inside, he was miraculously cured – a vision of his father had come to him."

"He was delirious," Avram said, "there are no miracles."

"*Master*, what a blasphemy, even for yourself. Mademoiselle was so moved that she was in tears. I cried with her. And do you know what else? She told me that she is not marrying Pierre Montreuil after all."

"Who is Pierre Montreuil?"

"Who is Pierre Montreuil? Master, sometimes I think you spend too much time with your corpses, if you please. Pierre Montreuil is one of the most important burghers in the district. And she has turned him down to marry you. I am sure of it."

Avram stood up from the table. The noon-time bells had begun to chime, and in a few minutes he was due to lecture at the medical school.

But Josephine was unready to excuse him. "Master," she pleaded, "you didn't say that you would *never* marry."

"I will make you a bargain," said Avram. "I will marry Jeanne-Marie Peyre if you will marry Emile Vaugrin." Emile Vaugrin was the astonishingly ugly man who had been Avram's first teacher of anatomy and was now the secret passion of his servant.

Beneath her crown of grey hair, Josephine's face turned a flaming red. "With Vaugrin, Master, I have nothing to be ashamed of. You know very well I am nice to him only because he reminds me of my absent husband." Then she crossed herself in the hope of his safety, as she had a hundred times a day for the past thirty years. "If I had wanted to be the servant of a monk, I would have gone to work in the seminary. A woman has a right to demand a family and grandchildren to enrich her old age. It is not so much to ask."

Josephine's voice, as she said this, reminded Avram of his mother's insistent recommendations of Gabriela Hasdai. And, as Avram walked towards the

189

university, he found himself thinking again of the boy he had been in Toledo and of the new age of science he had so fervently awaited. That this age might eventually arrive he still believed. But when he was young he had thought he could change the world by changing himself. Now he felt like the advance guard of an army yet to be formed, a stranger exploring a country still unnamed.

Later that afternoon, when the weak February sun was already beginning to yield to the rising grey clouds, de Tournière walked from his office to stand on the steps of the old rectory. From there he could see clumps of students emerging from the lecture theatre. Beyond them were singing voices: the daily procession around the walls of Montpellier, begging God for mercy, was growing in size even as the city melted away to the plague. Soon the whole remaining population would be wearily hauling itself from the church to the cemetery and back: so many now spent their days in various obediences that those who survived the plague would probably die of straining their lungs in song.

And yet, what else was there to do? A few minutes ago, when he had heard the news of Jean's illness from the servant, had he not thrown himself on his knees and prayed for the poor bastard child's life until his swollen joints brought tears to his eyes?

Now, seeing Avram, he stepped forward to get his attention. Legs unsteady, hands shaking, eyes blurred in the evening: in the eleven years since Madeleine had dragged him to her satiny pit, his body had, as if his whole life had been aimed at expending its energy in that one base and frenetic night, collapsed in on itself. But it would not die; instead, it was like some broken old jackass that survived, appetites intact, with no purpose but to frustrate its owner.

"Monsieur Halevi."

"Your Excellency."

"With what grace you pronounce my title."

"We Spaniards have tongues made of sand."

"Not you," de Tournière said. "You have a tongue made of glass. Everything you say can be viewed until it is transparent, then one realizes there is nothing on the other side."

"We Spaniards have empty minds."

"But not, I hope, empty pockets." He slid his hand onto Halevi's arm so that the younger man could help him back to his office. It was unfortunate that today was not the time for bantering, because this young Jew was amusing enough. If he had lived in a more fortunate era, he might have become famous as the best anatomist in all Christendom. He might even have been invited to teach in Paris. But then, Paris had expelled all its Jews a decade ago.

Avram helped him into his chair, and for a few moments de Tournière was silent, gasping to catch his breath. Every winter the damp settled further into his lungs. Sometimes they felt as if moist webs were growing inside, filling up the space that was needed for air and making his breath rasp and gurgle.

"The boy has grown sick again," de Tournière said finally. "A messenger came a few minutes ago."

"I'll go there right away, Your Excellency."

"What," de Tournière now asked, "was your prognosis for him?"

"Last night Jean de Mercier had the symptoms of the Death. But this morning my servant told me that his fever had lifted."

"And if it has returned?" Why he was asking these questions, de Tournière was not sure. Of course the boy was going to die.

191

"If it has returned," Halevi now said – de Tournière noticed that he looked slightly to one side as he talked, an attitude that was supposed to indicate deference, but was, like everything else this Jew did, more of a sign of his arrogance – "if it has returned he may not survive."

"He may not survive," de Tournière repeated sarcastically.

"I am sorry, Your Excellency."

"Don't apologize to me," de Tournière snapped. "Apologize to the boy."

"If you will excuse me, Your Excellency," Halevi said.

De Tournière had to keep himself from grinning. Where had Vaugrin found this young cock? He was more like a soldier than a doctor – and not a general, but a young and brainless horseman eager to be drowned in the sound of the sword clacking at his side as his mount carried him into battle.

"You are excused. And please tell Jeanne-Marie that I will visit in a few hours, when I have finished my business here and gone to light a candle for the boy."

"Yes, Your Excellency."

"Do you ever attend mass?" de Tournière suddenly asked.

"No."

"Do you go to confession?"

"No."

"Yet you say you are a Marrano."

"I was converted, Your Excellency, as a child."

"And the Lord came into your heart?" de Tournière could not resist asking.

"My heart was very small."

On the way to the de Mercier mansion, Avram had to cross the central square. It was late afternoon and the sun had already disappeared into a bank of grey clouds, letting a cold mist settle over the city: for a month now the evenings had been like this, as if the great Mediterranean sea itself was preparing a grey death shroud for Montpellier.

In every corner of the square pedlars were hawking roasted nuts, hot buns, millet baked in the embers of their charcoal fires. At night those fires would be banked with peat and while the pedlars withdrew into the comparative warmth and safety of their carts, beggars would try to keep warm by the remaining embers.

One of the pedlars was, Avram knew, a Jew. His place was always one of the busiest, surrounded by other Jews with their long beards and their knotted hair hanging down from their ears. These Jews lived together in a group of houses that made up their tiny barrio, and once, walking by their houses on the Sabbath, Avram had heard their voices raised in the familiar prayers. Now, suddenly, Avram had an urge to walk up to the Jewish pedlar and talk to him – buy something, anything.

He took a step towards him, then another step, staring at him all the while and wondering if this man would recognize him as a brother. So absorbed was Avram in this that he bumped into, without seeing him, a legless man sitting on the frozen ground. A dirty robe was drawn up to reveal his double misfortune and a handkerchief spread out on the ground to receive donations. Avram, thinking of Jean de Mercier, threw down a coin.

"Another, Monsieur," begged the man.

Avram remembered how once Jean de Tournière, when they were on their way to a faculty meeting, had reacted to a similar plea: drawing his sword, he had hit the beggar with the flat of the blade so hard on the side of the face that the poor man had stumbled to the ground, his neck bleeding.

"I would have done him a favour to cut his throat properly," de Tournière had grumbled later. But the next day, when Avram came with a document to de Tournière's office, he had found the beggar bathed and dressed and sitting at the door with a sword of his own, a new guard for the chancellor. "Pity," de Tournière had grumbled, "is surely the most corrupt of the emotions."

Avram reached into his purse, threw down a second coin, then began walking again – towards the de Mercier mansion. If de Tournière judged pity to be corrupt, what would he have to say about the enjoyment of solitude? For despite Avram's knowledge that Josephine was right, that he must marry and join the world again, he had felt contented enough in his loneliness these years. There had even been nights when, closing his eyes for sleep, he had thought to himself that the one consolation of his life was that there was almost no one whom he need fear would be killed while he slept.

When he got to the de Mercier house, the gates were already locked. They were of solid oak, reinforced with great iron flanges hammered into the shape of eagles' wings; two servants required ten minutes to open them, shouting their apologies to him all the while.

Inside, Jeanne-Marie Peyre was sitting by the hearth, where a huge fire was spitting and cracking its way through a giant burl of pine. Beside her was a short, thin man in the velvet robes that the rich burghers of Montpellier liked to wear. He had a dark and intense face, with clean-shaven cheeks but a long triangular beard on his chin and a black moustache with waxed tips. As Avram entered, he was leaning towards Jeanne-Marie, insisting on a point he was making with such concentration that he did not notice Avram until he had been standing in the doorway for a full two minutes.

Then he turned and whirled towards him, a blush of anger at being interrupted spreading over his face.

But when Jeanne-Marie saw Avram, she jumped to her feet and ran towards him. Grasping both his hands, then taking his arm, she drew him towards her other visitor.

"Monsieur Halevi, allow me to introduce my very good friend and neighbour, Pierre Montreuil."

Avram bowed, then extended his hand. Montreuil's grip was like a falcon's claw.

"It is an honour to meet you," Montreuil mumbled.

"The honour is mine."

"Monsieur Halevi has saved the life of my sister's son."

"I have heard many times of the miraculous cures of the doctor from Spain."

Avram bowed again.

"I myself," Montreuil snapped, "have always thought that blood-letters and barbers were more of a menace than any disease. But perhaps that is simply prejudice, because my father was killed by a surgeon who bled him to death."

Montreuil had the face of a man who has judged the taste of life to be sour. No doubt, Avram thought, any doctor who examined Montreuil would find him complaining of an excess of bile and the discomfort of haemorrhoids.

"So you see, Monsieur Halevi, I have always distrusted doctors." As Montreuil pushed his face aggressively forward, Avram was given a view of the thin black hair combed carefully to cover his balding skull.

"Does the dutiful doctor not defend his own profession?"

"The dutiful doctor does not defend himself against the accusations of the feeble-minded and the insane because our duty is to cure the disease, not battle the diseased."

"How delightful to see that the doctor's mouth does not desert him. Perhaps he has gained his fame by kissing the wounds of his patients. And now, Monsieur and Mademoiselle, less pleasant duties await me." With a tiny bow, a click of his heels, Pierre Montreuil wheeled away and started walking rapidly towards the front door.

"You'll have to excuse the charms of my friend," murmured Jeanne-Marie as soon as Montreuil was out of sight. "As I said, he is a friend of the family."

"Please don't apologize."

"But *I* am glad that he is gone because now I have you to myself."

Avram realized that Jeanne-Marie had not, since he had entered the room, let go of his arm. "But what about Pierre Montreuil?"

"What about him?"

"Surely such a family friend must make a potential husband to some beautiful and eligible woman?"

Jeanne-Marie laughed. Her dark eyes looked at him so frankly that they felt like small knives, cutting away his years of solitude and security. "The famous doctor should be more observant. He must have noticed that Monsieur Montreuil is wearing an engagement gem."

"And to whom does the honour belong?"

"To everyone concerned."

With this she squeezed his hand and led him up the winding staircase until they were in the room where they had stood the previous night, where Avram had watched the boy in the light of the candle and seen the sign of the plague clearly enough, where he had given up dinner with Jeanne-Marie in the hope that her nephew might live.

Now the drapes were open, grey evening light seeped into the room. Young Jean-Louis de Mercier lay like a tiny doll on a bed that could have supported a warrior. As Avram stepped closer, he could see that the boy's face was calm and serene, the face of a dying child whose spirit has stopped struggling.

"Do you have a stronger medicine to give him?"

"I don't know."

Near the head of the bed there were candles burning; Avram took one of the candles and held it to the boy's face. The skin that yesterday had been pale and translucent was now puffy and sallow. The child's mouth was open, he was breathing and half conscious, but when Avram reached under the blanket to check the swellings, Jean jerked in pain. The glands were as large as fists now: under the armpits, on one side of the neck, all over the groin. In another day these buboes would swell to the size of melons.

"Can't you help him?"

"Your nephew is dying," Avram said.

He covered the boy up again, looked into Jeanne-Marie's eyes. In the glow of the candles they were tiny lenses throwing back fragments of the surrounding room, of his own nervous love. Jeanne-Marie raised a hand slowly to Avram's mouth, then placed her fingers on his lips. At first, as if to silence this talk of death; and then, as she inched closer to him, so close he could feel the heat of her body reaching to him through the cold air of the dying boy's room, she took away her hand and pressed her mouth softly against Avram's.

FOUR

EVEN THROUGH THE CARPET, THE STONE FLOOR WAS SUCKING THE BLOOD OUT OF JEAN DE TOURNIÈRE'S KNEES, TURNING THE JOINTS COLD AND SWOLLEN. BESIDE HIM, ALSO KNEELing, was Madeleine. The bitch was crying like an aqueduct, tears running from her eyes in great rivers, her sobs shaking the room as if she were a mother wailing on the site of a blood-soaked battlefield. The whore: it was incredible that she could cry like this over the death of the little bastard; poor child, de Tournière himself had been relieved when he was finally permitted to die.

Above them, lying on the bed with its hands folded, was the body of the boy. What an excuse for a son: stunted, probably moronic; crippled, a bleeder – he was like one of those lumps of unformed and suppurating flesh that lurked half hidden in the inbred palaces of weak-chinned kings. But the boy had been innocent, his heart and soul as pure as the gold coins that now shone in his eyes. Undoubtedly he would go straight to Heaven. The archbishop himself had just left, after spending hours watching over the poor dying lad, giving him extreme unction again and again to make sure that not one wicked thought would have time to pass through his mind between blessing and release.

"Papa, Papa," the poor child had begun groaning. Innocent enough. And then he would clutch whatever hand was offered, gratefully murmuring the same refrain: "Papa, Papa." Even Madeleine had grown irritated.

"Here I am, your own mother," she would coo, no doubt embarrassed in front of the archbishop to be unwanted by her own expiring child. But the boy would only grasp her gratefully, put his poor face to her breast, and breathe, "Papa."

But what a horrible death he had died, whether of the plague itself or of a fever it was impossible to tell. Tongue black and swollen, face spotted, limbs alternately trembling with cold and bathed in sweat, the boy had begun to develop convulsions shortly after supper. Despite Madeleine's pleadings to bleed him, Halevi had refused. Instead, he had bathed the boy in cold water when he was hot, then heaped the bed with blankets when he began to shiver.

During the first convulsion the boy would have bitten off his tongue had it not already been so swollen. As soon as it was over he lapsed into a stupor. That was when de Tournière insisted they send for the archbishop. By the time he arrived, the boy's skin, just an hour ago elastic with sweat and fever, had become pale and shrunken, covered with a cold, clammy perspiration.

When he saw the archbishop, the news of his own death must have pierced the boy's demented mind, because he became so anxious that another convulsion set in immediately, shaking the bed until his artificial leg, which had been propped against it, was sent skittering across the floor.

"Let him die," de Tournière had prayed.

No sooner had the archbishop blessed him and sprinkled the holy water on his brow than a third convulsion began. During this his bones cracked audibly and while his eyes were almost popping out of his head, his mouth opened wide, of its own accord, and his tongue protruded in a little paroxysm of its own – this was accompanied by a sudden locking of the lungs that would certainly have led to death had Halevi not picked the boy up while de Tournière slapped him vigorously on the back.

After that had followed an hour of peace. The breathing that had been so laboured was now quiet and shallow, and a strange calm began to settle in the room as the features of the boy relaxed and became so peaceful that he could almost be imagined in Heaven. Had only the boy simply allowed himself – or been allowed – to die at that moment: what a sweet and tragic passing it would have been. But instead the boy had suddenly shrieked in a raucous voice not his own: "*Save me, Father, save me!*"

These words were followed by total silence. "Save me, please, I want to live," the boy cried out again. His face was covered with dark red spots, and he was panting as he struggled to breathe.

"He's dying," Halevi said.

Hastily the archbishop had sprinkled more water on the boy's forehead, muttered the necessary phrases.

The boy tried to answer, but his words were garbled by his tongue, which continued to swell, threatening to fill up his whole mouth and choke him to death.

"Give him air," Madeleine had cried.

"Let him die," de Tournière said. He put his arm around her shoulder, pulling her back from the boy. "Let him die in peace."

"No." And then the vixen had twisted away, rushed over to the side-table where Avram's instruments were, grabbed a knife, and before anyone could stop her, she had slashed the boy's tongue. "There," she sighed as the blood began to stream forth, "now at least Jean can breathe."

"Please," the boy murmured. And as his tongue shrank, the stream of blood grew, pooling first in the hollow of his wasted cheek, then dripping in a steady line down to the floor where it made a new lake, then flowing faster and redder until the lake on the floor began to send out its own tiny streams.

By the time the boy started to choke again, this time not from his tongue but from the blood that had collected in his throat, it was too late to help him: Halevi turned him on his side while the arch-bishop made one last benediction.

When the archbishop left, Halevi went with him. He looked, de Tournière observed, utterly exhausted. His mouth had drooped in defeat, and there were large dark hollows under his eyes. "Did you really believe you could save him?"

"Yes."

And then Madeleine had sent Jeanne-Marie, who had been in horrified and silent attendance the whole time, to her room to get some sleep before morning. "You, too," she had said to de Tournière, "you must be tired."

"I'll stay for a few more minutes," he had said, feeling sorry for her: the old bitch had rushed back from Italy to end up alone with her dead child. Even Madeleine de Mercier deserved better than that.

It was Madeleine's idea that they spend the vigil on their knees, praying, so that the boy's soul would be assisted on its flight to Heaven. "At least we owe him that," she had pronounced. But the floor was so cold, it was hours until dawn, if he stayed like this until the light came up, his joints would never move again. And, besides, he and Madeleine had already prayed their prayers, sung their hymns.

"If you're out of prayers," she suggested, "you could just talk in Latin. You have such a lovely voice when you speak Latin, just like a priest." And then, when he did not reply: "We'll just close our eyes, then, and imagine his winged soul flying into the arms of the Lord." A new fit of weeping, which even now continued, had overtaken any further instructions.

He grabbed the side of the bed for support and levered himself to his feet. Just as he found his balance, he looked across the room and his eyes fixed upon the boy's artificial leg, still lying where it had fallen. De Tournière walked towards it, his own legs shooting with such pain that he had to bite his tongue to keep moving. How could he have lived so long? Each morning his servant had to rub his legs and back so that he could stand at all; his bowels functioned irregularly or worse; his breath stank even to his own enfeebled nose; his eyes were beginning to cover over with cataracts. And yet who did not tell him at least once if not ten times a day that he was a miracle of longevity, of ever-sustained health, even of youthfulness?

"Jean," came the whisper, "Jean, can you hear me?"

"Of course I can." He had picked up the leg and was rubbing his fist in the socket made for the stump.

"Jean, do you think it was wicked for us to have a son?"

De Tournière looked across the room at Madeleine. She, too, had stood up now, and in the candlelight her face had taken on a soft, almost loving mask.

"Do you, Jean?"

"No." How could she ask? She really was a stupid whore. Of course they had sinned, not only against God, but against the poor decrepit result – what could be more evil than to bring a new life into this world? Why did she think he had never married? In the midst of his anger and pain he saw Madeleine coming towards him, her face twisted with emotion. He raised his arm to ward off her kisses. In his hand he felt the weight of the wooden leg. The crafty old bitch, she had gotten him alone again. Look, she was opening her arms. Leaping towards her, he swung the leg with all his strength.

"Jean." When he came to he was lying in a bed, soft, only one other bed had ever embraced him so softly. "Jean, can you hear me?"

"Hmm." He opened his eyes; again he saw Madeleine's face hovering above his own.

"Jean, are you all right?"

Madeleine was sitting beside him and, he realized now, holding his hand. Behind her, looking concerned and anxious, was Jeanne-Marie Peyre.

"What happened?" He struggled to a sitting position. Avram Halevi was in the room too. Had they all reassembled for a repeat of the death scene?

"Jean," Madeleine said, "it was so wonderful. You were on your knees, in the middle of the chamber, and then you simply passed out with a serene smile on your face."

Now Halevi drew near. The fatigue of the previous night had not been erased, but seemed etched deeper into his face.

"Am I going to die?"

Halevi smiled. "Not today, Your Excellency."

De Tournière felt confidence flooding into him with the sure sound of Halevi's voice. What a shame

203

that he was not young, so that Halevi could restore him to full health with that wonderful voice, that sad, hopeless smile.

"Am I going to die tomorrow?"

"Not tomorrow, Your Excellency. But your pulse is very erratic. I hope that you will take advantage of Madame de Mercier's hospitality and remain here for a day or two, until you are rested."

"I don't want to die here," de Tournière found himself saying. "If I'm going to die, I want to die at home. Do you promise me that?"

"I promise that if you close your eyes and sleep, you will die at home."

"You should have been a diplomat," de Tournière said. But the panic had subsided. "Don't you Jews ever tell the truth?"

"That is for Your Excellency to judge." Now Halevi extended a glass of wine. "After you drink this you will sleep for a few more hours. Then you should be able to get up."

De Tournière took the wine from the young doctor. How smooth and unscrupulous this Jew was. Halevi. He said he was a Marrano. Not a Christian, but a Marrano. Neither fish nor fowl. He sipped the wine. Marrano, convert, pig: they were all the same.

He slept, he woke up, he slept again. Then he woke up to Madeleine's face hovering once more above him.

Her face had aged, it was true. Her grey hair now was curled over her forehead in a new arrangement, and her cheeks had entered the furrowed and compromised country of old grandmothers. But she looked kinder than she used to when she was young. And her eyes were quieter, like rushing rivers that had become shallow pastoral ponds.

He sat up in bed. His clothes had been taken off and replaced by a silk robe. He wiggled his toes: they were naked.

Madeleine blushed. "I took care of you," she said.

De Tournière nodded. "What happened in the room, with the boy?"

"I told you," Madeleine said. "You passed out, praying."

He grabbed her wrist and squeezed. The old whore. He squeezed harder. "I remember something different," de Tournière said. "Tell me."

Madeleine smiled, the old seductive smile, and then leaned forward and kissed him gently on the lips. Her mouth was still soft, and the old perfume wafted over him in a sweet cloud.

"You're right," she whispered. "I didn't know if you'd remember." He had let go her wrist as she kissed him so that now she was able to reach up to her hair, to push it back from her forehead where a bruise, once dark, was tinged with purple and yellow. Good for Halevi: his contraption had not been of much help to the boy, but it had saved Madeleine's life. A solid hickory thigh would have knocked the old whore straight to Hell. "Jean, you wicked man, you almost killed me."

205

FIVE

THE AFTERNOON WAS BRILLIANT AND BLUE, AND ABOVE THE GRAVE OF JEAN DE MERCIER THE NEW LEAVES OF A GIGANTIC SPREADING WILLOW TREE WINKED PALE GREEN. THE BOY'S death had coincided with the last gasp of winter: as Avram stood at the edge of the family, he felt so exhausted that his only awareness was of the sun's heat on his face.

The archbishop was still giving his eulogy when Avram slipped away. By the time he got home it was almost dark. For an hour he sat gloomily at the kitchen table, drinking wine and refusing to speak to Josephine. Then he walked down the road to the university tavern where students were celebrating the end of another semester.

Through open shutters came the cool and smoky evening air. Three of his students came to sit with him, and soon Avram was drinking one glass after another of the raw red wine. But he was so tired and depressed that it was still before midnight when he rose to leave. Paulette was at his elbow. "Don't you want me to come?"

"Of course." His thoughts swept briefly and guiltily to Jeanne-Marie. Then he was standing outside the tavern and his lungs were gulping in the cool air.

After a winter so long that he had thought his soul would wither, spring had finally filled the air with the smell of wet and fecund earth. Paulette's arm slipped around his back, and when he turned her towards him for a kiss she pressed her breasts against his chest and hugged him tightly.

They arrived home so early that Vaugrin and Josephine had to scuttle into Josephine's room just ahead of them. Paulette, who was a cousin to Josephine and had shared her room before Josephine moved in to be Avram's housekeeper, called out a greeting as Josephine slammed her door. But there was no reply and Avram, embarrassed, drank three glasses of brandy to add to the wine he had already consumed. As they climbed up the ladder to his bedroom his legs began to buckle, and when he collapsed on the bed his heart spun wildly. Lying on the silk sheets as Paulette undressed him, he felt like the old beast of Toledo itself: thick-skinned, deaf, uncaring.

Like a fly, Paulette buzzed above him; the touch of her hair, her lips, her fingers like the faraway beating of brittle wings. Slowly the thickness dropped away. In the moon's light Paulette's body was slim and white. A pale snake, she writhed in his arms, twisted herself around him, roused him to such passion that she turned him into an eagle poised at the edge of a cliff. And at the edge, the sweet leap waiting for him, he stayed as he sweated out the brandy, the wine, the gory death of the boy – until finally his elephant's hide was thin and supple with sweat, his hair and beard matted with kisses.

At the next-to-last moment, as he was preparing to soar off the cliff and release the whole darkness of winter into Paulette, the sounds of laughter and shouting voices crowded through the open shutters, and even as the pounding on the locked door of his house continued, Avram heard Jeanne-Marie's voice calling up to him.

Almost at once Josephine had answered the door and thrown it open. A mere arm's length away, through the floor, a man was arguing violently with Josephine, who now realized her mistake and was trying to get the visitors to leave. Besides Jeanne-Marie and the stranger, Avram could hear Jean de Tournière, Madeleine de Mercier.

Then suddenly there was the yellow glow of candlelight shooting through the ladder-hole. Frantically, Avram withdrew from Paulette, threw the sheet over her and his doctor's robe over himself. Whispering to Paulette to keep quiet, Avram hurried downstairs.

"There you are," de Tournière cried. The death of his son had turned him from an old man to an ancient one and his face glowed like that of an incandescent corpse.

"Why is everyone asleep so soon? We have just come to invite you to the funeral supper!" Madeleine de Mercier's tone was forced and gay. She was, Avram realized, drunk: all four of them were drunk.

He also realized that the strange voice had belonged to François Peyre: the brother of Jeanne-Marie and the would-be suitor of Gabriela he had met in Barcelona.

"Look at you," Jeanne-Marie whispered. She stepped in front of Avram, he could smell the wine on her breath, and standing so close that her body almost touched his own, she put her hand to his sweat-soaked forehead. "You must have been in bed with a fever. Or were you having a nightmare?"

And then there were more candles, the room was ablaze with light and the enthusiastic voices of the guests enjoying just one more glass of brandy. Just as Avram himself was raising a glass to his lips, afraid that Jeanne-Marie would smell the juices of Paulette on his skin, he noticed that the voices had one by one, like layers of wrapping from a gift, fallen away. At the entrance to the attic stood François Peyre — he broke the silence with a loud bellowed laugh — and then into the circle of light he dragged the terrified and naked Paulette.

An hour later Avram was at the de Mercier mansion, feasting from a table laden with the new sweet delicacies of spring, wines from the de Mercier vineyards, venison and chicken that had simmered for hours in rare herbs and brandies. Jeanne-Marie was sitting beside him, her face flushed with wine, laughing excitedly as François apologized for the hundredth time to Avram for having dragged one of his patients from what might well have become her deathbed.

"Your care for beautiful women is famous all over Europe."

"I hope you understand," Jean de Tournière interjected towards Jeanne-Marie, "that doctors of a certain extreme dedication never hesitate to take care of a patient at home. These days, with hospitals the way they are, a doctor would be sending a patient to his death —"

"But not Avram," Jeanne-Marie concluded, "he is too noble, too wise, too dutiful —" She burst into helpless laughter and then suddenly leaned towards Avram, her mouth open and her eyes full of exuberant tears, and kissed him on the lips.

"Jeanne-Marie!" shrieked Madeleine de Mercier.

"Never mind," Jeanne-Marie said calmly. "I just had a sudden attack of the grave illness that almost killed the patient at the good doctor's house."

With that irresistible wit, everyone at the table joined in such loud and companionable laughter that Avram's ears began to ring. All over Montpellier, burghers' families who had lost members to the plague had finally reached such a low point of despair that they were now partying late into the night, drinking until they were overtaken by fits of weeping that lasted until the dawn when, crying and drinking still, the party would join rag-tag onto the first holy procession of the day: then would be seen the rich of Montpellier in all their soaked and food-stained finery, parading with the peasants and the lepers around the walls, wailing their helpless rage and singing hymns until the tired priests sent them home.

As the company's hysterical laughter reached its peak, Jeanne-Marie leaned towards Avram and pressed her lips, once more, fully against his own. Then, before he could react, she waved to the minstrels; as they struck up a song for the diners and the others began to sing, Jeanne-Marie put her mouth to Avram's ear: "Of course I know what you were doing at your house. If I didn't love you, I would ask my brother to kill you."

At first Avram was silent, but Jeanne-Marie grabbed his sleeve and whispered: "Answer."

Her face was flushed and insistent, her eyes glowing and pouring into his.

My answer is that I love you, too. Avram knew those were the words he should say. Jeanne-Marie was almost the same age as Gabriela had been when he had turned away from her: and what had happened as a result? She had become the hireling of Juan Velásquez. Jeanne-Marie's eyes were still open, waiting: she had a heart-shaped, fine-boned face, the confidence of money and safety.

He bent towards her, uncomfortably aware that the smell of Paulette had laid its musty blanket of lies over his skin. The lips that had kissed him so boldly now trembled. He lifted his fingers to her cheek.

"Answer or don't answer. I don't care. Because if you don't love me now, I will make you love me soon." And then, as the tips of his fingers grazed her face, she leapt backwards from the table, upsetting her chair. "And now, Monsieur Halevi, it is time for me to go to the chapel, to pray for my dead nephew. Good night, and God have mercy on your patients."

Her lips were parted, her brown eyes opened to his. Then the chorus of songs dissolved into more explosions of laughter and before Avram could speak, Jeanne-Marie had turned to leave.

Avram reached for her hand but she stepped away.

"Come visit me soon." Then her voice softened and she relented, as if she had read from his mind the shameful thoughts about Paulette and forgiven him. "I'm not angry, please believe me."

But when he got home, Paulette was still lying in his bed. As Avram, sitting beside her without undressing, searched for the words to tell her that it was time to leave, Paulette suddenly told him she was pregnant. Then she burst into tears, not because she was afraid of being disgraced, but because she was afraid of the birth itself. Four years ago she had had an illegitimate child and in the process of bearing it had almost bled to death. Telling this, she began to cry with her fear and Avram, ashamed to find himself inflamed by her weakness, lay down on the bed and clasped her close to him for comfort. Soon they were plunged back into the passionate love-making that had been interrupted a few hours before.

At the climax Avram had the sensation that his chest and guts were being forced open, that God was literally reaching down and stripping parts from his body so that the child might be made in the image of his father. For all the night that remained, Avram clung to Paulette, making love again and again. When it was finally bright daylight and she was ready to leave, he gave her a vial of the powders a midwife had sold him for such an emergency, powders that were guaranteed to reach down into a woman's uterus and tear away any baby that might be growing.

SIX

AS IF HE HAD JUST SURFACED FROM A LONG AND SILENT DREAM, AVRAM WAS SUDDENLY DROWNED IN A RUSH OF SOUND: A MILLION LEAVES FLUTTERING IN THE BREEZE, THE songs and twitterings of a thousand birds, the firm stamp of the horse's iron-clad hooves on the soft dirt path, the gentle breathing of Jeanne-Marie.

It was the month of May, 1400: the intense winter had given way to a late but dazzling spring that had now mounted to a near-summery crescendo. And on this particular day, after the first few cool hours of morning, the sun had turned the sky to a bright baked blue: Avram felt it pushing remorselessly down on him, and as the journey progressed he felt alternate layers of dust and sweat being painted onto his skin.

To this heat, however, Jeanne-Marie appeared immune. She was wearing a white and disturbingly bridal dress whose virginal aura was emphasized by her matching lace hat. Her neck and shoulders were wrapped in a shawl that seemed to slip off every few minutes so that her golden skin could be licked voluptuously by the very sun that was causing Avram such discomfort.

Riding slowly in an open carriage, they had spent two hours travelling progressively narrower roads.

Their destination was the de Mercier estate, which François Peyre managed and where Jeanne-Marie had spent the years of her girlhood. Just as Avram was about to complain of the heat, the carriage rounded a sharp corner and Jeanne-Marie warned him to be prepared for his first sight of the castle.

The road had entered a deep cleft: on both banks lush spring grass grew thickly, dotted with bluebells and wild violets.

"Now," Jeanne-Marie said, and suddenly the carriage followed a new curve and they were looking down on a crazy multipronged structure – a courtyard riddled by an epidemic of towers. "What do you think?"

"It's – "

"I love this place," Jeanne-Marie interrupted. She took the reins from his hand and snapped them over the horse's back. The open carriage began to bounce down the hill towards the château. Like a miniature of Montpellier, it stood in its own tiny valley with its own surrounding ridge. From the walls radiated a patchwork of green and yellow fields: some, freshly planted, showed their naked furrowed earth to the sun; others were already dense with clover, flax, and hay. François, Avram noted, was clearly as expert a farm manager as he was a discoverer of hidden guests.

As the cart gathered speed, Jeanne-Marie was thrown increasingly against Avram. After each collision she drew herself away, but not too quickly. Since the night that grief and wine had forced her to declare her love for him, there had been many invitations to dances and dinner parties hosted by Madeleine de Mercier. Avram, grateful for the opportunity of seeing Jeanne-Marie without having to court her openly, attended as often as he could. For hours he would morosely watch Jeanne-Marie gaily dancing,

Jeanne-Marie in a low-cut gown leaning over and laughing at the pleasantries of the men who always surrounded her, Jeanne-Marie listening with wide-eyed attention to the prattlings of a dozen different wealthy bachelors. Yet by the end of the evening she always sought him out, stood beside him as if he were an old friend or brother with whom she could find shelter. Every night as he walked home, cursing his own paralysis, he would have on his lips the taste of her parting kiss, the frozen words he had yet to invent. Because though every day he felt drawn in more deeply, closer to love, he was entirely unable to leap the insurmountable obstacle: for despite the fact that her parents had been Jewish, Jeanne-Marie Peyre had become a devout and practising Catholic.

Jeanne-Marie seemed content to wait. She had only asked him, gently enough, if he would like to drive with her one day to the de Mercier château. "You'll be able to see my home, and the countryside around Montpellier. Everyone says it is the most beautiful in all of Europe."

"That would make me very happy."

"You are in love," Josephine had said. Perhaps she was right: if love was thinking incessantly about the beloved, stepping back when he wanted to step forward, wanting to be touched and yet fearing his own reaction. He was thirty years old, a statistic Josephine never tired of reciting. Yet it seemed that in escaping Toledo and turning his back on Gabriela, he had killed something in himself. Compulsively digging his graves for the plague dead, he would sometimes look down into the moist pit he was making to imagine himself at rest in the damp earth, himself asleep forever while others fought the irresistible tide of the dying.

"Old bachelors never change," Josephine had declared. And it was true that the dizzy plunge of his feelings had been interrupted by fear and uncertainty. To climb out of the grave, to love, to marry, to allow himself to be reborn into the world of convention and compromise that he had so carefully avoided. To sacrifice his "impeccable behaviour" for a body barely glimpsed, eyes that by a quirk of light had captured his, a coquette's heart that had caught his own. Such thoughts only drove him ever more frequently into the comfortable arms of Paulette. Even last night, to gird himself for this journey, he had sought her out. And Josephine had approved: "It isn't easy for a man to stay pure. I know how it is."

As the carriage slowed down and came up to the open gates of the courtyard, he turned to look at the face of Jeanne-Marie.

"I hope you like it here."

"I won't be disappointed." A servant was walking across the yard towards them. Avram shifted on the driver's bench so that his thigh ran along the thigh of Jeanne-Marie. She pressed back firmly, desire jolted through him. He was risking his armour of "impeccable behaviour," but she had less to protect herself with, more to lose. She seemed suddenly naked of defence. He took her hand, her fingers laced tightly through his. For the first time in weeks he looked directly into her eyes. The caution he had so carefully nursed dissolved in a rush.

"I won't be disappointed," he said again. "And I won't disappoint you."

The doors of the castle opened, servants bowed and winked at him, François Peyre embraced and kissed him on both cheeks, even the old and arthritic dog who had been Jeanne-Marie's childhood pet tottered over to rest his head on Avram's knee.

By the second evening of his stay, when Jeanne-Marie excused herself so that François and Avram could enjoy a glass of brandy after dinner, nothing seemed to remain for Avram but to enjoy what was so clearly in motion. When François lifted his brandy and proposed a toast to Jeanne-Marie, Avram murmured "Jeanne-Marie" and drank with him.

"She is, after all," said François, "a remarkable woman."

"Truly remarkable."

"A woman in whom beauty and intelligence have found a loyal and faithful home."

Avram nodded.

"Such a woman deserves a husband of distinction."

Again Avram nodded.

"A husband," François continued, "who can shelter and protect her. Do you not agree?"

"Of course, I agree."

"A husband who can protect her with" – and here François Peyre, whose face was a fuller and swarthier version of Jeanne-Marie's, broke into a wide smile, – "money and land."

Only once before had Avram noticed François laughing; that was the time he had flushed out Paulette. But now, laughing again, he seemed entirely different from the modest and quiet gentleman he had played in Barcelona or in the house of Robert and Madeleine de Mercier. Here, on his own territory, he had expanded: even his coat was undone so that his belly itself could swell to include the produce of his fertile farms.

"You understand what I mean," François said.

What he understood was that François wanted land and security: through Madeleine he had made a start, and if Jeanne-Marie could be used for further gains, then so much the better.

"For example," François continued, "the perfect husband for my sister would be Pierre Montreuil. I understand that you met him."

"An impressive gentleman," Avram said.

"My sister doesn't think so."

"Perhaps someday she will."

"No," countered François, irritated, "she won't. Unfortunately she has been in love with only one person in her life, and that person has nothing to recommend him."

"How unhappy."

"Very unhappy," said François. "And not less so because she has absolutely no dowry to bring into a marriage. A few trinkets, of course. But no land. As you know, Monsieur Halevi, this estate belongs not to myself but to Robert de Mercier. When he married my sister Madeleine, he gave us its use as a gift in return for our conversion – all of us – to the Church. Since then it must be said that he has kept his bargain in the most generous style: not only are we permitted to reside here, but I have been allowed to keep servants and to live in a certain fashion so long as I manage the farms and collect the rents from his other estates. I am even encouraged to continue the constructions he started – you must have noted the towers for which our château is famous."

Avram looked down at his brandy. In Toledo, life had been direct, and even Jews who had converted did not live in castles.

"How could a man like you provide my sister with what she needs? Your house, of course, would be entirely unsuitable. You'd have to live in the de Mercier mansion in Montpellier. You'd be made dean of the medical school – that's very prestigious, though it doesn't pay very much. You'd need a new wardrobe, and a family coat of arms."

Avram laughed.

"In any case, Madeleine and Robert have already agreed to your staying in the mansion. They like having you as their physician. They were very touched by the attempt you made to save their son. Please don't be offended. It's for my sister, you understand. I would rather she married Pierre Montreuil, but she won't have him. It's up to me to protect her. I've done my best for almost twenty years. Now it's your turn."

François Peyre stood up. He was as tall as Avram, but much broader. He reached forward to touch glasses. "Welcome, brother-in-law. I hope it will be a pleasure to know you."

"You must be a wonderful collector of rents," said Avram.

"The best," François replied, without irony. "They come unto me like lambs for the shearing." And then, looking at Avram, he added: "It will have to be a church wedding. You will go to confession and attend the mass. My sister is a devout Catholic. Your children will be Catholics." He paused, and then added in a softer voice: "What you teach them at home is your own business, I understand."

When he had retired to his own room, Avram opened the shutters and sat on the stone ledge of François Peyre's cleverly constructed tower window.

There was a moon, and beyond the castle walls a few tall oaks could be seen in silhouette, like giant

219

black dancers with arms upraised, posing for their portraits.

Did he love Jeanne-Marie? Did it matter? It was time, as Josephine had said, to begin to love. Ten years ago, love had seemed like a storm – something that might happen to one all of a sudden or not at all. Now he knew better: love was like one of the trees outside his window – something that began as an almost negligible growth, fragile for a long time, and then, finally, perhaps only fully visible in shadow.

But that, he knew, was not how Jeanne-Marie loved him: she loved him with her whole heart, the way Gabriela had loved him. And yet she would be satisfied to have him as he was, just as he, in turn, would be better off with her, a wife to comfort him, than with a succession of Paulettes.

If he married Jeanne-Marie, there would have to be, as François had said, a Catholic ceremony. And yet how could he, in his heart of hearts, object? In his whole time in Montpellier he had walked through the Jewish quarter once, been to synagogue not at all, not even dared to speak to a single man as one Jew to another. He remembered the time he had been walking across the square, and though intending to talk to the Jewish pedlar, had bumped into the legless man. Now there, in the legless man, was the true Jew: because since everywhere Jews went, they were unwanted, they might as well have been born without legs; and since everywhere Jews went, they were without power, they might as well sit on the ground in order to beg and be spat on.

Why cling to such a hopeless life? His ancestors had been Jews, so he was a Jew. But before they had been Jews, no doubt they had worshipped everything from the god-pantheon of animals to the beautiful goddess Astarte. Why had they given up these gods for the God of Abraham? Had the Hebrew God shouted in the ear of his great-great-great-great-grandfather and frightened him into obeying? Had whole generations of men and women felt the hand of God yank their lives from one road to another? Or had they simply listened to some prophet with a long and dazzling beard, heard his words and needed his protection: yes Abraham, yes Moses, we will go along with what you say because life will be more bearable.

And now, Avram thought, his own life would be more bearable if he went along with the Christian God and the story of His crucifixion.

But with the image of the cross came the memory of Antonio: Antonio fully alive with his curly beard and his warm persuasive voice; Antonio making his own cross, his hands stretched out in Velásquez's cell and his flesh hanging down like a bloody ripped robe.

Antonio he had more than loved – he had worshipped him the way some of his friends worshipped their older brothers or fathers or uncles; the way their sincere followers must have worshipped Abraham and Moses. And yet, Avram knew, he had not admired Antonio simply because he was bigger and stronger: what Antonio had possessed, as his mother had told him once when he asked her why his cousin had such powers of persuasion, was moral courage. And moral courage was, she had explained, a quality that had nothing to do with physical strength or cleverness; moral courage was the ability to live life as it should be lived – a special gift of God that burned inside the soul of a chosen few.

"But," Avram had protested, "I thought all Jews were chosen."

His mother had laughed. "Some to lead, the rest of us to follow."

He had sat on his bed, thinking about this, his admiration for Antonio slowly mixing itself with jealousy. "But could this flame be developed in a man? Or does he have to be born with it?"

And then his mother's face had taken on that particular sad cast that meant she was thinking about her husband. "Some acquire it," she said. "Others, like Isaac Aben Halevi, were born with it. Either way it is a burden."

In the dim silvery light of the moon, Avram could see the ghosts of his past and future parading outside the château. Antonio's fate had been to be a warrior, and to die. His own fate had been to be a doctor, and to live. In his workroom at the university, where he had his instruments and designed new surgical machines, he believed that one man could intervene in the destiny of another, could with an expertly wielded knife carve away the attacks of death and poison and restore the body to health.

But in the night? In the darkness when he could almost hear the breathing of those who had died, could almost see the faces of his children waiting to be born, what did he believe then? Avram climbed down from the ledge of the window and locked the shutters against the night.

He had never thought of living outside the city. In Spain his whole life had been passed within the umbra of its safety, its protecting stone walls, its rings upon rings of barricades, the houses that were layered into fortresses, the markets where everything could be bought – the city was the natural, the only place to live. To be sure, there were some who lived in villages or even smaller settlements around a central seigneury: but these places were simply cities in miniature – tiny fortresses that equally needed to be able to provision and defend themselves. Even the farms were worked by peasants who lived in defended garrisons; so to hear Jeanne-Marie fervently boast about the pleasures of the rural life only made Avram want to laugh. It was not, he explained, that he held a grudge against trees or flowers; it was simply that he could not understand why people would aspire to live in a place where their livestock could be stolen, their houses burned down, themselves and their children slaughtered.

"But that's just *now*," Jeanne-Marie protested. "The world is in an evil state because of the wars and the plagues." They had reached the rim of hills that surrounded de Mercier's walled château, and with a sweeping gesture, Jeanne-Marie drew his eye along the whole visible circle of countryside – a glorious multicoloured patchwork of fields, some golden, others yellow-green, some the deeper green of the oak trees that were clustered together in the dense remains of forest.

"Look," she said, "have you ever seen anything more beautiful? Anything more entirely alive? This whole world is one huge and living being." She grasped Avram's arm and looked at him intensely, waiting for his reaction.

"That's heresy," Avram finally said. "But my old teacher in Toledo used to believe it."

"Then it's not heresy."

"He was a Muhammadan. And he didn't believe in God."

"Well," Jeanne-Marie insisted defiantly, "isn't it all the same, anyway, so long as you have faith?"

He turned away from her. Despite the previous night's conversation with her brother, he had said nothing about marriage. And yet now – was she telling him that they might bring up their children as

Jews? Were the Peyres, despite the priest who lived among the servants, secret Judaizers?

"Your brother said you were a devout Catholic," Avram now said, trying to keep his voice neutral. "Aren't you?"

"I swore on the Bible that I believed in the Holy Trinity, the Crucifixion, the Virgin Mary."

"And do you?"

"Do *you*?"

"Of course," Jeanne-Marie said. "I believe with all my soul." She was still holding his arm and now she forced him to look at her. "You mustn't, *mustn't* talk about things like this."

"It takes courage to be honest," Avram said, thinking of Antonio.

"Then be honest in your heart."

"Sometimes even the heart must speak."

"Then let it speak of the things that belong to it. Love, art, the desire of one person for another, the beauty of the moon above the water. Those are the matters about which the heart should speak."

Suddenly there was a clattering of hooves. As they turned to the sound, a panting stallion drew up beside them, a gigantic dark beast that dwarfed its rider. As the sweating horse came to a stop, it reared high in the air. The mare that drew their own carriage jerked upwards with it, pulling the carriage forward and sending Jeanne-Marie into Avram as he struggled with the reins. By the time Avram looked up, Pierre Montreuil was already exchanging greetings with Jeanne-Marie.

"May I extend my congratulations?" His face was flushed, his narrow jaws working with anger. Like his stallion, his breath was heavy with the exhaustion of a forced gallop.

"Not yet," replied Jeanne-Marie.

"Good. Then it is not too late for you to avoid a disastrous mistake."

"Monsieur Halevi is not a mistake." With him, Montreuil had brought a plague of anger. Now Jeanne-Marie's face was a dark and angry red. And Avram felt a rage that he hadn't known for years boiling to the surface.

"He is a mistake." Montreuil's voice was half-way to a shout. "A Jew, a charlatan, a liar."

Montreuil, Avram noted now, was heavily armed. He carried a sword and a dagger at his side, and was moving with the stiffness caused by chain mail beneath his tunic. Avram had the dagger that he always carried, also a sword that he had laid on the floor of the carriage before leaving Montpellier.

Now Montreuil turned to Avram. "What's wrong? Do you not have a tongue with which to apologize for your presumption?"

"Speaking of tongues," Avram said, "perhaps you should put yours in a safe place, before you lose it in an accident."

"Brave words from a Jew."

Avram shifted his position so that his sword would be at hand.

"Well?"

"Well," Avram said softly, "brave words should be challenged by brave deeds." His head was spinning with the desire for revenge.

"Are you asking me to put you out of your misery, Jew, when you are unarmed?"

"Stop it!" Jeanne-Marie shouted. "Both of you stop this at once."

"I cannot stop the fact that I have been insulted," said Montreuil.

In a quick motion Avram changed seats so that Jeanne-Marie was no longer between himself and

Montreuil. At the same time he reached to the floor of the carriage and withdrew the sword. It was the weapon of his old friend Claude Aubin, the weapon he had worn on the day he died.

Montreuil choked the reins of his stallion; the front feet clawed the air once more, then it danced nervously about the carriage. "You're a fool," Montreuil said. "In France we use the blood of Jews to clean the steel of our swords."

Avram laughed. He could taste the bile on his tongue. "You are the fool. In Spain we pick our teeth with the bones of cowardly Frenchmen."

"You see," said Montreuil to Jeanne-Marie, "I really must avenge myself for such insults."

"Insults?" asked Avram. "A Frenchman should be proud to have his bones gracing the mouth of a Spaniard."

Montreuil now drew his own sword. "Would you care to repeat that, Spaniard?"

"If you're deaf, let me recommend more frequent bathing, followed by a course of enemas. Perhaps such a treatment would also provide relief from your unwholesome odour."

"Please," whispered Jeanne-Marie.

But with every sentence Avram felt himself growing larger, more sure of himself.

"If you are so brave," Montreuil now said, "would you kindly climb down from your carriage? Otherwise, when I run you through with my sword, there is a danger that my weapon might harm Mademoiselle Peyre."

"If you wish to avoid harming me," Jeanne-Marie cried, "you will leave right now and pretend that this whole unfortunate conversation never occurred."

"No," shouted Avram, vaulting from the carriage.

Even as his feet touched the dirt, Pierre Montreuil charged him, and had Jeanne-Marie not screamed, Avram could not have defended himself against the sword sweeping towards his neck. But the scream unnerved Montreuil's horse: it leapt off the ground as if it had been punctured, all four feet pawing wildly. As Montreuil struggled to keep his seat, Avram darted forward and, with a flick of his sword, cut the reins out of Montreuil's hands. Montreuil fell immediately, landing heavily on his back. The sword bounced away from him and Avram picked it up.

Montreuil made no attempt to rise, but lay staring at Avram, breathing hoarsely.

"What's the matter?" Avram asked. "Do the French prefer to die lying down?" His right arm quivered as if its blood had become drunk on the prospect of running Aubin's sword through the armoured sunken chest of Pierre Montreuil.

"Note how he keeps insulting the French," wheezed Montreuil. "He was afraid to fight me on horseback."

"You fight, brave one." Avram threw Montreuil's sword across his belly. As the metal made contact with his mail armour, Montreuil squeaked in fear. Then, grasping the handle of his sword, he scrambled to his feet. But he let the weapon dangle uselessly at his side, so that his breast was undefended.

"Look at him," Montreuil appealed to Jeanne-Marie. "He wants to kill me. What an idiot. Because he is your friend I will let him go. But if I meet him again, I cannot be responsible for my actions."

Avram stepped forward, waved the tip of his sword in slow circles beneath the nose of Pierre Montreuil. With Aubin he had fenced every day for a year. Now his arm began to remember the weight of the sword, his wrist and hand the tiny movements that could slice like a scalpel.

"Please," whispered Montreuil. He had dropped his own sword and was looking imploringly at Avram.

"Where do you live?"

"Six leagues away, in that direction." Montreuil raised his arm to point, but kept his gaze on Avram.

"Good." His pent-up frustration could be held back no longer. With all his strength Avram lashed out with Aubin's sword, slapping its flat side against the stallion's withers with a loud smack that sent sweat and lather spraying into the air and the stallion itself galloping in great leaps towards its stable. Then he bowed to Montreuil, whose face was white with panic. "Consider yourself one of my charity patients. The advice was free, but on this occasion I will decline to operate."

Hopping to the carriage seat, he took the reins from Jeanne-Marie and cracked them over the back of the mare. As they galloped down the road Avram looked over his shoulder and saw that Montreuil had already begun his slow walk home. Meanwhile the mare increased her speed, as if her heart, too, needed to be exorcised of what had almost happened. Almost a quarter of an hour passed before she ran out of breath and slowed to a walk. Jeanne-Marie had been clinging to Avram the whole time. Now she turned and looked at him.

"I'm sorry," Avram said. His heart was pounding, swelling with each beat like a volcano waiting to erupt. He freed himself from Jeanne-Marie and stepped down from the carriage. If only Montreuil had had the courage to fight – all the hate he felt towards him was still boiling in his blood with nowhere to go. A few steps from the road was the crest of a small hill. He climbed it, hoping to see Montreuil making his insect-like way home.

"Don't be sorry."

"I wanted to kill him."

Avram's eyes swept across the fields. The shadows of the long afternoon were beginning to deepen and the sun, low over the horizon, had loosened its grip on the sky: now, for the first time since his nightly vigils on the walls of Toledo, he found himself noticing a sunset. The colours of the fields and trees were violently alive, the calls of nesting birds pierced the air like arrows, sounds so intense and painful that his eyes filled with tears: he saw Antonio spread-eagled on the dark stone wall. Finally, the image slipped away and he saw another – Ben Ishaq bending pleadingly towards him, an apron of blood flowing over the giant's sword.

"What's wrong?"

The tears were coming faster, it was the first time he had cried in the years since his arrival in Montpellier. He put his head in his hands and felt a huge block of grief detach itself from his stomach and start to force itself up his chest. The tears flowed, everything was mixed together: the baptism, Antonio, his mother's head lolled to one side, Isabel's last look as he leapt from the wall, the sound of the hunchback's breaking bones, the way the giant's punctured heart had sucked at his knife as he pulled it free. Suddenly he was aware of the wetness of his own tears, the grass and black earth pressing into him as if he had finally found the grave he had been digging for himself all winter. Tears filled his skull, his chest; deeper and deeper the weeping penetrated him until his whole body was a river of tears for the dead he had never mourned, his own pure soul that had died with them.

Against his face was a warm breath. Arms tightened around him. At first he felt like a dead man, hearing the unwanted call of the living. Then the tears slowed, his body came back to itself, and he

229

could feel his heart booming through his bones. He turned to Jeanne-Marie, embraced her, too, opened his eyes. The sun had slipped below the hills – and all the blood that used to empty over Toledo was here transformed into a dazzling cloak that draped the hills, the fields, the trees, Jeanne-Marie's face and naked neck, in a soft and living velvet. He kissed her eyes, her lips, her throat. Silky skin melted to his kisses, and as he wept, she wept with him. He could feel their hearts pounding together, beating to the deeper pulse of the warm embracing earth. And when she cried his name and drew him deep into her centre, he cried, too, finally safe between the flesh of love and the dark living blanket of the night.

BOOK III

TOLEDO
1407

ONE

I T WAS EARLY IN SEPTEMBER, 1407.
THE ANNUAL FAIR HAD THIS YEAR BEEN AN OUT-
STANDING COMMERCIAL SUCCESS, A SUCCESS THAT
MADE IT CLEAR HOW COMPLETELY TOLEDO HAD
recovered from its most recent catastrophe. Henry
III, the direct descendant and namesake of Henry
Trastamara, had died suddenly – poisoned, it was
said, by his Jewish physician, Señor Mayr. The
succession had been a smooth one, but for months
the rumours surrounding the doctor's interrogation
inflamed the city. Not since 1391 had feeling against
the Jews run so high, and it seemed to the Jews of
Toledo that the cloud cast over their fortunes had
endured so many decades, caused so many crises,
that eventually their sky would become absolutely
black, all life extinct.

But since Señor Mayr had died, the tension had
started to ease, and the month of the fair was an
occasion of celebration for Toledo's Jews, a month
of stability and commerce. For those who were young,
and who had no desire to listen or imagination to
understand the horrors recited by their elders, Toledo
was again a haven and a capital for its Jews. This
even though since the massacre of 1391, the Jews of
Toledo had been forced into ever-smaller quarters.

Even the beautiful Synagogue of the Tránsito that Samuel Halevi had given to his city had been taken over by the Church, and others of the former synagogues still lay in unreconstructed ruins.

But the century had not been without novelty and success for Toledo's Jews. New financiers had risen to protect their brethren – and so great was their power that even the accusation against the doctor of Henry III had not left them unable to make the transition to the new king.

What he liked, Juan Velásquez had said to Isabel a thousand times, was trade. The idea of making money by extricating it from the sweat of others had never appealed to him.

Sitting in his dining room late one September night, so desirous of being alone that he had long ago sent even the servants to bed, Juan Velásquez drank from the supply of wine that his brother had recently brought him. Strong red wine, the blood of Christ that ran from one real Christian man to another. There were times when he wished he had lived during the era of the Crusades, had ridden to do battle in the Holy Land. Not that he had the taste to die from illness and dysentery in a foreign country, but the idea of a brotherhood of Christians, like-minded men with the wit to conquer and organize huge kingdoms, appealed to him.

But the Crusades were over. Enough now, Velásquez thought, to gallop through his hunting estates and drive the spear into a fleeing deer. Or to go out with a group of his comrades into the forest, and surround and kill one of the great shaggy bears that lived there. Spring to the ground and stand beside the beast, feel his own heart expand with calm while life bled away from the hunted.

And, in any case, where were the men to be his brothers on a crusade? Not the merchants with whom he lived in mutual and total distrust. Not Rodrigo, who would send the whole world to Hell in exchange for the pope's throne. Even the women in his life were to be watched: Isabel, who had inflated Diego into a monster with her overblown barren mother's love; Gabriela Hasdai de Santangel, with her fatal weakness for loving men. After the death of Gabriela's first husband, Juan had spent a night with her, coupling in the warehouse. These Jews were pagans, throwing themselves on one another like cats in heat, then turning away, faces frozen into stone.

The thought of the Jews of Toledo, and the stones they were becoming, the stones under which they were being buried, reminded Velásquez of the Jewish doctor, Señor Mayr, who had been tortured to death only a month ago in the capacious cells of Cardinal Rodrigo.

The night before Mayr's death, Rodrigo had been to dinner. Isabel, who knew the man slightly, had asked Rodrigo if he could have pity. The sight of his imperious and saintly wife leaning to beg Rodrigo for pity had softened Juan, and as she had said the words, he had been surprised to find himself agreeing with her.

But Rodrigo had exploded. With all his heavy force he had slammed his fist onto the table: one bottle of wine was in his arm, giving it strength; another leapt from the table to shatter on the tile floor. "Don't tell me about pity," he had shouted. "I have seen the slaves who drive your husband's ships up and down the Mediterranean. They are chained to their benches, like cattle staked in the desert to die. And I have seen your face when you look towards the far wing of the castle, where your husband's bastard children sprout from under the blankets like prize cabbages."

The memory of Rodrigo's speech and Isabel's agonized look jerked Velásquez to his feet. He pushed open the shutters: the night was black and cold, the kind of night when a young man seeks love to warm the soul. Feeling restless, Velásquez went outside, then crossed the courtyard to Isabel's room. Although Halevi had told her that to have more children would have been fatal, Isabel had been able to welcome Juan Velásquez back into her arms while she had still been nursing Diego. But eventually the milk dried up, and although she insisted God had saved her once and she would take her chance with Him again, Velásquez had found Isabel easy to resist. Whether because of the operation or because the milky smell of her nursing had finally grown sour in his nostrils, Velásquez could now lie beside his wife in their wide marriage bed, but he could not bring himself to let his skin rub against hers.

In the years since her son's birth, Isabel had developed from the impulsive and pleasure-seeking girl who had given Velásquez a second youth into a woman whom the servants called a saint – likening her to the famous Saint Caterina of Sienna. Saint Caterina – who had proclaimed throughout Christendom that the ring Christ had given her was made not of gold but of the flesh taken in His circumcision – was so religious that she fasted every second month. The other months she ate only lettuce, and even that was said to make her delicate stomach convulse.

Seldom feasting and never drinking spirits, Isabel's naked body was a living reproach to the love she claimed she still wanted: her ribs ran like ladders from her waist to her shoulders, her small breasts were empty of all flesh and juice, her tiny waist tapered down to narrow, sharply boned hips.

Continuing on from Isabel's room, Velásquez crossed over to the servants' quarters. Opening a door, he went quickly to the bed where Renata, the mother of his two daughters, slept. During the night the sheet had been pushed out of place; one plump brown breast now rested invitingly on the white linen. By the time Velásquez had bolted the door, thrown off his clothes, and climbed in after her, Renata had turned to the empty space beside her, her arms open.

"Idiot," Velásquez muttered to himself, "she doesn't even know who's getting into her bed." But he slid between her waiting arms just the same, and soon he was taking his soft ride while she encouraged him with half-said words and caresses.

Spent, he slid from her, while she slipped instantly back into sleep, her fleshy buttocks curling into his belly for comfort.

"You're a cow," Velásquez muttered, but he put his arm around her and spread his hand across her stomach.

Safe and secure for the night, the palace was asleep. In one bedroom lay his wife, the almost-saint. In another slept his son, comforted by his old wet-nurse. Then there was the room with Lenora, the other servant who had given him children, the room with the children themselves, and last of all, this room, where he lay with Renata.

All these creatures depended upon him, loved him, served him without complaining. As did the dozen other servants scattered through the palace.

There was not one who could be bribed, not one whom he had retained by making him sign a contract, not one who would not cheerfully give his life in the defence of himself, his son, his wife.

And yet, once more, he could feel the familiar first sign of a sleepless night, the layer of sweat that coated his body even in the face of the cool night breeze.

Like an unwanted robe that could not be taken off, it itched and chafed his skin. He rolled away from Renata, pulled down the sheet so that his belly could dry off in the air. Sometimes, at the very moment of his release, he wished that he would die. Isabel remembered well enough when she joked about the little death of his pleasure; still, at fifty-four, it took him so intensely that he felt lost under its force. But only seconds later, paradise was gone and he was back to himself, nothing changed, lying soaked in sweat and come while his ears rang slightly in a last echo of whatever had happened.

He rubbed his hand down his chest and stomach. His hair was wiry and grizzled now, like an old bear's. Even his sweat seemed to be gritty with sand and tiny particles of flint.

He closed his eyes and tried to picture himself sleeping. Instead, he saw Gabriela Hasdai writhing under him, her white Jewess's teeth clamped to his arm. Suddenly nervous and entirely awake, Velásquez rolled out of bed and dressed once more. Walking slowly, his back and legs hurting with every step, Juan Velásquez made his way back into the dining room. There he lit the candles he had so recently pinched out.

Even as the tinder sparked, Juan Velásquez found himself staring at a certain shadow in the corner. And then, as the light of the candles ballooned out into the room, the shadow detached itself from the wall and began coming closer; like a devil in a black cape, Avram Halevi was walking towards him as if time had flown sixteen years backwards in a single cough.

"Don Juan."

"Halevi."

"Forgive me for coming so late. I did not know if I would be welcome."

"I owe you the lives of my wife and son."

"And your servants?"

"Servants can be replaced." Juan stepped forward, grasped Avram's arm, and drew him into the light. Time had been kind to the Jew who was so skilled with his knife, so uncertain of his faith. His face had filled out with the years, his beard grown more luxurious. The tall, pole-like young man had become a man of substance, even had the shadow of a belly.

"What are you doing in Toledo?"

"I came to testify at the trial of Mayr. But by the time I had arrived, the trial was over."

"I, too, was sorry to hear of the death of Señor Mayr. But when a king dies, those who surround him are in danger. It could have been worse – "

"I know," said Avram.

"You have changed," Velásquez murmured.

"And you, I hear, have grown more rich and more powerful than any other merchant in Toledo. Almost as powerful as your brother Rodrigo."

"Rodrigo was my brother long ago. Now he has become God's choice to lead the Church."

"Against the Jews," said Avram.

"Against its enemies, *whoever* they may be."

"Well said. And I apologize, Don Juan, for you, above all, are a friend."

Juan drew Avram to the table, gave him the chair where Rodrigo usually sat, poured him a glass of Rodrigo's wine. Then he himself sat down and put his hands on the table in front of him, lacing the fingers together. Every finger was a woman, a prostitute, a bastard child, a symbol of his unhappiness. His nights had turned into nervous prowls from one

239

bed to another, no interruption could have been more welcome than Halevi's – on the very night he had been thinking of kindred spirits – and yet the Jew's voice had become harsh and demanding, the voice not of a brother but of a supplicant.

"Speak," Juan said.

"This is a long story, but let me tell you at the beginning that I am married now, a father, and that the brother-in-law of my wife is Robert de Mercier, who is your business partner in Montpellier."

"I know de Mercier."

"He is being sued by a certain Pierre Montreuil."

"This, too, I know."

"I do not believe a man in our times can be happy," Avram Halevi said. "But like any father I am concerned that my child may live. Do you understand me?"

"I know what it is to be a father," Juan Velásquez said sharply. He felt suddenly irritated and sleepy at once, knowing what was coming.

"You understand, then, that I wish the suit against Robert de Mercier to be dropped."

"I understand," Velásquez said. Locked in a trunk behind the table, the very table where they were sitting, were the partnership agreements with Robert de Mercier. That night he had been going over them. They were bound together in a package, and when he had put the package back in the trunk he had thought how heavy it was, heavy as a heart.

"Your brother is the one pursuing this business."

"I know that, too," Velásquez said. "It is always a matter of my brother." The irritation that had started now threatened to become anger. Rodrigo Velásquez, Cardinal Rodrigo, the man who would be pope: on whose tongue was Rodrigo's name not both a curse and an inspiration? If only Rodrigo were in Toledo at this very minute, if only he would enter the door

240

to see this Jew sitting in his place, drinking his wine. "You are still a Jew?" Velásquez asked.

"I am nothing else."

"Since we last met, many of Toledo's Jews have converted. Sincere converts, men who go to confession every week, men who have learned how to live."

Avram Halevi leaned forward, his hand tightening around the glass. How he looks like Rodrigo, Juan thought; how his face twists and his hand knots when he is crossed.

"I want my child to live," Avram whispered. "Will you speak to your brother?"

"I will speak to him, my friend. But I will tell you, also, what I think of what Rodrigo does. For Rodrigo has tied his destiny to the destruction of the Jews. We both know that. As a man I am ashamed to have a brother who rides on the death of others. But as a Christian I know that something must be sacrificed if the Church is to be united again. Why not the Jews? Are they the first people that history has erased? Spain itself is a museum of peoples crushed by the Muslims — and the Jews — before coming together again to rule their own fate. But finally, Avram Halevi, I will speak to you as a merchant, for that is what I am most of all. And as a merchant I say to my old friend, to whom I am indebted, I say you must know what to choose and what to discard. When you became a doctor, you chose the future. And look, it has treated you well. I have heard of your successes in France, your unexpectedly brilliant marriage, *in a church*, your position as dean of medicine at the University of Montpellier. Now you must choose again; you must choose between being the Jew you never were, or becoming, with all your heart, a Christian. That is the choice, my friend, that you have refused to make. Now is the time to act, for soon neither I nor anyone else will be able to stand be-

241

tween you and Rodrigo. Because, you must understand, Rodrigo is not only a single man who wants to become pope, or even simply a man who symbolizes the power of the Church. Rodrigo is the face of history. History, my friend, has gone against the Jews. Soon what little remains of them will be entirely crushed, and neither I, nor Rodrigo if he willed it, nor even you can escape the force of the future."

Juan stood up. His own rhetoric had inflamed and awoken him, what he said felt so true that the dark night had unlocked its power and he could feel it vibrating through him, like a drum. But Avram only sat deep in his chair, eyes closed, rocking back and forth as if lost in the comforting rhythms of a fairy tale.

"Speak!" Velásquez demanded.

Avram opened his eyes slowly and looked at him across the candle flames.

"You are a sly one," Velásquez said. "I had forgotten how cunning you are."

"When I have something to say, I will speak. And wherever I am, I promise you will hear me."

TWO

ORNINGS, NOW, THE SUN ROSE LATER, EMERGING ONLY AFTER IT HAD EARNED ITS PLACE IN THE SKY BY BURNING AWAY THE COOL MIST. AND ON ONE SUCH morning, the morning after his unexpected conversation with Avram Halevi, Juan Velásquez was sitting with his wife and his son in the courtyard of his palace, soaking up the warmth.

Isabel, the pale queen, had become emaciated but beautiful in her middle years. Charity and good works had made her religious devotion famous throughout Toledo. But she was taut and sharp-eyed, too, and beneath her saintly smile was seen the iron will that had made Velásquez's fortunes rise. When he died, it was said, Isabel the iron saint would carry the banner of the Velásquez empire to new victories.

Already that empire was much larger than it once had been. On the eve of the Toledo massacre in 1391, Velásquez had been merely a wealthy merchant by Spanish standards, a middle-aged man who had spent a lifetime enjoying his inheritance and the favours that it brought him.

But with the uprisings against the Jews, and the growing power of the Church driving the Islamic empire out of the Mediterranean basin, Velásquez found the opportunity to expand. Going into partnership with French and Italian merchants, contacts and communications eased for him by Rodrigo's ties to the papacies in Avignon and Italy, he now owned a fleet of merchant vessels that plied the ports of the Mediterranean and carried goods ranging from the flax and cloth produced in the very north of Europe to exotic silks and spices drawn from the corners of the vast Oriental empire with which the Arabs traded.

"In the past," Velásquez once told Gabriela, "those who owned land were the most important: the extent of their estate measured the extent of their powers. But now power resides in movement and in trade. Gold is the international currency, and once you have the means of travel, there is so much land available that all of it is worthless." To prove his own point, Velásquez had multiplied his fortunes by selling his estates to buy his share of the fleet. On the walls of the warehouse office from which he directed operations, Velásquez had hung maps of Europe and Northern Africa. Marked on the maps were the headquarters of his partners as well as the cities that his vessels and his caravans visited.

To conform with his growing powers, the appearance of Velásquez had subtly altered. The hair that had once been a brilliant jet-black was liberally streaked with grey, and the rigid face had become mellower, more flexible. But Velásquez was still the rich gentleman with a taste for ostentation. His white summer linens had become even more carefully tailored, his winter cloaks were trimmed with rarer furs; even his posture was more erect – instead of walking with a merchant's swagger, Velásquez moved with the deliberate correctness of a statesman.

His son by Isabel was now sixteen years old, a large-shouldered, heavy-set boy, with a fine sprinkling of dark hairs beginning to appear on his upper lip. Tutored by a whole phalanx of experts in everything from fencing to Latin, to Juan he seemed to be a swollen and cold-hearted boy, one upon whom too much attention had been lavished. Or perhaps, Juan Velásquez considered as he saw the servant opening the gate to Gabriela Hasdai de Santangel, Diego was simply waiting for the opportunity to prove his manhood.

Like Isabel, Gabriela seemed to have grown more beautiful with the years. But if Isabel was the iron saint, Gabriela was surely a woman of steel. Tested by fate a dozen times, she had survived unmarked. Now she was married for the second time and the mother of two children. Still beautiful, always looking young, every day confirmed in her position as the right arm of Velásquez's foreign operations. It was, in fact, the world beyond Toledo that had held his attention after Halevi's departure. Unable to sleep, Juan Velásquez had spent the whole night pacing back and forth in his dining hall, the words that he had said to Avram re-shaping themselves and expanding until gradually the plan that had existed half-formed in his mind for years made itself clear.

As soon as his servants had brought him breakfast, Velásquez sent a message to the Santangel household. But now that Gabriela was here, Velásquez found himself thinking not just of his plan, but of Halevi's visit, and the request he had made.

"I have heard," began Velásquez, "that our friend and partner Robert de Mercier is being sued by a certain Pierre Montreuil."

"I met him when I was working for you in Barcelona." As always, when they talked business, she leaned forward to listen with total concentration. She had a mind to be feared: in almost twenty years of such conversations, she had never forgotten a single detail.

"This man, Montreuil, is someone Rodrigo thinks could be an ally. But tell me your impressions."

"He was a small man." Isabel laughed and Velásquez laughed with her. Gabriela's sharp tongue was a sword to be kept as a friend.

"I also heard," she continued, "that he paid court to the sister-in-law of Robert de Mercier, the woman Avram Halevi married."

Avram Halevi. She said the name, Velásquez noted, with care, as if the slightest misjudgement might cause it to twist in her mouth. He wondered if Avram had paid Gabriela a surprise visit, too.

"Now," said Velásquez, "Pierre Montreuil is suing de Mercier for collecting rent from lands that don't belong to him."

"Surely they must know which lands belong to whom."

"There are registered deeds but the matter is very complicated, and the judges told both parties that they must reach an agreement. But they didn't. Then Montreuil, on Rodrigo's advice, accused de Mercier of breaking the pope's prohibitions on Jews by employing François Peyre as his lands manager."

"Peyre is a Catholic – "

"But he is a converted one. And so the question is: does a man cease to be a Jew just because he has become a Christian? The judges have refused to rule."

"The wise men of Montpellier have a very easy job," said Gabriela, "if they are allowed to judge without judging."

"There is another matter, too."

"Yes?" Again Gabriela leaned forward.

"I am speaking about this with you first, because I know how much you love this city."

246

Gabriela nodded.

"I need someone trusted in Italy, someone to expand our operations there. In Bologna are the most stable banks in Italy, in Bologna is the strongbox of the Church's power, in Bologna reside the merchants who need our shipping contacts. Everyone knows that it is only a matter of months before the papal schism is ended. And when there is only one pope, where will that pope reside? In Avignon? Never, despite my brother's best efforts. The pope will live in Italy, where he has lived for centuries. But not in Rome or Naples – those cities are spoiled by controversy. The papacy will be in Bologna. It will need friends from Spain, financial arms to make it strong."

As he spoke, Velásquez watched the face of Gabriela. She was his most trusted employee and she was married to an Italian merchant. Nothing could be more natural than such a move.

"Let me think about it," Gabriela said.

"I will say nothing to León. In such matters there should be no wedge driven between husband and wife." Gabriela stood.

"Tonight," Velásquez said, "you and León might come to dinner. Avram Halevi is in Toledo, and an old friend would be honoured if the reunion could take place at his table."

THREE

WHEN THE NEWS OF AVRAM'S ARRIVAL IN TOLEDO. HAD COME, GABRIELA WAS IN ONE OF VELÁSQUEZ'S WAREHOUSES, INSPECTING A NEW SHIPMENT OF CLOTH. It was her sister Leah who delivered the tidings, a grim smile upon her face as if to say that finally Gabriela would be forced to pay for her sins as a youth, for her stubborn insistence on working for the brother of Cardinal Rodrigo, for her marriage to an Italian – a Jew, yes, but a Jew with foreign habits and strange ideas.

All afternoon Gabriela had prepared to tell León. For her Italian husband, despite his talk of a new age dawning, was just as jealous as other men. Before their marriage she had told him the story of Avram, and León had been concerned enough to ask, repeatedly, if she was not still in love with this charmless adolescent.

But when she arrived home, she received the news that León had left unexpectedly on a trade mission to Madrid. And thus the next morning, when Velásquez invited her to dinner with Avram, mentioning León's name as if he did not know where León was, Gabriela had already spent a night without sleep, dreading the meeting with Avram, wishing he had left the past intact.

But when the actual hour of the dinner had rung, and Gabriela found herself standing face-to-face with Avram, she was glad León was not there to witness her reaction.

Even the sight of him made her gasp, a fist slammed against her heart, and for a moment stars spun crazily about her head.

"Gabriela." He said her name. He walked towards her. She had heard of his marriage, that he had become dean of the medical school, but nothing could have prepared her for this, for Avram Halevi larger than life, walking hands outstretched towards her in the house of Juan Velásquez.

"Gabriela." The sound of Avram's voice made her dizzy again, and this time when the stars spun Gabriela fell forward, unable to help herself, and as Avram caught and embraced her, she burst into tears.

As Gabriela later told Avram, what happened next was almost like magic: sitting on the Velásquez patio, sipping fine wine and looking out at the setting sun, she felt as if the world of dreams had swallowed up the city of Toledo. Placed beside Avram, Gabriela felt her heart grow large again, like the heart of a young girl; the young girl, herself, was once more in love, once more safe in the aura of the most fiery spirit of all Toledo. And, what is more, in that magical world of dreams it seemed as if the young girl had been called back to life, and hovered happily above Gabriela Hasdai de Santangel and her first lover, watching to see what the middle-aged matron would do with the lover who had once spurned her, but now returned.

"You know," Gabriela whispered, "I used to believe you were destined to become a new prophet, risen like a flame to lead us safely through our darkest night. Remember how we would sneak down to the river to inspect the bones of the dead? I used to think our adventures belonged not simply to two orphans of Toledo, but that God had chosen us for a magnificent destiny and that we would be heroes of the Jewish people.

"Tonight, at Juan's house, I was as happy as if you'd already announced that the purpose of your return was to take the surviving Jews of Toledo back to Israel — that outside the walls of the city a caravan was already waiting, camels and horses saddled in gold trappings — to bear us away from all this suffering and back to the warm bosom of the Promised Land."

Gabriela paused. Her tongue was a runaway horse, ready to gallop all night. But here in her own house, what had been so magical and so right at Don Juan's was threatening to disappear. Across from her, reclining on cushions, Avram seemed to be retreating into the distance. Why had she invited him to accompany her home after the dinner? So he could meet her children? They had long been asleep. So that he could see how Gabriela Hasdai had survived the night in Barcelona, and now lived in one of the richest, most cultured houses of Toledo? Or because she was an insane fool, unable to resist throwing her heart, again and again, to the man who did not want it?

Now Gabriela found herself beginning to talk again, eyes averted. First she told him of the marriage she had made the year Avram left Barcelona. The name of the man was Jacob Eleazar, a biblical scholar. "When he asked for my hand," Gabriela said, "I explained that my heart had been broken by the murder of my friends in Toledo. Jacob said that he understood; his heart, too, had been broken by the sorrows of his people. I told myself that I would never love again, but that a woman has the duty of making herself useful to a man. In the end I married him out of pity."

At this Avram only nodded and Gabriela, feeling foolish, hurried towards the end of the story: "He got sick almost right after our wedding day. Soon he could only lie in bed; I, like a nurse, spooned broth into his mouth while he studied from his holy scrolls. He never stopped studying, the day of his death he was going over the commentaries on the Ten Commandments.

"After he died I really did resign myself to a life alone, even though with Jacob I had enjoyed the comforts of marriage."

Saying this, Gabriela looked up at Avram, but there was no movement at all, and she rushed on. "I had stopped working for Velásquez, but after Jacob died I wanted to return to Toledo. When I tired of daily life with my sister Leah, I accepted Velásquez's offer of a place in his business.

"One day, Leah told me of an Italian Jew who was said to be honest, intelligent, and looking for a wife. He was even from an old and respected Spanish family. This was my husband-to-be, León Santangel."

"And where is your husband tonight?"

"He is in Madrid, visiting cousins."

"I am sorry to have missed him."

Avram's voice had grown deeper with the years, more certain; and also, like the voices of other men, more opaque.

"Why did you come to Toledo?"

"To testify at the trial of Señor Mayr."

251

"That is all?"

"To see you, also."

"Now you have seen me." Gabriela heard the anger in her voice. But why should she not be angry? This reunion, dreamed of for so long, had become an uncomfortable farce. Blurting out her life story like a nervous girl, she had humiliated herself in order to hear one sentence – "*to see you, also.*" That was it. Her reward for a lifetime of love. *Also.*

"Has León made you happy?"

"I have a family, honesty, love."

"I, too, am married."

"And have you learned how to love?"

"Yes."

The fist slammed against her heart again, but this time Gabriela felt herself invaded not by dizziness but by fear: the fear of time's rapid flight, of her dreams being made ridiculous by this stranger who once had claimed her, of the anger and love that whirled their strange dance through her.

"I should not have come. I don't want to make you unhappy again."

Gabriela realized that she had begun to weep. She stood up and walked towards Avram, who watched without moving. When she spoke, it was not her own voice, but the voice of the young girl who had been left in Barcelona, left because in saving her life she had allowed her girl's skin to be defiled. "I need you. Don't refuse me."

What happened next began quickly. As Gabriela spoke, the oil lamp went out, and in the darkness she embraced Avram, whose arms were open and waiting for her. Soon they were joined, he was more abrupt and forceful than she remembered, and as he bucked and jolted in his desire she could feel jagged lightning streaks of pleasure rippling up and down her spine. She had never known herself to dream of making love to Avram again, but now that it was happening, she realized she had wanted it. Wanted to love him again, but not this way. Wanted to melt together softly, gently, to be swallowed by nights dense with stars and in the noise of the Targa. Wanted to feel his skin against hers for hour after hour, to wrap herself in him so she was surrounded by silky sheets of his smell, of his love, of his tender caresses. Instead something else had woken in her, a world of sharp want and need, and when her desire came to its climax she heard herself gasping like an animal in heat. Even the peak of her pleasure was torn forcibly from her, and when it was over she lay beside Avram, her whole body tingling, but love and anger, hope and disappointment, still mixed inseparably together. Her body trembled with the conflict, then she began to shiver.

"Cold?" Avram asked. His distant voice was now near enough.

"Disgusted," Gabriela blurted out. And sick with shame she rolled away, pulling her robe down over her hips.

"I, too, am married."

"And this is how you love your bride?" The young girl's voice, the voice that had begged, now dripped with scorn and self-loathing.

"No," Avram said, as she felt him moving towards her in the dark, "this is how I love you." And then suddenly his fist was at her throat, clutching the robe she had lifted up like a servant girl, his hand so swollen with anger that Gabriela could feel his knuckles digging sharply into her neck, bruising the very spots his lips had kissed so tenderly.

253

"I'm sorry," Gabriela said. But she wasn't, because she had finally gotten a tiny measure of revenge for the years of wanting Avram, needing Avram, loving Avram while he returned only indifference or worse.

"Don't be sorry." Avram's grip relaxed. "I *did* love you. I had even sworn to God, the night I was in the dungeon with Antonio, that if I escaped I would marry you. When I left you in Barcelona, it was not because I couldn't love you, it was because my life was aimed elsewhere."

"And now," asked Gabriela, "That you have become the renowned surgeon and dean of the medical school, now where is your life aimed? Towards love?"

Avram did not reply, and for a moment Gabriela, too, was silent. The words he had just said were still sinking in. Fifteen years ago, ten years ago, she would have believed life itself was not too precious to exchange for Avram's admission of love.

"Tell me," said Gabriela. "Do you raise your child as a Jew or a Christian?"

"Neither. Both."

"Like yourself," Gabriela said. He had loved her then, perhaps he even loved her now. But fate, not Avram's ambition, had torn them apart before, now it would again. Better to talk, to build a distance that could not be bridged, to admit a small defeat instead of engaging in a major battle that could only be disaster.

"That part of me is dead."

Gabriela laughed. What had happened between them had almost destroyed her, but here was her lover, Avram, her first love and her first unhappiness, as calm and unaffected by this night as by any other, ready to debate with her until the small hours of the morning rather than talk about what mattered.

"You are not dead," Gabriela said. "You are something different than dead: you are a man who has hidden himself in a trunk — hidden himself away while presenting to the world a puppet you have invented." She paused, but it was too late, a whole lifetime of bitterness was waiting to pour itself out. "My lover, my Avram, your fate will find you even if you refuse to search it out. When that happens, those who suffer will be the family whom you betray with such ease — theirs are the lives you propose to gamble on your desire to invent yourself in the face of history."

Avram was standing, his face turned away. When finally he looked at her there were tears in his eyes: the moonlight made them into pearls. Gabriela suddenly realized that where love had failed, anger had unexpectedly succeeded.

"Why are we fighting?"

"I don't know."

This time, when he embraced her, she melted against him. And when he left her house, in the hour before dawn, Gabriela stood in her doorway and watched his quick steps carry him into the darkness. The bitter armour had all been torn away: now she was the raw and innocent young girl again, her naked soul exposed to the night air, the dizzy pleasure of her lover's touch.

He didn't come back. It was Leah who brought the news that Avram Halevi had left Toledo. "As he came," she said, "at night, in a carriage. You would think he was a king, the way he travels. Did you see him?"

"Yes."

Over the years Leah's face had become as broad as a man's. She had stopped plucking her eyebrows, and she allowed the occasional black hair to sprout from the rounded point of her chin. "In such a situation," Leah said, "I would have taken great care."

Gabriela nodded.

"I would not want," Leah said, "to sacrifice what I had in order to remember a childish love."

The idea of Leah experiencing any sort of love at all, childish or otherwise, was inconceivable to Gabriela. And yet the speed and assurance with which she had spoken, the arch and piercing look that accompanied her words, made Gabriela's pulse skip.

She was about to protest when a disquieting thought paralyzed her tongue: she had given herself to Avram, everything of herself that could be given in one brief night, but not for one second had she considered leaving León, sacrificing the life she had with him to follow her feelings for Avram.

"Tell me," Leah now demanded. "Were you wise?"

"I was wise," Gabriela replied. "I have learned wisdom even better than I knew."

BOOK VI

KIEV
1421–1445

ONE

THE AUTUMN OF 1410 WAS WARM AND PRO-
LONGED. TRULY, AS NO ONE TIRED OF
REMARKING, THE SOUTH OF FRANCE HAD NOT
ENJOYED SUCH AN EXTENDED AND BENEVO-
lent summer since before the beginning of the black
death — that wonderful era when the population of
France was growing like wheat in the ever-increas-
ing fields; when new cathedrals were being raised
to the glory of God and his one pope; when even the
oncoming war with England was only a dream of
melodious ballads and noble deeds.

But Montpellier, though it woke every morning to
silvery mists and basked every afternoon under a
warm and gentle sun, was in the grip of a violent
scandal that had divided the town for over three
years.

It had begun innocently enough when Pierre Montreuil, one of the most important merchants and
landowners of Montpellier, publicly accused Robert
de Mercier of defying the pope's edict by employing
Jews as overseers of his lands. He had further accused de Mercier of using his Jewish employees to
collect rent from lands that he had stolen from none
other than Pierre Montreuil.

Such charges were nothing more than grist for the
usual mill of the Montpellier consular tribunal. After

endless hearings and debates the issue had simply drifted away, unresolved. It was rumoured that this result had pleased the powerful Cardinal Rodrigo Velásquez, who had made a special journey to Montpellier to discuss the matter. At this conclusion the townsfolk, too, were relieved: for while Montreuil was respected for his wealth and power, Robert de Mercier had many friends.

A few months later, however, at the very height of the glorious summer weather, a new and shocking incident revived the old lawsuit.

In the room of a medical student was discovered an extraordinarily heretical item: a copy of the Book of Genesis illustrated by a series of obscene drawings of naked men and women twined together like so many snakes in a pit.

Jean de Tournière, chancellor of the university, immediately convoked a tribunal to investigate. The proceedings became inflamed: during one fierce debate, a priest dropped dead at the conclusion of his own testimony. A representative of the Avignon pope was sent for, and a week later Cardinal Rodrigo Velásquez arrived in the official papal carriage.

Massive, impressive in his passion, Rodrigo Velásquez was known to be the only churchman with the strength and vitality to bring life to the failing corpse of the Avignon papacy and perhaps end the schism altogether.

Sitting on the podium and listening to the witnesses, Velásquez was an awesome sight, for with age he had grown from a large man to a gigantic one. The thickly muscled shoulders and chest were now augmented by an enormous belly that rose from his lap like a sack of stone-ground flour. The face, too, had changed: even the eyes that used to bulge with rage were now sheltered by swollen cheeks and overhung by thick black eyebrows gone white at their tips.

When the cardinal saw the offending work, after days of argument about whether or not it should be allowed as evidence, he was so shocked that he instantly declared that, henceforth, he personally would care for the souls of the poor inhabitants of Montpellier.

The promise must have seemed a potent one, for that night the accused hanged himself in his cell. The next day Jean de Tournière declared that since the guilty party had removed himself, the inquiry was closed. But so great was the continuing outrage of the townspeople that shortly afterwards Avram Halevi, dean of the medical school and the university's chief anatomist, took an indefinite leave of absence. This man, a Jew who had married into the converso clan of Robert de Mercier, had left the city after publicly stating that he had nothing to be ashamed of, and that he intended to give the poor peasants surrounding his brother-in-law's château the same standard of medical care that had previously been reserved for the rich burghers of Montpellier.

The moment Halevi decamped, Pierre Montreuil re-opened his suit against de Mercier, adding to his accusations that he was sheltering a known idolater and anti-Christ.

This time the consuls of Montpellier were rapid in their deliberations: before the end of October Robert de Mercier and Pierre Montreuil would settle their long-standing differences in the traditional way reserved for the burghers of Montpellier: a personal combat to the death.

Opening one eye, very slowly, Joseph saw that long strips of grey light had begun to grow between the cracks in the shutters. Pushing his feet down in the bed as far as they would go, he stretched until his spine was sweet and humming. No one else in the room seemed to know that the day had come and so, closing his eyes again, Joseph curled up and snuggled deeper in the cave of warm surrounding flesh.

His movements had attracted a large warm hand that now settled like a pillow on his stomach, pulled him deeper into the cave. He wriggled his shoulders so that he was squished between Maria's large breasts. Lying in this warm enclosing sea, he pretended he was a sailor, riding on the rising and falling waves of her breath.

Soon he felt himself drifting into sleep again. This was a morning sleep, unlike his night-time sleeps, into which he plunged so quickly that he knew only the feeling of Maria's hands drawing him into the feather mattress before fatigue sent him into a dark and mysterious country.

The next time he awoke, he was alone in his bed. He opened his eyes to see Maria sitting beside the window, now open, surrounded by yellow light as she held Sara, his baby sister, close to her breast in the circle of her arms.

The wet sound of his sister's nursing made him hungry. In the kitchen, he knew, there would be hot bread with apple cider to wash it down. This year, for the first time, he had been allowed to help with the pressing of the apples. Standing among the men, he had pushed the wheel round and round till the juice from the crushed fruit made sweet and sticky rivers between his toes.

It was only as Joseph's feet touched the floor and began the journey towards Maria that he remembered what it was that had kept forcing him back

262

into sleep. He stopped and rubbed his eyes; they were tender and swollen, as if they had been bruised each time his dreams had been pierced by his uncle's red and gapemouthed face, streaming with blood, sailing like a full scarlet moon across the sky of his sleep. Now more of the nightmare came back to him. Joseph, Joseph the dreamer, he was called. Last night he had dreamed his uncle was going to die.

It was Maria who had told him that after people died, their souls were tied to their bodies for fourteen days and fourteen nights while God decided where they were going to spend eternity.

During that fortnight, Maria said, the souls of the dead came to visit those whom they had known while they were living. To their friends who had been kind and gentle, the souls paid their thanks. But towards those who had been cruel, the souls of the dead could be cruel and spiteful in return.

Standing beside Maria, with one hand on her breast and the other on the face of his nursing sister, Joseph remembered one morning when he had come running into the room where his mother was sitting, and hurled himself into her lap, bursting into tears because just moments ago he had cut his legs while playing with the dogs.

"But Joseph," she had protested, pushing him away, "can't you see that I'm talking to your Uncle Robert? Run along now and find Maria."

That afternoon, when Joseph was supposed to be taking a nap, he had slipped out of his room and searched carefully through the maze of corridors until he reached the adults' bedrooms. That of Uncle Robert was one he knew well enough – it was utterly forbidden – and after Joseph had listened with his ear to the keyhole, the way he had seen Maria do, he crept inside and peed on the pillows of Uncle Robert's bed.

What a sweet revenge *that* had been. The impulse to burst into laughter had been so strong — but of course so dangerous — that he had had to hold his nose to keep from laughing, another trick Maria had taught him.

"Joseph!" Maria's voice was mixed with his sister's loud wailing, and Joseph realized that while worrying about his uncle and stroking his sister's face, he had somehow tugged at her ear and made her cry.

"Joseph." Already her voice was conciliatory and consoling. Her arm stretched out to him, drawing him closer, and by the time he was comfortably ensconced against Maria, his sister was contentedly sucking again.

That afternoon, Joseph sat in the courtyard with his father, watching him grind dried plants into powder. Around them were the walls and turrets of his Uncle François's wonderful castle, and laced into the October air were the mysterious smells of the kitchen.

While his father toiled with mortar and pestle, Joseph told him the story of his dream. Just as he was coming to the most frightening part, there was the sound of hoofbeats and a boy — older than himself, but still a boy and not a man — came galloping wildly through the open gate, his long black hair whipping in the wind.

One of the guards rushed forward to intercept him, but his father got there first, his giant hand darting out for the reins and pulling the sweating horse to a standstill.

Like his pony, the boy was covered in sweat and dust. And now Joseph recognized him: a month previous he had galloped in from one of the nearby settlements, his arm bound in cloth and bleeding like a slaughtered animal.

Now the boy was jabbering rapidly. Joseph, leaning close, unravelled the boy's patois to understand that his father had been crushed by an ox-drawn cart. A few minutes later Joseph was standing alone in the courtyard while his father, surgeon's tools in his saddle-bag, rode off with the boy.

The first time Avram had visited this tiny settlement, it had been winter. Freezing winds from the sea had swept the hill bare of all foliage and protection, and the view from the houses presented a barren prospect.

But the lush summer that had blessed the whole south had visited here as well: though the houses were only log-fronted caves dug into the hill, each one had its garden and its lattice hung heavy with swollen grapevines. Below, the terraced fields were still being harvested, but Avram could see that the wheat had grown thick and golden. At the end of the row of houses was a granary; outside of it, piled high, was the bounty that had already been gathered from the land. No wonder a man would want an ox to help bring in such a crop. As the boy had explained while riding, the cart had been loaded so high that the animal had staggered and fallen while climbing, for the fifth time that day, the twisted and stony path from field to granary. When the ox fell, the traces harnessing its broad neck to the shafts of the cart had snapped free, and the cart had tipped back, rolling into the poor man who had tried to halt it.

Now the injured man was lying on the litter they had made to carry him home from the field. Peeling away the blanket, Avram could see that the flesh on his side was a swollen and angry mass. It was amazing that he could still breathe because the ribs must surely have punctured at least one lung, and no doubt his belly was filled with blood.

The man himself was unconscious, his face white, his lips bloodless but parted slightly. There was blood on his tongue and when Avram turned his head, more blood rolled out the corner of the wounded man's mouth. Avram replaced the blanket.

"When did this happen?"

"I rode for you right away."

"Who carried him here?"

"I and my brother," the boy said proudly. "He has gone to get the priest."

Avram nodded.

"Are you going to operate now? I promised my brother that you would wait until his return, because he missed watching your operation on me."

Avram felt for the man's pulse, which was weak and irregular. The hand, almost lifeless, was covered with thick callus. The skin around his eyes was lined with fatigue, his bones were twisted to his work: to have lived even half his allotted span he must have been a powerful specimen.

"There will be no operation."

"He doesn't need one?" the boy asked. "We were sure such an accident would require an operation." The others, like curious but untamed animals, hovered at a distance, their anxious faces bobbing up and down.

"No operation," Avram repeated. And then, when the boy still looked puzzled he added, regretting the harshness as he spoke: "I thought you said you had sent your brother for the priest."

"I did — " And then the boy's voice broke as he understood. "The doctor says that my father will die," he announced gravely to the onlookers. "He says that it is fortunate my brother has gone for the priest, because the priest will watch over him as he dies."

Then the boy turned back to Avram. His eyes, Avram noticed, were the glittering black of gypsy eyes: they fixed on him the way a hunter's arrow searches out the heart of its prey.

"I will take you home now."

"Let me wait here with you, until the priest comes." Avram wanted to reach out for the boy, to draw him into his arms as if he were his own son who could be comforted. But the onlookers had come closer, to watch the drama of the boy becoming a man as his father lay dying beside him.

By the time Avram got home, the moon was high in the sky. A full harvest moon, it had loomed up from the hills as the sun was setting. Through the long twilight Avram had galloped, strangely nervous, plunging through shadowed valleys, then breaking out into the dying yellow light again, stopping only briefly at the forest stream before pushing on towards the main road and his own family.

Mist rose from the ground, gigantic trees that had stood since before the beginning of time were covered in rich layers of shadows and deep colours, the smell of summer still hovered in the earth. When he had fled Toledo he had had nothing to lose, only his own narrow life to save. But ever since his marriage and, even more, the birth of his children, it had seemed that he belonged to the earth and the earth to him, so that there was no sight nor smell nor sound that could not, in these sudden and crazy moods that came over him, make his eyes water and his throat fill with pain.

The last few months, this strange agony of happiness had reached a peak. But when his own best student had killed himself after he had been accused of making obscene drawings in a Bible, Avram had felt the shadows spring up around him, as if just out of sight, the walls of Toledo were rising again.

On de Tournière's advice, he had left the university. At first he had felt exiled. But now the daily excitement of caring for those who had never even seen a doctor had become a new enthusiasm. And meanwhile, unknown to anyone, he had completed and locked in a trunk the project that had gradually filled his workshop at the university, an illustrated textbook of anatomy. The detailed drawings he had so painstakingly made were based on the hundreds of dissections he had done: side by side he compared the organs of human beings and animals, so that the amazing correspondences of God's design could be seen. Sometimes, at night, he unlocked the trunk to inspect his book. For these pages he had lived his life, defaced the bodies of the dead, turned away first from Antonio, then from Gabriela. Twenty years of surgery and dissections reduced to a few dozen drawings.

As he came towards the château, twilight melted into night. The moon that had risen so swollen and yellow had contracted to a bright and gleaming ball, and the warm golden breath of day had been replaced by the silver sheen that spread now through the whole sky, a winter sky hanging above the still-smoking remnants of summer.

When Avram entered the dining hall, François Peyre was sitting alone at the long table. Despite the cool October air, he was wearing a sleeveless leather vest that left his arms and chest bare, so that although surrounded by mock-ducal splendour, he looked more like a labourer than a landlord. A handsome man, François Peyre, and it was said that in the winter season's parties, there was not a beautiful woman in the county who had not been invited, and accepted the invitation, to see past his fancy clothes to the well-muscled heart beneath.

Yet François Peyre was no eligible suitor. Every night the place at the foot of the table was elaborately set for his wife, Nanette. She, however, lived in the room to which she had confined herself since the stillbirth of her only child. "Crippled by a careless midwife," Jeanne-Marie had reported. For a year she refused to meet Avram, saying that she was ashamed of her infirmity. When finally he was presented to her, he met a woman who seemed large and robust, and though she remained seated, plying her needle the whole time, he still noticed that her ankles and feet seemed normally developed.

On the table, his brother-in-law had spread sheets of accounts. Although François, Avram was sure, could neither read nor write, he insisted on spending a night every month pretending to scrutinize the figures of the estate. Grumbling and sweating, he would stare intently at the numbers as if there were some secret that could finally be unlocked by sheer will. "Look at this," he would point out to Avram or Jeanne-Marie. "Whoever has written this has a hand like a moron's; can you read what it says?" And so forth until the whole document was committed to memory.

"It's you," he said now to Avram. "We thought you were going to stay out all night."

"I was waiting for the priest."

"When it comes to something you can't cure, you doctors always have a strange affection for priests."

"Everyone has his uses."

François Peyre laughed. "Father Paul will be happy to know you have finally decided to befriend him." François leaned forward. "And now that you speak

269

of priests, I am reminded someone else may be needing one soon. De Tournière sent a message tonight: Cardinal Velásquez is on his way back to Montpellier, and the combat is to take place the day after tomorrow."

"I will give Robert my dagger," Avram said. "It will find its way into Montreuil's heart easily enough."

"Forget the boasts about your Spanish steel. The court has said that there will be no weapons save truncheons."

François leaned back. His wineglass must have had a busy night; the huge pitcher he poured from needed to be tipped right over before it yielded.

"When Robert is killed," Peyre said, "the ownership of the estates will revert to Madeleine. And then, if Montreuil wishes, he could challenge her ownership on the grounds that she is still secretly a Jew. The council has specifically denied that section of his charges already, but in another week or another month – "

"I hear that they are allowing the Jews back into Paris."

"When it is a matter of lending money, yes," Peyre said drily. "But when it is a matter of collecting money, the Jews are still in exile."

"And so, my friend who is no longer a Jew, what do *you* intend to do if de Mercier loses?"

"I am still hoping the combat will be cancelled."

"Impossible."

"I have given all of our savings to de Tournière. He will offer the gold to Rodrigo Velásquez in exchange for our safety."

When Avram got to his room, Jeanne-Marie was already asleep. A slender candle had been left burning; its flame fluttered in the breeze that came through the half-open shutters, and in the shaky light Avram could see one of Nanette Peyre's most successful creations – a tapestry of a battle so gory that every single soldier was transfixed in spectacular death agony.

Sliding into bed, Avram opened his arms to Jeanne-Marie as she, still sleeping, moved towards him. For a moment her breathing grew more irregular, as though the dream that separated them was going to be broken. Then she took his hand, cupped it over her breast, and her breathing smoothed out.

Happiness: it had crept up and caught him from behind when he least expected it. Like sweet honey it leaked from his heart when he was with Jeanne-Marie, when the touch, smell, voices of his children lapped from their world into his.

As she turned to him he could feel her breath against his cheek. And then she was kissing him, softly around the eyes.

He folded his arms about her so that she was lying on top of him. He had blown out the taper, but his eyes had adjusted to the night, and the moon that had risen into the twilight was now directly over-head, sending long silver shafts of light into the room, spreading a grey sheen that turned Jeanne-Marie's face into a grey-silver statue, her eyes dark marble; even between the blankets the light spread, making a valley between her breasts, a long soft triangle that disappeared into the shadow of her belly.

Her lips on his now. When they were first married, he had still missed Paulette, and there were times when after his ritual nights of drinking with the students he would go to her house. But afterwards, he would feel not as if he had made love, but only that he had indulged in a sweaty but pleasant sport. And so his visits to Paulette slowed from every month

271

to every year. The final time he went to her room, he noticed that it was furnished with the kinds of trinkets that are bought cheaply at fairs, and the perfume that had once risen from her skin alone was now applied from a bottle, and mixed with the stale scents of other lovers seeking a night away from their wives.

Jeanne-Marie was kneeling above him, straddling him, her large eyes shining down on him as she searched him out, fitted him into her. And then she was bending down to him again, her black hair long enough to cover his shoulders and his chest.

"Do you think Robert will be killed?"

"I wasn't thinking about Robert."

"But maybe Robert was thinking about us, hoping we could help him."

Avram pushed the sheet away from his hips. There was a line of sweat where Jeanne-Marie's thighs had crossed his own, and now the cool air dried it, like a warning hand drawn across his skin.

"No one can help Robert," Avram finally said. "It was he who decided to try to take over Montreuil's lands, and once Montreuil sued him, it was the court who said that their conflict should be settled by combat. Robert knew he was taking that chance."

"But," Jeanne-Marie protested, "he only began to supervise the lands because the farmers hated Montreuil and were afraid of him."

"All farmers hate their landlords."

"You know perfectly well that Robert is not profiting by one sou. Anyway, if your student hadn't been caught with his stupid Bible, nothing would have happened."

"You're right. And if I could fight in Robert's place, I gladly would." Even as he said this, Avram felt depressed. The truth was that after three years he had begun to believe that the Montreuil lawsuit was a disease that had been cured. Now, it turned out, the disease was fatal: it had merely been marking time before making its final attack.

"Sometimes I wish you had killed Pierre Montreuil when you had the chance."

"I do, too," said Avram. "But if I had killed Montreuil, I would have had to leave Montpellier. We never would have married, never had Joseph and Sara —"

"I would have followed you. Anywhere."

Robert's trial, Robert's death: that was all they ever talked about. When Avram himself had been called to testify in the case of his student, Jeanne-Marie had ignored the event; and when he told her he was temporarily leaving the university, she said only that she was glad to be returning to the château where she had been so happy as a child.

"Tonight, when I came home, I talked with François. He says that de Tournière will be able to convince Cardinal Velásquez to call off the combat."

"De Tournière is sometimes the biggest fool in Montpellier."

Tears were beginning to slide down Jeanne-Marie's cheeks. Avram felt his throat blade with pain. Jeanne-Marie, who had lived her whole life inside a protected bubble, did not even know why she constantly cried these days: but Avram knew — it was because the bubble was about to burst.

"You," said Avram. "You, my wife, are known to be the woman with the most delectable pumpkins in all of Europe." He suddenly rolled her over and took such a bite that Jeanne-Marie shrieked out all her tension.

"Murdering bastard." Jeanne-Marie leapt on his

back and wrapped her arms around his throat. "Apologize or I will kill you in the name of my family. Do you surrender?"

"Never," Avram wheezed. He twisted and as Jeanne-Marie's grip loosened, he pulled her forward so that they were face-to-face, her arms still around his neck, his beard at her throat where he began to rub it back and forth until tears and laughter convulsively mixed together.

And then he was on top of her, sliding inside, his breath barely gained when she wrapped her legs around his waist and squeezed as the climax shot through her.

"I still can't stop thinking about poor Robert," whispered Jeanne-Marie later.

Avram was silent. Could you compare the death of Robert, who had lived a rich and easy life, to the death of a man who was crushed to death after thirty or forty years of toil and semi-starvation? But when Robert's time came, the trials of others would surely not console him.

"You have no pity, do you?"

"I don't know."

"You should understand these things," she insisted, "having been through so much yourself. Don't you think suffering makes one wiser?"

"Suffering makes me happy to have survived," Avram said. He took Jeanne-Marie in his arms, kissed her eyes, her mouth, the soft hollow of her throat where moonlight pooled like a silver coin.

TWO

FROM THE FIRST RINGING BLOW OF THE HAM-
MER, ROBERT DE MERCIER RECOGNIZED THE
SOUND. A FEW MINUTES LATER A SERVANT CAME
TO CONFIRM THE BAD NEWS. IN THE SQUARE OF
the palace of justice, only a stone's throw away from
the mansion of Robert de Mercier, a gallows was
being erected.

Until that moment, de Mercier had truly believed
the combat would be cancelled – it had already been
postponed for three years – and he had even heard
from Jean de Tournière, who was still, after all, not
only the chancellor of the university but the second-
ranked of the official physicians to the pope, that
Rodrigo Velásquez had arrived in Montpellier to settle the judgement in his favour.

But the sound of the first hammer was only the
prelude to a whole chorus of pounding blows. By
midnight de Mercier could see from his windows the
glow of torches in the square; finally, there were so
many that the noises of construction were drowned
out by waves of shouts and singing.

Unable to sleep, Robert de Mercier paced restlessly
through the halls. Exhausted, shaking with fear, he
tried to comfort himself first in his own bed, then
his wife's. But all night he stayed in that strange

zone between sleeping and waking, the zone that, he confided the next day to de Tournière, was a prelude to the Purgatory that awaited him after he was killed. When de Tournière replied that he must not be afraid of dying, and Madeleine insisted that he fight like a man, Robert found himself trembling uncontrollably again.

"Fight? I am sixty-five years old, fifteen years older than Montreuil. How am I supposed to fight a man in his prime? And do you suppose that I have ever even struck a blow in anger? Me? A merchant and a diplomat? Fighting is for children, for soldiers, for dim-witted fools who don't know how to use their brains instead of their thick skulls."

"But your brains haven't gotten you out of this, Robert," Madeleine whispered sadly. "And now we must obey the law."

"I hear Montreuil has been training the whole three years. He is like a little bantam cock, wanting to try out his spurs."

"Montreuil is half your size," said Madeleine, "and he is a coward. Spit in his face and the man will crumble without a blow. Then lean over him and thrust your dagger through the bastard's heart."

"Twist it," de Tournière added. "With a viper like that, the knife must twist so that the heart is torn to pieces."

"But," de Mercier said, "we aren't *allowed* to use daggers."

If only, Robert suddenly thought, substitution was allowed, if only Madeleine could be sent into the square to kill his adversary for him. No doubt, using her fingernails alone, she would have his eyes rolling on the ground before Montreuil had time to blink.

After dinner on the last night Robert went upstairs to compose himself. When Madeleine was finally

276

finished listening to her unending stream of minstrels, she came to his room and presented him with
the black hose, black stocking cap, and black tunic
she had made for him to wear in the morning. She
showed him the places where she had sewn in his
crest and initials.

"Don't you think this is distinguished?"

"Very distinguished," de Mercier agreed. He pushed
the costume aside, not wanting to see it. Morning
would be soon enough. "Do you think this is another
of your costume balls?" He was sweating profusely;
the stink of his fear filled the room. The previous
night had been destroyed by the ominous sound of
the rising gallows, but tonight, the eve of the actual
event, was quiet – as if the whole town were holding
its breath, eagerly waiting to see whose blood would
flow.

"They are planning on a great entertainment from
me tomorrow," Robert said bitterly.

"Not from *you*," Madeleine said. "Everyone knows
that you are right and that God will guide your hand."

"He will have to. Look." He held out his hand. It
began jerking about in the air as if it were having a
convulsion.

"You know, if our son were still alive, I believe
you would feel more confident. Perhaps if you could
pray to his spirit, you would feel better." She dropped
to her knees. "Will you pray with me?"

In the hall, de Mercier knew, was a priest she had
paid to spend the night outside his door, in case he
should have a crisis of faith before the dawn. How
ironic it was that she – the Jewess he had married
and on whose family's behalf this whole lawsuit had
started – was the one to be praying. Not only de
Tournière, but even the archbishop had testified that
there was no Christian in Montpellier more devout,

277

or more generous with her tithes, than the fervent Madeleine de Mercier.

On and on she droned. De Mercier held his hands out, watched them shake, clasped them together to gain control, tried to still the flames of fear that kept shooting from his stomach to his chest. Finally he knelt beside Madeleine.

"Mercy be to God," she whispered.

"God's mercy to me," de Mercier said.

He breathed deeply. His family had been traced back before the first crusades. Ancestors of his had ridden to the Holy Land. Inflamed by faith alone, they had swung their swords and lopped the heads from the brawny necks of the heathens. "Give me strength," de Mercier whispered. He closed his eyes, which were instantly sealed by tears. He would be humiliated in the public square and then they would hang his remains on a rope like a common criminal. He, Robert de Mercier, the last of his family and dead in disgrace. "God save me," he said sharply, "God give me strength to kill."

"Robert."

"God give my dagger strength, God give my arm strength, God help me smash my truncheon into the skull of the barbarian."

"Robert, God doesn't — "

"God doesn't what?" de Mercier had asked. Then he opened his eyes and saw Madeleine looking at him with an expression of such scorn, of such life-long contempt, that he raised his hand to hit her.

But Madeleine seemed so much more solid than himself that he simply lowered it again.

"You are gentle," she whispered. "God protects His saints."

"God makes His saints martyrs," Robert said. That was the trouble, he realized. He was willing enough to die, it was only that he wanted his death to be quick, and to take place in the merciful darkness of his own home. "All I ask," he said to Madeleine, "is to die here. Couldn't that be arranged, couldn't I die tonight? Couldn't de Tournière give me something – a potion, powders, anything – "

"Robert. *Robert.* I'll go to my room now, to leave you alone. The priest is in the hall. You will see him, won't you?"

"Tell him," de Mercier said, "that I want to meditate for a few minutes, to gather myself. Then I will call him."

"Remember, no harm can come if you are at one with God."

"Are you at one with God?"

"Yes, Robert, I have opened my heart to Him."

Madeleine, talking about her famous openings, reminded Robert of something he had read by one of the Greek philosophers: avoid desire, because the bonds of desire only tie you to the baseness of your own soul. He had not had much trouble in avoiding desire, but now the baseness of his own soul was presenting itself in any case. He wondered if his fear of death was not simply cowardice, but the absolute and true presentiment that he was going to die in the morning. The sun would rise and he would be alive. The sun would set and he would be dead.

When Pierre Montreuil dropped to his knees in the dirt of the Palace square, to offer his final prayers, Avram turned to look at Rodrigo Velásquez. Dressed in his scarlet cardinal's robes, crowned and bejewelled, he was mounted on a throne of kingly splendour. This throne was placed exactly in the centre of the pillars of the Palace of Justice. Surrounding him, on smaller but still elaborate chairs, were the

279

six chief consuls of Montpellier – merchants elected by their peers to be the ultimate arbiters of civil conflicts in the city.

Below the consuls were the family delegations, and like the consuls, each had its surrounding personal guard, its distinctive embroidered tunics and coats of arms. Seated on the descending ranks of stairs were the burghers of Montpellier, the chief artisans, the property owners. Crowded all around the square were more ranks of onlookers – so many it seemed that every one of the fifty thousand inhabitants of the city must have turned out to see the great event. So festive was this great occasion that pedlars had brought their carts to refresh the crowds. The smell of roasted nuts and millet was sweet in the brisk fall air, and puffs of smoke from the fires rose so prettily in the blue sky that as the two combatants readied themselves for the combat, it seemed they must be preparing for a dance, not a death.

Montreuil had gotten up from his prayers and was facing the centre of the square.

De Mercier adjusted his black stocking cap and pulled on his black gloves. Avram was holding the truncheon – it was as long as a man's forearm, weighted with lead. A blunt weapon: the nobles' idea of a joke upon the ambitious burghers. He tapped it against his palm – not something a man would want to be hit with – but not something that would easily kill.

De Tournière saw the two combatants making their last preparations. He turned to talk to the cardinal, Rodrigo Velásquez. Velásquez nodded to him, and stood so that the two of them could step out of earshot.

"Your Eminence," de Tournière said.

"Your Excellency," Velásquez returned. He was a man, de Tournière reflected, who looked more like a driver of oxen, which his grandfather had been, than one of the pope's most trusted cardinals.

"It is a pity that such a combat should be allowed to take place," de Tournière began, "with no benefit to the Church."

"The Church is pleased to see the king's will done."

"But surely it would be better for the Church if two taxpayers should survive, rather than one."

"It would be better," Velásquez agreed.

They had gone to the edge of the steps but de Tournière, even though he was now standing level with the cardinal, felt overwhelmed by him.

"And to think," de Tournière now said, "that the most likely victim of this barbarous exercise is Pierre Montreuil, such a loyal man to the pope but so tiny in stature."

"He is short," the cardinal replied, "but the snake who strikes from the ground is also short. No personal reference intended."

"Understood," de Tournière said. He wished that he had addressed Velásquez in Latin, a language in which such an expression would not have rolled so easily from the tongue. But Velásquez was not famous for his use of the holy language.

"The snake strikes from the ground," de Tournière said, "but the mongoose who masters the snake pinions his neck from above."

"Just so," Rodrigo agreed. "It will be, therefore, an interesting sport."

"But surely as servants of the Church we cannot allow men to sport with one another's lives. After all, it is commanded, 'Thou shalt not kill.' "

"Yes," Velásquez said, "I am aware of the commandments. Is it not also commanded, 'Thou shalt not steal'?"

"Of course. And yet, if you were to step out into the square right at this moment and, instead of giving each man the blessing of the Church, were to announce that the case had been settled, and that de Mercier, to keep peace in the community, had agreed to cede the lands he owned to Montreuil — "

"He should have done so in court."

" — and also," de Tournière continued quickly, drawing now from his cloak a velvet sack of gold almost the size of a man's fist, "if he were to make a gift to the Church, directly to yourself, that is, to make use of as you see fit. . . . "

Rodrigo Velásquez extended his hand; de Tournière watched as his large and hairy fingers wrapped themselves round the black velvet like a tarantula's legs. "A gift to the Church," the cardinal said, "is always appreciated."

He bowed to de Tournière, who watched as Velásquez, in his red ermine-trimmed robe and flat cardinal's hat, descended the steps to the square. There he stood for a moment while the crowd fell silent, no one failing to notice that this large and majestic man looked infinitely stronger than either of the combatants.

"The pope sends his greetings to the Christians of Montpellier, and on his behalf I would like to thank those who prayed and left donations at the church this morning." He held up the bag of gold that de Tournière had given him. "Even the most humble gift does not go unappreciated." He paused. "There will be a service later today in memory of those who died in the pope's struggle against the English heretics. In the meantime, having waited long enough, may I commend to you the spectacle of justice that we have all been awaiting. May the hand of the righteous one feel the strength of God in helping him to

282

strike down the enemy. *Pax vobiscum*." And then, waving the two men towards him, Rodrigo Velásquez added, "Will the victor have enough mercy to allow me to administer last rites to the vanquished. *Requiescat in pace*."

Rodrigo Velásquez stepped back so suddenly that Robert de Mercier was slow to realize that the contest had already begun. Montreuil, too, de Mercier saw, was surprised. As Montreuil turned to watch the cardinal retreat, de Mercier had a tremendous urge to throw himself upon his tormentor right away, smash his skull with the truncheon.

His arm tensed, his grip on the truncheon tightened, he began to shift his weight forward. He could imagine the shocked expression on Pierre Montreuil's face as he looked up to see the club descending on his skull: the eyes would skitter in fright, the skin of his narrow forehead split open as the truncheon hit home. Like a stuck pig he would bleed until the entire square was clotted red. Robert took a deep breath. Then Montreuil turned back to face him, eyes popping with fear.

Robert looked away from Montreuil, who was as frozen as himself in this blinding sun, to the steps where Velásquez and the consuls were sitting. He, too, had once been a consul: until he had strained his finances by over-investing in the fleet of Juan Velásquez, he had been one of the richest men in Montpellier. Now he was in debt to Velásquez: his brother, the cardinal, had come to watch the debt be collected.

"Pig," de Mercier said.

"What?"

"The cardinal is a pig," de Mercier said, in a low voice so that only Montreuil could hear him. Absurd:

even now, with only a few minutes to live, he was afraid to offend.

"Fight," shouted someone from the crowd.

"Cowards," came another.

"Fight," cried the first voice. "Fight, fight, fight." Other voices joined in; soon thousands were chanting and rhythmically clapping their hands.

Robert de Mercier lifted up his truncheon, holding it in front of him like a wand, like the sceptre of a king welcoming his subjects. And then, finally, Montreuil moved. Holding out his own truncheon as if it were a sword, he jammed it towards de Mercier's stomach.

De Mercier saw it coming, he had time to think how ridiculous it was that Montreuil, who had wanted this all along, was as fearful as himself and was reduced to behaving like a schoolboy pretending that a stick was a sword. And in the same moment some dim memory of his own school-days came back, the afternoons he had spent with the fencing master, and in a sudden move his arm slashed down to parry Montreuil and then thrust forward so hard that he lost his balance as his own truncheon smashed squarely into Montreuil's face.

There was a roar from the crowd. "Mer–cier, Mer–cier," they were now chanting. And when he recovered his balance he saw that Montreuil was on the ground, blood coming from his mouth. "I've won," he said aloud. And then he shouted it out: "I've won!" He turned to the steps of the Palace of Justice, waving Velásquez forward so that he could bless Montreuil –

But Montreuil was on his feet again, the crowd was roaring *his* name, and de Mercier could see that blood was pouring down his chin.

"Careful," Robert said. "You could get hurt." He extended his truncheon once more, ready for another clash. But Montreuil ignored it, he simply walked forward and tore it from his hand. And then, as de Mercier watched in amazement, his weapon fell towards the ground and Montreuil's club smashed him across his forehead. Covering his eyes, he fell to his knees, but even as he touched the ground, the club battered him on the back of the head and drove his face into the dirt.

The crowd's chanting had stopped. In the sudden silence came another – the sound of breaking bone as Montreuil, standing above de Mercier, swung his club into the poor man's skull.

The noise was so awful that de Tournière closed his eyes. When he opened them again, Montreuil was kneeling on the ground, trying to pry apart the hands of de Mercier, which had locked themselves in protection around his head. After hitting the hands with the club several times, with effect, Montreuil jumped high in the air and landed, knees first, on de Mercier's back. Now the silent crowd suddenly expelled its breath, as if every one of them had been attacked.

"Priest," one voice shouted. "Priest," others took up.

Again and again, Montreuil landed on the back of de Mercier. Gradually, in the silence of the crowd, it became possible to hear his moans.

De Tournière looked at Velásquez, who was staring fixedly at the two combatants.

Now Montreuil was himself exhausted, and was walking around his hapless victim, trying to figure out a way to finish him off. De Tournière saw his old friend's face turn; his moans had ceased, but he was breathing heavily. Once more Montreuil brought his knees down into Robert: the sound of his back breaking was like a branch snapping in a storm. De Mercier began to scream, long piercing screams that only grew more rending as Montreuil leapt upon him again and again.

The crowd was utterly silent. Finally Velásquez stood up and turned to the consuls. "Justice has been served," he announced, as if it were an epicurean delight. "It is time to use the gallows."

"Should we quarter him first, Your Eminence?" asked a guard.

"Is it in the statutes?"

"No," de Tournière interjected.

"Then slit his throat. I am tired of the sound of his complaints."

THREE

STANDING AT THE WINDOW OF MADELEINE DE MERCIER'S BEDCHAMBER, JEAN DE TOURNIÈRE COULD SEE THE DARK TREES ARROWING THEIR WAY INTO THE PURPLE REMAINS OF TWILIGHT. The evening planets and stars had already made their tiny punctures in the sky, and everything that could be seen was woven together by the last cries of the swallows. Like sentimental lovers they called from one shadowed tree to the next, the rise and fall of their woeful secrets piercing the night's cloth so perfectly that de Tournière found himself not mourning the death of Robert de Mercier, but simply thinking of the perfect balance of this world, the way God contrived to spin the wheel of beauty and sickness, of life and death.

"Jean, what will happen to us now?"

"I was just thinking that this will be my last autumn: this winter it will be time for me to die."

"You say that every winter."

"This time it's true," de Tournière said.

"You're going to live longer than Methuselah."

"I'm tired of living."

"Robert also said he was tired of living. But I've never heard a man scream more loudly at his death."

"Then you're lucky," de Tournière said drily, "because I have heard much worse. Robert died the death of a brave man, despite his screams. He even came close to fighting back."

"Close," Madeleine said.

"His spirit had been broken long ago."

"That is not a kind thing to say."

"It was not a kind thing to do," de Tournière said. Madeleine, the bitch, only she would have the gall to lie in bed, pampering a faked illness, while her poor cuckolded husband had just been tucked into his own final resting place, underground; no doubt Madeleine would start complaining about the weight of her fine woollen blankets at the very moment that the first worm began to eat its way through the wooden box that separated Robert de Mercier from the well-fertilized black earth of the Montpellier cemetery.

"It was very kind of the cardinal to come to the service," Madeleine said, her voice weaker now. That was her new trick: whenever de Tournière scolded her or made a sarcastic remark, her eyes filled with water and she changed the subject in a voice that quavered like that of a cringing slave. "And he, too, said that Robert was a brave and generous soul, who had gone to face God after fighting for his honour."

"The cardinal is a wonderful man," said de Tournière.

Madeleine shifted in her bed, drawing the oil lamp she had lit closer to her face. An unfortunate gesture, de Tournière thought, because the light no longer flattered the once-silky skin of Madeleine de Mercier. The planes and curves of the face that had once inspired sonnets by the dozen had become a field of deep furrows and scattered boulders. "I thought he was very gentle," Madeleine said. "He told me that he tried to convince the consuls to stop the combat,

288

but they refused, and that he personally would reprimand them to the pope."

"How reassuring."

"Jean, please come closer. Sit by me, please?"

He tightened his grip on his walking stick. He had been standing, hardly moving, for two hours now, ever since he had come from the funeral feast in the hall below to wish Madeleine good evening. She had sent a servant to fetch him, and he had contemptuously noted that even on the day of her husband's burial she was too weak to endure one moment of suffering alone. Even the presence of Velásquez at the funeral had caused her a nervous twitter of excitement – as if she had made a new social conquest. But, de Tournière knew, the funeral of Robert de Mercier was only the prelude to the death of all who surrounded him. Because despite the pretensions of civility, despite the crowds who had gathered to follow the brilliant and elaborate procession, the death of Robert de Mercier was not enough to purge Montpellier of the feud that had grown in its heart for three years.

"Why not?" Avram had asked, when de Tournière had explained this.

"Because only a great heart can contain a division between two loves. And Montpellier has the heart not of a great lover, but of a greedy shopkeeper."

"That is a strange thing for a man to say about his own city."

"It is," de Tournière had admitted, "but I would like to hear you praise the heart of *your* city, Toledo."

De Tournière walked slowly across the bedchamber of the newly widowed Madeleine de Mercier. Despite his age, there were still times when he could stand immobile and feel suspended in the happy weightlessness of a young man. But now, joints creaking with pain, balance all but gone, he had to lean on his walking stick and use it as a third leg to drag himself forward.

"Right here," Madeleine said, reaching out a hand and patting the bed beside her.

"You'll have to forgive me. If I sit, I can't get up."

"The servants will help you. Please."

Then her hands were suddenly around his arm, clawing to it like an animal terrified in a storm. "Jean, do you love me?"

"I am your most faithful friend."

"But do you love me, feel passion for me, want me madly? Would you kill for me?"

He looked down at her. Eyes wide, mouth quivering, she was perfectly serious. She squeezed his hand harder and he felt his heart squeeze, too, as if she would tear it right out of his chest.

"I would," he heard himself say.

"And even more: for the past twenty years I have lived only for you."

By the time de Tournière got down the staircase, he felt as though he was going to pass out. Eighty-one years old – what a disgrace to be alive. Sweating, seeing whole galaxies of stars every time he got up from a chair or even crawled out of bed in the morning, so weak sometimes that his legs threatened to collapse with the most meagre effort, what strange freak had God made him into? His oldest friend, the former archbishop, had died three years ago. Before his death he told de Tournière that living too long was caused by the unhealthy stockpiling of sexual fluids.

"Sexual fluids?"

290

"Semen, you idiot. If you don't make love, the body swallows its own unborn young and keeps itself youthful forever."

"We're not so youthful," de Tournière had pointed out, "only alive."

"Not for long," the archbishop had said. The cancer had been filling up his throat like a mushroom that had found a night to explode in.

"Anyway," de Tournière had said, "you're dying before me, and you took a vow of celibacy."

"Celibacy means not falling in love. But even the Church would not ask a man to retain the body's poisons."

"What did you do with them?"

"I got rid of them, you idiot. And I advise you to do the same, or you'll be alive until Judgement Day."

"But what did you do with them?" The question was too late. Right at that moment, as if to prove the efficacy of his own method, the archbishop had died. Without warning, expletive, or even a final coughing fit. De Tournière had had to lie to the Church officials and say that he himself had given final unction and heard the old man's deathbed confession. *Requiescat in pace*, God save the old pederast whose last confession had been to boast over his perversions.

De Tournière had come outside himself again, eyes opened to see a sudden blaze of lights at the door, a rush of footmen and servants, the cardinal himself in formal red robe and jewels, carrying a sceptre and sweeping up the stone steps and into the midst of the funeral feast like a king paying a surprise visit to the peasants.

And worst of all, he was coming right towards him, his rank breath preceding him like the unlucky wind fronting a storm.

291

"Your Eminence," de Tournière muttered as the cardinal drew to a full stop in front of him, "what an unexpected honour."

"Your Excellency, the pleasure is mine, for I will soon have to leave Montpellier for Avignon, and I wished first to say goodbye to old friends."

"And where better for that than a funeral?"

Velásquez burst into loud laughter. "Chancellor, your wit is even larger than your purse."

Velásquez's arrival had been expected, but when Jeanne-Marie saw him enter, she could not help feeling that a new curse had entered this household. As soon as she had control of her own sudden panic, she looked about to be sure that her children were safely upstairs.

In the middle of the hall, tables had been piled high for the feast. Roasted meats and fowl, steaming tureens of soup, endless loaves of bread, and great bowls of vegetables were lined up as if the sight of the earth taking in one of their own had only inflamed the mourners' need to swallow the earth in revenge.

Seated on a raised dais were the six consuls who had ordered the combat. As Jeanne-Marie watched, Cardinal Velásquez mounted the steps to join them. With them, also, was her brother, François, and representatives from the Montreuil family. Now that the combat was over, it was time for the merchant community to again seal itself into a common front against the nobles who would tax them to the death, and the artisans and peasants who would divide them against each other.

"Look at Velásquez." Avram's voice filled Jeanne-Marie with sudden reassurance. "De Tournière told me that when he tried to bribe him to stop the combat, Velásquez practically tore the gold from his hand. Yet he did nothing, and now he is here to drink de Mercier's blood."

Jeanne-Marie linked her arm through Avram's and leaned against him for comfort. They were standing by the hearth, standing in the exact place that they had stood with Pierre Montreuil ten years ago. On that night the veins in Avram's temple had pulsed with anger at Pierre Montreuil, just as they throbbed now. "Is the cardinal such a bad man as they say?"

"Worse." Avram's beard was fuller than it had been ten years ago, and the black hairs were laced with silver. But his voice was the same: flat and deep and totally certain.

"You must be a very wise man to see into the heart of a cardinal of the Church."

"You forget, I was a witness before him at the tribunal this spring. And the cardinal himself is an old friend. I was once a guest at his home, in Spain."

"You have known him for that long? You never told me that before."

"A husband must keep some things in reserve, so that he can regain the respect of his wife."

"But to regain respect, first it must be lost."

He put his arm around her. Jeanne-Marie stood close to him, feeling so safe and sheltered in the lee of his body that the danger humming through the room reduced itself to a barely audible whisper.

"Come," said Avram, "We will go to pay our respects, and I will show you how well the cardinal remembers me."

She walked forward, her arm still linked through Avram's. A few moments later they were seated at the table, flanked by Montreuil's relatives. On Jeanne-Marie's right was Leonardo Montreuil, the astrologer. Years ago, when the two families were friends,

293

she had told Leonardo of a dream she'd had, a dream about praying to Jesus. Leonardo had laughed, saying that only Jews had such a strong passion for Christ that they dreamed their prayers.

Leonardo had grown old – the young man who had mocked her was now fat and half bald. But when he leaned to speak to her, Jeanne-Marie heard the same sly tones in his voice.

Across from them sat the cardinal himself. She had seen him at the tribunal and at the combat, but up close Rodrigo Velásquez was a different man. The face that at a distance was merely gigantic now over-whelmed by its size. A broad slab-like forehead, dark jowls that drooped like muscular thighs over his studded collar; bright black eyes exuding an almost hypnotic power and intelligence; lips surprisingly sensuous that drew back to reveal large teeth gapped like those of an overgrown infant. When he opened his mouth to speak his first word, Jeanne-Marie was sure that his voice would boom out and shatter the room. But it was soft and powerful, the purr of a king surrounded by his subjects.

"I never knew," he said to Avram, "that you had been so lucky in marriage. How fortunate for you. And," turning to Jeanne-Marie, "how lucky you must be to have married a man with such a distinguished background. The ways of fate are surely curious."

"It is a curious fate that brings us together again," Avram replied. His voice was full of hatred and Jeanne-Marie felt her heart seize.

But Velásquez appeared unoffended. Instead his lips parted even further into a broad and guileless smile. "It is the privilege of the Church to bring all men together."

"A worthy mission." For the first time in years Jeanne-Marie was aware that when he spoke French,

Avram was speaking a foreign language, and that he had a curious slowness and precision in French that he abandoned when he spoke Spanish. "It is therefore even more unfortunate," Avram added, "that Robert de Mercier is not here this evening to enjoy the full benefits of such a gathering."

At this the six consuls looked up, entertained not so much by Avram's wit, Jeanne-Marie thought, as by his foolishness in needling the powerful Cardinal Velásquez.

"Robert de Mercier has suffered justice under the law."

"A man of your excellent position must be an expert in the witnessing of other men's suffering."

"We have all witnessed too much suffering," the cardinal said. "Do you not agree?"

Though the veins of Avram's forehead and neck were now standing out like knotted hemp, he did not reply. Instead, Jeanne-Marie saw his hand squeezing ever harder on the blood orange that he had been holding, until suddenly the skin broke open and the red juice ran down his hand and wrist.

Avram stood up, and the cardinal said something to him, quickly in Spanish, that Jeanne-Marie could not understand. Avram hissed his reply, then, helping Jeanne-Marie to her feet, made his excuses as if nothing unusual had happened.

"What did he say?" Jeanne-Marie asked later.

"He said, 'Don't injure yourself, my friend, that is an achievement that should be left to test the courage of your enemies.' "

"And what did you reply?"

" 'Unfortunately I am not blessed with brave enemies, only pigs and cowards.' "

"That was not a very polite thing to say."

"No."

"Is he one of your enemies?"

"Yes."

"Will we be forced to leave Montpellier?"

"I don't want to leave."

Now, in the night, she found herself possessed by fear. She began to gather the night noises together, hearing footsteps in the stone corridors, the muffled sound of horses. Guards were posted at night, but it was easy enough to hear their throats being slit in the random cries of birds. Until she married Avram, she had never slept in a room without servants to keep her safe. If she woke up, they were always there to reassure and comfort her. But she never dared to wake Avram when she found herself sleepless.

She took a deep breath. Her nipples were drawn tight and ached with fear. Father Paul had told her to pray when she was afraid, but she was no more capable of closing her eyes to pray than she was of climbing out of her bed, stark naked and undefended, to walk over to the shutter and close it.

The sound of her heart's beating grew louder. Some night in a future not yet dreamed of, she knew that the wind's sighs would become the breathing of men, and the shapeless sounds in the corridors, the birds' random calls, the shadows that threatened to become human – all would gather together to form the nightmare that her mind could not hold.

FOUR

WITH EACH LONG STROKE THE EDGE GREW
SMOOTHER, AND WHEN AVRAM FINALLY
HELD THE SWORD IN FRONT OF HIM TO
INSPECT THE BLADE, THE SUN'S YELLOW
glare ran like liquid down the fine and shining steel.

Between Avram and François was a whole arsenal of weapons: short, long, curved, straight, spears to be thrown from horseback, double-edged swords that would fell a running boar, crossbows that could send a bolt from the castle to the trees hundreds of yards away. All morning the scrape of oiled whetstones had buzzed through the courtyard. As they sharpened their weapons, François's two guards were modelling chain mail vests that had gone unused for years: groaning like old women wearing the corsets of their youth, they were fencing with one another, and the gasps of the restricted lungs mixed with the high, ringing sound of clashing steel.

From his bench, Avram could see Josephine kneading one of the endless loaves of bread that she baked for the household each day.

Since the funeral of de Mercier, five days ago, Josephine's prayers in the chapel had become so loud and so frequent that Avram was surprised to see her in the kitchen.

"Are you praying that God will lend us strength to defend ourselves?"

"No, I am praying that we will go to Heaven in spite of our sins."

Taking the whetstone carefully from one sword to the next, Avram found it hard to believe that only three years ago their situation had seemed so safe that he had dared to leave Jeanne-Marie and Joseph to make a trip home to Toledo.

"We have doubled the guard at night," François was saying, "and I have given the servants orders that no one but you and I may go out unaccompanied."

"Do you really believe Montreuil would dare attack us?"

"Not him alone. But Cardinal Velásquez travelled here with his hired guards. Those men, together with Montreuil's mercenaries – "

"And do you suppose we could resist such an attack?" But Avram knew the question was purely rhetorical. François talked about doubling the guard, but who could be pressed into such a duty? The tenant farmers were taking in the harvest; the priest was a round, weak man; the servants were completely untrained in the use of arms and could barely ride a horse without falling off; the only professional warriors were two veterans of the war against the English.

Peyre laughed. "Either we fight or we run. And if we run, with our families, our servants, our children, we will be fleeing without a sou, because no one would waste good money paying us for the lands they could simply take by force."

"But that is against the law."

"What an excellent devil's advocate you are, Halevi. But you know perfectly well that if we are excommunicated or, worse, declared to be Jews, then we are no longer entitled to hold land."

It had always seemed to Avram that François Peyre was an easygoing and optimistic man. Even now, as he outlined this increasingly hopeless prospect, he seemed cheerily intent on sharpening his swords.

"Do you want to leave?" Peyre asked suddenly.

"No."

"Are you sure?"

"If they attack us, we will resist them. If we do not fight them here, they will find us wherever we go."

"And now, my friend, are you becoming a philosopher?"

"Only a soldier," Avram said. He leaned forward and picked up one of François's swords. He was still holding the sharpened weapon in his hand, testing its weight and balance, when the rapid staccato of hooves announced a visitor, and the boy who had come to fetch Avram for his injured father swept into the yard. His face was covered with dust and his horse lathered with such a sweat that it might have been high summer rather than a November morning with a sun too weak to fully colour the sky.

"Today my brother is sick," was all that the boy would say.

When they got to the village, the boy dismounted outside of the entrance to his hillside cave.

"Where is he?" There were women outside their houses, cooking on the small fires that were dotted across the plateau fronting the houses, but there were no men to be seen; the fields were empty and the forest seemed curiously silent.

"In the house."

The door was a single great slab cut from a giant pine, hung from beams that had been forced into the hillside. The boy opened it and Avram stepped inside the cavern, momentarily blinded by the sudden dark.

As the door was slamming shut, Avram was aware of the unexpected smell of fresh soap. In front of him lay a boy on a pallet. Avram stepped closer. Without speaking, the boy drew back the blanket that was covering him, and Avram saw that below his right shoulder was a puncture wound, as if made by a spear.

"When did this happen?"

The boy shook his head, looked towards the door. Avram, suddenly smelling the soap again, whirled around. Pierre Montreuil was standing in the doorway, a broad smile on his face.

"He is a silent type by nature," Montreuil said. "That is the cause of his wound."

As he spoke, two guards appeared on either side of him, towering over him like generals protecting an infant idiot king.

"As you can see," Montreuil said, "for once I seem to have you at a disadvantage." He unsheathed his sword. "Of course, you seem to have forgotten your weapon, which is unfortunate. But you have also forgotten your wife, which is perhaps doubly unfortunate."

Avram stood with his arms folded across his chest. He had not worn his sword, but concealed in his tunic was the dagger he always carried, and one of his hands had closed around the handle.

"Well," Montreuil prodded, "where is your bravery now that you are without a woman to protect you?"

"Send your men outside," Avram said, "and close the door behind them. We will see who is brave."

Montreuil laughed. Avram's eyes had adjusted to the new burst of light from outside and he could see that Montreuil's cheeks were scarlet with anger and triumph. "Listen to the Jew bargain," Montreuil jeered.

300

"What does the rabbi have to offer? It shouldn't take too many shekels to save such a worthless life."

From outside there was the sound of horses. Avram turned his head to listen better.

"Listen well," Montreuil said. "To show you what a generous man I am, I have brought someone to help you spend your last night on earth, a priest to show your way to Heaven."

The horses had drawn up and there were scuffling footsteps outside, a groan. A slight figure was pushed into the doorway.

"Father Paul," Avram exclaimed.

"He was following you," Montreuil said. "He knows that the Jew doctor is the angel of death and that where you go, he will soon be required."

"I am sorry," the priest said regretfully. "Only this time, I didn't want the patient to die before I arrived. I thought I would come before they sent for me and so — "

"Don't apologize, Father," Montreuil interrupted. "There will be much use for you here, before your stay is over."

There was another round of shouts and hoofbeats outside, and then a new figure entered the hut – the boy who had ridden to get Avram.

"Monsieur," reported a guard to Montreuil, "he was caught trying to escape."

"Kill him, his use is finished."

The boy stood motionless and calm, his black eyes switching from Montreuil to Avram. The guards stepped forward.

"Leave him," Avram commanded.

"Listen to the Jew. First he bargains and next he gives orders."

"That is no reason to kill a child," the priest interrupted. "What harm can he do?"

301

"Take the boy outside and kill him," Montreuil repeated.

"No." In an abrupt movement Avram stepped forward and seized the boy, tearing him away from the guard and flinging him behind himself.

"Monsieur Halevi, stand aside while my servants obey my orders."

Avram withdrew his dagger. "Tell your servants to leave the boy, or they will have no master."

The two guards interposed themselves between Avram and Montreuil. Although they were both armed with swords and knives, they still faced him barehanded. He contemplated leaping forward to attack one of the guards, found himself hesitating. The thought raced through his mind that in Toledo he would never have hesitated, that twenty or even ten years ago he would have attacked without thought – and yet it was so long since he had fought that it was difficult to remember if he had really known how or if his past life was a legend he had invented.

"Step aside, Halevi." Without warning, one of the guards was upon him, a foot lashed out to kick the dagger from Avram's hand, and the strong hands of the guard were around Avram's throat. In a moment he was on the earthen floor, choking while his head was banged into the ground. Although Avram felt himself beginning to lose consciousness, he was aware of the boy being dragged past him, of a loud scream of terror.

Then he was suddenly raised to his feet and the guard dragged him outside, still with a stranglehold on him, and Avram saw that all the women and children of the settlement were standing in a circle. In their centre the boy had been flung to the ground, and his hands were being trussed behind his back. Seconds later a block of wood was dragged forward.

"Let this be a lesson to anyone who tries to betray me," Montreuil said curtly. While one soldier grasped the boy's hair to stretch his head across the block, Montreuil whipped out his sword and with a loud grunt brought it down on the boy's neck, half decapitating him. Montreuil next handed the sword to his other guard, who with a more powerful stroke finished his master's job.

Avram was dragged into the centre of the circle.

"Put his head on the block, and give me back my sword."

Avram felt the still-hot blood of the boy rubbing against his neck and throat. His hands had been tied behind him, and he was lying belly-down on the ground, his head arched uncomfortably upward onto the wood.

"Tell me, Jew, what bargain would you like to make?"

Avram's eyes were open and suddenly Montreuil's face came into view. It was contorted beyond recognition, a murderer's face scarlet with rage and the thirst for more blood. He saw Montreuil raise the sword above his head: as the steel swished down, Avram's eyes closed and the world went black.

From the wood there came the sound of a sharp tearing crack as the grain yielded and the block split in two. For a moment Avram thought that the sound of the wood cracking was the sound of his own spinal column being severed. Then, as his skull bounced with the force of the blow, he thought that his decapitated head must be rolling on the ground and that he was, crazily, still alive, still seeing, still registering everything –

The sound of Montreuil's laughter cut through the scream he had not even realized was coming from his own mouth.

"Jew, your pants are wet."

The guards suddenly hauled him to his feet and Avram, staggering, his hands still bound behind him, was left trembling in front of Montreuil.

"So, Jew, you are so brave, what are you going to do?"

Avram, trembling, lost his balance and collapsed to his knees.

"That's right, Jew, pray. Pray for your life or, better, pray for your death. Because, Jew, when Velásquez is finished with you, you'll wish that I had ended your life today."

Avram tasted the blood of his lip where he had bitten it in his fear. He was worse than the most cowardly Jews of Toledo. Like an old man he had lost control, fallen apart to fear, made a fool of himself in front of the enemy.

Montreuil held out his sword, still wet with the boy's blood, and wiped it against Avram's beard. "Feel this, Jew, feel the blood of the one who betrayed you."

Avram could not move. The fear, instead of leaving him as the danger receded, had invaded him so that he was absolutely paralyzed. Montreuil seemed to have swelled into a giant, and every one of his words was like a new wound.

"Goodbye, Jew, or at least goodbye for today. I am going to visit your wife, and I will tell her with what honour and brilliance her husband has acquitted himself."

Avram started to struggle to his feet, but Montreuil slapped the heavy sword against the side of his face and sent him stumbling back into the dirt.

The guards dragged him back into the hillside cave, threw him inside, and slammed the heavy slab door shut. He lay on the ground, listening to his own panting, the quieter breathing of the priest, the rising and falling breath of the brother of the boy who had been killed.

A few minutes later came the sound of Montreuil and his men rounding up their horses and preparing to depart. "Remember," he heard Montreuil tell the guards outside, "don't kill him. He is promised to the cardinal."

Avram dragged himself over to the wall and sat, his back against the dirt, head in his hands. Eventually he noticed the blood that had scabbed around his ear and neck: he reached up to find that the tip of his earlobe had been severed by Montreuil's sword.

"Excuse me, Master," said the priest, "if there's anything I can do – "

"No." Now was the time he needed the allies from his past: Antonio and Gabriela. Antonio would never have lost his nerve so easily. Antonio would not have allowed Montreuil to humiliate him in front of a whole village. He thought of Antonio spread-eagled against the cardinal's wall, Antonio begging to die. He had killed Antonio, but had he ever avenged him? Rodrigo Velásquez was still alive, more powerful than ever. And his brother had become one of the owners of the largest Spanish shipping fleet of the Mediterranean. So large and so powerful was he, in fact, that he could betray his former partners in the cloth trade, betray them and have them murdered, with no fear of reprisal.

"You're bleeding," Father Paul said, "let me bind it."

"It will be all right."

"Let me just the same."

Avram tore a strip of cloth from his tunic and handed it to the priest. His hands were quick and gentle, soft like a woman's.

"Is that better?"

"It is. Thank you."

"I saw what happened outside. You were very brave not to move. A lesser man would have jerked his head and been killed."

"A brave man would have killed Montreuil when he had the chance."

"And been killed himself? Surely it takes more courage to stay alive than to seek a foolish death."

Avram did not reply. Of course, the priest was right. Had not Ben Ishaq often told him the same thing? And yet where were Ben Ishaq and his mother – those founts of wisdom on how to live?

They were dead.

"Everyone says you are a brave man," Father Paul continued.

Avram shook his head.

"Did they kill my brother?" It was the first time that Avram had heard the wounded boy talk. His voice was young, unexpectedly vulnerable. Even in this village there was still, evidently, enough love so that one child was always the baby of the family.

"They killed him, yes." It was the priest who replied.

"My father died a week ago," offered the boy. "My brother took his place."

"Now you must take your brother's place."

"There is no one to be father to anymore, except my sisters. And they don't need me, they have my mother to take care of them."

"They will still need a man to keep them safe."

"I'm not a man," the boy said, "I'm only a cripple."

Avram stood up and went over to the pallet. He pulled back the blanket to look at the wound on the boy's shoulder. "It's not so bad," he said. "It won't leave you a cripple." Avram looked towards the hearth; but there was no fire left. With fire he could burn the edges of the boy's cut, make sure that the wound healed smoothly.

"It's not that," the boy said.

Fire: the word tugged at Avram's mind, made it fumble as he looked absently at the boy while he drew the blanket back further to reveal his whole body, his legs: one ended in a sturdy leather boot, the kind the peasant farmers wore. The other also ended in a leather wrapping – but there was no foot, only a swollen stump that was the thickened remains of an ankle.

"When I was a baby," the boy said, "they were going to kill me because it was such bad luck to be born imperfect. But my mother got me away from the midwives before they could cut my throat."

Avram was hardly listening. Instead he was craning his neck, eyes searching the roof of the cavern. Then he found it: a gap in the rocks where the smoke escaped. No light showed, but there must be a tunnel that would lead to freedom.

He looked around the room. There was a table, but even standing on it he wouldn't be able to reach the hole. The priest would have to let him stand on his shoulders and boost him to the smoke-hole.

"I brought food," the priest said suddenly. "Bread and cheese and wine." He reached into his robe and at the sight of the packages Avram felt a burst of hunger.

"Yesterday's bread," Father Paul said. "Josephine hadn't finished today's when I left."

Avram looked over at the boy: his mouth gaped with hunger while his eyes fastened raptly on the priest's beneficent hands.

"Let's eat," Avram said abruptly, "it must be time for dinner."

"For supper," the priest said. "Look, the light is almost gone."

Now Avram remembered that the hills faced west. The light that was allowing them to move about and see was actually the last light of the day. In an hour it would be dark.

It was the priest's idea to call in the guards after Avram escaped through the chimney.

"Too dangerous for you," said Avram. "I can go directly to the horses. The moon won't rise until midnight."

"Suppose the guards catch you."

"I would be as happy dying trying to escape, as dying at the hands of Montreuil."

"The cardinal," the priest corrected. "He is the one you have to fear."

"You admit that?"

"Of course. It is possible for the Church to be corrupt. Was not the Jewish church corrupt? After all, Jesus threw the money-changers out of the temple. Anyway," Father Paul said, "if you are killed, then you will not be able to save the people at — " He stopped. "Of course it is impossible that they would storm the château."

They were talking in whispers. Through the door's peep-hole they could see the guards sitting at the edge of the plateau, roasting meat over a fire.

"It *is* possible they went there today," the priest said.

"I know."

"If I hadn't followed you, I would have been one more person to defend the château."

Avram wanted to laugh. "How can you say that? You just told me that it is braver to live than to die."

"I followed you," the priest said, "because I wanted to see you do an operation. I have heard much about them, but never seen one."

"The sun's gone now," Avram said.

"Wait another hour."

Avram reached to take another swallow of the wine. *Wait another hour*. The priest was right. Either they were all dead, in which case it didn't matter how long he waited, or Montreuil had delayed his attack until the next dawn, which would be the logical time.

"If the guards come in," Avram said, "what will you do?"

"I will tell them that you are sick," said the priest, "and that you are lying at the back of the cavern, dying. While they bring their torch back to look at you, you will have a chance to bolt the door from the outside."

"Lock you in here?"

"And them." The priest smiled and from his robe withdrew Avram's dagger. "I hid this from the guards. Now I can defend myself."

The first time Avram tried to stand on the priest's shoulders, the table collapsed and the two men were sent sprawling onto the floor. When the table was reassembled, the boy got out of bed and propped up its bad leg with his good arm.

"Together we are one whole person," the boy said.

"Together we are one small circus," amended the priest.

With the boy supporting the corner of the table, the priest climbed once again to the centre. Then Avram followed.

"My father used to dance on that table. Don't be afraid."

The idea of the boy, who would certainly be killed when the guards came in, trying to give him the heart to escape surprised Avram so much that he could feel a sudden blush.

With a leap Avram reached the priest's shoulders. And then, while his human ladder shook and gasped, he reached to the roof, his fingers found a grip in the crevices in the stones of the smoke-hole, and he pulled himself upward. For a panicky moment Avram thought he would fall, the rocks were slippery with layers of smoke and soot. But after a brief scramble in which he felt his stomach give way as he started to slip, the rocks held and suddenly the priest's hands were on his boots, shoving him upward as he pulled himself towards the night air.

He was in the chimney itself when his elbow hit a thick metal object. Investigating, he felt a long curved shape; the chimney must have been a secret hiding place. When he pulled himself up onto the grassy top of the hill he was armed with a huge soot-covered sword, whose blade was dull but which was so heavy that the mere weight of it would crush anyone who got in its way.

He was gaining his balance on the hill when he heard the priest's shouting begin. Avram dropped to his belly and crawled forward on the grass, towards the lip of the hill, as the guards left the fire for the hut.

"What do you suppose they're shouting about?"

"Tell them to be quiet."

They stood for a moment outside the peep-hole.

"He's dying," cried Father Paul, "the Jew has poisoned himself."

"Let him die," called the guard.

"But His Eminence, the cardinal, wishes to see him. Quickly, come help me save him."

The first guard started to open the door. Avram waited. "Quickly, he's back here."

"Just a second," the other guard said. "We were told to keep the door bolted. Montreuil said he'd kill us if the Jew escapes."

"How can a dying man escape?"

The door opened and the first guard went in. Just as Avram was trying to decide what to do, the second guard raised his head and looked right at him. Their eyes were only a few feet apart. As the guard opened his mouth to speak Avram leapt downward and with all his strength rammed his black sword straight into the guard's face. As he landed on the ground, still holding the gigantic sword, he felt the guard's skull give way and split in two, like a nut cracking open.

Not daring to look down, Avram yanked out the sword and rushed into the cave. The other guard was just about to begin battering the priest's head into the wall when he turned to see Avram.

In the light of the guard's torch, soot and blood were mixed together on the peasant's heavy sword. As the guard dropped the priest and reached for his own weapon, Avram leapt forward again, thrusting the sword ahead of him like a spear, driving the tip deep into the soft triangle beneath the ribs.

FIVE

JEANNE-MARIE WAS THE FIRST TO SEE THEM.

SINCE THE EVENING OF ROBERT'S FUNERAL, THE NIGHTMARE HAD REPEATED ITSELF EVERY NIGHT – EVEN THE FACES OF THE RIDERS HAD BECOME familiar. And thus they were almost like old friends as they appeared single-file down the road, arrowing like ghosts through the dim grey-blue light that prepares the way for the rising of the sun.

"Avram." After returning from the village at midnight, Avram had stayed awake half the night with François, making plans. Now he was dead asleep, still wearing the bandage that had been put on him, the priest had explained, when he fell from his horse and cut his ear.

"I've warned you about riding too fast when you're tired – "

"I'm sorry," Avram had said, "I wanted to get back to you."

"Montreuil was here today," she had said. "He came to give us an invitation to his annual party. Perhaps he means to make it up with us. He said that, after all, we are still neighbours despite everything."

"Did he mention that he had seen me on the road?"

312

"No. Did you meet?" At this, Avram had only thrown a glance at the priest and François, as if such a stupid woman's comment was beyond even the most sarcastic response.

"Avram, they're here."

This time Avram sat bolt upright and then jumped from the bed, grabbing for his tunic and hopping comically into his leggings as he rushed to the window.

The air seemed to have darkened. For a moment Jeanne-Marie could believe that she had imagined not only the bruised colours of the sky, but the riders as well. Then they were visible again, they had only been momentarily shadowed by a dip in the road.

Avram was now buckling the peasant's sword to his waist. His tunic and leggings were, Jeanne-Marie noticed, filthy and torn. With his disreputable clothes, his huge weapon, the bloody bandage from yesterday still tied around his head, he looked like a ragged survivor from some ill-fated crusade.

"What do they want?" asked Jeanne-Marie.

"The children," Avram said suddenly, as if their existence had just sprung into his mind. As he turned, she saw that the veins of his neck and forehead were already throbbing.

She threw herself against Avram. One more time she felt his breath against her hair, his arms tightening around her.

"Go to the children's room," he commanded her, but he was dragging her with him even as he gave his instructions. "Lock the shutters and bar the door until I call for you."

From a window in the corridor the mercenaries could be clearly seen. They had drawn up at the gates and were spread out in front of them: a long thin line of soldiers looking like so many used coins in the dim light. And then there were shouts, not from

313

the soldiers they were watching but from the back of the château. As she turned towards the voices, Jeanne-Marie realized that another group must have scaled the back walls and were even now running through the courtyards.

"What are we going to do?"

"Stay with the children. They need you. And remember, don't let anyone in until you hear me outside." He pushed the door open. Jeanne-Marie saw that Maria and the children were up already, Sara was nursing and Joseph standing beside them, apparently oblivious to what was happening.

"Keep this," Avram whispered, "in case – " His lips were against hers once more, still warm with the heat of sleep, and into her palm he pressed a dagger. Her hand closed around it, sweating already.

Then he was gone. Jeanne-Marie forced herself to walk calmly to the door and put the bar into place. With the door and shutters closed, the room returned to night. Her heart was beating so loudly that even the sounds of fighting were sealed out. Gathering Joseph into her arms Jeanne-Marie felt for a moment as if their end had already come, as if they had all been transported to the deep silence of the grave.

Avram stood motionless in the hall, the initial panic fading and giving way to the beginning of the fear and paralysis that he had felt the day before, when Montreuil's sword had swept by his head. When Jeanne-Marie barred the door Avram turned to the sound, his mouth opening up to say her name once more. The choice abruptly offered itself: to stay with his family or to seek out the fighting.

Then Avram, sword in hand, heard François's voice calling from the central courtyard. Loud and mocking, it rose above the shouts of the soldiers as if the

314

very volume of his curses could deflate the enemies that surrounded him.

Turning away from Jeanne-Marie, Avram rushed down the corridor. To avoid being seen he descended by the back stairs: these took him through the servants' quarters, which were absolutely silent, and to a back door of the kitchen storerooms.

When he entered the kitchen itself, he walked into what he had escaped twenty years ago in Toledo.

The bodies of servants and slaves lay in a broken and bloody heap around the room. Josephine had been sitting at the table when she was cut down from behind, and now she was lying cheek down on the wood, arms flung out to the sides. A knife had been thrust through her back, pinning her to the stained oak like a carcass to the dissecting board. At her feet, sprawled on his back, was the priest. The knife he had tried to wield in Josephine's defence had fallen from his hand, and the curved slash in his throat leered up at Avram.

Avram stepped out the kitchen door to the central courtyard. There, lying twisted and broken in the dirt, were the rest of the servants, some wounded and crying for help. In the centre of the yard François was still standing. He and the two English war veterans had formed a triangle, back to back, and were fending off the swords of a dozen of Montreuil's mercenaries.

"Cowards!" Avram raised the sword he had found in the cave as the soldiers who had been surrounding François rushed towards him. With a great swoosh Avram slashed the sword through the air. And then suddenly he felt eighteen years old again, sweat bursting from his arms and back as he wielded the heavy steel with such ease that soon the entire battle was flowing around him, dancing to his rhythms, and one after another Montreuil's men either fell to the ground or retreated in bewilderment.

Once, twice, three times, his right arm found the chance that Antonio and Claude had taught it to search for. Three times his sword plunged in so deep that he could feel the life flee from his victim and the flesh sag into death even as his own weight was still bearing forward.

And then, suddenly, Avram was aware of a dusty silence. Avram looked behind him: no one but the dead and wounded – both Montreuil's mercenaries and the servants. Beside him stood François and the two veteran soldiers. In front of him were the open gates of the château, through which the remaining attackers were fleeing.

"Should we kill them or let them go?" François's voice was strong and sardonic.

"Let them go," said one of the guards contemptuously; as Avram turned to look at him the guard pitched forward, holding his arms across his stomach. Avram knelt on the ground and ripped off the soldier's tunic. The man moaned: through a slash in his mail armour, his intestines had started to ooze out like a nest of wet and shining snakes.

"Yes, let them go. That would be very generous." The voice belonged to Montreuil. He was standing, diminutive and unarmed, alone in the centre of the open gateway, dressed in a purple velvet tunic and the scarlet silk sash of the court.

"You forgot your sword," François jeered. From the hands of one of Montreuil's dead soldiers he pried a weapon, then threw it towards Montreuil. "Take this, so at least you need not die unarmed."

"Today," Montreuil said, "I need not die at all." He stepped forward and a dozen men on horses rode into the yard, surrounding the three defenders.

For a few moments everyone was motionless. Through a crack in the shutters Jeanne-Marie observed the frozen tableau: Montreuil the dwarf-conqueror posed between the gates; François, Avram, and the guard surrounded by the mounted mercenaries, like a neck waiting for the rope to be jerked tight.

Now Montreuil peered elaborately around the yard, counting both his own dead and the servants his men had felled. Even the wounded, Jeanne-Marie noted, took care to avoid breathing lest someone decide to test his blade on them.

"A quiet bunch," Montreuil said. "You have not shown my men your best hospitality."

"Pigs can fill their faces in the barn," François said.

Again the silence. Montreuil turned his head, slowly scanning the château windows. His eyes were seeking out tiny crevices and cracks. Jeanne-Marie stepped back from the shutters. In the closet, Maria was holding both children. The closet could be barred from the inside. When the time came, Maria would gag the children, Jeanne-Marie alone would be left to face whoever broke into the nursery.

"Your sister," Montreuil said, still addressing François, "must have told you of my invitation to our party tomorrow evening."

"She did."

"Yet when I come to visit you, she is nowhere in sight. Even your wife is hidden away."

"Perhaps they are still asleep. Your men" – he gestured at the bodies – "are very quiet."

"Very quiet," Montreuil agreed, and as he looked behind the defenders, Jeanne-Marie followed his eye to six additional men who had climbed over the back wall and were now standing awaiting Montreuil's orders.

317

"Brave man," François spat, "to fight his duels with the aid of an army."

"Not all my duels," Montreuil said heavily. He looked to the six men. "Find the women and children and bring them out. If they resist do with them what you like."

The men hesitated for a moment, looking around the courtyard for entrances into the château. Jeanne-Marie felt her heart accelerate until its beating was a stampede through which she could hardly breathe. The sun was now fully above the horizon, its great yellow eye bursting in her face.

"Now," barked Montreuil, and in a few seconds Jeanne-Marie could see the men no longer; they had disappeared under the roof of the kitchen.

"Maria, bar the door."

The closet was shut without further question, without kissing the children because she did not want to alarm them. As if, she suddenly thought, they would think it normal to be sitting in their own closet, gagged, with Maria holding them so they could not move.

"Now," Montreuil said. "The cardinal has requested the pleasure of interviewing Monsieur Halevi. Therefore, if you men will throw down your weapons and let yourselves be bound, I will give you my word that you will live and your lives will be spared."

"For how long?" asked François.

"I am not God," Montreuil replied. "I cannot guarantee your immortality, especially the immortality of Jews."

Jeanne-Marie heard the thunder of footsteps in the corridor. There were fists on the door, then boots and shoulders crashing into the wood. But the door held and there was a pause as the men conferred among themselves. Then the footsteps retreated.

Just as Jeanne-Marie was about to whisper something reassuring to the children, she heard heavy furniture being dragged through the hall, a grunt as it was lifted. It was suddenly too late to hide in the cupboard with the others. Jeanne-Marie held her breath to keep from fainting. There was a rush of steps as the men ran forward, crashing their battering ram into the door. This time the oak splintered; only the bar held the door in place.

On the next try, a crack appeared right down the centre of the door, and from the hall streamed in, sharp and sour, the odour of the men's sweat. For a moment it seemed as if they would not notice their success, that after two attempts they would give up and seek easier prey. Then with a sudden shout they rushed with such force that the hasps gave way and the door flew open. Jeanne-Marie was left standing in the open room, looking straight into the eyes of Montreuil's mercenaries. Without even thinking, she turned Avram's dagger towards herself, plunged it deep into her heart with all her strength.

When Avram saw the body of Jeanne-Marie held up to the window of the nursery, he felt a loud knock in the centre of his chest, as if his heart had suddenly emptied. Then, swinging his gigantic peasant's sword, he rushed the nearest horseman, who seconds later fell to the ground, his thigh hacked in two.

Avram vaulted onto the horse; he squeezed his knees into the compliant beast's flanks while he swung the sword crazily in the air, round and round in giant circles as if he would decapitate every one of the soldiers. Soon, as François and his guard joined in the fighting, horses and men were groaning in the dust of the yard.

Moments later there were more shouts as the men from upstairs rushed down to join in this new battle. François's guard was tackled from behind. François was surrounded by three men who had backed him into a corner. Montreuil had mounted his horse and with desperate cries was urging it towards the gates of the château.

Grasping the reins with one hand, still swinging his sword with the other, Avram urged his own horse forward. But it balked and almost fell over the bodies of two mercenaries. By the time it regained its footing, Montreuil was riding full speed away from the scene of the fighting.

On the mercenary's horse, a slow and clumsy beast that must have had oxen in its bloodlines, Avram followed as fast as he could. But he was losing ground and would have had to abandon the chase if Montreuil's horse had not suddenly fallen, sending Montreuil pitching over his head. When Avram arrived Montreuil was crumpled on the ground, moaning about his broken bones. His horse, somehow unhurt, struggled out of a hole camouflaged with branches and leaves and galloped towards home.

Avram dismounted and walked towards Montreuil. Montreuil twisted himself so that his eyes looked directly into Avram's.

"You're a doctor," he groaned, "I know you have taken an oath to help the sick — "

At a new noise, Avram turned. From behind a tree at the side of the road came limping the crippled boy from the mountain village. He was carrying a shovel over his shoulder and grinning. "My father always told me," the boy said, "that when you want to bury someone, first you must dig his grave."

"I command you," Montreuil croaked, "as your lord and representative of king and pope, I command you to deliver me from the hands of this Jew."

"My father also told me," said the boy, "that when you wish to kill an enemy, you must be prepared to crush him." Without hesitation he lifted his cast-iron shovel, then brought it down full force on Montreuil's unprotected skull. With a kick of his good foot, he rolled Montreuil into the pit he had dug in the road.

"The priest said it would be too dangerous for me to ride with him to the château, so I followed him on foot. This," brandishing the shovel, "is the only weapon I had."

Avram was swaying on his feet, and would have pitched over had the boy not caught him.

"Quickly now," the boy murmured, "we must hide in the forest until the men have ridden back. Then we will go to the château and the priest will tell us what to do."

But before the mercenaries returned, smoke rose above the horizon and its acrid smell drifted across the countryside. Then came the galloping of the mercenaries' horses as they travelled back, every one of them riding unknowingly over the grave of Montreuil, which the boy had re-filled and covered with leaves.

When Avram and the boy arrived at the château, it was almost twilight.

In the centre of the yard, bodies were piled, broken furniture strewn around them to fuel the blaze. Servants, children, soldiers from both sides, were being smoked together like animals being prepared for a gigantic feast.

Above them, whether left there by accident or by design, was the sole visible witness: Jeanne-Marie. Hung from the window by a rope, she swayed back and forth like a gigantic puppet, her dress billowing in the smoke.

BOOK IV

MONTPELLIER
1410

ONE

BY 1410, THE YEAR THAT ROBERT DE MERCIER WAS KILLED AND THE LIFE OF AVRAM HALEVI SHATTERED, FRANCE – ALONG WITH SPAIN, GERMANY, AND ENGLAND – HAD BECOME A dangerous place for its few remaining Jews.

But despite the successes of the Inquisition, the Christian religion was in a grave crisis. Since 1378, the papal schism had progressed from an accidental joke to a total disaster. The Christian world was becoming ever more frantic to heal the division that was weakening the power of the Church and threatening to turn its unquestioned authority over individual and state into a travesty too easily exploited by fanatics and reformers.

If neither pope would resign, how could they be gotten rid of The French government had attempted to besiege the Avignon pope and starve him into submission, but the manoeuvre backfired and Benedict XIII emerged with more determination – and popular support – than ever.

The Italian popes, meanwhile, continued to insist that they were the sole legitimate line. Financially and militarily secure, the Italian papacy was prepared to outwait its Avignon rival, no matter how long it took. This religious calm combined with the

*usual political chaos to make Italy the most tolerant
region in all of Europe. Despite ordinances against
the Jews, it was still a refuge for those escaping the
Inquisition elsewhere. It was also the place where
the great renaissance of the visual arts was to find
its roots – and its fullest expression. In 1410 the
birth of Leonardo da Vinci was still a few decades
away: but the movement of art towards centre stage
had already commenced.*

Yellow light splashed across the Piazza Maggiore,
the sun reflecting off the tens of thousands of new-
cut stones as if each were a shining facet in a huge
and glittering diamond, as if this jewel of Bologna
and all of northern Italy had the power to bend the
yellow rays until, like the astrologer's dream, it would
focus the power of the sun itself and become the
City of Light, the dazzling God-inspired prayer that
would suddenly cut free from its earthly base and
ascend straight into the heavenly eye.

From her place in the bankers' stalls, Gabriela
Hasdai de Santangel had a perfect view of the piazza.
Raised on a slight platform, she could see over the
heads of the hawkers and vagabonds who roamed the
crowd in search of a free meal or a dropped coin. In
fact, the only obstacle to her vision was the group
of merchants who surrounded her.

La Conduttrice, the Christian merchants called
her, though not to her face. This honorific was pronounced slowly, rolled down the tongue with a wink
and a nudge. *La Conduttrice*, the Driver, the witch
Jewess, had driven her first husband into the ground
and was now working on her second: León Santangel,
the dilettant scion of an old and honourable family.
The Driver, too, had a penchant for black-and-gilt
racing carriages in which she and her family sometimes careered about the city streets. Though never

on Saturday, because the Jewess kept the rules of her religion: every Sabbath she was seen walking from her house to the synagogue and back again, once even with tears streaming down her face. But the wink was always muted, the nudge only weak; because contempt for the Signora Santangel was mixed with fear, for Gabriela Hasdai de Santangel made her bargains with the force of an iron sledge smashing into its anvil, an iron sledge powered by the full weight of the great Velásquez empire.

To Gabriela's right, just beyond the merchants who were trying to convince her that their shipment of silk would arrive in time for them to pay off the debts they owed to Velásquez, sat her daughter, Sara. Thin and graceful, the seven-year-old had survived the typhus that had killed her brother when it descended on Bologna.

"Signora must understand," one of the merchants was repeating, "that we cannot guarantee the speed of one of our vessels. Perhaps it was delayed by the storms that swept Constantinople. If you foreclose now, before the season is over, we will be forced into bankruptcy. Signora, are you even listening to me?"

"Of course. Now tell me again what you wanted."

"Nothing, Signora. Our company wants nothing from you or Signore Velásquez, except the time to pay our debts honourably."

"Yes," Gabriela now said, "but the honourable time to pay debts is when they are due."

"*Signora*, I have explained already that the vessel carrying our goods has not yet arrived. When we can deliver them, then we can pay you."

"But how can I agree to accept payment when your vessel arrives, if you cannot tell me when that will be?"

The merchant was, Gabriela knew, one of those who felt free to defame her behind her back, then, minutes later, come sweating and begging for a new extension to his loan.

"Very well," Gabriela said, suddenly bored, "come back to see me next week."

Every Friday, before the Sabbath, she held court like this: seated on her raised platform, she heard the excuses of those who could not pay, the ingenious schemes of those who wanted to go into debt. Now Raoul Santangel, her husband's brother and an officer in Velásquez's company, leaned to whisper the particulars of the next case to Gabriela.

As he whispered, Gabriela looked beyond the petitioner. *Again.* For the second time that morning she was sure that she saw him. This time he was leaning against the pillars that lined the front of the Mayor's Palace, his face hidden in the deep shadows cast by the arcades. But when she tried to fix her eyes on him, he disappeared once more, and all she could see were indefinite figures moving about the ladders that supported the hundreds of artists – stonemasons, sculptors, painters – who were continually adding to and refining every nook and cranny, so that if the power of light did not make the city airborne, the thousands of depictions of saints, Virgins, and angels would guarantee the next best thing – a guided tour of Heaven's luminaries.

"Signora."

But now Gabriela *had* caught sight of him on the north side of the piazza, settling down on the steps of the San Petronio Cathedral. The steps were broad – as they should be for an edifice so huge that entire districts had been demolished to make room for it – yet the man on the steps had sat down casually and spread his long arms wide, as if he had found his own home. Beside him, half visible in the shadow of his cloak, hovered a young boy.

"Excuse me. I'll be right back. Sara, *Sara*, come with me."

Then she was on her feet, tugging her daughter by the hand and running towards the church steps. But once immersed in the crowd, she could no longer see; and by the time Gabriela reached the steps, the man was gone again.

"I thought I saw someone . . . *there*." Now he was in full view, standing in front of the most elaborately embellished building of all, the Palace of Notaries – the temple of money that completed the square of Church, political, and mercantile power.

"*Him*," Gabriela said. "I was sure that man leaning against the pillar was an old friend." But as the face came out of the shadows, Gabriela was no longer certain. The man was too broad, had too much grey in his beard, was dressed too filthily. In fact, as he drew closer, she saw that he was little better than a beggar. Only his walk was like Avram's: graceful and quick, it cut the distance between them in long strides.

Avram Halevi: it was a name Sara had heard often enough. And yet now that the stranger had actually appeared in her own house, the legend seemed even more mysterious. Avram Halevi: Gabriela had spoken of him as a powerful man, a giant whose tongue could wrap itself around a dozen languages, whose quick hands could dart in and out of the body, leaving only the tiniest of fast-healing wounds. Elegant, Gabriela had said: he had been so elegant that every woman in Toledo had been in love with him. Or at least, Sara knew, Gabriela must have been in love with him, because when talking of Avram her voice would grow soft and longing.

But this stranger did not resemble the man Gabriela had invented. Even bathed, Avram smelled of blood

329

and travel. His black hair was parted and hung down in ragged waves to his shoulders, his grey beard was long and twisted slightly to one side, as if it were avoiding something.

As for his son – Gabriela had never mentioned his existence – he was even more of a disaster than his father. With sandy hair unevenly streaked by the sun and a face tanned almost black, he was a skinny, cat-like creature who clung close to his father. Nor did his ears or voice seem to work: when Sara had, before supper, finally cornered him and asked his name, he had been unable to reply.

But perhaps this stupidity was a legacy from the father. For when Avram was asked, as the honoured guest, to make the blessing over the bread, the famous tongue gave a sibilant twist to the words, hesitated, then rushed over the conclusion as if deliberately slurring it together.

And as he ate, his fork trembled. How could a man with the shaking disease have been a surgeon? How long ago must it have been? Avram looked much older than either of her parents. The skin above his beard was brown and wrinkled, his forehead was drawn and lined, the backs of his hands were knotted with veins.

He had excused himself from going to synagogue, before dinner, by saying that he needed to rest. But rest had not helped – if anything, he seemed even more exhausted and distraught than he had been when they led him home from the square.

When the main courses were taken away, bowls of fruit were brought to the table. Sara watched as the stranger picked up an orange. His thumbnail, still dirty, dug into the skin. Then his hands twitched, as if with a life of their own. For a moment he held the orange helplessly in front of him. Sara looked across the table to the boy. Like everyone else, he was staring at his father, his whole concentration on the orange that quivered in his father's unsteady hands.

"They say it will be an excellent year for wine," León Santangel suddenly offered. "The weather has been so excellent, and the sun so strong, that the grapes are praying to be crushed and put into the vat."

Avram had reached into his tunic and drawn out a long and wicked-looking dagger.

"Signore Halevi, how is the wine crop in your region this year?"

But the stranger did not answer. Instead, his hands calmed and he twirled the fruit around in his palm while the tip of his knife was held to its skin. A neat orange spiral fell to the table. Sara leaned forward, gaping. Suddenly the stranger turned towards her.

"What is your name?" His accent was peculiar, but Sara understood him well enough.

"Sara."

"I had a daughter," he said. "She was killed. Her name was Sara, too."

Now the man's eyes had opened wider, focussing on her, and Sara felt herself being caught in the net of the legend.

"I'm sorry," Sara said. In her mouth the words sounded polite but useless. They were words she had heard León Santangel say once to a servant who was mourning the loss of a child.

"I'm sorry, too." Then he smiled and suddenly Sara saw that Halevi was young, after all. His teeth were white and shining, and when he smiled you saw not the grey and tangled beard but the jet-black hair that gleamed of soap and oil.

"May I offer you a glass of brandy?" León Santangel asked. "We are fortunate to have a cask of very fine

331

brandy here. It is a gift from the business partners
of my wife."

"A glass of Velásquez brandy? Yes, why not? Why
not a dozen glasses? Tomorrow will be time enough
to mourn; tonight I will celebrate my luck at being
among friends." And when the brandy arrived, he
raised his glass and said: "To my son, Joseph, who
has been so brave; and to Sara, may she be, like her
mother, as wise and as fortunate as she is beautiful."
It was the first time, Sara realized, that Joseph's
name had been spoken during the whole dinner. She
repeated it, Joseph, and as she spoke his name she
saw the boy had ears after all: they blushed a dark
cherry-red.

TWO

THE NEXT MORNING AVRAM WENT WITH THE FAMILY TO SYNAGOGUE. FROM HER PLACE IN THE GALLERY, GABRIELA WATCHED HIM SIT BESIDE LEÓN, SO CLOSE THAT THE TWO MEN'S shoulders were pressed together. When the rabbi came to be introduced to this stranger, Avram smiled and accepted the invitation, as honoured guest, to read from the Torah.

When he walked to the platform and bent down to the parchment, he looked so sincere and so humble that for a moment Gabriela almost believed in him again. He stood tall and handsome in front of the scroll, his ravaged face scoured with the grief he had suffered, with the witness he had borne to the suffering of his people; for a moment she almost thought that Avram had found the strength in his heart to accept his fate and be, if not a new Moses risen up to lead his people from bondage into freedom, at least a Jewish man ready to accept the bonds that tied him to his God.

He read the Hebrew words slowly, pronouncing them in the Spanish way and with great dignity. But then, at the end, when he turned to the congregation, he flung his arms open wide and Gabriela saw – who did not? – that beneath his silk prayer shawl he wore two gigantic knives strapped to his waist.

Only the rabbi, standing behind him, missed this. He stepped forward to Avram and put an arm over his shoulders. "You have suffered much," he said. "Rest among us in peace."

Afterwards León had told him that God did not like His children to wear their weapons when they worshipped Him.

"And I suppose," Avram countered, even while they were eating the Sabbath luncheon, "that God does not want His children to survive His enemies?"

At the table was another guest, a rabbi from Florence who was an old friend of León's father. He coughed, as if to speak, but León spoke first.

"God is the one with the strength. If He wishes you to live, He will keep you alive. If He wishes you to die, then mere knives will not protect you."

"Mere knives have protected me many times."

"I have never resorted to violence," León said smugly.

Gabriela, immobile, watched the children's eyes swinging from Avram to León and back again. In just one day Sara and Joseph seemed to have accepted each other, used each other to replace those whom they had lost. Now, like any children, they watched the adults curiously, alert to signs of discord or weakness.

"There have been many great warriors," the rabbi interjected mildly.

"And yet," León said, "the empires built by warriors have always fallen. Even Israel has been lost more than once."

Gabriela saw Avram's face seal over: perhaps he thought that León was a fool, and perhaps he was right; nonetheless, only Avram was stupid enough to show his contempt for a man who had given him shelter. Who did he think he was? A holy prophet that everyone would rush to admire? If he was thrown onto the street he would be lucky to survive a week – even with his shining knives. And when the news of what had happened in Montpellier made its way to Bologna, there was only one Jewish house in the city with power to protect him from the anger of Cardinal Velásquez; that was the house of León Santangel – the house of the partner of Juan Velásquez.

"Excuse me, Señor Santangel."

León's attention had swung to Joseph. The boy had spoken in Spanish and now blushed with his own audacity.

"May I say something?"

"Of course."

Joseph hesitated, his mouth working as if even the power to stutter in Spanish would be denied by his nervousness. "Señor Santangel," he finally said, "I am very fortunate that you have given me shelter here."

"It is my privilege," León said, and then reached for his glass, as if Joseph had only wanted to interrupt the conversation in order to express his gratitude.

"But Señor – if you were not strong, would we not be driven away from here, too, the way we were driven from France?"

León smiled. "I am strong, but all my strength is nothing in the face of the army of the city of Bologna. Or the army of the pope."

"Then we are here," Joseph said, "by their permission."

"Every man exists," said León, "by the consent of his neighbours. That is why we respect their rights, and they respect ours. That is the power of the law, and the law is more powerful than the sword."

Joseph nodded.

"Then Joseph must be wondering," the rabbi continued, "why his father, the honoured guest who is sheltered in this house, feels that he must carry his weapons – even in the synagogue, even in the house of his wise and gentle host."

As she lay in bed, Gabriela remembered well enough the look that had drawn itself on Avram's face: a dark and forbidding scowl slashed through by a sneer that tried ineffectively to be a smile. And then he had excused himself and gone to his room – the guest room given to him and Joseph – and had not come down until dinner time. Still with a face so dark and clenched that he looked like a man ready to die of his own private agony.

He had lost almost everything. That much he had blurted out to Gabriela as they walked from the piazza to her house. If Joseph had not miraculously survived, Avram said, he would have taken his own life.

"What will you do now?" Gabriela had asked.

"I have a plan."

But he had not revealed it to her. In fact, except for the brief exchange as they walked from the steps of the San Petronio Cathedral to her home, there had been not one instant when they could talk freely. The twenty-four hours of the Sabbath had passed encased in the rigid ritual upon which León insisted. The Sabbath guests, the meals, the prayers: the wheel of her life with León creaked and groaned with agonizing slowness. Avram had arrived and Léon had immediately given him his place: he slept in the room long ago furnished for guests; he sat on León's right in the synagogue pew purchased with Velás-quez gold; he prayed wearing the shawl once worn by León's grandfather, during the meals he was expected to converse with León and the scholars with whom León liked to decorate his table.

"Here in Bologna," explained León, "we live in a new age that Spain and France have yet to dream of. Beauty and the divinity of man's soul are what concern us here: there are more artists working here in Bologna, right now, than the rest of the world has known in its whole history."

"Most remarkable."

"I would be glad to arrange, with your permission, for your son to take lessons in drawing. His instructor would be a friend whom I value — Giovanni da Modena. He has been commissioned to paint the frescos of the great San Petronio Cathedral, and his studio is the most fascinating in all of Bologna."

In Toledo, where Gabriela had lived on the periphery of her sister's family, and had free access to Avram, she had pitied her friends who had to live within the constricted walls she had escaped.

Now it was she who was constricted. When she passed a silver tray of smoked fish to Avram, she could only smile at him; when León offered to have Joseph taught to draw Virgins, she could only glance at Avram across the table, let her eyes rest demurely for a moment, as if she herself were one of the Virgins; even when their sleeves brushed in passing, Gabriela could only continue on her way.

The first night of his visit she had fallen into sleep like a child, happy to know Avram was safe and close to her. But she had woken up in the middle of the night, certain she could hear the slow, patient slap of his sandals as he paced the stone garden below. At the same time she had heard her husband's breathing, felt the weight and heat of his leg, which he had possessively thrown across her. For three years – since Avram's visit to Toledo and the bitter after-taste of guilt and betrayal it had left – she had hardly thought of him. And yet now that he was back, it seemed those years had been without life or purpose.

The second night there was no sleep at all. After hours of trying to lie still, Gabriela finally swung out of bed. All day she had tried to find a time alone with Avram. Now if he was in the garden she would see him; if not, she could at least mourn him in peace.

In the corner of the room a night-candle was burn-ing. It cast a golden light on her skin, making it look, for the moment, tawny and young. Unused to noticing herself, Gabriela raised her hands protectively to cover her breasts. Against the far wall was a mirror, and she saw her reflection: in the dim light she looked like a young and shapely woman, coyly hiding her nakedness and her desire for the lover she knew was waiting for her.

Now she reached for her clothes: first a silk underdress that slid snugly over her, teasing at her belly and pushing against the nipples erect with the half-formed thoughts that were crowding into her mind. Then she put on a heavier woven-wool tunic. It made her shapeless again, a middle-aged woman. But still her long hair hung almost to her waist. Since her marriage to León it had grown thicker than ever, a glossy black streaked with a scattering of silver that she washed away with henna.

She pushed her hair back over her shoulders. Then, walking soundlessly in her bare feet, she slipped out of the door of her bedroom and stood on the balcony overlooking the courtyard.

He was sitting stone-still on a stone bench, his legs crossed under his robe and his palms folded together in his lap.

Again she felt a rush of desire. Avram. She *had* loved him truly. And why not, was he not a man worthy of being well loved?

Then she was descending the steps, one at a time. Avram swung his head towards her. Gabriela looked away, down towards her feet, which were flinching from the cold stone.

"It's you," he said.

Gabriela sat down on the bench opposite Avram. In this light, the light of a moon that glowed whitely from the scrubbed granite surfaces, the huge urns with their potted trees that stood at carefully random intervals through the yard looked like ruins from some old Roman graveyard. And in fact, according to León, the benches, the red-clay vases and urns, even the flagstones of the patio itself, were valuable treasures that had been found by excavators, relics from the time of Christ or even earlier.

"You left without saying goodbye."

"I meant to write," Avram said. "But now, even better, I am here myself."

"Even better," Gabriela agreed quickly. She could feel herself blushing. What had gone wrong with her? Her heart was pounding, with every breath her lungs caught tensely, her whole body was uncomfortable and almost writhing.

From the shadows Avram now leaned forward; his face entered a pane of white moonlight and suddenly it was framed, a prophet's face with eyes burning like coals, dark lips parted.

"Avram." Without knowing it she had moved forward to meet him, was kneeling on the floor in front of him, her hands on his thighs. They were thinner than they used to be, muscles like separate cords of iron, so cold they might have been carved out of the same stone as the benches. Then his hands were on top of hers.

"Avram." She dropped her head into his lap. His long fingers found the back of her neck, reached beneath her hair to touch the buttons of her spine. She could feel her breasts pushing against his legs. Desire exploded like a flower from deep in her groin. Avram's hands found her eyes, her cheeks, her lips. And then, just as she was sure that no force on earth could prevent her from drawing him down on top of her, bringing his whole being into her while her husband slept only a few yards away, Avram spoke.

"Gabriela, I want you to help me."

"How?" she whispered.

"I want to kill Rodrigo Velásquez."

With his words, desire suddenly turned to fear. *As long as you take me with you*, she wanted to say. *Kill the cardinal and then we will escape together.* But her lips refused to open. Instead, for one second, she let herself dream of the unknown country where the man she had loved for her whole life might finally give his love in return.

"You know he is the one who has destroyed my life. He tortured Antonio. He organized the burning of Toledo. Then he caused the death of Jeanne-Marie and Sara. Surely it is time that these debts were repaid."

"And after?"

Avram shrugged. "No doubt his guards will take their own revenge."

"Perhaps we could arrange your escape," Gabriela said as casually as possible, laying out the thread lightly.

"I'm tired of escaping. The only reason I came to Bologna was to kill Velásquez."

"And how am I supposed to help you?"

"Velásquez is coming to Bologna next week, is he not?"

Gabriela nodded. Everyone knew that in one week a new chapel of the marvellous cathedral of San Petronio was to be consecrated. For the consecration the pope in Avignon was sending an emissary, his strongest cardinal, to join the emissary of the pope in Rome. In Italy the gesture was taken as the long-awaited admission that the papacy belonged to Rome, and that Pope Benedict of Avignon was at last ready to end the schism by stepping down. But who could not suspect that the eventual winner might be Cardinal Velásquez himself? A Spaniard with excellent contacts in both Italy and France, surely he was the logical candidate to be the pope who ended the schism.

"And what do you intend to do?"

They were still pressed together, almost intertwined. Gabriela held one of Avram's hands in her two smaller ones. The sharp edge of desire had receded but her body had already given itself over to Avram.

"I have heard León speaking of a reception," Avram whispered, "where the merchants of Bologna will welcome the great cardinal from Avignon to their city."

"And you want me to take you to it?"

"Exactly," Avram said. "You will take me as your guest and I will kill Rodrigo Velásquez."

"I hope you are planning," Gabriela said sarcastically, "to say a few last words to him, to make sure he understands who is taking his revenge."

"You're a fool," Avram said sharply. The hand she was holding squeezed hers so hard that she gasped. But Avram did not loosen his grip and Gabriela felt

341

the fingertips she had just so tenderly kissed quiver with eagerness to destroy.

"Avram, I *love* you. I want you alive."

"If you love me, help me to kill Rodrigo Velásquez. And then let me die. Because León was right: the life that has been saved only by violence is worthless."

Gabriela jerked free of Avram. His face had become the mask of a madman, carved equally by the murders it had seen and the murders it had committed.

"Did you love Jeanne-Marie?"

"Yes."

"And your children, too?"

"Yes. And it is for my children — for Joseph — that I am asking your help. I want you to keep Joseph with you after I die."

"If you love Joseph," Gabriela finally said, "and if you loved Jeanne-Marie — surely those loves are more important to you than your hatred for Velásquez."

"Joseph would be better off with you," Avram said flatly. "I am too bitter." Now his face softened and in the moonlight Gabriela could see a tiny silvery line of tears starting from each eye. "You promised. You are the only friend I have."

Gabriela watched the mask threaten to dissolve, then pull itself back into place. Somewhere, perhaps buried in bitterness or perhaps even watching her with compassion, the man she had once admired must still exist. "I will help you," Gabriela said. "But not at the reception: that would be too dangerous. I have a better idea. When Velásquez arrives in Bologna, he will be staying at the house of a Monsignore Spannelli, a Neapolitan who is very powerful here in Bologna. Spannelli is well known to the Velásquez brothers. I am familiar with his home because I was a guest there when I first arrived in Bologna.

"The house is surrounded by a wall, and the gate to the house itself is locked. But beside that locked gate is a narrow alley where a man could hide at night. If the man were to be there when Velásquez returned from the reception, he could kill him then."

Avram was silent.

"Avram, my plan gives you the opportunity to change your mind and live. You could start a new life here. Bologna has the best medical school in all of Italy; I am sure you are still a brilliant surgeon."

"No," Avram shouted. He stepped back abruptly, tripping over the stone bench and crashing into one of León's clay vases. It shattered loudly.

"A valuable piece."

Gabriela looked up. León was standing on the balcony. His elbows were propped against the railing as if he had been a spectator to the whole conversation.

"It was an accident," Gabriela said. "An argument among old friends. Perhaps we were intoxicated by the wonderful Velásquez brandy."

"I thought Spaniards were famous for their drinking," Léon replied equably, descending the steps. He put his hand on Gabriela's shoulder and she willed her skin not to cringe at his touch. After a moment she was able to put her arm around her husband's waist and pull him close to her.

"He has been too long away from home," Gabriela said. "Now that he is safe here, he will rest from his travels and become himself once more."

THREE

AS ALWAYS, EVEN WHEN HE SLEPT IN THE BED RESERVED FOR LESS SOLEMN OCCASIONS, CARDINAL BALDASSARE COSSA WOKE UP HALF AN HOUR BEFORE THE DAWN. BRIEFLY he lay motionless, reassuring himself that he had spent the night alone. Then he rolled out of bed and took the few steps to the prayer alcove, where he sank to his knees and began to say matins. At first his voice was slurred by sleep; gradually it gained strength until after a few minutes it became the voice that the cardinal's many admirers were accustomed to: authoritative and yet gentle, a voice that came from the chest and spoke the Latin prayers as words that had their own known and subtle meaning, a voice that rolled from one sentence to the next with the confidence of an orator but without the insistence of a politician; the voice, in short, of a man of the Church who was also an admired architect, a humanist, a soldier, poised between the love of power of the old age and the reason of the new.

When his prayers were finished the cardinal took off his nightshirt, a long ropy garment that still tortured his skin, and splashed cold water over himself. Then he put on a silk undershirt – surely a night of privation deserved a day of luxury – and followed it with the white robe he wore in the mornings.

By now the morning light was beginning to stain the floor of his cell. From further reaches of the mansion he could hear the noise of others awakening. Nonetheless his private garden was empty, as always, when reached it.

The morning had commenced with a sky of a delicate lemon colour, a veil spun so fine that the luminous blue peeked through like the hint of a vein pulsing behind the white skin of a beautiful woman. The thought of beautiful women temporarily distracted the cardinal. Again he reminded himself that for almost a whole week he had been chaste. In chastity, his father had always said, resided luck and good fortune.

It was, the cardinal reflected, an extraordinary morning. But if the weather was fine – had he himself not prayed for it? – so much the better. There was no beauty that was not enhanced by the sun: granite, marble, the intricacies of the new frescos, and most of all the spectacular stained-glass windows were at their best when the sun performed its wonders and raised them from mere beauty to harmonious perfection.

The servant had now appeared and brought, as always, a cup of broth and a bowl of cereal for the cardinal.

The broth was from bone marrow boiled with a touch of wine; the cereal reinforced with chunks of meat. Cardinal Baldassare Cossa plunged eagerly into his breakfast. Today he was to meet his great rival, a man who was supposed to be as great a *condottiere* as himself.

The man's name was Rodrigo Velásquez, trusted servant of the infamous Benedict, self-styled pope of

Avignon. When Velásquez, a few years previously, had come to Italy to visit the Italian Pope Boniface IX, the interview was so ferocious that Boniface had died three days later. Whether of suppressed apoplexy or of humiliation, no one could say.

Breakfast was taken away and replaced by a bottle of wine and the architect's drawings of San Petronio Cathedral. Cossa reached first for the wine. When he entered the service of the Church, the priests had told him that the man who begins the day in holiness has set out on the road to Heaven.

"I am not the sort of man to spend my whole life travelling," the newly appointed Cardinal Cossa had said, "but I shall make a little of the journey each day."

For twenty years the sound of stonemason's chisels had marked the rhythm of the city's days. And for almost half that time the cardinal Cossa himself had supervised the work: can a man who has tasted of wine and death and love be entirely ignorant of beauty? Trusting his advisers, he had hired the best sculptors and painters in all of Italy. And fending aside politics, revolutions, even a siege outside the city walls, he had made sure the work continued without interruption.

His supporters knew him as a man of the world who had chosen to lend his experience to the Church. It was only his enemies who accused him of being an ignorant womanizer whose personal life was a disgrace to the Church.

The mist had already burned away and from his garden the cardinal could see, unveiled, the piercing green of the hills that surrounded the city of Bologna. The day had now begun: turning to his steward, already waiting, he summoned his advisers for a final meeting.

By noon the burning sun had turned the lemon mist of morning into a molten gold. In the Piazza Maggiore pedestrians and vagabonds alike began to search for the cool shade of the arcades that fronted the Mayor's Palace and the Palace of the Notaries. Even above the bankers' stalls, awnings had been raised so that the merchants and their messengers could be protected from the heat.

Only the workers on the steps of the church were fully exposed to the sun. Wearing hats and white smocks, arms burned golden red by constant exposure, they were working at a furious pace to complete the Bible stories that were being carved onto the pillars. Normally these workers would have stopped for lunch and to avoid the heat of midday. But today there would be no respite until the cardinal had made his inspection and approved what had been done.

The cardinal, however, was still inside the church, talking interminably, as he had been for over an hour. The workmen, starving for lunch, ready to faint from the blistering sun, had been told that the cardinal was entertaining a most important delegation, a group of visitors who had come all the way from Avignon.

Certainly the cardinal and his guest had been wonderfully attired. Wearing the deep red robes of the cardinals' college, and the matching wide-brimmed hats, the two men had entered the church from a long and splendid carriage, which still stood at its front steps. They had been accompanied, both within the carriage and on foot, by dozens of councillors and soldiers. These now stood scattered in groups about the steps, while the cardinal and his guest had their private conversation inside.

At a hundred paces' distance from the carriage, shadowed by the deeply recessed arches of the Palace of the Notaries, waited Avram Halevi. Like the cardinals he, too, was dressed for the occasion. In his styled merchant's robe, with a black hat to shade himself from the sun, he looked like a prosperous Levantine trader. His beard was cropped close, a salt-and-pepper colour; the skin of his face and hands was burned by the southern sun; he had a curved hawk's nose with the skin drawn tightly over the narrow broken bridge.

Rested, dressed properly, subjected to a barber, he now looked like any of a thousand other well-off visitors to the city of Bologna. And in the company of Gabriela's most trusted coachman, he had spent the previous few hours on a walking tour of the quarters of Bologna. After showing him the endless squares dominated by churches, and explaining the towers that poked up in such profusion from the houses of the aristocracy, the coachman reported to Gabriela that Avram was absolutely uninterested in the history of her adopted city. Even the workings of its inner and outer gates had seemed of little concern to him. In fact his guest had only truly woken up when they walked through the merchants' quarter. To the coachman, this part of the city had always seemed the least interesting of all. Almost devoid of towers, the houses were surrounded by walled gardens so that the wealthy could protect their goods from the needy; in fact, in the opinion of the coachman, the merchants' quarter was even more boring than the quarter of the Jews.

But the Signore Halevi had insisted on retracing the route twice, once in each direction, and he had even asked in which house lived the merchant Spannelli.

The tour had taken so long that they had missed the arrival of the cardinals.

"Do you think the Christians will bring their Church together?" the coachman had asked. He had heard León Santangel predict this would happen.

But his guest had not answered.

"I hope they do not," the coachman said, in a low voice so that no one would hear. "If they are united, they will be stronger. And if they are stronger, they will persecute the Jews." In Munich, before his family fled, the Jews had been forced to wear a yellow wheel, the symbol of a gold coin, on their backs. The first time he had gone out walking with his sister, a gang of boys had chased them, pelting stones. One of the stones had landed directly on the wheel. Sharp-edged like a knife, it had cut through his cloak into his skin. There it had made a tiny scar, a small lump he could still sometimes feel when he twisted too quickly in bed or leaned against something hard.

Inside the cathedral, triple pillars mushroomed up to the huge and magnificently vaulted ceiling; it was as if the heart of the city had suddenly been cut open, revealing not blood but a cold and echoing silence.

Light tinted by the stained-glass windows pooled on the unfinished marble floor, illuminating great swirls and galaxies of mason's dust. Aside from the two cardinals there was one man to be seen in the church – the painter, Giovanni da Modena. For a month he had been working frantically to have his fresco completed for this visit; now the cardinals had arrived, but no one had thought to warn him of the exact day of their coming.

"Look at him," Cardinal Cossa said. Da Modena was high on a scaffolding, carefully detailing the hands of an adoring witness to the Crucifixion. "He has made so many Virgins that his brush knows the way without being told." He led Velásquez towards the

349

painting. "Look at the figures beneath the cross. One is beautiful, chaste, her arms spread wide to receive the truth of Our Lord. While the other, on the other side, is a crippled and ugly old man, an ancient husk of humanity ready for the grave." He put his hand on the shoulder of Velásquez. "I asked Signore da Modena to show these figures this way because they represent the depths of our struggle. The beautiful and chaste maiden is the true Church, waiting to receive her instructions from Christ. The old and empty man is the Hebrew synagogue, the worn-out bearer of God's truth that is now ready to be replaced by the Church." He paused, as if this idea – that the Church was the true successor to Judaism – was so original and powerful that it had been invented at this very moment.

"And yet," Velásquez said, "although there is only one Lord Jesus Christ, and one true Christianity, there are two churches."

"True." The Rodrigo Velásquez who had frightened Pope Boniface to death was nowhere in evidence today, Cossa reflected. First they had spent almost an hour exchanging letters and greetings from their respective masters; only now had Velásquez introduced the subject of the schism.

"One religion with two churches must be confusing even to the wisest of men," Velásquez said.

"Agreed."

Cossa noticed that Velásquez had now begun to sweat in the cool air of the church.

"It is said," Velásquez now ventured, "that you yourself wish to be elected."

"My name was put forward," Cossa admitted. "But it was against my wishes, and I am pleased to be the servant of Pope Gregory."

"And yet," Velásquez said, "it is more interesting to be master than to be servant."

They had sat down on a workman's bench and now Velásquez slid closer, leaning towards him. He was a big man, Cossa realized, bigger than he first seemed. He had heard that Velásquez, in his prime, had been a terror in the torture chambers of Spain.

Cossa nodded, but did not move back.

"You and I," Velásquez said, suddenly switching from Latin into Italian, "what do we know about books? I come from a family of merchants. My brother has a fleet of sailing vessels. And you were a sea captain yourself. We know this bickering is like a stupid family feud."

"You are right," Cossa said. "Does the man you call pope know this, too?"

"Everyone speaks of you as the Italians' choice for the next pope," Velásquez said. "And if this next pope, be he you or someone else, were to make certain concessions – "

"But," Cardinal Cossa interrupted, "it is your own star that blazes brightly in these heavens, Cardinal Velásquez. If Pedro de Luna were to meet an unfortunate death, you would surely replace him." Velásquez was now leaning so far forward that his face was only inches from Cossa's; and Cossa could smell the mixture of garlic and onions that floated on Velásquez's breath.

"Anyone can meet an unfortunate death," said Velásquez.

"Are you threatening me, Cardinal?" Cossa now had his hand tucked into his tunic, where a dagger was safely in place. "I have heard that your victims scream for mercy. But they are tied to the rack. I am not."

"And I have heard," Velásquez rasped, "that the Italians are too squeamish for the rack. Instead, in their great mercy, they simply allow their victims to fly like birds."

Velásquez was referring, Cossa knew, to the notorious story about Pope Urban, who had killed several dissenting cardinals by having them dropped repeatedly from ceiling to floor. Finally the last survivor, a Venetian cardinal in his eighties, had wheezed out: "But Your Holiness, has not Christ already died for our sins?"

Cossa stood up. "Why did you come to Bologna?"

"As an emissary of peace," Velásquez said, "and good will."

"Then," Cossa said, "if you wish to leave Bologna alive, I suggest that you remain peaceful."

Now Velásquez got to his feet. His face was a flaming scarlet, a deeper, bloodier red than even the most spectacular of the gifted Giovanni da Modena's representations. "I will leave Bologna when I please. And whoever wishes to stop me — " Velásquez extended his hands. They were enormous, wide-palmed, each finger like a rope ready to snap a man's windpipe. Cossa, even with his knife, stepped back.

"You are right. It is unfortunate we are not allies."

"Perhaps we could be."

"There are obstacles."

"Even obstacles do not live forever."

Cardinal Cossa laughed. No wonder Boniface had been frightened to death. This man was even more outrageous than he had been told. "My friend, you are truly a terror."

"But you are not terrified."

"No," Cossa said, "I am not." He motioned with his head towards the far wall of the church. And then he watched as Velásquez's eyes followed the direction of his nod. Standing insolently, with their swords unsheathed, were a dozen guards.

"Now we should make our final inspection," Cossa said, "because I am growing hungry and thirsty." Velásquez, he noted with satisfaction, was trembling with rage. "You see, Cardinal Velásquez, in my lifetime I have been both an architect and a sailor. In both these professions it is necessary to plan ahead, otherwise the unexpected storm can bring disaster."

"Remember that," Velásquez said. And then, suddenly, Cossa felt Velásquez's huge palm resting on his chest. His heart leapt uncontrollably.

"You are nervous," Velásquez said.

"No."

"Look," Velásquez commanded. He turned his hand for Cossa to see. A knife had appeared in his palm. Its flat blade had been resting, unperceived, against Cossa's heart.

"Kiss my ring," Velásquez said. He offered Cossa his other hand.

"Don't be a fool."

"Kiss it."

The eyes of Baldassare Cossa grew bright. In the semi-darkness Rodrigo Velásquez prepared to lash out with the knife. And then Cossa's eyes looked down towards the large cardinal's ruby that Rodrigo Velásquez wore on his wedding finger. There was a moment more of hesitation, but Velásquez knew he had won. And then Cossa's knee dipped, and his head bent towards the ring.

Velásquez felt the pirate's breath against his skin. Then Cossa was upright again, his eyes blazing.

"Now," Velásquez said, for he prided himself on knowing when to turn the knife and when to withdraw it, "I will do the same for you, because I respect you as my equal."

Velásquez flexed his own knee, and as his eyes let go of Cossa's and he bent his head, exposing his neck to the man he had just humiliated, he felt a sudden surge of happiness and danger. Like the stallions he had learned to break as a boy, like the heretics to whom he had offered a knife when their agony brought them to the breaking point, Cossa had become conquered territory.

"Friend," he said to Velásquez as they walked out into the golden sunshine, "my friend, perhaps your visit will prove to be fortunate for us both."

Cossa's guards were following them, but Velásquez was unworried; they had, after all, only seen two cardinals exchanging their respects after a private conversation.

For a moment, when they first stood on the steps, the bright sun was so fully in his eyes that Velásquez was unable to focus. But while Cossa was talking to his workmen, Velásquez noticed the crowd of the curious drawing nearer. As he and Cossa walked to the waiting carriage, his eyes suddenly locked on those of an onlooker.

"Halevi." The name blurted out. But there was no response. The man stepped closer and Velásquez saw that he must have been mistaken: the man was a merchant, not a doctor.

And besides, he knew the story of de Mercier's estate. Montreuil had been killed in a riding accident, true, but the captain of the mercenaries had also sworn that every one of the Jews had been destroyed, including the children, whose heads had been skewered to pikes as a warning to those who needed to be warned. As for the rest, their bodies had been too numerous to bury; the mercenaries had burned them instead. This Velásquez knew to be true because an east wind had carried the unpleasant smell

354

of burning flesh across the valley from the ruins of de Mercier's home to the door of Montreuil's, where Velásquez had ridden to console the widow and assure her that her husband had performed a valuable service to Church and state alike.

FOUR

FOUR

AVRAM LANDED ON THE GROUND LIGHTLY, BUT NOT ENTIRELY WITHOUT SOUND. AND THAT SOUND WAS ENOUGH TO START JOSEPH MOVING. PUTTING ON HIS CLOAK, the boy stepped to the window. He had a knife he had stolen from the kitchen, but the thought of actually plunging the blade into someone else's flesh only made him tremble.

Joseph stood on the ledge of the window for a moment. Then he saw Avram hurry out of the shadows of the Santangel stable and disappear around a corner. Without thinking, Joseph leapt. He landed heavily on all fours, banging his knee against the pavement. But he stood up immediately and began hobbling after his father.

After a few minutes Avram stopped outside a large walled house. Breathless, so frightened that his ears were pounding, Joseph crouched in the narrow alleyway. He saw Avram walk briefly back and forth under the garden wall; then suddenly Avram leapt high in the air, clinging to the top of the wall as his feet scrabbled their way up the stones.

Only yesterday, his father had taken him on a walk through this quarter. And passing this very house, Joseph had noticed a window open as a maid shook out the mattress. Now Avram could be seen approaching that same window. He pried one of the shutters open, then abruptly dropped into the room and out of Joseph's sight.

With every inhalation the cardinal's mouth opened wide. Sucking, gasping, and wheezing, Rodrigo Velásquez was journeying through the night.

Avram stepped closer and took out his sword. To kill was bad enough; even in revenge it was impossible to kill a sleeping man.

"Pig," Avram said. Velásquez only stirred in his sleep; no doubt the ghosts that visited Velásquez called him much worse. Avram raised his sword. Why be squeamish? If Velásquez woke up, he would only be harder to dispatch. "Pig," Avram said again. And then suddenly, a lump he had taken for a cloak piled upon the floor launched itself at him, silent, knife outstretched – a guard who had fallen asleep.

Avram fell to his knees. When the guard was almost upon him, Avram thrust the blade with all his strength into the exposed belly of his assailant. The man – but he must have been a boy, he was so light – emitted a short, high-pitched shriek. Avram bounced to his feet, the momentum of his attack carrying him forward, and, still holding the sword in front of him that supported the now-soundless weight, staggered to the window where he dumped the body into the street.

"May Christ forgive you."

Avram whirled around.

Velásquez was sitting up in bed, as calm and composed as he was in his own torture chambers. On his head he had placed his cardinal's hat and in his hands he held a large jewel-studded crucifix.

357

"Go ahead," Rodrigo Velásquez said. His voice had lost the weakness of sleep and was not the deep and gravelly voice Avram remembered well enough. "Kill me, Jew. But my death will not change your destiny. Nor the destiny of your people."

"And what is that?"

"Like all those who refuse to believe, your own destiny is to die and to go to Hell. That is no concern to me. It is the destiny of your people that I care about."

"Yes," Avram said. He balanced the sword in his hand now. Toledan steel, the best steel in the world. How perfectly just for steel fired in Toledo to rip out Velásquez's bowels. "Tell me," he said, advancing, "tell me how you care about the destiny of the Jews."

"The destiny of the Jews," the cardinal said, "is in their own hands. Either they will be swayed by madmen and demagogues like yourself, maintaining a fanatical and dangerous minority that undermines Christian society, or if they are more fortunate they will accept the fact that they have been misled by stubborn leaders and will convert to Christianity. Then in a few generations the Jews of today will be, like my own forefathers, the ancestors of Christian believers."

"A man with your wisdom should be pope," Avram said.

"He will be pope," Velásquez said, "if some fool does not first make him a martyr." He pushed back the covers and climbed out of bed.

"Don't move," Avram warned.

"Kill me. I am ready to go to my reward. But remember, if you kill Rodrigo Velásquez you will unleash the whole fury of Christendom upon your people."

"Your reward," Avram said, smiling because he had suddenly remembered an expression from his childhood in Toledo, "your reward will be to spend eternity with your feet in a dung-pile and your head jammed up the asshole of a camel."

"Kill me."

As he said this, Velásquez swung the heavy crucifix.

Avram tried to duck but Velásquez had taken him by surprise and the jewelled studs dug into his eye.

In a second the cardinal was on top of him, his huge hands wrapped tightly around Avram's throat, squeezing it while he lifted Avram's head up and smashed it again and again into the floor. "At least I have had one great privilege in my life," Velásquez said, measuring his words to the rhythm of Avram's skull crashing into the wood, "and that is the privilege of killing you with my own hands."

With one hand Avram pressed against his eye. With the other he worked his way into his tunic, finally finding the dagger that was concealed there.

"Halevi," Velásquez laboured, "die, die – "

Avram wrapped his fingers round the handle, then with a sudden burst of strength pushed the blade straight into Velásquez's heart.

There was a grunt as Velásquez collapsed. His throat filled up with blood. A last wheeze and a desperate sucking for air. His hands fell away from Avram's throat and Avram was pinned under the inert mass of the dead cardinal.

By now there was shouting throughout the house. Avram, unable to free himself from Rodrigo Velásquez's smothering weight, heard the door to the room open.

Arms reached down, pulled the body away.

Avram staggered to his feet, one hand grabbing uselessly at the insane pain of his ruined eye, the other still clinging to his dagger.

The men were holding lanterns and Avram, looking down, saw that the floor was covered in blood. His velvet merchant's cloak was torn and stained, Velásquez's nightdress was a sodden mass.

"Who is it?" a voice finally asked.

Avram backed towards the window, waving his dagger weakly to keep the others at bay. He remembered riding away from Toledo, the healing wind on his face. Now he would steal a horse from Gabriela's stables and soon Bologna would be only another nightmare that he had left behind. He swung one leg up onto the ledge. It was slippery with the blood of the boy who had been guarding Velásquez. A new and gigantic throb of pain burst through his eye. A hand grabbed at his arm. Even as he turned to slash at it, the knife fell from his fingers and he collapsed on the floor.

"Don't kill him," someone said.

The pain receded and he felt an enormous sadness. Then he fainted.

When Avram climbed in the window, Joseph had lost sight of his father. For a minute the boy stayed frozen, caught between fear and curiosity. Then, inching his way forward in the silence, he crept along the base of the garden wall until he was below the window into which his father had disappeared.

In the wall's shadow he heard the shriek of the guard as he hurled himself at Avram. And when the body dropped onto the road, Joseph retreated to the alleyway.

There, poised to flee, he waited until finally he realized that what had fallen on the road was not going to pursue him.

Then came the fear that Avram had been killed; yet he was not sure that the shadow had resembled his father's. Nervously Joseph twisted his stolen knife in his hands. It was unlucky to look at the dead.

He hesitated, undecided. And then he heard his father arguing with another man. The argument ended with a scream so blood-curdling that once more Joseph prepared to run. But the noise had brought others out of their houses. Like a demon that could be called forth at any time of the day or night, a crowd sprang from the darkness to celebrate the disaster.

Trapped, Joseph moved towards the unlucky house. From behind the garden wall came a red glow as dozens of torches were lit. In a few moments the crowd surrounded him and Joseph was enveloped in a sea of unwashed smells, long arms pushing and shoving, voices gabbling in Italian.

The gates were flung open and he was pushed into the gap. Lying on a stone slab in the courtyard, his red cardinal's hat placed on the bulging hummock of his stomach, was Rodrigo Velásquez. And on his knees beside him, held down by half a dozen soldiers, was Avram. No sooner had Joseph recognized him than he saw him take his hands from his face, shake off the restraints of his captors, and struggle to his feet.

Between his father's legs, Joseph now saw, stretched a thick chain connecting the heavy iron rings that had been placed around his ankles. And as Avram turned his face Joseph saw that half of it was covered in blood, as if an eye had been torn out and the socket was pouring forth everything it had ever seen.

"Father." The word escaped from him involuntarily. Not a shout, only a whisper. But the whisper was heard and the hideous face peered towards him. From the crowd erupted a chorus of shouts and jeers.

At that moment, Avram stood tall and erect, a giant avenging angel. The crowd surged forward, roaring, pushing Joseph with such force that he stumbled right into his blood-soaked father. The arms came down around him, surrounded him with the smell of death and violence. Then other arms dragged him away and threw him back into the street.

As the onlookers hissed and shouted, Joseph saw first the body of Velásquez, then his father – the dead and the dying – lifted into a carriage. The door was locked from the outside and whips cracked over the heads of the crowd as the horses began their journey towards the centre of the city.

FIVE

THEY PULLED HIM FROM THE CARRIAGE, AND THEN HURRIED HIM DOWN A CORRIDOR. EVERY STEP MADE HIS HEAD WANT TO BURST OPEN WITH THE PAIN OF HIS RUINED EYE. A door opened, a hand pushed down his neck, he was shoved forward and sent sprawling onto the floor. A damp sewer-like smell rose up and surrounded him. With every beat of his heart, every throb of pain, he wished he would die. There was no sound other than his own breathing. The hours passed and somehow the pain began to melt together, from one pulse to the next, until finally it was like a bitter sea: nonetheless a medium in which he could float and then, before he could stop himself, doze.

The next day he woke up with a new feeling in his gut: the sensation of a wire, long slack, having been pulled taut and alert again. Then he realized that the pain – having failed to kill him – had woken him up.

The cell was of stone: floor, walls, ceiling. The exceptions were the door, which was wood and metal, and so low that even a dwarf might have to stoop his way through it, and the window, which faced into a tiny courtyard. The stone was what he had slept on, what he breathed, what he dragged his chains across as he explored his tiny universe, what he leaned his back against when he was too exhausted to move.

To protect his wounded eye, now covered over and scabbed by blood, he tore a strip of linen from the shirt Gabriela had given him and knotted it around his head like a pirate's bandanna. For a few minutes it smelled clean: then the fresh odour of sunlight faded and like everything else in the cell, it assumed the dank and grainy odour of the stone.

His own breathing, the scraping of metal against rock, the subtler whisper of his clothes rubbing together when he shifted: all these collected into a chorus of waiting.

But nothing happened except that after a while the light faded and there was blackness again.

The second night he was sure he was going to be killed. Only a few days ago he had been bragging to Gabriela that he wanted his life to end, but now he sat rigid in the darkness, his hand going occasionally from the floor to the bandage.

Again he betrayed himself and slept. When he woke up there was a curious silvery shimmer in the air of the cell. For a few moments he actually believed that his misery was so great that God Himself had come to console him. And then he realized that it was only the first light of day.

The door swung open – but with no advance footsteps, so perhaps someone had been watching him for hours – and two bowls were shoved towards him. The door slammed shut. In one bowl there was a grey and rock-like loaf of bread. In the other, water. First he drank. Then he undid his bandage and used the rest of the water to wash the blood from his wounded eye. There was a moment when the pain returned in its original intensity. The eye throbbed, swollen hugely in its socket. He had operated once

364

on a diseased eye, removing it so that the spreading ulcer of the eye would not eat into the patient's head and consume the brain. He wondered if his own eye would resemble the eye he had extracted, if he would have to be strapped to a table while someone dug at his skull with a scalpel.

That night Avram woke up in blackness, strong voices resounding with the force of cannon in his mind, Old Testament prophets roaring in the desert of his dreams, giants so vivid that even after he was awake their battles raged on, voices and bodies smashing together while he cowered in the corner of his cell.

Every night the hallucinations returned. Sometimes, in his fear, he would try to cover his eyes. When that happened, his wound being touched, the cell would explode with vivid flashes of lightning.

Weeks passed, every night a torture. Once, washing the wound, he thought its size might be decreasing. The next day he felt a sudden movement: it was his eyelid, finally freed from the accumulation of caked blood, gliding over the surface of the damaged eyeball. He felt a strange sensation, as if there was a worm beneath his eyelid. Then he realized he was feeling the scar that had formed; the injured eye was blind.

That night, when he woke to his nightmares, he heard weeping from the adjoining cell. Avram crept close to the wall, pressed his ear hard against it. Who wept? "Gabriela," he roared. But there was no reply, only the continued soft-voiced woman's weeping.

The next night, and the next, every night for weeks, he would wake from his nightmares to hear the unknown woman's weeping. Gradually he found himself joining in, his own sobs first muffled and then finally, one night, unrestrained wails. The force of such crying made the lightning flashes of pain slash through his skull. But he realized the woman had heard him; her own wailing grew louder, joined his.

Avram embraced the wall, ground his face deep into the stones as he wailed, and with his eyes shut tight, he knew that the woman on the other side was pressing herself to him as he was to her. The damp smell of the cell was overwhelming; he felt as though he were being forced to drink in the misery and despair of the whole lonely city that had died here. He heard the woman gathering her breath through the wall, and then suddenly he was smashing against the stones, desperately pounding first his knuckles and then the bones of his own skull into the chinks. A loose pebble jabbed into his eye and he screamed with pain. The woman screamed with him, their voices fusing in the night: his heart opened in agony, he felt his blood flow together with hers, flow and scream with the voices of all the Jews who had lived out, like him, their dirty and degraded finale in this cell; the Jews who had been bound together and burned in the wooden shacks they themselves had built; the Jews who had been slashed to pieces by mercenaries; the Jews who knelt day after day, year after year, moaning out their terrified prayers to God.

"God," he whispered timidly. And then he heard a new and louder scream from the next cell. His heart shuddered and then, without warning, the blackness unlocked.

Avram turned from the wall. There was a ringing in his ears, a dizzy surge of fear and anticipation. "God!" This time his voice was a roar that filled the cell.

Again the silence. And then a new feeling: the sensation of fear replaced by sweet gold running through his veins. Now the sound of breathing again.

But not through the wall: this time beside him, around him, through him.

He fell to his knees, asleep instantly, his arms hugging the slab stone floor.

He woke in the morning with the taste of mortar on his lips. But the next night, when he began to weep, no voice answered his. When, weeks later, there was another voice, it was that of Gabriela.

She came in the door, stooping almost to her knees as she entered, then a brief cry followed by a perfumed rush towards him. In an instant he was surrounded by her: breasts, belly, hips – soft flesh cushioning him after months of stone. The smell of human skin, warm breath on his cheek, fingers caressing his own: she was crying as she held him but Avram felt as if God, in response to his plea, had led him from the driest of deserts to this fabulous oasis of his old friend Gabriela.

She pulled away from him, shaking, her face contorted with grief.

"What's wrong?" His voice croaked. It was the first time he had spoken since the night he had called out to God.

"Wrong?"

"You look so sad. Has something happened?"

"Nothing outside. No. I was only afraid for you."
She was standing so near to him that he could feel her breath on his face as she talked. Her hands were against his neck. His hands resting on her shoulders.

"I love you," she said.

Avram tightened his hands on the shoulders of Gabriela. He looked at his hands. His fingers and wrists were emaciated. He had called out to God, God had answered him; and now he was like one of those prophets he had always mocked. In payment, his flesh had been stripped away. Unlike the flesh

367

of Gabriela, which was soft and pliant under his touch. He pulled her closer, greedy for the heat of her breasts against his bony chest.

"It must be terrible," Gabriela said, her voice full of love. "Being here."

Her fingers twined into his hair. She pressed herself closer, the mounds of belly and breasts flattening themselves willingly against him.

"You've changed." She laughed uncertainly.

I've found God. Avram tested the words on his lips, but they would not come out. He took a step away from her, lowered his arms.

"I'm lucky," Avram said. "Before they destroyed Antonio they chained him to a wall and whipped him. I, on the contrary, am served bread twice a day and can even sit on the floor and eat it at my leisure, like a rich man." Over his wounded eye Avram still wore a bandage but through his good eye he saw well enough: Gabriela recoiling from his bitterness.

Another month passed before his next human contact. One morning the guards dragged him out of the cell blindfolded and marched him into a bathing room, where he was given a tub of hot water and told to clean himself. For the first time in months he saw his naked body. Bowed, scabbed, skeletal, covered with welts and scars he had forgotten, discoloured by rashes and blotches where his unwashed clothes had chafed. In a few months he had turned into a stinking old man.

After the bath he was given a robe and then a barber came in to trim his beard and hair.

"You shouldn't let it grow so long," the barber said. "It's not the style these days."

"I'll try to remember." When they had come to his cell and blindfolded him, he had expected that he was being taken away to be killed.

"You should take better care of yourself," the barber said. He touched the wounded eye lightly. "You should have come to see me when this happened, too. I could have sewn you up. Must have been a real butcher that did this. Looks terrible now."

He held up a mirror and Avram, before he could look away, saw his face: thin cheeks, hair dark and lanky, beard a dirty grey-white. His good eye was opened wide, expanded into a circle with the effort of seeing for two.

The other eye was closed completely, the lid drooping over it, an ugly red-purple scar right over his eyeball. He must, he realized, have closed his eyes instinctively by the time Velásquez's crucifix hit him, and the metal must have cut right through the eyelid to the eye itself. He turned away.

"Not a sight for women and children," the barber said.

Avram looked down at his new white robe.

"I'll give you a patch," the barber said. "Tell the ladies you're a sailor."

When the barber was finished, a guard came to lead Avram back to his cell; again he was blindfolded. But when they took the blindfold off, he saw that his cell had been furnished in his absence. Against the wall was a wooden platform with a blanket thrown on top of it.

As he moved to inspect it, the guard came in yet again, this time grinning broadly and carrying a huge tureen of thick broth.

Avram ate it so greedily that he scalded his tongue; he ate so much that his stomach expanded to a ball that protruded roundly from his skeletal ribs.

Then he was blindfolded once more. This time as the guard led him, Avram cunningly counted his steps and kept track of the turns. But when the blindfold was removed, he had only turned once, and the number of paces he had taken was less than two hundred. Yet in this brief distance he had travelled from his filthy cell to a richly appointed drawing room: when they pushed him through the door he was blinded by the bright light and tripped on the thick carpet. The figure of two hundred paces rattled uncomfortably in his mind. He had been humiliated: only a brief walk separated this palatial and dazzling splendour from his own universe of stone and filth.

For a few moments he was left alone. Then Juan Velásquez was standing in front of him, robust and bursting with health.

"Don Avram."

"Don Juan."

"Don Avram, you are looking remarkably elegant for a man who has spent six months in the dungeons of King Enzo's Palace."

Six months. He had had no idea so much time had passed.

"But then, while you were bathing, they showed me your cell and I was pleased to see that you were being treated with such respect. All things considered."

Now Juan Velásquez stepped forward. His face was rigid and controlled, the way it had been the night of Isabel's operation. "When they told me Rodrigo had been killed, I knew it must have been you."

"I am sorry," Avram said.

"But he fought for his life. Even at the end."

"He did," Avram said. They were standing in the centre of the room. He wanted to back away from Juan Velásquez, from his anger. He clasped his hands together, to keep them from trembling. "He was a brave man," Avram added.

"But you were braver." Velásquez spoke in a low monotone, a tone Avram had first heard when Velásquez told him that if a choice were necessary, it should be his son and not his wife who survived.

"Speak," Velásquez commanded.

"I am not used to speech."

"But surely you are not used to modesty, either. At least you can admit how courageous you were."

"If you want to kill me," Avram said, "I am ready to die."

"Is that what Rodrigo said to you, as he lay in his bed asleep? Did you hear him dreaming, as you planned like a coward to stab him, that he wished you would crawl through his window and put an end to his life?"

"No," Avram said. "Did your brother tell you that he was doing the Jews of Toledo a favour when he paid the peasants to storm the barrio? That he was doing my wife and children a favour when he withdrew the protection of the Velásquez empire from the de Mercier family? Or was that your doing, old friend?"

Velásquez stepped closer. His eyes were as black as ever, but around them Avram could see fine-netted wrinkles of age and sadness. "It was not my doing, *old friend*. I wanted to teach de Mercier a lesson, but Rodrigo was to stop the combat. He gave me his word."

"I am sorry he did not keep it."

"I, too, am sorry," Juan Velásquez said. "You saved my wife and my child; I bear part of the responsibility for the death of yours."

The wrinkles around Velásquez's eyes grew deeper and more complex.

371

"They died because they were Jews," Avram said.

Velásquez sighed. "It is a strange fate," he said suddenly, "to be born a Jew. I have always felt sorry for you Jews. You are like a town that is about to be deserted."

Avram heard Velásquez but could not reply. The darkness had unlocked only a few months ago; now, again, he had the unexpected feeling of unlocking and release. The room swayed under his feet. In the corners of his vision, shadows seemed to move. God come once more to answer a poor Jew in distress? Or someone different, Death, the one he had escaped so often, now here to take his turn?

"I suppose you think," Velásquez continued, "that because of my kindness you are still alive. The truth is that you are alive not on account of compassion, but because you are the living proof of Baldassare Cossa's innocence. If you were to be killed or to disappear, no one would believe that you had been anything but an assassin paid to eliminate Cossa's worst enemy, Rodrigo Velásquez. As it is, anyone can see that you are a Jew who killed my brother for your own motives."

"And what," Avram asked, "were you hoping for? A public execution to commemorate the memory of Rodrigo Velásquez? Perhaps you could have me burned alive on the steps of the cathedral, so that the Italians could learn how firmly the Castilians deal with their heretics. Or, so that Spanish horsemanship could be demonstrated as well, perhaps you would like my arms and legs tied to four of your pure-bred stallions, and Castilian knights, dressed in the most splendid colours of the court, could spur their beasts on so that my body is torn to the four winds. Or perhaps even that death is too noble for a poor Jew. After all, a refugee from an abandoned town shouldn't cause even a donkey to raise a lather on its Christian flanks. Maybe, like your esteemed brother, you'd prefer to see me chained to a wall, whipped – "

"Stop!" Velásquez shouted.

Avram, dizzy with anger and the sound of his own voice, obeyed. But his mind reeled on: hardly able to keep his feet he swayed back and forth, seeing only the blurred image of Velásquez, who was now holding him and shaking him by the shoulders.

Then his head snapped back. Once. Twice. He was sitting down now, Velásquez was standing in front of him, preparing to slap him a third time. Avram put his hands up instinctively protecting his injured eye.

"I'm your friend," Velásquez whispered. "I told you that I was in your debt. That night in Toledo, I promised to help you. And you said that when you spoke, I would hear your words. Now I know what you have to say. *Death*."

Avram shook his head. His skull ached with the blows.

"I could arrange something," Velásquez said. "I've explained why you have to remain in custody here, for at least a few months. But then you could declare yourself a Christian, and say that in your nights of contemplation you had finally conquered your own stubbornness and embraced the true God in your heart."

Avram took his hands away from his eye. The room was dazzling; the bright light was making his head spin. Suddenly he felt lonely for his cell; an intense wave of desire to be safely within it crashed over him.

"Listen to me," Velásquez continued, "if you become a true Christian, it would be the first step

373

towards your release. After a few months you would be permitted to teach again, perhaps even to do operations. What do you think?"

"No."

"You *must* declare yourself a Christian," Velásquez whispered, as if the idea might be more attractive if spoken more quietly. "It's for your own sake, don't you understand? If the town is being deserted, why not leave now?"

Avram said nothing.

"You used to be so ambitious. You used to believe in science and the power of reason. When you came to operate on my wife you were like a cocky young stallion in search of a mare. Would you not rather be a doctor, a professor at the University of Bologna, than waste your life in some prison cell, waiting for an angel to come and save you?"

The presence was in the room again, but whether it was God or Death was impossible to know.

"Your marvellous operations," Velásquez said. "Life in your hands. Surely you must want – "

Avram heard himself laugh, for the first time since the disaster at Montpellier. It was a harsh and cynical laugh, the kind of laugh he had often heard from men who hated themselves.

"You say you are in my debt, that you owe me the life of your wife and child. Now it is time to pay the debt; you are a businessman after all. And so you offer me, in return for your wife and your child, my own life. But business is business, it has its own rules, and so you insist that I accept interest as well: not only do I receive my life from you, but I receive my life reformed. A new man, born again into God and medicine. Surely you are being generous to a fault."

"And surely you," Velásquez returned, "are the

greatest and most arrogant fool I have ever encountered." He stood up. "Think about my offer. And remember: your knife is not simply a sign of your superiority, it is also a tool for helping other people. When you are not using it to kill them."

SIX

IT WAS THE LAST GASP OF TWILIGHT. ABOVE THEM THE SKY WAS A HEART-RENDING SCARLET, BUT IN-SIDE THE WALLED GARDEN THE AIR WAS STILL WARM AND RICH WITH THE HEAT OF THE AFTERNOON SUN. According to León, this year's spring was unu-sually beautiful; but León, enamoured of his own country, was always boasting that each season was extraordinarily poignant, each sunset more subtly layered than the last, each new wave of painting and sculpture the ultimate celebration of the human spirit.

His most recent passion was for furniture. Thus Gabriela was sitting on what León claimed had once been a Venetian doge's chair – a high throne-like wooden structure so ornately carved that even to rest her hands on its arms Gabriela had to risk her fingers in the mouths of sharp-toothed snakes. A position that was, she knew, only too appropriate: for oppo-site her, his own muscular hands folded into each other, occasionally twisting to whatever combina-tion of sorrow and rage, was Juan Velásquez.

They had been sitting in silence for almost an hour. Earlier, Gabriela had recited all she knew of the dead cardinal's role in the Montpellier affair: then she had summoned Joseph, who told what he had seen the night, six months ago, when Rodrigo Velásquez was killed.

"Now I am alone," Juan Velásquez finally said. The words were spoken slowly and for effect: words that had been repeated many times, like a prayer that is expected to gain God's ear. But the voice was genuine – a mourner's voice, low and rasping. From the moment Juan had arrived at the house, Gabriela had seen that his brother's death had been an unexpected and hard blow.

"You have Isabel, your children."

Juan opened his palms wide. "They are my family. Rodrigo was part of my soul."

"I'm sorry."

Velásquez laughed, an abrupt, harsh laugh that came from his old and vigorous self. "You are not sorry. How could you be? If Rodrigo had become pope, even Italy would have turned against its Jews." He lapsed back into silence for a moment. "When Isabel heard Rodrigo had been killed by her old friend and favourite doctor, she begged me to take no revenge."

Gabriela watched Velásquez's hands as they rose from his lap into the air. His fingertips pressed tightly together, opposing themselves with all his strength – the way his own heart must be opposed to itself.

"He gave life to my son. He took life from my brother. Is one worth more or less than the other?"

"He wanted to die," Gabriela said.

"To die? No, Rodrigo did not want to die, he wanted to become pope."

"Avram wanted to die."

"Then he should have killed himself, not someone else, not my brother."

Echoing from the kitchen Gabriela could hear the raised voices of the cooks as they worked through the drama of their daily squabble. The meat had been placed over the fire to sear, now the smell of singed flesh filled the garden.

"Of course Rodrigo was correct," Velásquez suddenly said. "In one world there can be only one faith."

"A faith in humanity," Gabriela said.

Velásquez laughed, another sharp bark.

"But you must believe that. You have, after all, protected me all these years. You have even protected Avram."

"I am a merchant, not a priest." Another silence, only his knuckles interrupting it as they cracked. "For my brother I felt love, for the brave Señor Halevi, admiration. When he opened the womb of my wife, it was an act of courage. He knew that if she did not survive, neither would he. But then to attack Rodrigo in his bed, trying like a hired assassin to kill him in his sleep: that is surely the act of a coward."

"Or a man driven insane."

"*Insane.*" Juan Velásquez spat out the word. "When has Avram Halevi been anything but insane? He dared to travel to Montpellier to learn his surgical wizardry. He dared to operate in the houses of Christian merchants. He preached to all who would listen a gospel of science and a changed world. When he escaped the massacre at Toledo – killing two of my household – and went to Montpellier, he even became a professor of the religion he had invented, gathering students about him who worshipped the obscenities that he preached. Yes! Rodrigo told me everything about what this man did. And then your friend, my friend, Avram Halevi, decided that he must go even farther. Not only would he call forth the apocalypse of reason like some demented prophet, he would by his own hand change history itself. With his hand and his famous knife. But he chose to change history not by his miraculous operations – no, those

378

were the works of the child: the work of the mature man was something else. Murder. He killed, you will please remember, not only the man who was my brother, but a prince of the Church, a man who might have been pope.

"And the man who might have been pope, my brother, almost won the battle that he was forced to fight from his bed. Halevi survived, but he will carry the scars to his grave."

"And now," Gabriela said, "you would like to put him there."

"When Rodrigo was brought back to Toledo to be buried, six months ago, I was sure that when I came to Bologna this spring, it would be to see our friend Halevi killed. But six months is a long time, time enough to think. To think, even, of madmen. Halevi is mad, as you say, but so was Rodrigo. They were perfect enemies. I loved Rodrigo, but I hated him, too. He was right about the Jews – but he almost destroyed my city. He was a prince of the Church, but he was a prince of darkness, not compassion. He tried to bring the Inquisition to Toledo. If he had become pope, the Church would have been crushed, not healed."

He suddenly stopped and Gabriela felt, as Juan Velásquez caught his breath and sipped at his brandy, that the tenuous string of Avram's life might be snapped in this last uncertain light by a single cough from the mouth of Juan Velásquez.

"Today," Juan began again, "I went to see our friend Avram Halevi. I wanted to see him before I visited you, because I wanted my decision to come from my own heart, not be influenced by the kindness of my old friend and trusted partner."

"Was he well?" Gabriela could not help asking.

"He was well. I had paid a certain amount to Cardinal Cossa to ensure that he would be prepared for my visit. Cossa even gave me permission to offer our friend his freedom, on condition that he convert. And what do you think Avram Halevi said to this generous offer?"

"He refused it?"

"Yes."

"He is a fool," Gabriela said. But she felt herself blush just the same, as if she were a stupid young girl being told of the daring deeds of her secret lover.

"He is a fool," Velásquez agreed, but in his mouth the words were not the protest of a friend but a final and contemptuous judgement. "I will tell you," Velásquez continued, "that I no longer care whether your friend Halevi lives or dies. When we were young — twenty years ago — we all of us saw into the future. My vision of the future was a Mediterranean Sea criss-crossed with merchant vessels unloading their cargoes for the benefit of the Velásquez empire. Thanks to my vision, to your help, to the knife of Señor Halevi, I have such an empire and a son to pass it on to. My brother Rodrigo's vision was of a Church and world united in one faith. And if he died in pursuit of what he personally did not attain, he was at least a man who knew where he was going. But your friend Halevi? He had his own vision. He wanted to stop history, first as a scientist, then as a murderer. With his knife he performed miracles that even the ancients would not have dared. Today I offered him a chance to continue his work, to teach others, a chance to convert his dream to power, influence, even wealth."

The twilight had turned to darkness and in the corner of the garden, Gabriela could see that Joseph was sitting, immobile, waiting to learn the fate of his father.

"I will tell you something else," Juan Velásquez said. "A man in my position learns that he must know the hearts of his friends. The night I invited you and Avram to dinner, four years ago, I could see that you still loved him. Just as you love him even now."

Velásquez moved his head closer until Gabriela could feel his breath on her face. "Avram Halevi is a madman, but he is your madness, too. While we watch from safety, he is the dancer, dancing among the demons, dancing out our dreams. And so mad is his dance, so mad his separation from man and God, that when he dances we want to dance with him; and when he falls, we all fall down."

In the night Gabriela, unable to sleep, found herself thinking not of Juan Velásquez, but of an evening when she was still a child, and her love for Avram was still growing.

In Toledo, there had been a Purim festival every spring. To celebrate, every Jew dressed up in a mask and costume – men disguising themselves as women, women as men, boys and girls as famous characters from the Bible. One year Avram costumed himself as Judah Maccabee, the famous freedom fighter who had sparked the rebellion of Israel against Antioch.

Gabriela remembered her own costume: a tunic, tightly belted; leather leggings; and strapped to her waist a long wooden sword that threatened to trip her every time she ran. Like her, the rest of God's Mistakes were dressed as part of the rebel gang that surrounded Avram/Judah: even Antonio had joined in, taking the role of Bar Kochba – the mighty soldier so strong that with his powerful hands he could up-root trees while galloping on horseback.

Of course there were no longer any Romans in Toledo – though the old Roman circus still existed – so instead of driving out the occupying army Avram persuaded his gang that as a joke they should swoop down on the Purim celebration, wooden swords waving, and scoop up the great punch bowl to carry to their hiding place by the river.

That year Avram was a tall and skinny boy with a shadow on his upper lip: but with the help of charcoal he made the shadow grow into a heavy moustache. When Gabriela asked for her turn with the charcoal he held it back, laughing, saying she must play the part of his wife.

"Your wife! But I want to fight."

He handed her the charcoal, his palm casually open but his eyes fixed and glittering in the light of the fire, challenging her.

"Can't I fight and be your wife, too?"

Then the others surrounded them and whatever Avram had been about to say was drowned by their shouting.

But he *had* asked her: Avram, the wildest, the strongest, the most heretical young Jew in all of Toledo had declared himself to her. But the next day, when Gabriela told her sister, Leah only frowned and said that Avram Halevi would be a worthless husband.

"He's not worthless, he's a hero."

"No. A hero is a man who accepts the role that God has made for him."

"The Jews in this city are so fat and proud of themselves they *need* to be woken up by someone."

"By the right person, yes," said Leah. "But not by a foolish boy who is the bastard son of a drunken peasant soldier."

"Go to Hell," Gabriela had screamed, and run out of the house.

But now, thirty years later, who was to say what was right? Perhaps life *did* belong to the pompous and the cautious. True, Juan Velásquez professed to admire Avram – but from a distance, and with gratitude that Avram, and not himself, was the one to teeter on the brink of disaster.

But, hero or fool, Avram was still alive. And so was she, the wife he had never quite taken, her mind and love as fixed on him as always.

Hero or fool, Avram had risked not only his life but that of his son – *and* his hosts – by killing Rodrigo Velásquez. A risk that León Santangel had pointed out only a few hours ago as he drank from the new supply of brandy that Juan Velásquez had brought.

"Of course I forgive you," León had said. "I will even offer your friend the shelter of our home, once he agrees to Juan's proposal and is released."

"Thank you, but I assure you, he will not accept."

"It is not always easy," León suddenly said, "to be the husband of the most desirable woman in Bologna." And then he had swallowed down one final glass of brandy before turning on his heel and walking slowly upstairs to fall into the sleep that still claimed him.

Lying beside her husband, Gabriela could smell the brandy and the bitterness. Tonight they were equally mixed. Tonight he had had too much of both.

She got up from the bed and stretched. The weeks without sleep had made her feel twisted and old. When she saw herself in the mirror tonight, she saw not the young maiden hiding coyly from her lover but the old crone, hiding from herself.

From the bedside she walked to the shutters and peered out, wishing it was dawn. When she turned around she saw that León's eyes were open. He was, Gabriela thought suddenly, the kind of man Leah had always hoped she would find, the kind of man for whom happiness and comfort were ever-present twins.

SEVEN

SHORTLY AFTER THE DEATH OF RODRIGO VELÁSQUEZ, BALDASSARE COSSA ACHIEVED HIS GREAT DREAM AND BECAME THE ITALIAN POPE. BUT IT WAS FIVE YEARS BEFORE HE WENT TO VISIT Avram Halevi in his cell. "To think that you are my benefactor," he said. "To think that it took a Jew to kill Rodrigo Velásquez." Then he looked at Halevi carefully, almost lovingly, the way a hunter looks at a favourite battle-scarred dog. "I will keep you alive forever, for you are the living proof of my innocence."

Then he left the cell but for weeks afterwards there lingered a reminder of his visit, a strangely mingled smell of garlic and perfume.

And every time Avram heard the name of Cossa, this same odour would return to him; even from one year to the next, the memory did not diminish.

But how did one hear the name of Cossa? Most often as the butt of jokes. For the only significant act that he achieved as pope was the convening of the Council of Constance; and that council, after due deliberation, deposed and imprisoned him.

Next, from his cell, Avram heard that the council had also deposed Benedict XIII, the antipope of Avignon. Then the council proceeded to elect a pope

385

of all the world, a Roman nobleman named Odo Colonna, who became Pope Martin V.

This news and more Avram gleaned from Gabriela and Joseph, who came to visit him, from rare chance contacts with other prisoners, from friendly guards.

After the woman he'd wept with during the first months of his imprisonment, other neighbours followed. But there were long stretches when, with no visitors allowed him, the sounds of crying were, aside from the perfunctory grunts of the guard, the only human sounds he heard. And how vulnerable those crying voices were! As he listened to their soft and human tones, spilling out notes of loneliness and pain, Avram would feel his own loneliness spring to life, his need to touch and be touched. And while he listened, almost greedily he admitted to himself, from night to week to month the voices would change. For prisoners without Avram Halevi's influential connections did not receive a lengthy pension at the Palace of King Enzo.

But to each he listened, and for each he felt pity. Sometimes he even imagined their faces, the lives behind the voices. And when there was an old Jew who consoled himself with loud prayers, every night for two months, Avram learned to pray with him.

For a year he shared his cell with a cabbalist, who taught him how to use Hebrew letters as numbers. The letters of Avram Halevi, the cabbalist had assured him, were absolutely special: they guaranteed that he would be transformed into pure spirit.

"Everyone is transformed into pure spirit," Avram had laughed, "after the worms have eaten him."

"You pretend to be a cynic," the cabbalist said, "but you fool no one. Declare your belief, you will be a happier man."

"This is no place to worry about happiness."

"And why not?" the cabbalist asked, as if any fool could see that this cell was nothing less than paradise itself.

The day the news came of Martin V's election, the cabbalist was still with Avram. When the guard related the story of this grand event, and the celebrations that were sweeping the whole world to mark the end of the schism, the cabbalist's face looked suddenly shocked, as if he had been unexpectedly bitten.

"You know what that means?" he asked Avram after the guard had left. "The schism is over. The Church is united. Now the sun can rise and set in happiness again." He giggled, a sharp-pitched nervous sound that Avram had not heard before. "My death sentence," the old man said. "To celebrate they will begin the trials again."

He fell silent for a moment. Avram felt his own heart accelerate at the mention of the word *trials*; then he suddenly thought with disgust that he was like one of those insane and doomed ants that ran from the thumbs of children who, poised above them, merely waited for the most entertaining moment to crush them into the dirt.

"Excuse me," the old man said, "for thinking of myself." Then he smiled at Avram, a brilliant and radiant smile that lit up the cell like the flash of a steel sword in the sun.

The night before the cabbalist's execution Avram dozed off just before midnight. When he awoke, the old man had become young, his body straight as an oak tree, his smile the same brilliant flash he had given the day the Christian world had finally reunited.

He was sitting cross-legged on the stone floor, hands clasped together, and from his body, heat pulsed through the dark cell. The letters of his own name, he told Avram, could be transformed to Jacob's Ladder, and that was why he was chosen for his profession. "You, too, will be with God," he said. Then the cabbalist closed his eyes and began to breathe deeply, the space between his breaths gradually lengthening, the rhythm finally growing so slow that the dark cell became cold and lifeless.

By the time the sun rose, the old man was locked in the stiffness of death. When the guards discovered what had happened they knocked Avram to the floor, kicked him until his own body lay across the old man's, kicked him until his ribs began to snap, the broken ends grinding together, until he passed out.

But two days later, when the cabbalist's body was taken away, the guards replaced it with a table and a roll of cloth. Avram wrapped his sides as tightly as he could, then collapsed back onto the bed.

A week later, he was well enough to sit up. At the table, holding his aching ribs, Avram invented his tribute: in memory of the cabbalist he spent the daylight hours staring at the surface of the table, the once-living grain of the wood, and trying to turn his contemplation of God's work into the contemplation of God.

Nine years! Time enough for one winter to become confused with another, time enough for one man to feel his life contract and disappear before his eyes.

Nine years! That was how long Avram Halevi had been in prison when they released Baldassare Cossa from *his* confinement. A broken man, it was said, a man given to ranting about how *he* could have been the pope to save Christianity and bring the world back to its senses.

By the time of Baldassare Cossa's release, Avram's ribs were fully healed.

But he still spent his days hunched over the table, staring at it in a stupefied trance.

In the sun's full light the grain was so stained and dry as to be almost obliterated, and the once-dark oak was a pale field of fibres rubbed raw. Yet for all those hundreds of days that he had watched the sun make its way across the worn surface, that he had dulled his eye staring at the light's invasion of each solitary fibre, had God truly entered his soul and transformed his being? There had certainly been moments of peace when in the sun's heat he had felt himself drifting in a sea of serenity, like a baby in its mother's womb. But then he would snap out of it to find himself doubting again. Here you are, he would sneer at himself, the great man of science, conqueror of superstition, wielder of the silver knife. And what do you have to offer yourself? Fool's gold. Like the alchemists who believed their own superstitious rantings, you are an imprisoned man trying to believe that the current of life has not passed you by.

Nine years! But today the sun was strong, and the wood glowed under the power of its light.

In Montpellier, in the loft of his house and in his workroom at the university, he had laboured in the light of such a sun, one as powerful as the Italian sun, transferring sketches from his notebooks into a larger sheaf of drawings for his textbook of anatomy.

Humans, animals, even some plants: all had been dissected and compared, one living structure to another, one life to another. And even the morning that Pierre Montreuil and his men had attacked the château at Montpellier, Avram had not neglected to think

389

about his life-work concealed in the locked trunk that resided under the bed he shared with Jeanne-Marie.

But when he had come back to the château with the lame boy from the village, when he had seen Jeanne-Marie hanging from the window and the burning bodies of the others, then he had run crazily through the halls shouting the names of his children, searching like a madman through the rooms. Insane with grief and rage upon finding no trace of the children, he had begun throwing his and Jeanne-Marie's belongings out their bedroom window to the burning pyre below. When Nanette called to him from the door he was hacking clothes, furniture, tapestries, even the walls to pieces with his heavy sword.

When he remembered the trunk, he broke it open and laid the drawings – as though they were the corpse of his marriage to Jeanne-Marie – on the bed. Crying and screaming, he had slashed at them with his sword, throwing such frenzied strength into each blow that finally the bed split apart with his efforts.

When he opened his eyes he saw his hands, an old man's hands, clasped together the way the cabbalist's had been the night he willed himself to die. Fingers white as sand, knuckles swollen by the damp, palms softened by years of dreaming. He was lifting his hands towards his face, lifting them as if in a prayer to demand his own death, when the guard swung open the door.

"I have something to tell you," he said. "Baldassare Cossa has been killed."

Avram felt his own head jerk up, felt from his lips whistle forth a shrill and nervous giggle, the same sound that the cabbalist had made the day he knew his own fate was finally determined.

"You Jews are always laughing," growled the guard. And then pushed shut the door.

EIGHT

THE CELL OF AVRAM HALEVI LOOKED NOT INTO THE SQUARE BUT INTO A NARROW COURT. BUT FROM THE OUTSIDE WHAT WAS TO BE SEEN WAS NOT A GRIM-LOOKING PRISON BUT the rich and magnificent edifice known as King Enzo's palace – so named because centuries ago a certain King Enzo had spent his whole life imprisoned among his riches.

Once King Enzo's Palace had been the preserve of Baldassare Cossa. In it were located jails, his art collections, and – some said – the treasures he had accumulated during his decades as a seaman and pirate. It was also said that Cossa – first as cardinal, then as pope – used the palace for his more private pleasures: certain rooms were often lit late into the night, and at the same time the sounds of torture rose up from the lower levels, laughter and music drifted down from above.

King Enzo's Palace was only a few footsteps away from the Palace of the Notaries.

To that guild belonged Joseph Santangel, who had been born Joseph Halevi but had then taken the name of Santangel to honour his protectors and for his own safety.

In 1419, Joseph still worked for the family who had been his benefactors. As part of his apprenticeship he had been assigned to the changing of money in the bankers' stalls. The assignment suited him well enough. At eighteen years of age he was glad to have the opportunity to stand outdoors, watching the commerce of the city being transacted in its main square, watching the city itself, unimaginably rich, as its hundreds upon hundreds of workmen struggled industriously to raise one palace after another into the beauty the Italians seemed to covet so much.

Sometimes, bent over his figures, or talking idly to a customer, or even walking across the square watching the swooping shadows of hungry gulls, he would hear what seemed to be a voice calling to his ears alone.

It was a soft voice, the voice of a man who was almost old. "Joseph," it would say to his imagination. And Joseph, whatever he was doing, would shake himself as if the voice was waking him from a dream.

"What's wrong?" Sara would ask him, "Were you dreaming again? Joseph, Joseph the dreamer."

And Joseph would remember himself and laugh. "That's it," he would say, "I must have been dreaming."

On the day the news of Baldassare Cossa's death reached Bologna, Joseph looked up from his stall to see Gabriela and Sara crossing the square towards him. It was noon, the sun was so high in the sky that it poured directly down into the square, a glaring shadowless light that made the brilliant white cloak of Gabriela Hasdai de Santangel shine that much more brightly.

Sara was sixteen years old – two years younger than Joseph. The other Sara, his sister, had been killed during the raid on the château. He remembered that day well enough. Crouched in the cupboard, hiding under the skirts of Maria, Joseph had heard the door being tested, then splinter open. There was a brief moment when he thought they might survive undetected: Maria's hand was tight over his mouth and nose, so that even if he tried, no sound would escape. Then, from Maria herself, a muffled sneeze escaped. Seconds later, their own door had been wrenched away and Maria had been dragged out, holding Sara in her arms. He remembered the sudden movement of her legs, his own instinctive, desperate scuttle to stay concealed beneath her skirts. And then, just as she had screamed and her skirts had come up, Joseph had seen the open door of the room. One step, two, three, he was out the door and running unnoticed down the hall, the thundering footsteps of the pursuers only the beating of his own heart —

"Joseph. Weren't you expecting me?" Said almost mockingly, as if he might be a lover ready to be spurned. As if, at least, Joseph must hear this possibility, must live with every question and doubt that she could raise.

"I am always expecting you," Joseph said. In the past two years Sara had become so beautiful that he hardly dared look at her. But now, somehow, he was staring directly at her. She had a long oval face, high cheekbones that accented her dark eyes, glossy hair that matched her black silk dress, and now, a sudden white flash of a smile.

"What are you always expecting me to do?" she asked. Joseph, his eyes still fixed on her, saw Gabriela approaching.

"I don't know." He turned away. To be afflicted with love for his own adoptive sister was surely a most stupid disease. While he was the disgraced son of a criminal, Sara was one of the most beautiful — and well-dowried — young Jewesses in all of Italy. Twice she had been engaged to wealthy and important men. Yet year after year passed without her getting married. Soon, León joked, her beauty would grow so heavy that she would simply collapse, over-ripe, to the ground.

Once Joseph, visiting Avram, had dared to broach the subject of love.

"Was your heart ever broken?" Joseph asked, summoning all his courage.

"Love is not what breaks your heart." Then Avram had shrugged curtly, his old man's shoulders still wide, his smile, grown lopsided with his vision, suddenly alive with the happiness of being able once more to surprise his son. How many loves had there been? In vain Joseph would try to imagine his father's romantic and improbable youth, the string of women that must have beaded his warrior's nights.

"Joseph."

His father's was a soft voice, the voice of a man who no longer has to make himself heard. Yet it said his name differently than others did: perhaps, Joseph had tried to convince himself when he was younger, the difference lay in the fact that Avram added to his name a father's love.

Gabriela and Sara had gone, leaving them alone. As always Gabriela had been full of news of the latest appeals, the new evidence that would be introduced. In fact, it was six years since the latest hearing had been promised.

Of course another prisoner would not have lived so long. But nor would he have lived so well. The Velásquez money had, everyone said, divided itself

394

in two over Avram Halevi: but even with the cardinal dead, the living merchant was not quite able to wrest a final advantage.

"You're well, Joseph."

"Very well, Father."

"Are you still painting?"

"I go to the studio."

"And?"

"The other apprentices live in the studio," Joseph burst out. "They spend their whole days serving the master. I come there a few hours a week, not even every day." He stopped.

"Go on," Avram said.

"That's all."

"Do you wish to live in the studio, with the others?"

"No."

"And why not?"

Joseph folded his hands awkwardly. "Because I am a Jew. No Jews live at the studio."

"So?"

"To eat the right food, to say the right prayers — " He stopped, unwilling to continue.

"You are telling me that you can't be a painter because you are Jewish?"

"It is forbidden," Joseph said quietly. "You know that."

"It is forbidden to paint the face of God," Avram said.

"Do you expect me to paint Madonnas?"

Avram laughed and the air between them was suddenly clear.

I did paint Madonnas, Joseph wanted to protest, *I painted Christs, too* — but he knew that whatever he said would sound ludicrous to Avram, and would be carefully deflated before being laid to rest.

"It's all right," Avram now said gently. "You have my permission to stop going to the studio. I command you to stop going to the studio."

"Thank you."

"When I was young I didn't have a father to tell me what to do."

"I know."

"It was no tragedy."

Joseph looked across the cell at his father. How to be the son of such a man? "He has no room in his life for children," Gabriela had once explained, when Joseph returned home in tears, "that is what you must forgive him."

The cell door was open and on a stool in the entrance a guard had been sitting the whole visit. Now he stood up.

"It is time for me to leave."

"Let us pray first."

"Quickly."

Joseph watched as Avram took the scroll from the table. "On our knees," he said. Gabriela had told him that his father had spent most of his life as an unbeliever. Perhaps that was why, now, he insisted on his relentless prayers. "Listen to me now," Avram said, "listen to me and heed the meaning of my words." And then he opened the scroll and began reading from it in Hebrew: "'And the time grew nigh that Israel must die: and he called his son Joseph, and said unto him, If now I have found grace in thy sight, put, I pray thee, thy hand under my thigh, and deal kindly and truly with me; bury me not, I pray thee, in Egypt.'"

When Joseph left the prison it was late afternoon. Outside, there was still bright white light in the sky, though Avram's cell was already growing dark. Before Joseph left, his father had kissed him: his lips and wiry beard like a foreign country against his cheek.

As he walked home, the taste and smell of his father still lingered on Joseph's face, as though the old man were finding a new way to claim his son. But Avram was labouring at a task already fulfilled: on his way to work in the morning, during his lunchtime stroll, on his way home again in the evening, Joseph would work through the crowded square to look at the building where his father was imprisoned. He had done this for so long that in its course he had grown from a boy looking up to a giant into a man who stood eye-to-eye with his father.

That night, after supper, Gabriela made Joseph go over every detail of what had happened after she had left. She did this every month as if the visits were a biblical commentary to be ceaselessly examined for new clues to God's mysterious ways.

Grudgingly, Joseph reported the conversation about the studio.

"I didn't know you wanted to be an apprentice," Gabriela said.

"That's just it," Joseph exclaimed, "I don't want to be an apprentice. But when I'm talking to him, I feel as if some great rock is being lowered down on me, that I must justify my existence or be crushed."

"You shouldn't feel that."

"Then he made me pray with him."

"That is good," Gabriela said, "I am glad to hear that he prays now." Her own home was still completely religious. Even now, as they talked, León was at the synagogue, reciting the evening prayers. Most evenings Joseph would have been with him. And why not? He was eighteen years old, a man old enough to take his place before God, old enough to be married. When he was thirteen, León had sponsored his bar mitzvah at the synagogue. Now he was a man among men: at the synagogue, in the banking stalls, in the social life that revolved around the Santangel household. All of these segments of his life fitted together: together they were round, like a wheel. To take one away would make the wheel fall in upon itself and crash.

The room was empty, he was alone with Gabriela, a rare opportunity to ask the questions he never dared to raise.

How, he wanted to know, had his own father been a man among men when he turned away from their God, from their synagogues? How could people have let him operate on them when they did not know where his heart was? Or had his unbelief been only another of his endless poses? Sometimes Avram, with his elaborate jokes, his enigmatic commands, his silences on obvious matters and his outbursts of loquaciousness on things of no consequence, seemed like a remnant of another time, not simply a generation before his own, but an era before his own. And yet his father's friend Gabriela was a woman of the new age. Religiously liberal, despising the big landowners, an enthusiast who urged Joseph to participate in the outburst of painting and sculpture that gripped Bologna, a rationalist who was sending him to university and who praised, of all people, Avram for being a scientist ahead of his time.

"Just now," she said, "the eminent professors at the University of Bologna are realizing that to cure the human body it is necessary to look under the skin. But your father Avram Halevi was doing dissections and operations thirty years ago, when the penalty for being discovered was death."

"He must have been a very brave man," Joseph said, trying to keep the doubt out of his voice.

"What else happened today?"

"We prayed."

"What prayer?"

"No particular prayer. It was a section from Genesis, about Jacob's death. I thought he was telling me that he was getting ready to die."

"He is not ready to die," said Gabriela flatly.

"He's an old man." Joseph said this firmly, keeping his eyes on Gabriela. "The last two visits he told me that he couldn't live forever in his cell, he — "

"Why didn't you tell me this?" Gabriela interrupted angrily. Her voice was like a sword, cutting off his line of thought.

"It was just a complaint."

"What did he read you today, exactly?"

Joseph closed his eyes. He could hear his father's voice. " 'Listen to me,' " Joseph repeated, " 'listen to me and heed the meaning of my words: "And the time grew nigh that Israel must die: and he called his son Joseph. . . . " ' "

Joseph stopped because Gabriela had leapt to her feet and crossed the room to get her own scroll out, the book of Genesis. In a moment she had found what she wanted, and as Joseph recited she read aloud with him.

When they were finished, Joseph said, "You see, he wants to die."

NINE

BURY ME NOT IN EGYPT," AVRAM HAD COM-
MANDED JOSEPH. ANOTHER OF HIS JOKES,
PRANKS, CRANKY REQUESTS? OR A SIGNAL THAT
THE TIME HAD COME: THE DEMAND
that he be freed? And if Avram were to escape his
prison, Gabriela asked herself, should she not escape
hers?

The next morning, instead of going to the warehouse, Gabriela walked through the streets of the
quarter until she came to the synagogue. The official
round of morning prayers had ended, and inside the
walled courtyard a rabbi had gathered his pupils around
him and was rehearsing with them some tiny point
of theology. The rabbi bowed to her, she bowed back:
Velásquez money had helped to build the wall that
kept the synagogue invisible from the eyes of whatever citizens might be offended by the sight of a
competing religion.

Inside the synagogue she climbed the stairs to the
women's gallery. There, alone, she looked down at
the few old grandfathers who prayed their days away.
Clutching bits of scrolls that long ago had been memorized, wrapped in huge shawls that reduced them
to gnomes, masked by knotted beards that stank of
milk and stale bread, they rocked back and forth,

chanting out their private sorrows, their submissions, their obediences to God's iron will.

So many dead, so many to mourn for.

So many scattered, it would truly require a Day of Judgement for the Jews to find their way back to Jerusalem.

From the gallery she could see the ark, the ever-burning candle.

"I am a jealous God," God had warned.

Jealous, yes. Perhaps that was why He had chosen the Jews – He had chosen them to be the people who would not be permitted to forget His jealousy, His wrath, the harshness of His service.

Just twenty-four hours ago Gabriela had heard that Baldassare Cossa, the old pirate become pope, had been killed. With Cossa gone, what would Avram be? The prisoner of a man who had been assassinated. A prisoner whose only reason to exist would now be a trial for murder and heresy. Another martyr to appease the God of the Hebrews.

The voices of the old men quavered on, accusing her like a chorus of wagging fingers.

"I want to die," Avram had said, the last time she had seen him alone.

"Then die," she had snapped back. And felt guilt knifing through her as Avram shrank back against the stone wall. But a few moments later he was his old self again: embracing her, laughing, saying that he was so strong that he would still be a young man when the long-delayed pardon finally arrived. Telling her that Cossa had recently sent him a message, through a bishop, that as soon as his position was strengthened he would be released and given safe passage back to Toledo.

Then, skinny and bent, Avram had reached out for her and his long-fingered hands had barely gripped her waist when suddenly she was swinging up in the air like a child being amused by its favourite uncle.

Now only one of the old men was still singing. His voice rose and wavered; like a wounded bird it swerved and clawed at the vaulted ceiling, hopelessly seeking a place to come to rest. Through the open window of the synagogue came the peal of church bells, so loud that the old man's voice was reduced to the size of a buzzing fly.

The decision had somehow made itself; all that was left was the details. And one small final problem – how to soften the blow.

Gabriela turned and walked down to the courtyard from the gallery. The students had gone home, but the rabbi was sitting on a bench, meditating in the warm sun.

"Good day, Rabbi."

"Good day, Signora. Give my regards to your husband."

Gabriela walked slowly down the crowded streets, letting herself be pushed by the crowds criss-crossing from home to market. The rabbi would tell León, this evening, that he had seen Signora Santangel at the synagogue. Gabriela would have to invent an excuse: perhaps the anniversary of some death that León had not already consoled her for. He was kind, he was considerate, he had even once been passionate. But her decision was taken. One door had been opened while others were closed.

Joseph was at his place in the banker's stall when a feather was laid across the figures he was calculating.

He looked up. Sara was standing in front of him, smiling at his startled expression. Joseph glanced hastily down the row. León was engaged in a long and involved transaction with a merchant from Florence. For three days they had been arguing about the terms of a letter of credit that the merchant wanted to take to a fair in Genoa. With this he and his partners would be able to buy enough wool to fill a whole sailing vessel. But if the vessel sank or was robbed, the money would never be repaid.

Such a problem would have prevented any consideration of letters of credit, had there not been one additional factor. In order to make sure enemy pirates did not steal his debtor's cargo, Velásquez had a navy of his own brigands plundering the ships that he paid for. Joseph had overheard Gabriela whispering this to León. So not only did Santangel have the task of securing advantageous terms, he also had to be a play-actor of consummate skill.

Even as Joseph walked with Sara towards the centre of the Piazza Maggiore, he could hear the voice of Santangel singing his scale of imagined treachery and fear.

"My mother tells me that you are leaving Bologna." As she walked, she let her shoulder press against his, and as always Joseph felt his body grow suddenly alive, a quick reaction that he could not control.

"What do you mean?"

"She told me of your plan," Sara said. "Wasn't I supposed to know?"

Joseph felt fear fanning through him. It was true: a plan had been made. And the plan was so dangerous that, as Gabriela said, after this adventure he would surely be a man.

"I'll miss you," Sara said.

"I'll miss you, too."

"You promised to dance at my wedding."

"You should have married sooner."

He regretted the words as he said them, and when he saw that Sara was blushing, he felt himself blushing with her. Her two engagements had both ended when the suitors became ill, and at the funeral of the second the dead man's mother had screamed at Sara that she was not a woman but a spider who cursed everyone she touched.

"You should have married, too," Sara finally replied.

Now it was Joseph's turn to be embarrassed.

"You never asked anyone? It's lucky now. You can find a woman in your new life."

"You're right," Joseph said. "There is luck in everything." They were weaving through the noontime crowds, sometimes separated by the mass of people, other times pushed together. In the sun her scent was so strong that Joseph felt stunned by it.

"Do you want to have children?"

"I hadn't thought of it."

"In the Torah, God is always sending His believers out into a new land, to multiply." She grinned at Joseph and he knew she was referring not to his virility but to the facility for arithmetic that made him useful to Santangel.

"I hope you will be very happy and successful." She said this in a formal voice, stopping now at the edge of the square. "My mother also said to tell you that it was very kind of you to be my brother."

"Stop it," Joseph said. Again his eyes fixed themselves on Sara. He tried to look away but it was impossible. He wanted to drink her in, every detail, every tremor, every pore.

"Joseph," Sara said.

"*Come with me.*" The words formed on his tongue. He even opened his mouth to say them. "Have a happy life," Joseph said.

"You have a happy life," Sara said. "God bless you." Then she turned and walked rapidly away.

That night Joseph's dreams were like dull stones. Towards morning he woke up, opening his eyes briefly to see the bed that had once held his father. Then night became day, his dreams as bright and vivid as the full force of the sun.

First he saw himself as a child, lying in the same bed he lay in now, pretending to sleep while trembling nervously. His father waking up. Dressing to go out into the night. Except that in the dream the night was high noon, and as his father climbed out the window, and Joseph followed, every window in the city opened so that curious eyes could follow their curious fate.

Then his father was climbing into the house where Rodrigo Velásquez was staying. Joseph, the light hurting his eyes, tried to find a place to hide. But everywhere he stood, strangers came and stared at him, poked curiously at his ribs, asked him questions in a language he couldn't understand. He ran from one corner to another.

Finally he was standing in front of a gate. It opened.

"Joseph. Joseph."

Sara in her nightdress was leaning over him. Her hair fell straight to her shoulders; but his eye caught a small black tendril that curled round her earlobe like a lover's caress.

He reached towards her and then she was in his bed, lying beside him, lying on top of him, her weight the pressure that relieved the panic he had felt looking for his father. He kissed her lips. Once. Twice. They tasted like wild strawberries, sweet and full. He kissed them again.

"Joseph."

He opened his eyes. Saw his hands on Sara's shoulders, saw that his hands had grown older, pulsed with ropy veins, had long tanned fingers that had spent a lifetime in the sun. He remembered the curse, the spider's poison.

"Joseph." This time the voice was louder, breaking his dream. He woke up. His heart was beating wildly but the room was empty. Then the door opened. It was Sara, after all. "Joseph, forgive me for this morning." When her lips touched his, he already knew their taste, and when in the dark his hands searched out her face, his fingers already knew the curls they wanted to get lost in.

TEN

WHEN JOSEPH CAME TO THE CELL FOR HIS VISITING HOUR, THE DOOR WAS OPEN AND THE GUARD SITTING IN THE DOORWAY, STARING ACROSS THE CORRIDOR AS though new stories were daily inscribed onto the wall for his amusement. At the end of each corridor, there were additional guards. All were armed with enough swords, knives, and truncheons to subdue a whole crowd of unruly prisoners. But, of course, such an event would never occur because only one cell door could be opened at a time.

Joseph nodded to the guard and gave him a silk handkerchief. As always, the handkerchief contained sweetmeats and two gold coins. This tribute was not absolutely necessary, Gabriela explained, since for visiting privileges one had to bribe more than a single guard; but the gifts made the guard look forward to the visits. In order that his companions in the corridor would not grow jealous, they, too, received gifts, though not so often.

Joseph went into the cell. As if it were a normal visit, Avram rose from the single stool to embrace him.

Joseph, in the arms of his father, could not believe that his heart had not yet burst from his chest.

"Shalom," he said. And then added, still in Hebrew, "I have brought you a gift because of your prayer. Forgive me if it is the wrong gift." He hugged Avram closer, so that his father would feel the handle of the dagger pressing between their chests.

His father, moving with surprising speed, reached into his cloak, took the dagger, and put it in his own. Then he stepped back.

Joseph, crazily, felt a total relief now that the burden had been taken from him. He sat down on Avram's stone bench, as if everything were already over.

"Gabriela is not coming today?" Avram asked.

"She was busy."

"She had other arrangements to make?"

Joseph felt his heart constrict again. "You mustn't speak Hebrew any more than necessary in front of the guard," Gabriela had warned him, "it will only make him suspicious."

But the guard was not suspicious. In fact, anticipating his gift, he had taken out his knife to whittle himself a toothpick from the supply of sticks he always carried with him. Sometimes it seemed that, aside from watching his invisible entertainments, the guard's main treat in life was the cleaning of his teeth. So intense was this pleasure that he liked to make his first toothpick before he ate so that not a moment would be wasted.

Joseph nodded.

"I am glad that my son is such a student of his Bible."

Joseph could see only the guard's back, but the sound of whittling continued. According to Gabriela, the poison would require at least a quarter of an hour to work. "It is guaranteed," she had said, "to make the man drop dead on the spot. But of course such guarantees can be worthless. If the poison doesn't work, or if it only makes him choke, you will have to kill him."

Joseph had turned away from her: Avram and Gabriela – they were like beasts from a time when men had torn each other to death. Of course he had taken lessons in swordsmanship, and he had been in enough fights with his friends at school. But to kill another human being, that was almost unthinkable.

"Don't worry," Gabriela had said drily, as if she could read his mind, "when the opportunity comes, you will know how."

There was the knife he had given to Avram and, belted to his side, there was another weapon: a short sword that Sara had given him.

His father had now moved to the window. Its only view was to the few feet of dusty air that separated it from the next stone wall. In the strong light Avram's skin was pale and moist-looking, like parchment that had been stored in a damp place. Over his injured eye, his eyelid, itself scarred, drooped like a shutter permanently closed. His beard was ragged and almost entirely white, but his hair was still jet-black. It, too, was uncut and fell past his shoulders.

The sun settled in Avram's good eye, shone right through it, transformed it from a human eye to the glowing and unreadable eye of a cat. The guard had finished eating and had begun to pick his teeth.

The seconds dragged on. Joseph remembered escaping from the bedroom in which Maria was being killed, running down the hall even as his sister's wail began to sound. Without planning, he had ducked into the room of his Uncle Robert and hidden under the bed. It was so high that with the bedspread around him like a tent he was able to sit with his legs drawn up to his chest and his arms wrapped around his knees, pressing them even closer to his own pounding heart.

After a long time he had gone to look out the window: this was one of the clearest memories — looking out the window to see the yard suddenly empty except for the burning bodies of the dead. And then, somehow, Nanette had found him. Joseph had been so surprised to see her that he had screamed with fear, his first sound in hours, and fallen forward on his face. He woke up to see Avram sweeping in the door, his face gone mad with rage, his arm raised with a sword and the smell of blood surrounding him like so many cloaks —

"Now," Avram said.

Joseph jerked on the bench. Fear had drawn his bones so tight that he could hardly move. He looked towards the door. The guard was deep in communion with his toothpick.

"Let's go."

Avram started towards him. Joseph felt his stomach spinning crazily, he was going to be sick. With each step, Avram was swelling, the rickety old man who had spent nine years in prison was falling away from his shoulders.

"My son," Avram said, extending his hand. "Stand up, my son."

Joseph tried to get to his feet, but his knees were buckling and he could only stand half-erect. The shame of his own cowardice was sweeping through him; he could feel the sweat that had covered his skin.

"My son," Avram was repeating softly.

Joseph looked up at his father. He knew he was trying to give him strength, but his voice only made him more ashamed.

Joseph somehow managed to lift his hand, stretch it towards Avram, who pulled him to his feet. And then, just as Joseph was finding his balance, he saw that the guard had turned in the doorway.

"Hey," the guard said, his voice croaking at first, then becoming a shout. "Hey, what are you doing?"

The guard's cry started the other guards running, and with the sound of their footsteps crashing through the hall Joseph felt his mind wanting to crack open.

"Now," Avram said a final time.

And then, as Joseph watched, Avram turned from him and sprang towards the entering guard. He saw his father whirl the guard around and draw the shining dagger across the poor man's throat. A river of blood chased the steel. Avram ran out the corridor, towards the stairs, Joseph on his heels.

At the stairway one of the other guards caught up to them. As he leapt towards Avram, Joseph whipped his short sword from beneath his cloak. He felt the weight of the guard as his belly impaled itself upon the sword. Sara's gift. Then, jerking it free, Joseph rushed down the stairs, followed by loud screams, and into the courtyard.

For a moment the bright sun numbed his eyes. And then he saw, as if in a dream, the waiting carriage. It was Gabriela's finest, a fast black carriage with iron-reinforced walls and wheels that had been forged by the best blacksmith in Bologna. The driver was Gabriela's strongest and most trusted guard, and as Joseph flew across the courtyard towards the waiting open door he saw the guard first raise his arm in greeting, then bring it down with a hard snap, sounding the whip over the horses' backs.

The stallions surged forward. Joseph, as he stretched his legs to meet the carriage, felt the blood flowing from a wound that had been opened across his shoulder. The horses had already started to gallop when Joseph's last stride carried him to the open door, and Avram's hand stretched out to catch his.

Shouting soldiers chased them as they wheeled through the Piazza Maggiore, galloped by the banker's stalls where León Santangel was standing and working. Seconds later, they had lost their pursuers and were careering through the crooked streets towards the western gate of the city. Wiping Joseph's shoulder clean, wrapping it in soft linen as they went, was Gabriela's daughter, Sara, dressed like a bride and smiling at him with the radiance of a thousand suns. Across from her, sitting beside Avram and holding his hands in her own, was Gabriela.

At the gates of the city there were more guards. This time Joseph felt courage beating its gigantic wings in his chest. The driver was killed even as Joseph was flying out the door, but with Avram at his side, he felt the power of God surging through his arm, carrying his sword through the flesh of his enemies, reducing them to a bleeding chorus of surrender. And when Avram, the old man swinging the sword with the sinewy grace of a wrathful angel, was staggered from behind, Joseph sprang forward, sending his sword so deeply through the chest of Avram's attacker that, when he fell backward, he could not even have the comfort of dying on the good earth because the tip of the sword had pierced his back and now suspended him from the ground.

Joseph, transfixed by the dying, felt himself turning to stone. Then his father's arm was around him, Avram grown to gigantic size was sweeping him into the carriage, carrying him as effortlessly as he had when he was a child in Montpellier. In the shelter of his father's arms, covered again by the many-layered cloak of blood and death, he saw Gabriela herself leap out to replace the fallen driver of the carriage and with a loud crack of the reins start their long race away from the city, and towards the safety of the sea.

BOOK V

BOLOGNA
1410–1419

ONE

WHEN THEY WENT TO KIEV, THEY FELL OFF THE EDGE OF THE WORLD.

THE PEOPLE OF KIEV WERE TARTARS – A DARK-HAIRED SLANT-EYED CROSSING OF Mongols and Turks who had conquered Kiev centuries ago, wiping out the orderly empire of the ancient Kiev princes and substituting a brawling and expansionary state.

Among their many virtues, the Tartars knew how to live in the cold. They wore thick fur-lined boots laced to the knees, leather leggings, coats made out of hides and trimmed with the multilayered fur of wolves.

"Look at them," Gabriela mocked, "they resemble a bastard breed of the animal they are wearing."

Even the houses of Kiev feared the winter. To protect themselves from the cold they huddled deep into the frozen ground. From the street level it was always necessary to descend several steps into the kitchen whose hearth could never warm it.

In Kiev, a city that seemed in every respect to have dropped out of the sight of God's eye, the streets were made not of dirt but of wood, which had to be constantly relaid and built up. Because instead of transporting their goods in carts pulled by donkeys – a method good enough for every civilized nation

*of the world – Kievans preferred to use ox-drawn
sleds with iron runners. Night and day the sound of
metal scraping over wood and ice resounded through
the city like the cry of a monstrous infant who could
not be made to sleep.*

They had ridden like thunder from Bologna: Avram
Halevi and his son, Joseph, Gabriela and her daughter, Sara. With bags of gold and silver coins hidden
in the secret places of their carriage, they galloped
from one Jewish community to the next until they
reached Venice. There they boarded a merchant vessel
bound for Constantinople.

"What are we going to do there?"

"Find Jews," was Avram's reply.

But the Jews of Constantinople had strange cus-
toms and prepared food that burned the throat. At
the marriage of Joseph and Sara, even the cook was
made ill by the feast. Worse, the rabbis were so
superstitious that when Avram was seen to be a doctor who dared to operate without first consulting an
astrologer, they started a rumour that he secretly
worshipped the Devil.

"Give them time," Gabriela urged. "Then they
will discover what a great doctor you are."

But to this Avram would not reply; he only stared
at her, stony-faced and indifferent.

The next year they were travelling again – first
across the Black Sea and then up the Dnieper River
towards Kiev.

Avram grew healthy. The man who had been bent
and foul-breathed in prison was now fifty-one years
old, hardened like ironwood, a biblical patriarch.
Standing beside him, as they made their slow way up
the broad river, Gabriela would feel her own self
shrinking – as if in the powerful shadow of a man

touched by God. And at night, lying beside him in the darkness, she felt Avram drawing into himself, closing his strength around himself like a cloak that could not be pierced. Gabriela, now that the excitement of the escape had waned, found herself alternating between happiness at being with Avram and bitter disappointment that his love for her had refused to flower.

The journey took a long time. There were ports to stop in, cargoes to be unloaded and taken on. In Constantinople they had lost most of their money when an unsuccessful operation led to threats of bringing Avram to trial. Now, to pay their fare, Avram was doing surgery again – all the while complaining that with only one eye he was unable to see properly, that his years in jail had made his fingers slower, his touch unsure. But every storm brought a cluster of accidents down upon the seamen. Then there were broken bones to be set, torn flesh to be stitched together, crushed fingers and limbs to be amputated.

By the time they reached Kiev the riverbanks had turned white – first with frost, then snow – and ice had begun to narrow the river to a barely navigable channel. During the whole voyage not a single sailor lost his life; on the last night the crew made Avram an offering, as if he were a saint, and when they were convinced no bribe could persuade him to remain on board, they begged permission to use his name while praying to God for protection from the sea.

Gabriela, Avram, Joseph, and Sara lived in a one-room hovel that they rented from Leo Kaputin, Kiev's richest Jew.

"It will be a mansion when you learn to love it," Kaputin promised. The landlord Kaputin was a short swarthy man who jabbed his fingers upward like a hacked-off root struggling to push new shoots through the earth and into the sun. The mansion was an old shed that had been converted into a kitchen. Before it was a kitchen, the shed had been an addition to the stable where Kaputin's oxen were kept. Through the gapped planks in the separating wall flowed a rich but undeniable odour.

"Don't worry about the smell," Kaputin reassured them. "After a while you will come to recognize it for what it is, the free gift of warmth."

Joseph and Sara slept on a ledge above the hearth while, for the sake of the young couple's privacy, Avram and Gabriela slept in the corner farthest from them, making their own heat inside a small skin tent that Kaputin had provided.

"Who has ever seen such a thing? A house so cold that we need a tent inside the walls in order to keep warm." Gabriela was shocked at the sound of her whining voice. The way her sister would have whined had her husband failed to keep the household supplied with the requisite weights of linen and silver. "I'm happy," Gabriela corrected herself, "to be with you."

Beneath their blankets, surrounded by the multi-layered conglomeration of hides that should have been left rotting in the stable, Gabriela pressed herself close to Avram. But just as during the day he seemed to look right through her, in his sleep he sometimes squirmed away from her embrace.

In the front door of their house was a piece of glass. "That is a special gift for you," the landlord Kaputin had declared, "to help you remember that Kiev is God's City of Light. Think of me when you enjoy it." Winter had just started when they first arrived in Kiev, and when the fire was roaring and the afternoon sun strong, Kaputin's window would be clear so that, pressing her face to it, Gabriela could see up the steps to the street.

But winter deepened and the days became as short and dark as Kaputin himself. Soon there was no time of day sufficiently warm for the glass to be clear – steam from the boiling soups froze layer after layer of ice onto the window. Eventually it became so thick that even a fingernail could not chip it away – a knife was required. Finally, the frost from the glass became a stained yellow-white curtain that spread from the window to cover the whole door, then to the wall surrounding it. One night Gabriela, desperate with misery, stepped outside to look at the stars. The frozen air cut into her lungs and pinched her nostrils together when she tried to breathe. Looking up, she saw that even the sky had been invaded by foreign constellations.

On the shortest day of the year their one friend in Kiev – a Spanish Jew called Moses Viladestes – came to visit. According to himself, in the long-ago epoch of his youth Viladestes had been a well-to-do and respected rabbi in Sevilla. Now, old-fashioned and timid, Viladestes seemed barely able to keep straight the dates of his own history.

"It's me, it's me," he mumbled, as he kicked the snow from his boots and came towards the hearth. "I hope that everyone is not too busy to see a fellow Jew on the first night of Hanukkah."

Gabriela was standing at the table, cutting away the rotten parts of the vegetables that had been the Hanukkah gift from Leo Kaputin's wife. Carrots and other roots for which the Spanish language had no name: twisted fibres torn from the earth that only a starving Jew would eat. Next, there would be nothing left but the fermented mash they fed the oxen.

421

"Come in," called Avram. As if Viladestes had not already taken off his snow-crusted outer tunic to reveal a patchwork of layered garments.

"I have brought your wife a present for the season." Viladestes held out his hands. They were folded around his secret.

"Meat," Gabriela whispered, then wanted to bite her tongue. It was only a week since Sara had stolen a chicken from the market. If she had been caught, her hand could have been cut off. Avram, extracting the story from her, had been so furious that he refused to eat. Until Sara, who was pregnant, and Joseph, who was starving to death before their eyes, said they would not eat either unless Avram joined them.

"Does your wife know who is Judah Maccabee?"

"My wife," said Avram. And hearing the warm and dreamy tone of Avram's voice, Gabriela was certain that as he had been sitting and sewing, his surgeon's fingers now reduced to the one paid employment he could find – stitching leather aprons for the town's butchers – he had been remembering his life in Montpellier, the long-lost Jeanne-Marie whom he claimed to have mourned and buried but whose name he sometimes murmured as he twisted in the night.

"I know who Judah Maccabee is." It was the first time she had even spoken to Moses Viladestes: he was not the sort of Jew who liked to hear the voice of a woman. "He was a man who knew his duty, a true son to his parents, a leader of his people." *As I believed Avram to be,* she added, but only to herself.

"Your wife is an educated woman," said Moses Viladestes. He opened his hands.

Tallow, Gabriela saw with disappointment. As a present he had brought her a handful of wax.

"Now I am going to make candles," announced Viladestes. "Tonight we will celebrate the triumph of the Maccabees and the miracle of the eternal flame."

He stopped and looked at Gabriela. The frost and snow had melted from his beard, leaving it grey and stringy: an old man's beard on an old man's face with a beaked nose too often swollen from the cold; watery eyes that protruded with the constant effort to see what they could no longer quite reach; bony red cheeks that were permanently pinched and flushed from the frost. Only his lips were young: sensuous and muscled, they advertised Kaputin's claim that Moses Viladestes was the most skilled glass-blower in all of Kiev.

Gabriela felt as if the old man were looking into her heart, seeing her thoughts and damning her for daring to complain that the legendary Avram Halevi did not love her in the manner of a more ordinary man.

"It's time to tend the oxen," Gabriela finally said. "I'll be right back."

"I understand," Viladestes murmured, his eyes still locked to hers. And then he fell. At first to his knees, as if to beg pity; then his head lolled forward and he continued his fall, face first. His old man's body met the floor with a dead and rattling sound. For a moment he lay there, dead still. Then suddenly he spoke.

"Excuse me." The old man rolled onto his side, began to struggle to his feet.

Gabriela rushed to him, took his hands in her own. The skin of his fingers was so dry and scaly that they felt like the claws of the chicken Sara had stolen.

"You are welcome here. You *are*." Then, opening her arms, Gabriela hugged Viladestes, rocked him back and forth to make him warm.

423

The air of the shed was thick with the sound of the oxen eating and grinding, the grain slops shaking like oceans in their huge mouths.

Gabriela had brought a tiny candle stub with her. This, set upon a roughly hewn beam, made a small break in the darkness. With the help of its pale yellow light she poured steaming water into the trough, then from a barrel she scooped more of the smelly, half-fermented grain that kept the animals from dying of cold during the long nights.

To live, to die: panting from her own exertions, Gabriela felt for a moment like one of the huge animals she was feeding. Woven in with the sounds of their eating, Gabriela could hear the wet and laboured breathing of the oxen. Matching her own, she thought bitterly, breath for breath. And then, seeing herself in her layers of rags and mouldy hides, looking down in the candlelight at her hands, which had swollen and turned red from cold and damp, she had a sudden memory of herself in Bologna, sitting in the hot sun of the central square, wearing silk dresses and licking the taste of wine and fruit from her lips. Sometimes, now, she did not know whether she wanted to brace herself against misfortune in the hope that the wheel would turn once more, or simply sink into the darkness of straw and frozen wood, become part of the graveyard of winter.

Through the wall she could hear Viladestes, apparently recovered, telling his stories to the others. Moses Viladestes — he had chosen to live through one winter after another into an old age that he surely would have feared if he had known it lay ahead of him.

And what about Avram?

If he had died in Bologna, losing his life for killing Rodrigo Velásquez, surely that would have been both

424

suitable and just: no man could ask more than to die for an act of passion that avenges those he has loved. But instead, almost against his will, he had survived. After all these years, Avram the bastard Marrano had found his faith and become a Jew. The rebellious young man who had scarcely recognized his Jewishness, who for greed and love had put himself through a Christian marriage and let a priest save his life, had somehow used prison to become soft and understanding towards his own religion and soul. A true saint, that was Avram now: yet in the process of learning to know himself, he had closed himself to others.

Gabriela realized that she was clinging to a stanchion and shivering.

She remembered for a moment a morning on their voyage up the Dnieper. On one side of the river had risen a massive cliff, a gigantic rock fortress crowned by evergreens saw-toothing up into the frozen blue sky. On the other side, low alluvial plains, a vast expanse of loamy black soil. The cliff, she had understood, was the unbreachable barrier between herself and the world she had left, a world to which she could not return – León's world of light and art and luxurious living, the world of comfort and beauty and power, the world of gold and the city of man.

Rocking back and forth, growing colder with every breath, Gabriela felt that the obscure string that had once bound her to faith, to hope, to the past, had finally snapped. She had left her life in Bologna, her comfortable marriage with León, to follow her own feelings for Avram. But would he ever love her in return? Or perhaps he was more comfortable as the stranger he had played that night in Toledo, the man who arrives in the dark and is eager to leave before morning. The freezing blackness of the shed was

425

filled with the vacant sounds of the oxen gorging themselves. And as they shook their heads and clucked their tongues, Gabriela could imagine her sister. Leah clucking with them, helping to witness the self-pity of the foolish Gabriela who had wasted her life.

At dinner Viladestes insisted on retelling the story of Hanukkah. But not simply the usual tale, the story of the Maccabee family starting a rebellion against their oppressors in order that the Jews could be free to worship their own jealous God. In Viladestes' story, Judah Maccabee had become one of God's prized helpers, an immortal spirit known by cabbalists to be the guiding force for Jews strayed far from their own land.

"And where *is* our own land?" Gabriela demanded. "Is it Eretz Israel, where we have never been? Spain, where Jews now die on the stake and are roasted like meat? Here?"

Viladestes leaned over the table, smiling at Gabriela like a teacher welcoming a favoured student. His head was so close to the candle that in his watery eyes the yellow flame danced.

"You have almost understood. No wonder you are so famous as an intelligent woman. You are like the woman rabbis of Spain in ancient days. The land of the Jews cannot, as you say, be seen on any map. The land of the Jews is a kingdom of the soul. For when God said he would help Moses lead the Jews back to the Promised Land, he meant not the Promised Land of Israel but the Promised Land where God and His people are tied to each other: heart to heart, soul to soul. It is when a Jew wanders from *that* kingdom that he is in danger."

Gabriela had heard Viladestes rave often enough about the one kingdom of the Jewish God. In Spain

426

he must have been considered a heretic by the orthodox, simply an overenthusiastic fool by the more tolerant. But he had a curious hold over Joseph and Avram. They seemed unable to resist the hypnotic effects of endless talk: Viladestes' long and rambling discourses settled round them like chains — long, twisted theories linked together by brief and blood-soaked battles.

"Tonight," Viladestes announced, his handful of tallow made into a candle, "it is our happiness to celebrate the Festival of the Lights. This one candle burning is the sign that we recognize God's absolute power. The flame of the candle is the flame of our devotion, its light is the light of God's law, our submission to it is our submission to our fate."

As Viladestes spoke, Gabriela looked about the table: Joseph and Avram were listening with such attention that their mouths were agape.

"Our submission to the candle is our submission to our fate," Viladestes repeated, his head bobbing up and down with the rant of his words.

"And how do you submit to the flame of the candle?" Gabriela was unable to resist asking.

"With your heart, first," Viladestes said. He was leaning close to the candle, speaking in a voice of total conviction. Even while she watched, his face grew firmer, his beard thickened and became more patriarchal, his eyes and skin began to shine with the heat of his belief. "The heart is the most important because without the heart the soul can never ascend to God. Once you have believed with your heart, then you must feel what is deeper, the beat of your soul. For the soul is your immortality, the tiny grain of God within you. And when you love God, your soul is connected to God again and God's strength is in you."

"That is beautifully said," Sara now interjected, "but like my mother, I, too, wonder what having your heart and soul open to God has to do with submitting to the flame of a candle."

"The women in this family," Viladestes said. "So wise and so beautiful." He held out his hand. "This is flesh. My soul is immortal but my flesh is not. Yet God, through His commandments, makes it clear that He wants not only our souls linked to His, but our bodies, too: why else does He command what we may eat, whom we may marry, even what we may wear?" He put his hand in the flame. "If our love for God is perfect, He will treat our bodies as His own."

The flame of the candle was spread out against Viladestes' palm. Seconds passed, piled together, became a minute. Only the light of the fire remained to illuminate the faces at the table. Then Viladestes removed his hand and the candle's flame leapt back into the circle of eyes.

"You are crazy," Gabriela muttered.

"Crazy with love."

That night, when Viladestes left, Gabriela took his hand. She could see that there was no wound, not even a faint blister, where the flame had touched.

Later, Gabriela felt that by some magical trick Viladestes had plunged her into the flames. Her body was soaked as she twisted in the blankets. She could smell the sweat rising from her skin, the musty odour of her own discontent mixed with the rank and ancient lather of the beasts whose skins surrounded her.

"If our love of God is perfect," Viladestes had said, "He will treat our bodies as His own."

428

But how perfect a love did God require? Had she not loved God when she was a girl in Toledo? Had she not gone to synagogue every day, often more than once, to pray the prayers that the rabbis had prescribed? Had she not been a dutiful daughter when her mother was alive? Obeyed the commandments? Loaned money at low interest rates to Jews and always repaid her debts? And how had God loved and respected her body?

Sent it into the hands of an ignorant peasant at the fairgrounds, forced her to submit to him before she could escape.

But Avram preferred innocence to survival. What he truly admired was the ability to kill oneself in order to stay faithful. His beloved Jeanne-Marie had known how to carry her purity to the grave. And Avram, as if to join her, had destroyed his life's work as his first act of mourning. No doubt when Avram died, he would pray that his soul be allowed to join hers in the land of milk and honey.

What a trickster Avram had been. To get rid of Gabriela in Barcelona he had tried to kill her with shame. But when his own life was in tatters, he came back to her for help. And with her unstoppable child's passion for him unbroken, she had gathered him into her house, her arms, clasped him close and offered her body as his pillow, her daughter as sister for his son, her home and her husband as his shelter while he planned his revenge.

The darkness broke open. Avram was pushing his way into the bedchamber, carrying in front of him the candle of Viladestes. It made a map of his face, showed crooked paths descending into the oblivion of his beard, circling his eyes, joining the corners of his nose and mouth in lines that could never be spoken.

"You're awake? I thought you must be sleeping."

He crawled to his place beside her. The shrunken prisoner had regained his health now. But the graceful boy from Toledo – *el Gato* – where was he? Had he ever existed, or had she only invented someone to love and admire? Avram was sitting beside her now, his breath laboured after the exertion of twisting himself into position.

"Did you have a bad dream?" His voice solicitous, a grandfather's voice. But the voice that had asked her, in Barcelona, if she had escaped without injury, had been equally caring, equally sympathetic.

"Look at our house." From the candle's flame leapt a fabulous golden sphere. Like the glorious Synagogue of the Tránsito in Toledo, the temple revealed by Viladestes' gift stunned the eye with its harmonious variety. But instead of being constructed of sweet rare woods and precious stones and metals, the vaulted heaven of this new world was a dark patchwork of horse and oxen hides. In place of the round windows of glass and the delicately worked reliefs were the decorative stains left by the sweat and blood of strangers. Even the throne-like pews had their counterpart: large patches rubbed hairless by saddle and yoke attested to the submission of man to God's will. And replacing the Hebrew words of the Law written in a circle around the wall were the thickly sewn seams that held together this temple of winter.

Avram lay down beside her.

"Even the pigs next door live better than we do."

"There are no pigs next door."

"Oxen. Is there a difference?"

"Pigs are bred for slaughter, oxen to the yoke. We are free human beings. Unlike either pigs or oxen, we have seen many countries, lived many lives. We are here, as Viladestes says, of our own free will."

"Free will!" Gabriela exclaimed. This was another of Viladestes' grand flights of fancy. He had told Avram that he should recognize himself to be a man of the future: a human being who by his own efforts and with God's help had — ahead of everyone else – shot out of the Dark Ages like an arrow from a crossbow. In the midst of the chaos of a disintegrating Europe, said Viladestes, with the Church divided against itself and Jews degrading their religion with one heresy after another, Avram Halevi had emerged: a proud and arrogant bastard boy born in a decaying Hebrew capital, nurtured by a free-thinking Muslim, a student at the best Christian university in Europe, always only a heartbeat away from the God of his people. The result, according to Viladestes, was a man so gigantic that Europe had been unable to contain him, a man so independent that he owed allegiance to no king, no noble, no city, no priest or rabbi. Only his own conscience and the direct voice of his own God could instruct him. In short, Viladestes had proclaimed, Avram Halevi, his constant host, was not quite the Messiah promised in the holy writings, but he was a Jew to be watched and admired; a Jew sufficiently strong to survive the new blanket of fear and death being laid across his race; a Jew leading his people into a new and unthinkable country. What a hero Viladestes painted Avram! And with what eagerness Avram absorbed his every word! As if these two Spanish Jews of Kiev must contain the whole cosmos in their two souls.

"We have decided to be here," Avram said.

"Viladestes says that Judah Maccabee is the guide of wandering Jews. And why do we need a guide? Because we have wandered too long, strayed too far from our fate. We should have stayed in Spain, lived or died with our own people. We thought we were

431

fortunate to escape. *Fortunate.* All we did was create our own Hell."

"You didn't listen to Viladestes," Avram said quietly. "He said our true kingdom was no country but God's soul."

Gabriela looked at Avram. Could it be true that he was happy here, so secure in his faith that even in the midst of this frozen Hell he debated disaster and death as if they were a schoolboy's argument about some remote point in the Talmud?

"You could go home," Avram said gently, "back to León. Soon it will be spring. The river will unfreeze. I will travel with you to keep you safe."

"You are very generous."

"There is no need to waste your life in unhappiness," Avram said.

Gabriela laughed. Like a person thrown from one of the horses whose hide now provided her sky, she was seeing double. Through one eye came Avram as he now was, the kindly old man so joined to God and his own soul that he could offer to risk his life so that her own might be improved; but through the other eye she saw the real Avram, the man who had put on this kindly mask: the real Avram was a proud and arrogant boy who had killed his cousin to spite Rodrigo Velásquez; a jealous and mean-hearted lover who had spurned his betrothed in order to seek adventure; a vengeful warrior who had killed and stolen without scruple to preserve his own overblown conception of himself.

"You think you can make me happy by dispatching me from your bed to León's. Like a disobedient bitch who can only be cured by a return to her old master." In her anger her hand had waved violently across the golden sky of their tent, knocking over the candle by mistake. She scooped it up instantly

432

— the brief moment of burning skin and darkness was ended in the blink of an eye.

Avram sighed.

"Go ahead, moan your sorrows." She was whispering and shouting at the same time: that is, her face was red with the effort of shouting, her breath forced, but the sound she made could hardly be heard, a whisper to be contained within the skins so that Joseph and Sara, snuggled together on their warm platform above the hearth, could believe that all around them was peace and serenity. "Moan, groan, twist in the night. Do you think I don't know the truth? It is not me you wish to return to León, it is yourself you wish to return to Jeanne-Marie. You think I am so stupid I don't feel you hiding from me in your sleep? So deaf I have not heard you groaning her name, seen you wrap your arms around yourself and shiver as if to say you would rather be underground clutching her skeleton in the grave than be alive, with me, here of your famous free will, holding another woman in your bed."

"Gabriela."

"*Gabriela.*" Her voice had become a stranger demon filling up her chest and throat, speaking words she had never thought, twisting them with a spite she had never felt. "You think I am some kind of rag to bind yourself with after you have fallen? And throw away after you feel better? Go back to your Jeanne-Marie if you want to. Go to her or anyone you like. I stay here. *This* is my home now, even if you have made it a living Hell. Maybe I *was* happier with León. He did love me better, and I loved him too. But, no, I am not some little character in one of your famous plays; I can't take on one disguise after another. You may be some God-like creature who can do whatever you like. I am simply living out my

433

fate, which is to follow, as meekly as possible, your duplicitous shadow as you fornicate, murder, and martyr your way across half the world."

Avram was sitting erect now, his torn eyelid drooping, the scar like a jewel in the yellow circle of light.

Gabriela felt her bones beginning to shiver and tremble again. She leaned towards Avram, her hands on his shoulders, her lips diving forward, open, closing on his beard, the salty taste of his mouth, her lips drinking up the unseen tears that had formed on his cheeks, tongue licking the curve of his broken hawked nose, tongue rubbing through the bristle of his eyebrows: lips closing again, first over the good eye, then over the bad, taking the scar between her lips, touching the twisted skin with the tip of her tongue.

Now she was on her knees; in the light of the candle she saw that silver had begun to invade his jet-black hair; she opened her robe and pressed his face to the bare skin of her chest. Her bones were crying their own troubles now, crying out to the old bones long buried on the Targa, and even the pressure of Avram's face against her chest hurt, made her want to cry out; but she pressed him closer, pushed her flesh into his mouth: if only he would tear her open now, devour her, let loose the years that were boiling up in her like a volcano begging to erupt. Then the candle was out, he was kissing her, squeezing, biting. With every touch of his teeth she felt warmth flooding out, as if her blood itself was released. And then he was on top of her. He was too much for her, something had gone wrong, she could feel her pelvic bones cracking open with the violence of his lust. "No," she cried. Avram, León, Juan Velásquez, Carlos — all merged together into one insatiable man-stallion, a mindless and murderous beast

434

that wanted to kill her, by whom she needed to be killed. She had her hands around Avram's neck; his strong throat pulsed as she squeezed it; then she drew her hands down his back, digging the nails deep into his flesh.

There was a sudden torrent, a hammering in her heart, a force so strong inside her that she was blown out of this frozen skin-heaven and into the stars, flying through the sky over the Targa and they were young again, Avram's honey lips against hers, the noise of their pleasure drowned in the falling thunder of the river.

She was falling slowly through the sky, a naked woman floating among the planets, Viladestes' candle in hand, gliding slow and serene through the warm white river of stars. For one last moment she had the whole view: then she was plunged into Avram's arms again, their own small heaven of skin and warmth, the past snipped away like a cluster of stray threads with nothing to join.

TWO

O N THE SEVENTH AND LAST DAY OF HANUK-
KAH, BY WHICH TIME VILADESTES' CANDLE
HAD BURNED ITSELF TO A TINY STUB, LEO
KAPUTIN CAME TO VISIT. FOR HIS OFFICIAL
Hanukkah appearance he wore a thick fur coat, and
his wrists and fingers were heavy with bracelets and
rings.

"I hear you were once a trader," he said to Joseph.
Kaputin had a rough mixture of Spanish and Italian,
which he claimed to have learned while sailing merchant vessels up and down the Dnieper.

"I traded money," Joseph said, "not goods."

"You traded money for money?"

"The currencies of many countries."

"Keep gold and silver," Kaputin said, as if this was
a wisdom he alone could dispense. "Forget the rest."
He pointed to his rings, which were greedily sucking
up the last light of Viladestes' candle. "I will tell you
something else," Kaputin offered. "I will hire you to
trade money for money on my behalf, in the summer
when the fairs come. But first you must trade me
sweat for money, so I know you are honest."

"He already sweats," Sara said sharply. "This house
has made him sick."

436

"He sweats in my house," Kaputin said. "I have a factory where he can sweat more usefully."

Joseph pushed back his chair and stood up. Every day the Jewish midwives came to inspect Sara and prepare the welcome for the new baby. But first they attended to Joseph, the proud father, who had been stricken by a mysterious series of fevers since their arrival in Kiev. Teas, powders, herbs, the dried organs of a dozen different rodents had been poured into him. Avram would not permit the use of leeches, but at least one day a week the midwives brought enough wood to stoke the hearth to such a roaring fire that Joseph felt his breath would be burned away. Then they would strip off his shirt and apply plasters to his chest until his skin rose in doughy mounds.

This ordeal had been repeated just hours before Kaputin's arrival.

"I want to work," Joseph now said. "I am tired of being sick." Sara shook her head but Joseph, unheeding, continued. "Let me help you down at the shipyard. You have men building a boat there: I will calculate the wood that is needed. When the time comes for you to purchase more, I will buy it for you."

Kaputin leaned forward, smiling, a fat jewelled finger raised. "I accept your offer," he said, "to become an apprentice in these matters. There is much to learn, but I will charge you no tuition. However," he added, "I still need help in the factory where glass is made. Perhaps you can do both?"

"Let me work in the factory," Avram interjected.

Kaputin laughed. His teeth were yellow and stubbed, as if they too had lived in the earth. "A factory is no place for an old man. Carrying wood and splitting it for the fire tires even a youth."

"Try me."

"Your wife told me you were a doctor. Why would a doctor want to break his back swinging a heavy axe?"

"Even a doctor has to eat."

"Believe me," said Kaputin, "I understand what it is to be poor. When you and your son are rich, you will be a doctor again. In the meantime, men must feed their families. Tonight, free, on the house, I have brought you some vegetables that were grown by my wife. And when I pay you at the factory, I will deduct the rent so that it will be as if this house, too, is free. Please take this as a gift from the heart."

That night, lying under the covers with Sara, Joseph put his ear to her belly to hear the infant's heartbeat.

"You must be out of your mind," Sara whispered. "I want my child to have a father, not a corpse frozen to death at the shipyards — working for nothing."

"Absolutely free," Joseph said. "A gift from the heart."

Sara giggled and he moved his head up to kiss her lips.

"I can do it," Joseph said. "I feel better than I did. And if I don't start earning money, my father will find a way to kill himself on our behalf."

"You worry about him too much, he is stronger than all of us. Remember the storms on the ship? He was the only one who didn't get sick."

But Joseph found himself thinking not of the strength of his father, but of the last visit in prison. "I had no father," Avram had said. "It was no tragedy." At the time Joseph had thought only that Avram was making light of his own past, being his usual evasive self. But now he had a new interpretation: in many ways the years he had lived without his father had been easier than the years since the escape. Alone, he would have to struggle to be a man

438

– and without a father to help him. But in Avram's household the struggle was only intensified – for who could grow in the shadow of such a man?

"Are you asleep?"

"Not yet," Joseph said.

"Are you hoping the baby is a boy or a girl?"

"A girl," Joseph said.

"Tonight, watching you and Kaputin, I wanted a boy. Boys are more peculiar."

The glass factory owned by Leo Kaputin was a low wooden building, located at the end of a path that split the centre of Kiev's tiny Jewish community.

Long and narrow, the factory had walls made from the same warped logs as Kaputin's house. But despite the crooked strips of winter that showed through the carelessly fitted logs, the factory was hotter than an oven.

Each of the cast-iron cauldrons that lined the centre of the room was supported by a stone fire-box. "That," Kaputin said as he pointed to the roiling surface of one of the cauldrons, "is the glass. Your job is to keep it boiling." He clapped his hand on Avram's shoulder and Avram, carrying a gigantic log, had to keep himself from staggering.

"Shove it in," Kaputin said. "Stick it right up until she groans."

Two glass-blowers, drawing liquid from the top of the cauldron, laughed loudly at Kaputin's joke. Kaputin, wearing his fur coat and slick with sweat, grinned and jabbed a stumpy finger towards the roof.

While Kaputin watched, Avram knelt to the door of the furnace. Then, shaking with the effort of controlling the log, he began to put it into the fire. A blast of heat slapped against his face. The fire was so strong that nothing could be seen but a blinding pink-red flame that roared out sparks and heat with the intensity of a sun.

"Don't be shy," Kaputin said, "she wants it all."

Avram leaned closer. The flame was melting his face, annealing it, turning it from the wrinkled hide of an old man into the liquid skin of a baby. The firebox was like the stories of Hell that had been described by the old men of Toledo, and as he stared, transfixed, he imagined himself suddenly cut free from life and tumbling through the flames. For a moment he felt another presence, Death: then the feeling was gone and he was lying on his back, on the floor, the face of Kaputin leering down at him.

"You said you could work like a young man," Kaputin said accusingly.

But Viladestes was pulling him to his feet. Skull filled with the smell of his own singed beard, Avram staggered forward, out the open door of the shed to the woodpile, where he hoisted a new log onto his shoulder; then he returned to the factory where, averting his eyes from the flames, he rammed the log deep into the womb.

At the end of the building where Viladestes and the rest of the glass-blowers worked were shelves of bottles and jars. To one side was the working place of the factory's foreman, a monk from Venice who was being paid a small fortune by Kaputin to teach the secrets of Venetian glass-making. At midday, Viladestes introduced Avram to the monk. For a few minutes the three men talked in Latin as if they were not lost in the pit of a barbaric city but back in the capitals of the world.

"His Order sent him here," Viladestes explained later. "They told him that this was an opportunity to make money for his brethren and to convert the Jews."

"And has he converted any Jews?"

"No. But then he has not received any money either. Kaputin's glass is so poor that it fetches the lowest of prices."

The next day, Avram fell under the weight of a log he was carrying. When his knee hit the ground it cracked against a rock, and he felt the shock of pain go through his body, as if a spike had been driven into the marrow of his bones. Struggling to his feet he saw that Kaputin had been standing behind him, watching. But he had no comment, only looked away with disinterest as Avram continued on his way.

On Sabbath eve Avram sat and steamed his aching bones in the small tile bath that Kaputin had built for the Jews of Kiev. Viladestes sat beside him. The light had almost gone from the sky, leaving the bathhouse in a strange and limpid half-darkness, a hanging womb of steam in which the two men were surrounded by huge silvery cauls. In his luminous arch Viladestes was gaunt and ancient; loose skin hung over his bones with no intervening cushion of muscle or flesh.

"You are tired?"

Avram tried to find a place to shift his weight without sending his back into new torment. "Now I know what God meant when He said that man would live by the sweat of his brow."

"It is worse when you are older."

Avram sank deeper into the hot water. His hands were raw and blistered from the axe, his shoulders so sore from chopping and carrying that his muscles and ligaments felt as though they had been half torn from his bones.

"You know," Viladestes said, "that you are doing the work of two men."

441

"Ten."

"I am serious. The week before Kaputin hired you, there were two men doing your job. They both died of the fever that is sweeping the city."

"And so Kaputin decided to make me a gift of their positions."

"To test you," Viladestes said. "He told me that he has looked into your eyes and seen who you are."

Avram laughed. "If Kaputin has discovered the nature of my soul, then he has found out something every man wants to know about himself. Who am I?"

"You know who you are," Viladestes said. In the steam his voice had become charged with certainty. Avram felt his heart beating faster, as it had decades before when Ben Ishaq was about to impart one of his secrets. "Admit to me that you are a man who knows himself."

"I know now," Avram said. Delirious in the silver steam he was one of God's chosen, floating in the half-light between Heaven and earth.

"But your journey is still unfinished."

Viladestes twisted his skinny frame and, half-bent still, scurried towards the changing room. By the time Avram, lame and sore-footed, could follow him, Viladestes had disappeared.

The day after the Sabbath, Avram was back at the factory. He had hoped the rest would heal his body; instead, his ailments had only increased, and as he walked into the factory he had to force himself erect, reminding himself of Ben Ishaq when the old man was trying to fool his apprentice into thinking that he was healthy.

But this day there was no one to deceive: Kaputin and Viladestes had gone to arrange for the purchase

442

of some of the special sand from which the glass was made. Avram, so sore he could hardly walk, caught himself groaning aloud as he worked. But without Kaputin to make him nervous by gloating over his troubles, he was able to keep from falling. At noon the chief glass-blower, the monk from Venice, approached Avram with a jar of wine.

"If you drink some of this," he said, "your back will stop complaining."

"Then it is worth drinking," replied Avram, and accepted the offer of the jar. The wine was rough; as it went down it clawed at his throat the way the stolen raw wine of Toledo once had. But soon he felt the muscles of his back, which had been squeezing his spine in a spasm of protest, begin to unclench.

"Signore Viladestes tells me you are a doctor."

"I was."

"Signore Viladestes told me that you performed the most famous operation in the history of Bologna, that you, a Jew, rescued the Church from its fatal division with one stroke of the knife."

Avram felt his stomach give way. Of course this was what Viladestes must have meant when he said his identity was known.

"Was it a difficult operation?"

"For whom – the surgeon or the patient?"

"Signore Viladestes told me that the patient died." The monk smiled and clapped Avram on the shoulder. "My superior was one of the ones paying Rodrigo Velásquez to kill Baldassare Cossa. When the plot failed, we all had to flee. If not for you, I would still be in Venice making plots against the pope and having nightmares about how I would be tortured when they caught me."

"You prefer it here?"

443

"Of course I do. Here I live with a woman who gives me more pleasure every night than I used to receive during a year in the cloisters. But you – " He leaned closer to Avram, and Avram found himself gripping the wine jar as if it were a sword with which to cut his way to freedom one more time.

"You, too, are safe here," the monk said.

"And now, if you will help me finish the bottle which you are preparing to break over my innocent pate, I will help you to carry your wood this afternoon. My lips have decided that they would rather spend the day sucking foul Russian wine than blowing inferior glass in the service of the Jew Kaputin."

There was a small synagogue, a wooden building in the yard of the glass factory, where Avram went to pray in the evenings and on the Sabbath. The building had no windows; it was only a large shed with an alcove for the ark.

In the synagogue he prayed to God but he heard no response. Night after night he walked home in the freezing dark: the universe had spat him out, the sky slammed black and cold as a coffin's lid.

By his side, most nights, walked Viladestes. Since the week of Hanukkah, Viladestes had become almost one of the family. Before dinner he would recite the prayers over the food; and when the meal was ended he would initiate discussions on controversial theological points in the Torah, forcing everyone to join in as if they were the eager – but stupid – pupils, and he the tolerant rabbi.

Then, refusing to leave until the others went to bed, Viladestes would make Avram sit next to him at the hearth. Pulling out tattered scrolls, which he claimed to be original copies of the Zohar itself, the holy book of the Cabbala, Viladestes would trace the letters by the light of the dying fire.

"Behind each letter is the light," Moses Viladestes said, "and if you follow the light it will lead you to the end of history, the end of time, to God's heart itself."

"If God has a heart, why does He make it so cold here?"

Viladestes laughed. "So that you and I will crouch in a corner praying, my friend, instead of lying about like sleeping snakes in the sun."

At night Avram's back often throbbed too much for sleep. He then would lie with his eyes closed and try to imagine himself sitting on the wall of the city of Toledo, his youth and his future tightly coiled inside him.

The morning Sara's water broke, Avram went to work as usual. It was mid-March and the sky was so clear that as he stood in the yard splitting wood he could feel the sun's heat burning into the skin of his face. By now his body had grown almost accustomed to the labour; but in the process he discovered that he had become an old man.

At noon and again two hours later he laid down his axe and rushed home to check on Sara. Her labour had begun, but it was still slow and intermittent. "Go back to the factory," Gabriela said. "If anything happens we will send for you. Even the midwives have not yet arrived." It was true that Sara seemed in no discomfort. Pausing only for the worst moments of the contractions, she continued to knead the dark bread as she did every other day. Joseph, home from his labours at Kaputin's shipyard, watched her every move.

445

Just before work ended, Avram was approached by one of the midwives. At the sight of her he panicked, threw down his tools, and grabbed his tunic in preparation for running home to whatever emergency must be happening.

"The labour is still slow. Your wife sends the message that there is time for you to go to the synagogue to say your prayers."

Kaputin was standing beside him.

"Congratulations, it is a blessing to become a grandfather." Kaputin, it was well known, had thirty-two grandchildren. Once Avram had seen the whole family assembled at the synagogue. Gathered together outside the door – adults, adolescents, children, babes-in-arms – they looked like pale sunless roots torn out of the same plot of earth from which Kaputin himself had been miraculously extracted.

"Even one grandchild is something," Kaputin said. "When there is one, there can be hope for more." Kaputin pressed a coin into Avram's palm. "Take this gift, from one brave grandfather to another."

Avram looked down at Kaputin's square face, the beard still littered with bits of the huge lunch he had stuffed into himself.

"You have pride," Kaputin said. "I have money."

He took Avram's arm and led him past the woodpile to the synagogue. The bell for the day's ending had not yet rung: Avram and Kaputin were the only ones inside the shed that served the Jews of Kiev as a house of worship.

"You don't like me," Kaputin announced, "but I like you. I am the boss, the mayor, the rabbi, the king. I am a true Kaputin, like my great-great-grandfather the king. I will be remembered by my descendants as the Jew who made a place for the other Jews of Kiev. You, Señor Halevi, have pride – but

446

even the miracles you used to perform cannot have saved more lives for our God than this synagogue. Count them, I dare you; you will agree that I have saved more lives than you. Yet you think little of me in your heart, and no doubt in your private times with your wife you say that I pay small wages, rent you a house that is not the palace you dream of. But look at the more important thing I have given you, free, from the heart."

Kaputin waved his stubby fingers in the air, making the sweep from the door through which they had come, past the curtained-off ladies' section, towards the synagogue's most important feature – the ark in which the Torah was kept. This cupboard was itself separated from the main room – not by the old and mouldy cloth used to divide the sexes, but by a ragged curtain of purple velvet onto which was crookedly sewn a giant silver star of David.

"Here," Kaputin said, "your grandchild will learn what it is to be a Jew. Here you will carry it in your arms; and here it will listen to the prayers that we offer to our God, smell the smell of our people, listen to the mourning of our exile. When it is old enough to understand, here Viladestes will teach your grandchild the language of our people, help him to memorize the Torah so that running through his mind will be the words that God has given to us. If you are so fortunate as to have a grandson, I myself will give the boy a silk prayer shawl. He will be barmitzvahed here and where you and I sit today, you and your son will sit and cry with joy thirteen years from now. If you have not a boy but a girl, I will be the first to contribute something fine for her dowry. And when the time comes, God willing, this is where she will be married. Who knows, perhaps even to one of my own grandchildren. When that happens, you and your esteemed wife — whose fame has already spread through the city — will sit here and weep with happiness."

"I shall look forward to that," said Avram.

"I know," Kaputin replied. "You will, and your love will go out to me. For it is my pleasure to provide all these things and many more to the Jews of my kingdom, absolutely free of charge, and every time I give, it is truly a gift from the heart."

At home the kitchen was blazing with candles. Although Sara still paced about between contractions, each seizure of the womb now exacted its tribute of silent tears.

While they waited, the four midwives ate the bread that Sara had baked that afternoon and drank the wine that Kaputin's wife had donated to the family to help them through the night.

It was not until midnight, Sara almost constantly in tears, that the midwives consented to let Avram examine his daughter-in-law. By then she was on the kitchen table, lying on her side and scarlet with her constant exertions. The midwives led him into the enclave they had made. Their amulets, old animal parts, their lucky herbs and dried plants were pinned to the blanket like so many pagan charms. After making Avram swear not to look at Sara's naked body, they pulled up the cover. Avram, eyes closed, let his hands be guided to Sara's belly. Then, after he had felt it to satisfy himself that the womb was still healthy, he pushed his fingers inside her until he could touch the cervix. As he felt for the size of the opening, he remembered the exact feeling of Isabel Velásquez, the way she had been closed almost as tightly as a woman who had not even started to labour. But Sara was having better luck: three fingers wide. Exploring, Avram felt the baby's head. Down its centre was the narrow groove where an infant's skull is separated like a halved egg waiting to be joined. As he touched the baby's skull he felt it move. And somewhere, deep inside himself, an answering shudder: as if, his doctor's skills useless, his own soul was calling directly to his grandchild, persuading it to come into the world. There was another movement of the skull. Avram felt it twist as the cervix opened almost a finger wider.

"Are you going to bleed her?"

Avram was kneeling now so that his head was close to Sara's. Hours of pain had left her eyes puffed with crying: the anticipated miracle of childbirth had become an endless nightmare.

"There will be no bleeding."

"Are you going to open her up? We have heard that you perform miracles, plucking children from the very bellies of their – "

Now Sara's eyelids quivered with terror.

"No," Avram said. "There will be no operation." He pushed Sara's hair back from her forehead and, doing so, realized that he had never once touched his daughter-in-law, never held her in consolation during Joseph's illness, never reassured her that the birth would be easy.

Once more, he looked into her eyes. They were like Gabriela's had once been: fierce and eager for adventure, yet curiously submissive to whatever tragedy might be waiting.

"There will be no operation," he repeated. "The baby is taking a long time preparing to be born, but soon it will be ready." As he spoke he stroked Sara's face. "The only medicine you need now is a small glass of wine. So far it has been your job to endure:

449

soon it will be your task to push the baby out of the comfort of your handsome belly and into the world."

Avram made his way through the curtain and into the kitchen. Gabriela was sitting at the hearth drinking tea with Joseph. In all these months, Avram realized, he had not only failed to touch Sara; he had hardly exchanged a word with his son, even with Gabriela. Work at the factory had turned him into a slave, with only the strength to sweat and to sleep.

"The child?" Gabriela asked.

Avram looked at her: while he had been living his nightmare, Gabriela had made life flow through the frozen household.

"The child will be born soon. And Sara is well."

Two hours after midnight the baby was born. While the midwives fought among themselves for the honour, Avram delivered it.

"Who ever heard of such a thing," the midwives grumbled, "a man delivering a baby? Luckily, it is a boy."

Avram pulled back the curtain. A new being: the kitchen pulsed with the energy of birth, and everyone began to glow like embers of an old fire that has been blown back into life. From his purse Avram took four coins that he had saved, and distributed them among the midwives. A few minutes later they were gone.

Avram looked around him: Joseph, Sara, Gabriela. Risking everything, they had rescued him from prison and delivered him to freedom. When he had burst across the courtyard and into the carriage, they had been waiting: dressed in white, full of hope, ready to die for him.

"Thank you," he said. But no one heard him: Gabriela, the tension released, was finally weeping with relief; Joseph was staring happily at his son; Sara was placidly holding the infant to her breast.

Towards the dawn, still unable to sleep, Avram lay beside Gabriela.

"Avram." Gabriela's whisper filled the tent.

"Are you awake?"

"I'm awake," Avram said. He could barely choke the words through his clogged throat.

"Are you happy?"

"Yes. I am happy."

"I love you," Gabriela whispered. "I wish we could have had a child. Do you love me?"

"I do love you," Avram said. "I do love you."

As he said the words he felt their truth: Gabriela was as much a part of his life as his own arms or legs. "I do love you," he said once more. His heart clenched with doubt but he leaned down to her, put his mouth to hers, kissed her lips slowly and carefully. "You are my wife now."

Morning light leaked through the seams of the tent, turning Gabriela's face to a pale ghostly blue. He could see that his words had made her eyes fill with tears; in answer his own tears began to flow. But as he embraced her he felt his heart still resisted; he was weeping, he realized, because no matter what he said or even felt, his heart was determined to betray him, clinging stubbornly to its own invincible truth.

An hour later, just as the sun was rising but only after the baby had been inspected another dozen times, Avram set out with Viladestes on a horse-drawn sledge to the village outside Kiev where Kaputin bought his wood.

The grip of the cold had loosened. These mornings when Avram breathed deep he no longer felt a scream of panic from his lungs. In fact, as Avram and Viladestes rode the sledge, the sun was so dazzling in the sky that Avram began humming to himself and tapping his heel in time to the horses' progress.

Soon the city was behind them and the horses, themselves infected by the good weather, were trotting along a narrow track through the forest.

Avram looked at the trees, the icy crust of snow that multiplied the glare of the sun, the pure blue of the sky that held it. Into his own hands his grandson had dropped, still wet from the long struggle down the birth canal. Holding the baby, he had seen its eyes open: eyes blue as a sky that had never known a cloud. He had handed the baby to Joseph while the cord pulsed out its final signals. Then, with the last of his Toledo knives, Avram cut the cord. As Joseph passed the baby to Sara, who put it to her breast, the baby coughed into life and Sara, with one final push, released the afterbirth from her womb.

"Antonio," Joseph had said. "Antonio will be his name."

"I never thought it could happen," Avram said. "To think that we have travelled so far from Toledo, yet the blood that was cut loose there is still running from one generation to the next. And to find a new Antonio, one who can hope for a more fortunate life — " He stopped. He could not even remember if he had ever spoken to Viladestes about Antonio, if he had ever told the secret of his death.

"God has kept his promise and answered our prayers," said Viladestes. He was looking directly into Avram's eyes and Avram felt a sudden loosening in his heart, as if Viladestes knew about Antonio after all — knew and had forgiven him — knew about Antonio, about his betrayal of Gabriela, about all of the lives he had taken or ruined.

452

The horses had stopped. Winter air was laced with spring, and the soft melting hummocks of white snow threw back the heat of the sun.

"Now," said Viladestes gently, "is the time to forget the past."

The eyes that Avram was accustomed to seeing in the glow of candlelight or the dark shadows of the glass-blowing factory were in the sun a fierce and glinting Spanish black. "It is the bird," Viladestes said, "and you are the cage. Open your heart and let the bird fly free."

Avram looked from Viladestes' burning eyes to the snow, from the snow to the naked winter wood of the towering oak trees that grew only a few paces back from the road.

"Let the past fly free," Viladestes urged softly, "let the past fly free. Your grandson has been born, God has shown His faith in a new life. Now is the time for you, too, to have a new day, a new life."

Avram felt Viladestes' words echoing through him and then, looking into the old man's eyes, felt himself suddenly breathing the same air he had breathed in the prison at Bologna, felt his heart beating the same rhythms, his soul again naked and undefended.

Turning from Viladestes, he leapt off the sledge and walked into the pure embracing snow. Soon he was deep in the forest, surrounded by the mysterious smell of the waking trees, the thunder of rising sap and thawing earth.

Beneath his feet he could feel rivers rushing underground, ready to spurt new life. But when he looked up, the earth betrayed him and he was thrown onto his back, landing in the soft snow with a sigh.

Through the army of branches above, clawing and galloping towards the sky, he could see the sun. Suddenly he felt like one of those ancient fanatics who spent their lives stumbling through the desert in hope of a vision of God. But because he was in exile, the desert had been replaced by snow, the mountains by trees, the dryness of thirst by the hollow cold.

He was travelling light – as Antonio had so long ago recommended.

His eyes were on the sun, on the light fractured by the bare branches.

In his dizziness the branches began to dance, forming the letters of the alphabet, each letter on fire as it was consumed by the brilliant yellow light, each letter burning its way into oblivion until it was replaced by the next. The letters grew larger, began to fill the whole sky as they spelled out the secret name of God.

Then he felt a breath behind him, heard the tired groan of an old man labouring through the snow.

He leapt to his feet, ashamed to have Viladestes catch him in such a ridiculous position.

But he was alone in the forest.

THREE

THAT SPRING, AVRAM AND JOSEPH HALEVI WERE SENT BY KAPUTIN TO FIND A MARKET FOR HIS GLASSWARE IN NOVGOROD. THE YEAR WAS 1422.

"Don't misunderstand my trust in you," Kaputin said to Avram, the evening before he left.

"What," Gabriela asked, "is there to be misunderstood?"

"It is my gift to your husband to send him on this great journey," Kaputin said. "I am asking only that he remember that, and keep my interests foremost."

"My husband feels nothing but gratitude towards you," Gabriela said. "You do not have to remind a loyal slave to obey."

The journey was to last two months. After the farewell dinner Gabriela, trembling at such a long separation, sat with Avram by the hearth. The loft of the house had been converted to living quarters: in it now slept Joseph and Sara, as well as Antonio. Sara was already pregnant again.

Where the sleeping tent had been there was now a permanently walled-off bedroom for the grandparents, as they were now known. And to remind them of the journey they had made, Gabriela had hung the skins of the sleeping tent on one wall, tapestries from Toledo and Bologna on the others.

"Are you looking forward to this voyage?"

"I am feeling tired," Avram said.

"The winter was long."

Gabriela put her hand on Avram's back, rubbed the broad space between his shoulder-blades.

"I miss Viladestes," Gabriela said. "I still find myself waiting for him to walk in the door."

"I miss him, too."

When Viladestes had died that winter, frozen to death in the small room that he kept, Gabriela was torn by such grief that she thought the lucky angel that had preserved their lives since the escape from Bologna must have deserted them. Now she was perpetually nervous and full of foreboding. Sometimes when the others were out of the house she would find herself imagining the horrible fate that might have befallen them.

"I wish you were staying," Gabriela said. "The whole time you're away, I will worry about you."

"Come with us in the morning to the docks. When you see us board the ship, you'll know that we are well and that we will return to you."

In the morning, as Avram had suggested, she accompanied him and Joseph down to the river. It was a bright and turbulent dawn. The muddy flats leading to the shore were beginning to sprout their spring grasses, birds returning from the south chirped and swooped from one budding tree to the next.

"When you return, it will be summer," Gabriela said. They were standing by the river: broad and molten, coloured by the rising sun, it flowed by like some great and untouchable force capable of carrying away even the most tenaciously gripped wishes.

Gabriela looked up the river, tried to imagine the ship sailing back, two months later, carrying her men back from the heart of Russia into her heart. Instead she saw only the icy water, glints of bubbles the colour of steel.

"Be careful," Gabriela said. Avram swept her into his arms, squeezed her so hard against his chest that for a moment she lost her breath. As she was losing herself in Avram's strength, she wished that they could be dying now, together in one another's arms. Then she felt Avram's dagger pressing through his tunic and into her breasts.

"Don't worry. We'll be back safely."

"I love you. And now I want to go home while you're still here, near me."

As soon as the ship began to move, Avram Halevi felt like a young man again. He straightened his shoulders and cracked his spine: winter split open like a thick and musty shell. Through his excited blood moved the constant rocking of the water as the valleys became narrow and the mountains erupted into the sky, wave after wave of great pine forests. He breathed in the rich air; the scent of pine burst through him like hashish – and when he stretched his arms over the side of the boat, he could feel the ghost of his youth expanding with pleasure.

One afternoon he saw Death: the face that had winked at him from Kaputin's furnace was a cold white sun on the surface of the water.

Joseph was standing beside him. "What are you staring at?"

"Death."

"Are you sick?"

Avram made no reply, but he was startled at the fear laced through his son's voice. Death was what you feared when your life was still unlived.

Novgorod was a city of wood. Even as they entered the harbour, they were overwhelmed by the scent of pine oil. Pine streets, pine houses stretching up three stories of vertical pine logs, sixty factories where pine furniture was hammered out by carpenters who went to and fro with the creamy-white shavings curled into their garments like fur.

Only the churches were made out of stone. In the zigzag wooden streets they rose up like rocky fists, ready to pound the truth into any head too soft-wooded to believe.

With the money Kaputin had provided, they stayed in one of the city's most luxurious inns. "If you're going to sell," Kaputin had instructed them, "you must appear to be rich already." That evening they drank brandy, and when it was time for them to eat, great chunks of succulent lamb were brought to their table.

With the meat there was a jug of wine, and then after the wine more brandy. Sitting at the long table, drinking and laughing with the other guests, Avram found himself looking into the great roaring fire that filled the hearth. But instead of seeing the red and dizzy Hell that he had discovered in the ovens of Kaputin's workshop, he saw instead great chunks of Novgorod pine blazing and spitting enormous good cheer and happiness, so much hope that the whole room was filled with the exciting sound of knots exploding and the sizzle and flare of boiling sap. By the time midnight had come and the other travellers had gone to bed, Avram felt his own blood nourished by the power of this fire. When he stood, the room wavered: then there was a moment of brilliant clarity: the empty tables, the stone chimney, the scarlet flames shooting up into the blackness of the night

458

– here was a world fit for a man who had carried the same tiny cares for too long.

Each evening he ate and drank more than the evening before. As he collapsed into sleep each night, his blood was dancing with the brandy; in the mornings he slept late, while the meat he had eaten the night before found a place in his own flesh. He felt like a baby again: fire and happiness at night followed by long dizzying sleeps from which he awoke so refreshed and full of energy that he sprang to the window and tore open the shutters to see what wonderful things were happening in the streets.

At the fair, he did no business at all – that was left to Joseph – but rushed from one stall to the next, speaking French, Italian, even Spanish in a wonderful orgy of loquaciousness; and when his tongue had loosened and expanded and found a way to speak real words again, it became a boaster about the prowess of his son, the beauty of his grandson, the horrors of Kiev – city of winter and desolation.

Day after day reeled by. Avram felt like an old and rocky riverbed brought to life by an unexpected flood. One afternoon he bought a mirror and spent hours with it in his room, trimming his beard and scraping the yellow from his teeth until they were white and gleaming. The next day he exchanged one of Kaputin's coins for silk underthings to comfort his reawakened skin, a soft cotton tunic to replace the rough garment that had seen five years' service.

That night he and Joseph invited a group of Italian travellers to be their guests. At the end of the banquet, when all the others had either gone to their rooms or simply passed out at the table, Avram found himself alone with the servant who had been bringing them their food.

His blood was in the grip of the brandy again, pulsing with a sad and wonderful clarity that took him back to the years of Montpellier. He looked at the fire and let his ears fill with the sound of pine knots splitting in the heat. Then his eye, of its own volition, swung to the face of the serving-girl.

"Jeanne-Marie!"

Had he spoken or just thought the words? She stepped towards him, the dream he had never since dared to dream.

"Jeanne-Marie," he said again, this time letting his mouth feel her name. Now the brandy raced through him, pain and love mixed into a knife that was tearing him apart. He staggered forward. The girl was looking directly at him.

As Avram's arms prepared to embrace what he knew must be a hallucination, he felt flesh and breath rush against his own, winy lips kissing his, hands frantically sliding under his new clothing to reach his skin, pull him closer.

Avram held his breath. He was catapulted back into the netherworld of his years in prison, the world where memories were so strong that he would sometimes burst into them like a man rushing into a room.

He raised his hand.

"Don't you want me?" She had deep brown eyes, shaded by long curving lashes whose feathery touch his skin was beginning to crave. "Jeanne-Marie," he said again. Desire, unbidden, slammed through him.

"I know who you are," the girl said. "You used to be a famous doctor: they were talking about you at the fair – the operations you performed, the lives you have saved."

"Jeanne-Marie." But this time he only whispered her name. Through him now was flooding, a river forgotten, all the love he had had for her.

"Tell me," the girl started, but Avram could hardly hear her because the sensation of loving Jeanne-Marie was so crippling that he had grabbed the girl's shoulders to keep from sinking to the floor, "is it true that you are the Jew who killed a cardinal?"

Avram's right hand flew free, ready to slap the face of this impudent whore. Then he stopped, looked at his hand, saw the fingers that had once so gracefully held the surgeon's knife. "My doctor," Jeanne-Marie had once whispered to him in bed, "my saint who would cure the whole world with the same hands he uses so wickedly on his loving wife."

"Let the past fly free," Viladestes had said.

But the past had not gone anywhere -- except into hiding. The boy who had burned to make the human body into a transparent machine, the man who had dreamed of raising peasants into angels, the father who had been consumed by rage and the desire for revenge -- they had all been merely locked away.

"Are you?"

"You have a sharp tongue for a whore."

The girl raised her face and laughed. Now Avram saw she was truly not Jeanne-Marie – not even Jeanne-Marie reincarnated. But she was beautiful nonetheless: and her mischievous smile reminded him of Jeanne-Marie's when she prodded him to declare his love.

Avram drew a gold coin from the pocket of his tunic. "Take this," he said, "it will bring you more enjoyment than the body of an old man who has already been given his share of love."

But in his room, lying in his blankets, the breath of his son only a few feet away from him, Avram was overwhelmed by sadness.

Even when he opened his eyes to break the spell, the face, the perfume, the love of Jeanne-Marie hung over him. From the window of the children's bedroom, the mercenaries of Montreuil had dangled her like a grotesque and broken puppet. And looking up at her, Avram remembered, he had felt a brief moment of panic and rage; then nothing at all, only a silence inside himself. Death. Death was what was left when life somehow slipped away. Death was what remained when the blood had emptied itself onto the ground or the operating table. Death was what happened to those he had impaled on his furious sword. *Thou shalt not kill*, God had commanded. Now he had killed more men than he could remember, more men than Antonio had boasted about, perhaps even more men than he had saved with his doctor's knowledge.

Looking up at Jeanne-Marie, he had felt the silence of death: not only her death, but the death of his feelings, of the life he had struggled to build, had enjoyed so much, had known must eventually come tumbling down because it was built on lies. Death: a dark and endless well of oblivion he had spent his whole life dancing around — fearing it, craving it, pulling some back from the edge while sending others to its silent ending.

Avram sat up and rubbed his face with his hands. True, he had escaped from prison, but that was three years ago. But the winter in Kiev had been worse than any of the winters in his cell, and now memory had imprisoned him again; he was locked once more into the catechism he had whipped himself with every night for twelve years.

What lies had his life with Jeanne-Marie been built on?

First of all, the lie of his conversion. He had pretended, along with Jeanne-Marie and François, to be
no longer a Jew. But the world knew they were Jews,
thought of them as Jews, treated them as Jews. The
lie had covered them with false security, but had
fooled no one else.

Secondly, there was the lie of his belief in the first
lie. For he had known from the very first dizzy moment with Jeanne-Marie that he was trading love for
truth. That the life he would live with her would be
built within the dream-world imagined by this beautiful but innocent girl. Of course he could have tried
to break her innocence, to introduce her into the
darker truth of God's Mistakes, of cities consumed
by hatred and flames, of love turned sour by ambition
and betrayal.

But that would have turned Jeanne-Marie into
Gabriela.

Who had died for the lies he had lived?

Not himself, who deserved to, but Jeanne-Marie,
who was their innocent victim.

Avram stood up and began to pace the room as he
had once paced his cell.

He had prevented Jeanne-Marie from turning into
Gabriela — but it was now Gabriela in his arms,
Gabriela who was his wife, Gabriela who whispered
love-words to him.

Love. Why could he not *love* Gabriela with his
whole heart? For it was she who had saved him from
prison, she who had carried the family through the
winter in Kiev, she who had brought Joseph and Sara
together so that their grandson could be born.

"Corruption and wisdom are twins," Viladestes
had once said. "The innocent have no need of knowledge; they have their hearts."

And, Avram now wondered, were the hearts of the innocent filled with the sweet sounds of the harp and singing angels? His own heart was full, but not with anything that the Bible talked about. It was full and breaking with the bitterness of love wasted, love lost, love transformed into death.

He had begun to cry without realizing it, and now each new sob sent sharp stabs through his aching heart so that he found himself gasping in pain and sorrow, clutching his chest, and sinking to the floor, falling into darkness as the floor rushed up to greet him.

When his bones first cracked into the wood he felt himself burst through a barrier, the wall – like the wall of Toledo – that separated the wanderings of the living from the city of the dead.

Then around him were wrapped the arms of his son, strong as a man's arms they lifted him. Soon Joseph was weeping with him; the night that had never been mentioned, the people whose name they had never one time since spoken, seemed to be flickering in the room between them, joining them, until finally Avram – who by now was comforting the tears of his son – lifted Joseph's face to his and looked at it in the dawn light.

Brown eyes – eyes like the eyes of Jeanne-Marie, a forehead that was high and bony, like his own, the kind of skull holding a mind that knew how to be arrogant; a strong chin covered by a black and thickly curling beard; high cheekbones burned red by the frozen winds of Kiev. A man. A Jew. A stranger.

"I was thinking about the night your mother was killed."

"I think about it, too. All the time."

"Your mother and I loved each other very much." Here Avram's voice broke, and he looked away from Joseph's face.

"I know. But I am glad you told me."

Avram turned back to his son. The eyes of his son, Jeanne-Marie's eyes, were wide open with love. "I also love my son," said Avram. "Forgive me if I have not shown it."

"You," Joseph cried, "you have nothing to be forgiven."

The piercing note of his voice opened the last door: without warning Avram found growing before his eyes the scene of his mother being raped by a huge and screaming shadow, and through his blood shot an arrow of hatred and fear.

Avram stood up. He put his hand on his son's shoulder.

"Let the past fly free," Viladestes had urged. But Avram, for the first time in his life, felt free of the need to escape it.

FOUR

I N 1445, WHEN HE WAS SEVENTY-FIVE YEARS OLD, AVRAM HALEVI FELL ILL. LYING IN HIS BED HE COULD FEEL HIS HEARTBEAT GROWING FAINTER, AND WHEN HE CLOSED HIS EYES HE FELT LIKE A BIRD SKIMMING effortlessly over the sea.

As he wavered between sleep and consciousness, he let his back settle deep into the mattress, as if it was already sinking into the ground. According to Gabriela, the bed was filled with the finest feathers of Kiev. And why not? When he opened his eyes, even in his own bedroom he saw evidence of such wealth that he had to struggle to remember how completely his fortunes had changed.

He and Joseph had come back from Novgorod six months later than planned, but bringing with them a gigantic shipment of pine.

Only two years after this journey, Avram Halevi, wearing the thick ermine-trimmed robes of a successful Kiev merchant, had the pleasure of supervising the demolition of the hovel Kaputin had rented to him. Constructed around a courtyard, in memory of the palaces of Toledo and, like them, with walls thick enough to be a fortress, the new Halevi home was built, so wide and so tall that even the lumpy dwelling of Leo Kaputin was thrown into its shadow.

"You see," Kaputin said, "I told you that with my help you would succeed. And now look at the wonderful temple you have built. While I wasted my money on charity for the poor Jews of Kiev, you have had the wit to protect yourself."

As Kaputin also predicted, Avram Halevi lived long enough to see his grandson become a man in the synagogue Kaputin had provided. However, by the time of this happy occasion, the ragged ark had been replaced by a much grander one – imported courtesy of the ever-flourishing Halevi lumber business – and the synagogue had been expanded to hold the new Jewish immigrants who were coming to Kiev to escape the escalating horrors of the European Inquisitions.

In 1437, yet another of Kaputin's predictions came to pass, although he himself had died years before. In that year Avram Halevi was sixty-seven years old, an old man who, hand in hand with his wife, ruled a family empire of timbering and money-changing. It was an empire large enough to give employment to many of the Jews of Kiev – now so numerous that a second synagogue had become necessary. But the prophesied marriage between Antonio and one of Leo Kaputin's granddaughters took place in the old synagogue. And before the ceremony was completed, the rabbi, a young man come all the way from Paris, had eulogized Leo Kaputin – whom he had never known – as a man who had been a father to the community he had created, a man who had given from the heart even while his pockets were empty.

The heart: since the night his heart had broken open in Novgorod, Avram had never again spoken the name of Jeanne-Marie.

467

Beside him, watching him die, was Gabriela. He had loved Jeanne-Marie better, but fate had tied him to Gabriela. Though for years now his eyesight had been growing misty, he could see her face clearly enough: beautiful, devoted, youthful still – she was as attentive to his dying as she had been to his life.

Only a few minutes ago she had leaned over and whispered something into his ear. "Do you remember the story Moses Viladestes told us about Judah Maccabee becoming the guiding angel of the Jews?"

"I remember."

"Now look at Kiev. It is so filled with Jews that soon there will be a third synagogue. You and I, Leo Kaputin and Moses Viladestes – *we* were the guiding angels. We came here first and made a place for others to follow."

And Avram, despite his dying, had laughed so hard he had almost choked. If only Antonio Espinosa were here, crouching beside them and listening to these words; if only Antonio could hear that after all these years God's Mistakes had become God's guides to the future, that the man of science who was going to escape his fate and leap into the new age had instead, like a crazed and backward Moses, pointed the way to a city at the edge of the world. Where, to be sure, in his old age he had taken up his doctor's instruments again to teach surgery and anatomy to the European Jews whose minds were open to such techniques; and had even begun wielding the scalpel again – to strip away the foreskins of the crowds of boys being born to the new Jewish mothers of Kiev.

Behind Gabriela, joining her death-watch, were Joseph and Sara. And with them waited their children – whose names he sometimes forgot – and even a few children of their children.

Death had long ago changed from an occasional mischievous visitor to a constant presence. Behind his own laboured breath, Avram could hear the more certain rhythms of his fate. He closed his eyes. He was skimming above the waves, a land bird so far from shore that he would never turn back.

El Gato – the Cat. The man with the silver knife. The slayer of superstition. The Jew who killed a cardinal. The venerable and wealthy businessman. Avram smiled to himself. The night the ghetto of Toledo was sacked he had turned his back on safety and, spreading his physician's cloak wide, leapt from the wall of Juan Velásquez. In a way, he had been flying ever since, a fancy bird who knew how to change his plumage with the season.

Every few years – or was it minutes? – his heart would stop, locking within itself like a wheel no longer able to turn. Then he would feel something inside of him lurch, a last burst of energy sparking him back to life.

He opened his eyes.

They were crowding around him, bending over him, stooping to kiss the old grandfather goodbye. It was time for him to die now, to be sent to his fate, an old bone thrown to a jealous and wrathful God, so that others might be permitted their turn in the sun.

Men's lips scratchy with beard. Rough women's lips cracked by the freezing winters of Kiev. The soft open mouths of children.

All pressing against his forehead, sending him to God.

When they were alone, Avram reached out, took Gabriela's hands.

All his life he had been the smartest, the strongest, the most ruthless.

Now he was dying. His soul, helpless, would be sent to God for judgement. Avram felt his heart splutter and flare once more. He held his breath, wondering if this time he would find himself exhaling in the land of the dead.

But the moment passed, he was breathing ordinary air again, panting slightly with the effort.

"Are you in pain?" Gabriela's voice – loving, solicitous.

"No pain," Avram said.

"I have something for you here. A gift from your students."

As Avram struggled to raise himself in order to see, Gabriela set a thick wooden box on the bed. The box opened. Inside was a piece of parchment. Avram bent closer. Gradually the words swam into focus.

In Loving Tribute To Our Beloved Teacher
Master Anatomist & Surgeon
Guide To The Unknown Country Of Man
Avram Halevi

Gabriela read the dedication aloud, then turned the page: a drawing of the human body, skin peeled back to reveal the layers of muscles. She turned the page again: an arm, this time the bones and joints exposed in their workings.

"They have been labouring day and night for months," Gabriela whispered. "Inside are drawings of all the dissections you have made, and the texts of your lectures on surgery and anatomy." She turned through several pages of script to a new illustration. This was in colour. It showed an old man, beard down to his chest, bent over a body on a table, surrounded by onlookers.

"Joseph did that drawing. You see? His days in the studio were not wasted. He – " But her words were choked off by tears and Gabriela simply pushed the page closer to Avram.

The old man was himself, his eyes turned towards the viewer, burning with the insanity of his project.

"He loves you so much," Gabriela said. "We all love you."

Avram felt tears streaming down his cheeks. Where was Ben Ishaq now, to laugh at him? Where was Moses Viladestes, to make jokes about the man so stupid that he cries at his own death?

"I wish I was dying with you, being buried with you in the same coffin."

"I'll wait for you."

"I'm afraid to be alone."

"I love you," Avram said. As he spoke he heard a short gasp – the laughter of Death.

"I love you," Avram said more loudly.

Now the water was folding over him, cool and silent. He was on the boat from Barcelona to Montpellier, sailing away from Gabriela into the unknown with only his wits and his will to protect him.

When Joseph came back into the room, he found Gabriela weeping over the body of his father. On the bed, still open, was the wooden box; text and illustrations were scattered on the covers.

Death had wiped Avram's face clean, left it serene and contented. Kneeling beside Gabriela, Joseph closed his eyes. For a moment he felt like a small boy again, surrounded by the powerful smells of his elders, never knowing when his life might violently break and change direction. He opened his eyes, reached out, and took his father's hand. Cold and gnarled, it was growing still already.

As he touched his father's fingers, Joseph felt a sudden beating in his own chest. Then the air of the

471

room was thick with the spirit of Avram Halevi. There was a humming in his ears and the candles flared so brightly that Joseph's eyes began to burn. He staggered to his feet, reached into his cloak for his sword, thinking for a moment that they must be back in the cell in Bologna, preparing to run the gauntlet of the guards.

Then he turned to Gabriela.

She had slumped to the floor beside Avram, her head was resting on his chest.

"Joseph. Joseph the dreamer." Joseph felt his ribs tearing open, as if the voice of his father were forcing its way in to touch his soul.

Then the room went quiet and dark again.

Joseph bent down to comfort Gabriela, but even as he reached out to her, he realized that she was dead.

The next day Avram and Gabriela were buried, side by side, in the Jewish cemetery of Kiev.

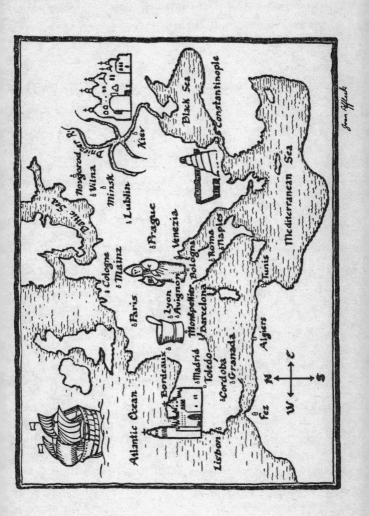

Atlantic Ocean · Baltic Sea · Black Sea · Mediterranean Sea

Lisbon · Bordeaux · Madrid · Toledo · Córdoba · Granada · Fez · Algiers · Tunis · Naples · Roma · Bologna · Venezia · Montpellier · Avignon · Barcelona · Lyon · Paris · Cologne · Mainz · Prague · Lublin · Minsk · Witna · Novgorod · Kiev · Constantinople

Novgorod R.

W N E S

Jean Allack